THE

FIRST

SOUL

ALSO BY W. J. CHERF

THE FIRST SOUL

THE ADVENTURES OF J. J. STONE

BOOK I

BY

W. J. CHERF

FBP
FOXBAT PUBLISHING

DEDICATION

The production of a book, much less the initial offering of a new series, is a daunting task. So much has to be considered. Yet, every day, writers fearlessly do just that.

Writers do not tread this path alone. They employ several editors, seek writing groups for criticism, and even beg others to beta-read early versions. These last are brave individuals, because often what they get, they cannot believe. Roger is one of these, as is Diana, Maryanne, Jim, Lou, and even a kind geneticist who wished to remain nameless. To all of these persevering readers, I wish to thank you from the very bottom of my heart.

And what of my dear Sweet Sue? Yes, it is true, she did make me do some serious rethinking, and in doing so, she made this effort better. Bless you.

A GPS Adventure Book

How many times did you wish you could go where the story took place? That mummy's tomb? That Caribbean pirate ship? Normandy Beach or the Alamo?

For Harry Potter, there is Platform 9¾ at King's Cross Station, the Reptile House at the London Zoo, Leadenhall Market, and the Tower Bridge. Universal has an entire Wizarding World devoted to the famous J.K. Rowling series.

But did you ever read a book that told you where to go? To actually see what inspired the writer? Or where the action took place?

Well, now you can. Sleuth out any of the following GPS coordinates of J. J. Stone's first adventure. One even has a USB thumb drive secreted at the location that contains a secret chapter! Be sure to have a USB adaptor handy that is appropriate for your device.

Good hunting!

1: GPS: Lat: 35° 39' 53.67 N. Long: 105° 58' 20.67" W.

2: GPS: Lat: 33° 13' 6.83" N. Long: 97° 7' 47.97" W.

3: GPS: Lat: 39° 57' 13.35" N. Long: 75° 12' 10.07" W.

4: GPS: Lat: 37° 40' 53.81" N. Long: 121° 46' 6.36" W.

5: GPS: Lat: 39° 37' 01.27" N. Long: 104° 47' 54.88" W.

6: GPS: Lat: 39° 14' 50.88" N. Long: 114° 53' 20.90" W.

7: GPS: Lat: 35° 45' 50.00" N. Long: 105° 54' 46.54" W.

CHAPTER 1
Monday, June 4, 1973

THE FIRST LESSON

From somewhere deep within the vast void of the earliest Universe, the Creator smiled as the grand plan went into motion. For out of that abysmal darkness, it created light and matter. From those constituent parts the realms of existence came into being along with their various guardians and overseers. Then, with great care and deliberation the Creator caused its greatest creation: the First and Second Souls.

The First Soul, a construct fashioned with free will, was tasked with the overriding desire to preserve and protect that which the Creator created. The First Soul, afforded with many protections, evolved through incarnation, but was not allowed to attain perfection and ultimate transcendence. For to do so would remove it from its primary task–the preservation and protection of the Cosmic Order.

The Knot of Eternity. (trans.) G. L. Love. 2nd. edition with T. Good. (Old Oaks Academy Press, 1960), vol. I.1, 13-14.

When the aged rabbi and founder of his hamlet's synagogue passed away, surrounded by adoring family and friends, the First Soul of Creation departed his withered body.

Bernard Isaac Cohen had a hard, but satisfying life, filled with challenge, crisis, and sheer superhuman effort. Many who lived through the horrors of Bergen

Belsen attributed their survival to the rabbi's strength. Despite famine and disease, he had somehow managed to keep their spirits up until the British and Canadian forces liberated the camp in mid-April of 1945. This solitary man, somehow, managed to stand apart.

Free again, the First Soul sought another host. During its travels it sensed the extreme love and devotion issuing forth from a rural household. The First Soul, attracted to this intense unconditional love, found this particular circumstance an auspicious choice. So it merged with the unborn infant full knowing, through its long experience, that simple choices often portended great things.

The primordial First Soul took root within the fragile babe, this Texan, this child of promise. The First Soul had high hopes this would be a special soul carrier.

* * *

The office of Hawthorne Insurance nestled in a copse of tall lodge pole pines on the corner of South Kansas Street. Painted in maze yellow with white trim, this once detached two car garage had on three of its sides bay windows all trimmed with gathered lace curtains. At its entranceway, mounds of potted bright yellow and white flowers greeted its visitors. Its many windows just sparkled in the sun.

Mrs. Hawthorne, founder and sole owner of Hawthorne Insurance, struggled with the lock of her office's front door that early June morning. The summer humidity in Topeka, Kansas, always swelled the old wooden door frame. Finally in, she bee-lined to her desk, plopped down her heavy purse stuffed with mail, and made for the kitchen to make some coffee. Soon, its aromatic waves crested and flooded the office. Furnished in tasteful Early American furniture backed by dark maroon Colonial-style wallpaper, the office's comfy familiarity soothed the soul.

Thirty minutes after her arrival, Mrs. Hawthorne, ever the efficient one, had sorted the mail, downed two cups of coffee, and had prepped for her nine o'clock appointment. Then she heard a distinctive rattling from nearby.

Glancing over her cheater reading glasses at the fax machine, the slight, gray-haired woman noted several curled up transmissions in its output tray. Gathering up the four yellowed thermal transmissions, Mrs. Hawthorne scanned the first three and shredded them without a second thought.

But the fourth stopped her cold.

Mrs. Hawthorne's fax machine possessed a special second function, other than electronic transmissions, which produced up-to-the-minute notices of all paranormal births occurring between the eastern border of Colorado and the Mississippi River. A marvelous mechanism generated this information. Named Ollie, a pleasant auto-writing gnome resided within.

The fourth transmission's header said *Infant Insurance Policy Application*, an obvious ruse to confuse the nosy and hide the document's true importance. Ollie had encoded across the page a numbing bureaucratic quagmire of unidentified tick boxes, numeric values, obscure entries, and even some fields with ordinary text.

Mrs. Hawthorne smiled at the intellectual challenge like a fresh crossword. Ollie's special transmissions, after all, represented puzzles for her to solve. So she went to her desk and retrieved a Reese's Cup from her candy stash, returned to the fax machine, and rapped upon its ivory colored plastic casing with her knuckles. At the signal, a tiny pink hand and forearm covered in downy white fur extended from the darkness of the tray, into which Mrs. Hawthorne placed the treat.

"Thank you, Ollie, for that special transmission," she said.

"You're most welcome, Mrs. Hawthorne. I thought you would be pleased," came the tinny response. "And thank you for the most generous treat! You shouldn't have."

Mrs. Hawthorne sat down and began deciphering Ollie's notations in her head. Juggling this against that, transposing the result, all the while taking into consideration the date and time of the document. Being a formidable mathematical savant, the process did not take long. In fact, Mrs. Hawthorne's long hand transcription of it took longer.

Her aged, freckled hands trembled as she read. "My dear Lord. Never before have I seen such an intriguing birth notice."

Ollie's special fax said, after Mrs. Hawthorne's decoding,

> Jonathan Joseph Stone. STAT: Unaffiliated
> IPAR: 10. SN: 1
> SSD: June 3, 1973
>
> Mother: Constance Marie Stone. STAT: Unaffiliated
> IPAR: 1. SN: 47949222
> SSD: October 17, 1911
>
> Father: Andrew Richard Stone. STAT: Unaffiliated

IPAR: 3. SN: 89754522
SSD: February 4, 1909

Birth Location: Denton County, Texas
TIIIS Contact Name: Reverend Paul Roberts
TIIIS Contact Number: (940) 382 2577

Gazing upon her transcription and taking in its importance, Mrs. Hawthorne paused to consider postponing her nine o'clock appointment. As the Central United States Membership Coordinator for TIIIS, The International Integrated Interface Society, this information needed to be disseminated to both TIIIS' local and regional contacts.

The membership coordinator in Mrs. Hawthorne smiled at the word, "unaffiliated," as it represented an opportunity for TIIIS to increase its numbers. But best of all it meant the Stones could not be counted among those godless heathens, allied to that other paranormal organization–CMES, *Consilium magorum et sagarum*, The Council of Magicians and Witches.

Pox upon them, she added with hard eyes. Her own allegiance with TIIIS had been forged from her desire for raw vengeance–a harsh word that could not bring back Mr. Hawthorne, ever.

Back to the transcription. Mrs. Hawthorne had twisted it in her hands while she had recalled Mr. Hawthorne's gruesome fate.

The newborn's Innate Paranormal Ability Rating, or IPAR, could not be any higher at ten, she noted, while his father's had a stout rating of three.

I only have a rating of two. Mrs. Hawthorne thought. *Is young Jonathan perhaps the product of good genes?*

That notion, however, Mrs. Hawthorne dismissed when she considered the child's Soul Numeral, an SN of one.

Never have I seen such a low soul number! According to this, young Jonathan carries the very first, The First Soul of Creation. If true, then he is both blessed and cursed. Poor thing. Both he and his family will be put through such tribulations. She thought with an empathic shake of her head.

When Mrs. Hawthorne took note of the Soul Separation Date or SSD of young Jonathan. She again paused to reflect.

The First Soul waited only one day, if that, to reincarnate. Usually, souls wait a considerable time before they re-enter the mortal world. But not this one. I wonder why? What would cause it to return so soon?

At that moment, Mrs. Hawthorne jerked out of her reverie as the bell over her door chimed.

"Good morning, Mrs. Hawthorne!" a cheery voice greeted.

"Ah, good morning to you too, Mr. Keeney. You're early."

"It's because your office always smells so inviting, Mrs. Hawthorne."

"Would you like a cup?"

*   *   *

A non-script, pre-World War II, red brick building near the Thames River held the London office of TIIIS on its second floor. Within this oversized broom closet of an office, the society's president, P. I. E. Smithers, sat wedged behind his worn wooden desk with his assistant seated likewise less than six feet away. Their world consisted of a doorway, a window that viewed a brick wall, and rows of filing cabinets, their tops covered in stacked files. Neither men remembered what color the walls had been painted.

"Mr. President, have you had a chance to read the fax from Chicago?" the assistant asked as he pointed to the president's in-box.

"Yes, I have, Geoffrey. Among the many details that make this birth report so remarkable, I note in particular The First Soul chose its next mortal carrier with considerable dispatch. That extraordinary detail alone told me it must have been for a very good reason.

"Geoffrey, start a file on this Jonathan Joseph Stone. I have a feeling we will be hearing from him."

"Very good, sir. And Mr. President..."

"Yes, Geoffrey."

"I have managed to secure for us a more spacious office."

CHAPTER 2
Denton County, Texas, 1973

Andrew Richard Stone never before heard his wife Constance cuss or swear, but she bellowed with a vengeance. A former drill sergeant in the U.S. Marines, this tall, reed-thin, and well-weathered Texan thought his wife's performance rivaled his boot camp best. Just how his itsy-bits did it, he didn't know. She sure had guts.

A. R. held her hand. Their eyes met glistening with love and anticipation. Suddenly, a quiet stab of pain passed across Constance's blue eyes. She hollered again, this time squeezing his hand, hard. Her pale complexion turned red with exertion and with her light brown hair pasted to her head with sweat, A. R. counted to ten until the episode passed. Unconsciously, he had held his breath too. Once the episode passed, they breathed.

"That's the fifth one today, Honey Bee," A. R. said using his favorite nick-name for his wife. His eyes showed all the tenderness of a loving husband, but his facial lines remained rigid. He prepared his game face for the trials ahead.

"They're coming faster and faster." Constance said.

She gasped again. Another horrific stabbing contraction came and went. He marveled again at his Honey Bee's crushing grip.

Constance said wearily. "The doc said when they start happening thirty seconds apart, then all heck is about to break loose."

"Don't you worry, Honey Bee. I will always be here for you."

When the big push finally came, time slowed in the Stone household. Sitting upright in a sloped birthing chair so that Constance had plenty of leverage, it all came in a rush. First the head, the shoulders, and then the rest came squirting out, which the well-seasoned mid-wife caught and immersed in a warm pan of water.

"It's a boy!" A. R. shouted.

"Is he alive?" Constance asked.

A strong cry broke out in reply as the mid-wife tied off the umbilical cord and began washing off the infant.

"Thank God," she said with a deep sigh. "Good Lord, I'm beat." But she wore a happy, radiant grin that only a mother can produce.

For the first time in his life, A. R., humbled by his wife's accomplishment, had been a helpless bystander.

*   *   *

Within an aristocratic villa with a red tile roof nestled in the hills of Tivoli, Italy, a slight and beautiful young woman with flowing raven black hair threw flour and kneaded bread dough. She had just blown aside an errant lock when she froze, startled by the onset of a powerful premonition. Gripping a white marble edge of the kitchen's island for balance, the woman waited while the vision ran its course.

With wide eyes and a heaving chest she marveled.

Such a vivid portent...

Valeria Costa, coming down from the emotional rush covered in sweat, felt like she had just ran a marathon. Still wobbly kneed, she washed the flour from her hands, abandoned the mound of rising dough, and went to the family chapel.

Within its dim and low-ceilinged confines burned an ancient bronze brazier, corroded and dented by time. Its fire scented the cramped chamber with rich oaken smoke. Valeria maintained this flame both morning and night, the *actual* eternal flame of ancient Rome, which had not been extinguished for over twenty-seven hundred years. By caring for it, Valeria perpetuated The City's magical continuance.

Also inside the chapel's rough stone walls stood a short stone pillar with a polished silver lustral basin filled with clear mountain water. While it looked like a Christian baptismal font, in reality, it provided a focusing lens for *visus procul*, the reading of portents.

Valeria stood over the lustral basin, gripped its sides, and began to chant into it using the old Latin of Republican Rome.

> I, Valeria, heed your call oh ancient one.
> I, Valeria, devoted high priestess of Vesta, seek a vision.
> I, Valeria, daughter of Coelia Concordia, *Vergio Vestalis Maxima*, command you to do so.
> I, Valeria, keeper of the most sacred flame of Rome, command you to do so NOW!

The mirror-like water rippled, and formed itself into the image of a healthy baby boy. But the baby's aura, a rich, metallic gold, flooded out of the basin like a search light, filling the chapel with its warming glow.

"The First Soul of Creation! It has reincarnated!" Valeria exclaimed in rapture.

"But where? Tell me where?" begged the high priestess of Vesta.

The prerequisite for a chief vestal virgin, beyond the obvious, included powerful oracular abilities and a mastery of divination. In these, Valeria did not disappoint. She held her patron's future and that of the Gathering in her callused and often bloodied hands. After all, young Valeria Costa, descendent of Coelia Concordia the last vestal virgin, was a powerful witch. When Valeria spoke, people listened. Though beautiful and desirable, Valeria never married. She instead cited that her time should be watching over the futures of her patron and the Gathering than washing diapers.

Again the waters swirled at her command. This time, however, the vestal saw before her an unknown symbol, perhaps a flag. Memorizing the image, Valeria blinked with exhaustion and sagged against the basin's pillar as its waters stilled into smoothness.

"I must inform my *patrono* of this portent, *subito*."

*   *   *

On a bright Saturday afternoon in June, the entire family dressed in their Sunday best and gathered before the stone steps of The First Baptist Church, Denton County's oldest. Among this circle stood A. R.'s two older brothers, their families, and Reverend Paul Roberts in his white vestments, who, in spite of the heat and his advanced age, had agreed to perform the baptism.

When A. R., Constance, and their newborn son Jonathan Joseph arrived at the appointed hour, only broad smiles greeted them, and hearty well-wishes gushed forth.

Near the end of the baptismal rite, the reverend became agitated. His hands trembled to such a degree he had to end the proceedings early, claiming heart issues. A. R. helped the old family friend to his white clapboard ministry house next to the church, while the old man grasped his forearm in support.

After assisting the octogenarian into his favorite rocking chair, A. R. fetched a glass of cold water. "Reverend, how are you feeling? Is there anything else I can do for you?"

Still breathing hard, the reverend again gripped the rancher's forearm, but this time like a steel claw. Then he answered between labored gasps.

"A. R., I have a secret I must tell you. But you mustn't speak a word of it to anyone, except your wife, Constance. Will you so swear?"

A. R. knelt beside the seated reverend and nodded in agreement and concern.

"Before my dear Bethany died those many years ago, God blessed this young and energetic Baptist minister with many gifts. I am a powerful faith healer, even though I couldn't save my own wife."

He hacked into his handkerchief, marking it with bloody spittle, folded it, and then wiped a tear from his cheek.

"Reverend, can I take you to the hospital? You don't look so good."

"No, A. R., not now, later. Just listen. Please. I am also a man of vision. I can see things others cannot. I know all of this sounds like an old man's ranting, but listen to me carefully. Your son did not need to be baptized today."

"What?" The new father exclaimed in surprise.

"That's right, A. R. You heard me right. Your son is special, very special indeed. Care for him. Guard over him. Raise him to be strong and self-reliant."

"What do you mean, Reverend?" the confused ex-Marine countered. "Of course I will."

Shaking his head vigorously from side to side, the agitated reverend continued.

"You know, A. R., you're sometimes as thick as your daddy. Now boy, listen to me, and listen good. Your son didn't need to be baptized, because he's special. He's been given a gift. He is, in the words of Ezekiel 1:28, 'a man with a glowing halo.' And, A. R., there are those who will want to do him harm. Serious harm. Do you hear me, son? Your boy is a golden child and that makes him a target. Care for him, because Lord knows all of humanity needs him, desperately."

The rancher, shaken by the reverend's words, called the hospital about the old man's shaky health. There, the new father waited until the ambulance arrived, explained to the first responders the situation, and then made sure the minister received proper care.

As the medics wheeled the old man to the ambulance, A. R. escorted him, holding his hand.

"A. R."

"Yes, Reverend?"

"Never forget what I told you about your son."

After the ambulance pulled away, A. R. returned to his wife and baby boy, who waited for him in the front pew. His son lay wrapped in her arms, sleeping, an image of serenity.

"Honey Bee, it's time to go home," he whispered so as to not disturb the dozing babe.

"What happened to the reverend?"

"He'll be fine, Honey Bee. I'll tell you all about it on the way home."

*　　*　　*

La famiglia Presto represented an ancient aristocratic Roman family that once provided Rome with more than its fair share of *pontifex maximi*, or high priests. A Presto ancestor had even taken part in the assassination of Julius Caesar.

This family's latest scion and playboy, Giovanni Presto, not only aspired to be an F1 racing driver, but considered himself a formidable telekinetic practitioner and reader of auras.

Presto, rich, spoiled, and insufferable, made few friends. Frankly, the racing community treated him at best, if not generally, as a jinx. Competing drivers suffered mechanical troubles. Nothing anyone could prove, but something bad always happened whenever someone passed Presto on the track. Center wheel lug nuts all too often came loose. Meanwhile, within the paranormal community, his family had supported CMES for generations, and in the process had made several overtures regarding Presto's candidacy for chairman. To date, the family had been told to season their own.

Young Presto, all too aware of young and beautiful Valeria Costa, his family's trusted and treaty-bound oracle, took notice when Valeria first contacted him.

"*Signore* Presto, we must talk, today. Something has occurred that will impact your family and our Gathering."

"Excellent, *Signorina* Valeria. So what's your pleasure? Dinner perhaps? Should I order a car?"

Valeria bridled at Presto's demeaning form of address. *I am no longer a girl, but a woman, a Signora.*

"No, *Signore* Presto. That will not be necessary. I will meet you for lunch at my favorite restaurant along the Via Valeria, off the Via Scuole Rurali."

"*Ciao.*"

*   *   *

A. R., hardly a man of books much less libraries, the following Monday morning wanted to find out what this "golden child" stuff meant. So he made for Denton's Emily Fowler Public Library on Oakland Street. He arrived as it opened at nine.

Marching directly up to the reference librarian's desk that Monday morning, the librarian asked, "May I help you?"

"Yes ma'am, I certainly hope so. I need to know what a 'golden child' is."

"Hmm. That's an interesting question. One that will need some research. Can you give me a couple of days to track this down for you?"

Surprised that the librarian would do this, A. R. nodded his head with considerable relief.

*   *   *

The quaint restaurant insisted upon linens and a bottle of local red wine on every table. Valeria had selected it for its excellent food, discreet waiters, and intimacy.

Dressed in an ivory colored shift with a simple pearl necklace, Valeria looked stunning. Presto, dressed in a dark silk suit with an open collared dress shirt, complemented her. The surrounding patrons sensed that they basked in the presence of near royalty. Once seated, Presto poured each of them a glass of wine.

"So, *Signorina* Costa, what is the news you wish to deliver?" Presto opened with an ingratiating smile.

"*Signore* Presto," she began with her hands folded on her lap, "the portent I received might elevate your family to greatness once again, and perhaps even you, to our Gathering's chairmanship." She softly said and then took a delicate sample of her wine. A slight tilt of her head spoke to her pleasure for having done so.

She saw her message had been delivered perfectly. She had achieved what few could: command Presto's virtually non-existent attention.

"Precisely, *Signorina* Costa. What do you mean?" Commanded Presto.

"The First Soul of Creation has reincarnated as a boy child. As to where, I only have but one image. It seems to be a flag, but one I am not familiar with."

At that, she passed to Presto a folded piece of stationary. Opening it, Presto's forehead furrowed.

"I do not recognize it either. I will have my staff look into it. But what of the chairmanship?"

At that response Valeria realized Presto had missed the point and thus the opportunity.

How sad for his family. I must direct him, lead him like a cow.

She folded her hands before her on the table, leaned forward, and began the school lesson.

"*Signore* Presto, forgive me if I have not been clear, but what would the Gathering think if *you* proactively removed the First Soul of Creation from the mortal chessboard? Even if only temporarily? What would that mean for *your* family's reputation within our Gathering? *Your* potential career?" she emphasized.

A dull silence met Valeria's questions. A direct

woman, she probed again her intellectually vacant luncheon host. After all, while she swore herself as treaty-bound to support the Presto family, she also had to balance that responsibility with CMES' long-term fortunes as well.

"*Signore* Presto. If you find and remove this infant carrier of the First Soul of Creation, that decisive act could elevate you as the youngest chairman in the history of our Gathering.

"Consider this, *Signore* Presto. You might delay for generations the First Soul's interference in our Gathering's affairs."

*   *   *

Miss Lilly Nelson, information librarian, lived for intellectual challenges, be it elucidating the planting cycles for emmer wheat, determining the number of boots an alligator's hide provided, the population of New York City, tracking down the kind of cherry tree George Washington cut down, or the weight of a sperm whale. It didn't matter. Lilly shined at her best when she found the unfindable.

Being intuitive by nature, Lilly bit down on the eraser of her Number Two pencil, surveyed her domain, and gravitated to the B-stacks devoted to religion. She drifted from the seven levels of the Hindu chakra, to the five-layered colors of the Prabhashvara aura of Gautama Budda, to the halos of Christianity, and then to parapsychology.

She realized the term "golden child" had nothing to do with the child, but a theory, which stated all living things possess an electromagnetic field. This envelope, called a halo or aura, could display many color hues, which represented an individual's spiritual, physical, and emotional state, as well as many other things.

"Fascinating," Lilly whispered to herself, as she dialed Mr. Stone's telephone number. "I wonder if I've an aura? What color would it be?"

A. R. at first didn't hear the hay barn's telephone ringing off its post.

"Hello?"

"Mr. Stone, this is Lilly Nelson over at the Fowler Public Library. How're you today?"

"Just fine, ma'am."

"Well, Mr. Stone, you paid us a visit the other day and made a research request."

"Oh, yes! I remember. What did you find out, Ms. Nelson?"

"Well, sir, it's all very involved, but here's what I found out..."

CHAPTER 3
The Hit. June 1973

THE SECOND LESSON

Coincident in time with the creation of the dark, light, and mortal realms, the Creator caused energies to coalesce into several immortal entities. One came to be named by the ancients the Ledger Keeper. This self-aware, this neutral overseer of the three realms, records the presence of every soul and tracks their every mortal passing and incarnation, to ensure that balance is maintained within the Cosmic Order.

The Creator also fashioned a terrible entity out of dark energies, one subservient to the Ledger Keeper. This entity came to be named by the ancients the Devourer of Souls. This self-aware incorporeal construct was tasked to destroy the demented and berserk of its dark realm. However, weak and susceptible mortals, enfeebled by hate or ignorance, could be influenced to do its bidding.

The Knot of Eternity. (trans.) G. L. Love. 2nd. edition with T. Good. (Old Oaks Academy Press, 1960), vol. I.1, 14.

That evening, Presto, motivated by his family's oracle, made a transatlantic call. The man he contacted, *Signore* Shapiro, an assassin within the Gathering, carried serious baggage that Presto chose to overlook.

"Is this *Signore* Shapiro?"

"Yeah, dat's me. Who's dis?"

"I am Giovanni Presto. I am in need of your services."

At hearing the name Presto, Irving Shapiro, the last surviving hit man of Detroit's infamous but extinct Purple Gang, almost choked. *Presto is big-time*, the assassin realized. *And big-time is big money.*

"What can I do for you, Mr. Presto?"

"I want a baby boy eliminated. Can you manage that?"

Pause. *Should I dicker with dis guy? Or, just get into dis guy's good graces?*

"Ah, not a problem, Mr. Presto. We can make dis a straightforward contract deal. But if you wish, we can work dis out on a retainer basis, too."

"No, Mr. Shapiro. This is a simple contract. However, if done well, then we can talk about something more permanent."

Most might hesitate to take on such a contract given its target, but not Shapiro. Back in 1922, the roguish and young-looking gangster, then in his mid-twenties, had bartered his soul to a dark entity in exchange for a magical elixir that preserved his youthfulness and health. Shapiro had to brew the concoction four times a year to maintain its potency. While the preparation of the elixir presented few difficulties, one ingredient represented a thing of horror: the fresh liver of a male infant.

"You've got yourself a deal, Mr. Presto. Send me the particulars and you can consider the job done."

"Excellent, Mr. Shapiro. Expect a fax shortly. Good day."

Fourteen minutes later, the former gangster's fax machine began to hum and three pages appeared. Discarding the cover page, the second depicted a crudely drawn picture of the state flag of Texas. The third transmission contained all the particulars from Presto's oracle, including the contact information of several of the family Presto's *Stregas*, or witches, who had offered to cast a *locatur augorium* or locator spell upon all of Texas. After all, Texas was, "Texas big."

The next day, per their instructions, Shapiro stood before an enchanted wall map linked to the spell and in no time a colorful marker appeared, north of the Dallas-Fort Worth area, near a town called Denton, Texas.

Now with the baby boy's general location, Shapiro decided to fly into Dallas, rent a car, and drive north to Denton.

"Piece of cake," he murmured.

Two days later, Shapiro arrived in Denton to overcast and rainy skies. Since he needed some local information, the hit man homed in on the Fowler Public Library, located on Oakland Street.

There, he asked the friendly reference librarian where she stacked the town's newspapers, and then sat down to read the June 4th, Monday edition. Nothing. No birth notices. So Shapiro checked the following Tuesday issue. Nothing again. Finally, in the Thursday printing of the *Denton Record Chronicle*, he found something on page six of Section C.

Jonathan Joseph Stone

Monday, June 4, 1973

Andrew Richard and Constance Stone of Denton County have announced the birth of their son, Jonathan Joseph Stone.

Jonathan was born by midwife on June 4 at the Flying Wedge Ranch in Denton County. He weighed seven pounds, 14 ounces and measured 23 inches at birth.

He is the first child of the family. His paternal grandparents are Marie and William Joseph Stone, who live in Denton County.

His baptism was performed by Reverend Paul Roberts, First Baptist Church of Denton County, on Wednesday, June 5.

(XLIV, 1973, Thursday, June 7, 6C)

Not born in a hospital...that's why his birth notice appeared in the Thursday instead of Monday edition.
With the announcement in hand, Shapiro asked the reference librarian for the local phone directory. At the mention of the name Stone, she perked right up.

"Why, I remember that name. In fact, the baby boy's father came in last week requesting information."

At this news, Shapiro smiled like a Cheshire cat with a mouse.

"So's how might I find the Stone's Flying Wedge Ranch?"

"I'm sorry sir, but our phone book doesn't include ranch addresses outside of Denton proper. Why don't you contact Reverend Roberts at the First Baptist Church? He'll know for sure."

"Why thanks ever so much. How do I get to the First Baptist Church?"

After some directions, the man left with a wave of a gloved hand...while mouthing a forgetfulness spell directed toward the librarian.

*   *   *

The church stood only six blocks away. Next to the imposing flagstone structure stood the modest white clapboard ministry. Seeing no one in the church's parking lot, and being a Wednesday afternoon, Shapiro knocked on the ministry's front door. After waiting thirty seconds, he knocked again, and the door opened.

"I heard you the first time! The world is not coming to an end," the frail male voice said from a wheelchair.

Looking down, Shapiro asked, "Would you be Reverend Paul Roberts?"

"In the flesh, young man. How may I help you?"

"I'm looking for directions to the Flying Wedge Ranch. I understand the Stone's have been blessed with a baby boy. I would like to pay my respects."

The old reverend thought a moment and then backed his chair away from the door, while his eyes took in this unexpected visitor. The man before him wore his thick and luxuriant hair long, over his collar and ears, as if to protect them from the sun. Tight kid gloves covered his hands. His facial skin looked unnaturally shiny, healthy, and wrinkle-free.

"Excuse me, young man, where's my manners? Please come in out of the heat while I fetch the address you're looking for." Then, stopping and wheeling about. "Can I get you anything? A glass of water, perhaps?"

"No thank you, Reverend. Won't be necessary. Just the directions to the Stone's ranch, if you please."

"Well then, close the door behind you and follow me into the kitchen. That's where my Rolodex is."

Sitting before a desk high enough to roll his chair under, the reverend got a pen and paper out of the drawer and began flipping through the many note cards of his Rolodex, every so often looking up as if to think. He saw that his visitor had taken off his gloves and held them in his well manicured left hand.

"You're not from around here, are you, son?"

"No, I'm not. I'm from Detroit."

"Hmph. Detroit. Such a godless place."

"How so?"

"With all of their crooked politicians and gangsters, they make Lucifer himself look good."

That elicited an all too knowing chuckle from the visitor.

Reverend Roberts finished scribbling and folded the note paper twice into a perfect square, and then wheeled about, stopped before his visitor, and asked again.

"So where did you say you come from, young man?"

"Detroit."

"Hmph," the reverend grunted. "That's funny, because these old ears thought they heard a Brooklyn accent."

That startled Shapiro, because he had grown up in Brooklyn before he moved to Detroit to join the Purple Gang. But before he could comment on this, the old reverend extended the folded note paper.

Shapiro reached out to take it, when with surprising quickness, the old reverend grabbed his right hand with both of his. He pulled it to his mouth and bit down on the back of it savagely, sucking away blood and flesh in the process.

"What the devil!" Shapiro squealed as he fought to disengage his ravaged hand from the old man's mouth.

"Are you out of your fuckin' mind!"

Eagerly licking his lips and swallowing his guest's blood, Reverend Roberts smiled a bloody smile and declared with a vengeance, "Devil indeed, dear visitor—whatever *you* are! Your black and squirming aura betrays you as one of the damned!"

The old cleric bowed his head, folded his age-freckled hands in prayer, and rapidly recited a spell in old Church Latin. Shapiro, cradling his bleeding hand, felt his throat closing and his breath becoming short.

Realizing what the wily cleric had done, the gangster fled the man's house. That helped, but only fractionally. He got into his car and drove off heading south out of town toward Dallas.

Damnation! That geezer priest's bite tagged me with an exilium maledictio*, a corporeal banishment curse! Where the hell would a Baptist minister pick that up?*

Two blocks later, Shapiro's brain, struggling for oxygen, lost the battle, and he passed out. His vehicle ran off the road, jumped the curb, and smashed into a fire hydrant, splitting it open. A geyser dowsed the car and its occupant. The impact also displaced the hood shattering the windshield, rammed rearward the sub frame and engine into the steering gear. Shapiro, impaled on the steering column, never woke up.

As the hydrant's water continued to wet his skin, it blistered, sagged, and deformed, turning the driver into a jellified mass. The elixir that preserved Shapiro's youthfulness did not agree with clear, pure water.

*   *   *

The Ledger Keeper made an entry recording the sudden

passing of a soul from the mortal world into the dark realm.

*   *   *

Deep within the abyss of the dark realm The Devourer of Souls snapped its jaws in anticipation at the arrival of this long overdue soul. Feeling cheated at this particular miscreant's unnatural tardiness, the demon noted the soul's advanced state of its depravity.

"Tasty, it will be," the demon gloated, "but first I will play with it, and only after I tire, will I destroy it."

During this entire private conversation, Shapiro's soul squealed and shrieked in anguish, trapped, and with nowhere to go.

*   *   *

A curious crowd gathered at the scene of the crash. Moments later, the first responders arrived. Among them, Jake Sapper, a fireman with twenty-four years experience, took one look at the driver's corpse and thought he had seen it all. A member of the local TIIIS chapter, Sapper knew what he saw.

One dead demon in Denton.

*   *   *

The old reverend had continued to repeat his spell ten times, and like a church bell tolling or a pebble striking a still pond, each repetition caused the spell's effective range to expand in an ever widening ripple.

The reverend died of heart failure while reciting the spell the eleventh time. He passed over, full in the knowledge he had protected as best he could the Stone ranch and its newborn golden child, J. J., under his protective magical umbrella.

The church congregation buried the reverend's remains in the church's cemetery. Impregnated with Shapiro's blood and tissue, this caused the banishment curse to persist for a long, long time. But that was unneeded as the curse had already done its job. Shapiro had been destroyed.

CHAPTER 4
Alexandria, Egypt, 1981

THE THIRD LESSON

The Creator fashioned the dark, light, and mortal realms as distinct and separate. At a mortal's passing, its soul first arrived in the dark realm. There the soul chose whether to rise toward the light and pass into it, or to remain unperfected and sink ever deeper into the endless darkness.

Souls that failed to rise toward the light did so because they were bereft of hope and love. They chose misery, became demented and vengeful. Souls, so doomed, as their depravity mounted, continued to descend until they met their utter destruction. This journey was called damnation.

Those souls that chose to rise up through the dark and enter the light did so based upon their innate sense of contrition, hope, and capacity for love. From the light realm a soul continued its progress through a portal, provided for the purpose, to the mortal world. This journey was called incarnation.

The Knot of Eternity. (trans.) G. L. Love. 2nd. edition with T. Good. (Old Oaks Academy Press, 1960), vol. I.1, 14.

Ahmed Makris, while not a wizard, indeed ranked as an adept *and* sensitive. This pious Coptic Christian saw himself as a man of God, blessed with talents that few possessed. Loyal and trustworthy to a fault, Makris saw things, the small and insignificant things, that made a person. Call it what you will, but the man only needed a brief face-to-face moment to assess an individual's emotional state, intentions, or the truth or falseness of their words. As the confidant of a powerful politician, in this case, President Anwar Sadat of Egypt, Makris' provided an invaluable litmus test like no other.

Yet, perhaps Ahmed Makris' greatest strength lay with his keen telekinetic mind, which could move objects both great and small. He could alter the flight of a soccer ball or find an unwashed fork beneath a foamy layer of soap suds. While taxing, Makris did not share his mastery of telekinesis with anyone outside of his family. The Egyptian thought of it as a last resort, for the most dire situations, as with that errant auto and the endangered child.

*   *   *

Cool, freshening Mediterranean breezes wafted in through the penthouse's windows and billowed near-diaphanous curtains. On that flawless Alexandrian evening, these gentle caresses ruffled the seated man's stylishly long, sandy brown hair.

"Are you certain of accuracy of this information?" the almost five-hundred-year-old Dark One asked in old Parisian French–another aficionado of the dark elixir of life, but one far more canny.

"*Oui Monsieur*. Absolutely. I saw it with my own eyes. With a few quick hand gestures, he diverted the out-of-control automobile and saved the child from certain death."

The shaken subordinate then stuttered out, "The man's a telekinetic a-a-adept, *Monsieur*. Perhaps even a w-w-wizard." The slender man trembled in The Dark One's presence.

"So you say," the pale and smooth-skinned man murmured more to himself from his deeply padded office chair than to his nervous subordinate.

"And, please remind me, *Monsieur* Graf, he has rejected *how* many polite entreaties to join our Gathering?"

"At least four, *Monsieur*," the quavering voice said.

"Four. Hmm. That seems a fair enough number of opportunities. So, *Monsieur* Graf, the question is–what is he a member of?"

"He is well regarded within his church, *Monsieur*. He's a Copt, and quite devote, I'm told."

"*Monsieur* Graf, I know he's a Copt. But is he a member of a paranormal organization? That is what I wish to know," the seated man said as if explaining himself to an idiot.

Looking down at his shaking hands, Graf realized he had been tracking this man's daily movements for over three months, and not once did he note any indication of such an allegiance, and he said so.

"Hmm, it seems once again our Gathering's sullied reputation has preceded us. Interesting. But that fact alone suggests to me he is indeed aware of his surroundings. That, in itself, tells me he is indeed connected to the paranormal network. And, *Monsieur* Graf, if you are correct in your observations, and I believe you are, that means he has developed his opinion on his own. That makes him one of the non-aligned, maybe even an outright freelancer, and that tells me this presidential aide commands considerable talent *and* intelligence."

The Dark One paused to take a deep breath. "What

a lost opportunity for our Gathering. Such a figure as *Monsieur* Makris would have been a fine acquisition. To have co-opted such a high governmental functionary would have been a genuine coup."

Then, rather brusquely, the seated man made up his mind. "Such a pity, *Monsieur* Graf. I cannot have such rogues wandering the streets of my city. No matter how highly placed they are. Watch him."

"*Oui Monsieur. Tout de suite, Monsieur.*" A head of thinning hair bobbed as he exited the office with relief.

*   *   *

Soccer had provided the medium that kindled an innocent boyhood friendship between a Moslem and a Copt. Each knowing the other's mind, they had made a formidable pair passing the ball deftly between defenders. This one-minded closeness extended into their teenage years, their enlistment in the military, and now within the bureaucracy of the modern Egyptian nation.

Inseparable, one began a sentence and the other finished it. The pair also shared a secret. They could converse without speaking. Needless to say, a shared glance could convey volumes.

In the post-1979 world, following the peace treaty with Israel, many plots broke out against the president. The Egyptian administration's crackdowns on its critics, rabid Islamic fundamentalists and Coptic Christian extremists alike, created a tension-filled atmosphere. Makris, presidential aide to his life-long friend, Sadat, possessed invaluable talents. To date, he alone had prevented catastrophe in three instances.

"Mr. President," Makris said, "do you think it wise to yet again take part in this celebration of our last war against the Jews? Especially since they are now our allies?"

"Ahmed, I know your mind. And, between us, you are absolutely correct. However, the military runs this country. They need their morale strengthened, to let off a little steam, and burn some jet fuel, diesel, and gasoline. Think of the celebration as a harmless escape valve, nothing more."

On that Tuesday, October 6th, 1981, Makris stood beside his brave president, all the while harboring grave reservations. He sensed something wrong, but could not for the life of him place his finger upon it. From the shade of the concrete reviewing stand, dignitaries from around the world gathered to see his country's proud parade of military might and readiness.

What a sham! Makris traitorously thought. But from the rigid look on the faces of the surrounding military staff, this military parade provided their surrogate for war. Yes, my dear Anwar, they indeed needed this...display.

Brave troops marched as one with their heads cocked in our direction. Sand-colored tanks, with their turrets turned in salute, rumbled by. Ridiculously expensive French Mirage jets thundered overhead pummeling the grandstand with their afterburners' roar. Trucks towing artillery pieces drove on past, except for one, which turned toward the reviewing stand, and stopped. Presently, a lieutenant appeared from the cab wearing a wide green sash with objects in his hands.

Makris saw the lieutenant's aura, a rippling mass of muddy blackness, his mind filled with pure hatred. The sheer force of the revelation shook the Copt to his core. When the lieutenant's eyes scanned the crowd, they locked not the president, but instead on Makris. Never before had the presidential aide sensed such pure evil directed at him, such malevolence focused in such a manner!

The Egyptian lieutenant began heaving grenades into the reviewing stand. Makris turned to his right and yelled at his friend Anwar to get down. The first two the adept managed to deflect to the right and left, but the third made its way through unaffected. Then, three others from the truck, also wearing green sashes, began firing in Makris' direction and into the surrounding crowd.

The third grenade exploded with a loud crump less than ten feet away from Anwar, lifting and tearing apart several of the Egyptian high command, who, in total shock, had failed to abase themselves before the brazen assault. Bullets filled the air, their sizzling passage inches above Makris' head, thudding dully into this body and that. The assault continued for what seemed an eternity, but in reality only mere moments, as the screams surrounding him built up into a chaotic cacophony.

Finally, seeing what had happened, the nearby parading troops surrounded the traitorous truck and its crew, taking them, brutalizing them, nearly tearing them limb from limb.

Amidst all the screams for help, the moans of pain and injury, the lifeless bodies of the Coptic Bishop Samuel and a nameless infantry general had collapsed and buried Makris. With the floorboards of the grandstand awash with blood, he crawled out from under the dead weight, making him looked like the dead coming to life.

Looking over towards his prone boyhood friend, I could only see the soles of his shoes, which did not move. Crawling over to him, his chest looked as if it had exploded. Only later would Makris hear that Anwar had been hit by several bullets and multiple shrapnel fragments.

In all, only eleven had died, with some thirty-eight dignitaries wounded. As for Makris, his wife's amulet had protected him.

*　　*　　*

While the nation mourned the loss of their beloved president, Makris grieved for his friend, who had been killed in a savage crossfire somehow meant for him. Confirmation of that fact arrived two days later in the form of a telephone call.

"*Monsieur* Makris?" the conversation innocently began. Makris noted the caller's odd accent, perhaps a mix of French, and Italian?

"Speaking."

"*Monsieur*, you are one very lucky man, are you not?"

"Who is this?"

"Who I am, *Monsieur*, is not important. But what is, is that you, *Monsieur*, are still alive. Especially after the events of the past few days.

"How is that?

"How is it you are still alive? How did you survive so many grenades directed at you and the hail of so many bullets, *Monsieur*?"

The conversation had a chilling effect on Makris.

One, the caller had his name and government office telephone number. Two, he had called it. Three, his exacting enumeration of the brutal attack's details suggested he had witnessed it.

"I am a religious man, *Monsieur*," Makris replied with frost. "I consider my present state of health a matter of God's own design. As for you, *Monsieur*...?"

"Nonsense! Your Christian God had nothing to do with it! You survived because of magic, and magic alone, pure and simple. Everyone else around you died. Only you, *Monsieur*, remained unscathed."

At this last accusation, altogether too true, Makris placed the receiver into its cradle.

Someone knows. Someone knows my name, my faith, and apparently, has an inkling as to my special abilities.

But who?

As The Dark One received a dial tone in response to his last assertion, he chuckled to himself.

"Yes, *Monsieur* Makris, I know not only who you are, but what you are as well. Think long on that."

CHAPTER 5
Growing Up on the Ranch

Ever since I could remember I have been able to see auras. I thought nothing of it, as no big deal, I knew every living thing had a cloud of pretty colors around them, and depending on the season or time of day, those pretty colors would change. At first, I didn't know why, but early on I noticed whenever a steer got pregnant or a horse ill, or if someone felt sad, or angry, or happy, their colorful cloud would change, becoming more faded, or dark, or hard in its intensity. Being able to see these changes, sometimes subtle, other times great, I found to be pretty handy around frisky bulls and sickly calves–a constant to ranch life. As a child I thought everyone could see these colorful, wispy clouds and so thought nothing of them, excepting which steer to avoid or who to play with. Like breathing, I found seeing auras such a simple thing.

I suppose I grew up normally, as any child would. Being an only child, I learned to amuse myself, go out exploring, and managed to get into a fair share of mischief, which I thought of as fun. I liked to dig in the dirt, too.

Throughout my early years, I never felt alone, because I had all of these friends who would play with me, slither and hop about, buzz around and tickle my ears, flutter and fly, and moo and whinny. Never once did I feel afraid of any of my friends, because never once did any of them harm me, nor me them.

I learned later what responsibility and hard work on the ranch truly meant. Dad would first ask why something didn't get done, and if my answer didn't satisfy him, he would tan my hide. This straightforward cause and effect logic I learned right quick.

By age ten, my tannings had ended, but something far worse–*the look*–replaced them. Whenever dad used the look, it conveyed his disappointment, and I didn't need to read his aura to confirm the fact. His gaze could bring on deep shame and regret, which triggered on the spot my acknowledgement of the error of my ways, all while I looked my dad straight in the eye, and at attention.

Leaving or abandoning a machine in a pasture constituted one of the worst things that you could do.

"J. J.," Dad would say, "are you sure you're sorry you did that?"

"Yes, Dad. I blew it. I should have thought ahead and checked the gas tank. It won't happen again. Promise."

A forthright answer always earned me a quick nod from dad, as his eyes continued to drill into me for emphasis. A formal handshake followed to seal the deal. Once done, all was forgiven and forgotten.

To my dad's credit, I only heard him cuss once in front of me when a steer kicked him square, knocking him down in a pile of fresh manure. No matter how mad he might be, dad would sooner bite his own tongue than swear in God's name. When I turned thirteen, I asked him about it.

"J. J., as you well know, your grandpa served as a Marine. That's how he raised me and how I raised you. Discipline's in our blood.

"Marine sergeants transform men into soldiers, train them to adapt, improvise, and kill the enemy.

Otherwise, they'd never survive in battle.

"Unfortunately, to do that successfully, I had to first get their attention, and that meant cussing. As penance, I made my peace with the Lord never to cuss again. Especially not in front of you or your mother."

*   *   *

By the time I reached my freshman year in high school, I had pretty much grown up. Ranching life does that to you in North Texas and so does sports. In Texas there is only one sport–football, and I wanted to play–bad. As a result, dad and the high school football coach had several frank discussions. Dad, knowing the value of a team experience, signed the many permissions and liability papers.

Every young Texas male dreams about being a star quarterback, a flashy halfback, or a speedy wide receiver, but my sheer size and strength destined me for a far less glamorous place–the offensive line.

During those years playing football never once did I get injured. I chalked it up to living a charmed life. Ever the plow horse, I played steady and reliable, and people noticed. There in the trenches of black eyes, bloodied noses, and bruised knuckles, I became a disciplined and selfless warrior who protected his own.

Mom and dad never missed a game. To me, that meant a lot, because lots of my teammates' folks didn't. I often heard mom's distinctive voice during a game cheering from the stands, and even her commenting about the blindness of a particular zebra. She also brought bags of sliced oranges for halftime, which I shared with my teammates.

As for dad, during a pause in the game, I would

glance over, see him, and we'd share a nod. In his own quiet way, he had my back on every play. I could feel it. Afterwards, mom, usually quite hoarse, would give me a hug. Dad, as usual, smiled with pride and gave a shoulder pad a healthy squeeze.

During high school I came to realize that only I could see a person's color cloud. So to avoid any teasing, strange looks, or unnecessary trips to the optometrist, I kept my secret to myself. Besides, seeing people's color clouds told me a lot about people's hidden truths.

In competitive sports, and especially with football, I could tell who wanted to blitz based on their color cloud's excitement level. As an offensive lineman, I would use every fiber of my body to protect my quarterback. In a sport where any and every idiosyncratic twitch someone on the coaching staff jotted down, my hidden ability translated into my quarterback's security.

In social matters, however, that same hidden ability made it easy to see who liked whom. As with so many things, be it cattle, horses, or people, it became a distinct advantage as to how approach or deal with my peers and superiors.

By senior year, I became a team captain and prided myself not in touchdowns scored, but in pancake blocks, where my opponent found himself on his backside and flattened to the ground, with me on top of him. To have my quarterback sacked felt like a personal affront and I got the idea across to my fellow linemen, early on. "Number Ten's uniform is to remain clean. Period. Or feel the heat!"

During my senior year's Homecoming game, I

played pumped up and sky high. I terrorized the opposing defensive line and as a result recorded seven pancakes, which sprung loose our star halfback for over two hundred yards. But the game's results paled in importance to what happened on the sideline. While hustling back out unto the field I ran over one of the pompom girls, knocking her down. Her name was Grace.

Red-headed, freckled, petite, and drop-dead pretty, Grace's family had moved into the area the summer before. In fact, on the first day of senior year, I spotted her, but she somehow disappeared until that Homecoming game. I was head over heels in love.

Two weeks after Homecoming, I got the gumption up to ask her out. I began my first serious courting, this big ranch clod, trying to be a smooth mover. I would smile at her in the hallway between classes. She would smile back and blush. Five months out from senior prom, I asked Grace, a sophomore, to be my date.

Like two peas from the same pod, that described us to a tee. Everybody knew it. Me, this big, hulking Brahma bull. She, this delicate Texas wildflower. We did everything together–went to church hand-in-hand, went to the movies, and took long walks. I even accompanied Grace when she picked out the fabric for her prom dress. Yes, I was certifiably whipped.

As for our families, they got along well enough and blessed the match. Without question, Grace and I as a couple had a thing going that our parents didn't want to mess with, all the more in this world so rocked with corruption and chaos.

*   *   *

I woke up and found myself covered in blood in our hospital's emergency ward.

Grace immediately came to mind. Where was she? All in a panic I started hollering out her name from my gurney while two nurses tried to clean me up.

"Grace!" I yelled at the top of my lungs as I struggled to rise. They managed to hold me down just long enough to sedate the hell out of me.

Several hours later, I came to, all cleaned up, but strapped to the gurney and sporting a monster of a headache.

A physician parted the drapes and said, "Well, young man, your blood alcohol levels are on the decline. We sedated you earlier because you became a handful."

"Where's my Grace?" I demanded.

At that point, the physician's face fell a mile, but to his credit, he didn't mince words.

"Son, I'm sorry, but she didn't make it."

Strapped down like Frankenstein's monster, a wave of confusion crashed into that hard reality. I do believe that I would have hit the roof had my body not been secured. That's when I started screaming again, and this time, the doc knocked me out.

Sometime later, I came to. This time my dad stood over me, blood-shot eyed and all. I'll never forget that moment until I'm a hundred.

He said, "J. J., son, your Grace is dead."

Streams of tears flowed down his weathered face. "Your mother is with her folks right now. We're all torn up, real bad. As for the other two, Josh and Linda, they're gone too. You're the only survivor.

"It's probably best you hear this from me, son. As

best as the state troopers and firemen could tell, when Josh's truck rolled, Grace, who was sitting on your lap, saved you, son.

"But jeez-o-Pete's, why didn't any of you kids have your seat belts on? And drinking, too...?"

Dad, speechless, looked like a deflated beach ball, and shook his head.

"J. J., your mother and I have been worried sick about you. Somehow, someway, you came out of that god-awful wreck with just some minor scratches, bumps, and bruises. Think on that, son. Gracie gave herself up for you."

Then it hit. Me, the big bad lineman, had been shielded from harm by my beloved Texas wildflower.

"Oh, Dad no..." I then totally melted down. My macho self peeled away like an overripe banana skin, leaving behind this exposed bundle of nerves and muscle, screaming in psychic pain. With my world turned upside down, my heart crushed and aching, I even doubted God. How could He allow this to happen to my Grace? What had she done to deserve this?

Filled with selfish pity, at first I denied reality. Then, I got angry about it, consumed in rage. I lived the next several days in a nightmare. The burial preparations for Josh, Linda, and my Grace had begun. Everyone at our church and high school stood around in a state of shock and mourning. I staggered around the ranch, doing chores in a haze that wouldn't clear. I ached with a shattered heart. I couldn't bear being without Grace, her smile, her goofy jokes, and her soft, understanding eyes that read my soul. More than that, I had lost a dear and close friend, one who had protected me with everything she had.

CHAPTER 6
Alexandria, Egypt, 1983

THE FOURTH LESSON

Nature, the most powerful Mistress, full of wonder, beauty, wields a terrifyingly swift judgment when even its smallest creatures are placed in peril.

While the honey bee nurtures Natures very being, its sting releases her life force with a formidable surge, second only to the lightning bolt. That act is the ultimate sacrifice a bee can make in defense of its Mistress.

Woe unto any demon or demon-possessed stung by the lowly bee, for its destruction will follow.

Similarly, all things created by the industry of the bee possess powerful qualities. Sweet honey not only protects and speeds the mending of mortal wounds, it also is the bane, the poison without equal, of demons and those possessed by them.

The Knot of Eternity. (trans.) G. L. Love. 2nd. edition with T. Good. (Old Oaks Academy Press, 1960), vol. I.1, 14.

With his boyhood friend dead and buried, the political landscape tilted as vice president Muhammad Hosni El Sayed Mubarak took office as the new president of the Egyptian state. Makris remained astonished at how orderly the transition of power had occurred for his country in this war-torn and politically hot corner of the world.

Nonetheless, change came. The government asked

Sadat's old colleague where he wished to relocate. Fortunately for his family they had a summer residence in Alexandria. There, the administration retained his services as a minor bureaucratic.

Frankly, Makris had expected this. While Mubarak knew he had championed him as Sadat's vice president, Makris, nonetheless, represented the old regime. The new president's inner circle would be made up of his former Egyptian Air Force comrades.

Throughout the transition Makris remained grateful for this assignment and performed to the best of his ability within the regional office of the Egyptian Antiquities Organization. Besides, working with the French archaeological mission in Alexandria had its own distinct advantages, particularly for his young daughter, Melaina, and her budding future. In many respects, the move led to a match made in heaven.

There remained, however, that other issue, far less savory, regarding that unknown voice who knew where he had worked. That remained the sole source of his personal heartburn, fitful nights, and stress. Makris even considered the prospect of moving abroad to somewhere more secure.

* * *

The stalk of the paranormal rogue known as Ahmed Makris began without fanfare. François Graf, who had tailed the man on and off for the last several months, could follow the man's daily itinerary in his sleep. Like clockwork, Makris would leave his family's third floor flat on Mohammed Rafat at seven-fifteen. A brisk walk of twenty-three minutes later, the man would arrive at the Faculty of Law building at Alexandria University.

Once there, in his suite designated as the Regional
Office of the Egyptian Antiquities Service, Alexandria,
the man would spend the day shuffling papers, meeting
with foreign and domestic academics, only to depart at
four in the afternoon and return home. Occasionally, the
man left his office to visit one of the city's many
archaeological sites, often accompanied by his young
daughter. Otherwise, the sheer regularity and sameness
of Makris' daily schedule drove Graf nearly mad.

*   *   *

Ever since Makris received that mysterious phone call,
he placed his highly-tuned senses on alert. After several
months had passed, he detected a tail, who, while quite
effective in his selection of urban camouflage, could
not alter his general stature and gait.

Each morning became a game of "where is my
tail?," "how quickly can I spot him?," and "what is he
now pretending to be?" Makris' favorite was the falafel
vendor who never seemed to sell anything. Another, a
shoe shiner with the same, odd, non-profitable business
model. In fact, Makris prided himself on his sameness
of routine and its predictable punctuality. Still, his tail
followed him every day like a homeless, hungry puppy
in search of a scrap.

*   *   *

"*Monsieur* Graf, do you have anything new to report
concerning our rogue practitioner?" The Dark One
asked his subordinate.

"*Non Monsieur. Monsieur* Makris has not
displayed any inkling of his telekinetic powers since the

incident with the out-of-control automobile. He plays the role of a minor governmental functionary to a tee."

"I see. Have you been conducting the past month's surveillance of the subject?"

"*Oui Monsieur*. I have."

"*Bon*. You have done well.

"Now, *Monsieur* Graf, I want you to task three of your subordinates to follow this miscreant on a rotating basis. With perhaps the addition of three fresh sets of eyes we will better catch him red-handed in his unauthorized use of magic."

The Dark One, seeing Graf's flushed face, thought to add, "*Monsieur* Graf. I have better and far more important things for you to attend to then street surveillance. Let others do it. In the meantime, I would like you to look into the following..."

*   *   *

After three weeks, no further evidence had been gathered of the man's unauthorized use of magic. Bored and vaguely disappointed, The Dark One made his decision.

The unexpected death of a government bureaucrat, such as Ahmed Makris, must *appear* as something it wasn't. The assassin had to be unknown, and above all, untraceable. Yet, Makris' demise had to send a clear message to Alexandria's paranormal community that unaligned, rogue practitioners, would not be tolerated within The Dark One's city. To advertise that fact, the assassin had to be magical in origin, otherwise the paranormal community would not take notice of the murder.

Looking for an obvious message to send, The Dark

One consulted his own magical compendium, *The Book of Spells: Instructions for Summoning Those of the Netherworld*, in search of inspiration. Almost five hundred years in the making, his compilation contained fifty-two spells, each which named a specific demon, for a specific purpose.

So many grand choices, The Dark One ruminated. *What is my darkest desire?* He crooned to himself. Then it came to him.

Yes, yes, that would be deliciously perfect!

*   *   *

One homicide investigator, a middle-aged Coptic Christian, had a pretty good idea of what had happened. As he reread the police report, he first noted that Makris had arrived at his office around seven-forty that morning. At eight o'clock, his first appointment had arrived. His secretary then discovered Ahmed Makris still warm, but very dead, sitting in his office chair, slumped over his desk. The official cause of death: heart attack.

What balderdash! Someone clearly received some serious baksheesh for that inaccurate report.

The investigator moved on to the sealed coroner's report, which in his mind, while better, still didn't do justice to what he considered a crime scene.

In it, the coroner reported that the victim had a double puncture on the left side of his neck above the collar. The toxicology report revealed the subject had been bitten by and died from the poison of a *Cerastes cerastes,* or horned viper, based on the presence of its unique thirteen toxins. Death, while quick, must have been agonizing. Apparently, the reptile had been lying in wait in the center top drawer of the victim's desk. While investigator knew horned vipers lived throughout Egypt, it remained a mystery as to how the snake had found its way into the victim's desk drawer. As a result, he began a quiet investigation as to who had access to the victim's office.

Two pieces of evidence within the coroner's report grabbed the homicide investigator's notice, which the forensics team did not appreciate. Makris had slathered his neck wound with honey before he died. In fact, the coroner took a picture of him with the three middle fingers of his right hand still in a half-emptied and overturned jar as if caught in mid-motion, his arms outstretched on the desk blotter between two desk photographs of his wife Fatima and daughter Melaina. The investigators saw from where the jar of honey had come–the open right hand upper desk draw, with an appropriate gap within its contents, with a residual ring on its bottom that matched the jar's base.

The second piece of damning evidence made the hair on his neck rise. The victim died while holding in his left hand a honey-coated, sloughed horned viper snakeskin. While otherwise complete in all respects, the fresh white snakeskin no longer contained its owner.

To at least this homicide investigator, a long-time member of the Alexandrian TIIIS community, the honey meant only one thing to him. Makris knew he had been attacked by a snake demon, put up a struggle, and tried to foil the effect of the snake's bite. However, he noted, if that explanation held any water, then Makris understood the paranormal and how to ward off demons. It also signaled Makris death as not a heart attack as reported, but rather a murder by dark magic.

He reported these findings to his society's leadership with dispatch.

Now rummaging through the evidence box, the homicide investigator examined the label on the honey jar. There, he saw his absolute proof, as if he needed any at this point.

GOLDEN NECTAR
100% Africanized Bee Honey
Product of Brazil

*   *   *

Extreme age seemed to be a commonality among the Alexandrian TIIIS community. The region's foremost spell whisperer reflected this fact, for he while blind in his left eye and hobbled by arthritis, the man soldiered on. A devout Sunni, the spell whisperer knew of Makris, a Coptic Christian of impeccable reputation.

Makris' blatant murder exercised the spell whisperer. He considered the sending forth of conjured demons to do one's dirty work as shameful, immoral, and uncivilized. Much of the modern world's ways he found to be so, but no one seemed to listen to him.

The spell whisperer appeared at the local police station at the agreed time. The homicide investigator, who had called him, greeted the man respectfully and provided his own office to examine the critical evidence–the honey-covered snakeskin. With the investigator's desk cleared off, in its center sat the evidence in a common shoe box, marked with name, date, and several other bureaucratic tracking codes.

With his one good eye, the spell whisperer observed the box as he shuffled his way around the desk, before he made any attempt to remove its lid. But when he reached for it with his bare hands, the spell whisperer received what amounted to a psychic electrical shock.

Grunting his displeasure, the old sensitive took two white cloths from the long and broad sleeves of his *jellibiya*. Wrapping each hand with the linens while leaving his thumbs free, he lifted off the shoe box's top to reveal a milky transparent plastic evidence bag.

"Ah, so there it awaits," he murmured more to himself than to the expectant homicide investigator.

"*Monsieur*, can you perceive auras?"

"*Non Monsieur*. Unfortunately I cannot. But in my line of work that skill would come in most handy."

"Perhaps we should work on that, together. The skill can be acquired."

Then the spell expert refocused upon his quarry.

"Well, *Monsieur*, even with the honey so applied, this object is still active, dangerous to the touch—not by a commoner, mind you, but to anyone sensitive as are we. Its aura appears like a small bundle of writhing, black snakes. A most awful thing to ever see. I find this most troubling as someone has managed to defeat our greatest natural ally, the honey bee."

"So that's why..." the homicide investigator began.

"*Précisement Monsieur*," spell whisperer finished his thought with his right index finger raised in triumph, "why Makris' use of Africanized bee honey came for naught." Shaking his sparsely populated, near bald head, "Amazing, just amazing."

Now stroking the stubble of his white bearded chin in thought, spell whisperer considered his options.

"*Monsieur*, is that evidence bag waterproof?"

"It should be. Why?"

"Then get me a janitorial bucket, the kind on wheels, full of water."

Not questioning the elder man's request, the homicide investigator scrounged about the station house until he found what his guest wanted, and in the process, received some very curious looks and more than one comment regarding the odd augmentation of his meager investigator's salary.

Closing his office's door, he declared, "*Monsieur*, this better be good, because my colleagues have berated me about procuring this bucket."

Only a wry smile answered him as the spell whisperer lifted out the plastic bag and plopped it in the bucket where it floated on the bladder of air trapped inside. Looking around the investigator's office, he took an umbrella sitting in the corner and used it to force the bag underwater, displacing half of the bucket's contents in the process.

"Hey!" the homicide investigator said as he barely got his feet out of the way of the inundation. But then he gaped as the plastic bag began to melt as its contents caught fire, *underwater*.

"How is that even possible?" the investigator asked, the spilled water now long forgotten.

"I tore open the bag with the tip of your umbrella and in the process immersed the bag's contents. Now, *Monsieur*, note all the apparent char in the bag. Watch closely as it too will soon disappear."

And, it did.

Now still holding the water-filled bag underwater, the spell whisperer explained to his dumbfounded colleague.

"*Monsieur*. What you just witnessed is the destruction of a demon-construct, which when it came into direct contact with water, dissolved into something called ectoplasm, that charred-looking material. Ectoplasm is the building material of the Underworld, and it disappeared, evaporated right before our very eyes, because it is not of our world.

"As for the conjurer of this most evil deed, there can only be one–The Dark One, also known as *Monsieur* William Alexander. I can pronounce this judgment on several grounds. The first being I have seen with my own eyes the dark aura of other instances of his evil mischief. They all possess his particular mark or signature, without question. Secondly, consider the complexity of this conjuring–the placement of the snake demon within Makris' desk's upper drawer, the demon's resistance to the Africanized bee honey, and the dangerous snakeskin the demon left behind."

"What would have happened if either you or I touched that demonic snakeskin?" the homicide man had to ask.

Again with the wry smile, elder sensitive continued his instruction. "Then, my dear friend, the snake demon would again have appeared, delivered its bite, and vanished from the scene. The devilishly clever part of this spell is the demon snake imparted venom, instead of trying to possess its victim. Makris, not knowing this, did the proper thing to defend himself from possession. I believe the Americans have an expression for this kind of subterfuge. It's called a 'curveball.' So, *Monsieur*, this spell was designed, from the very beginning, to kill and kill alone.

"And consider this as well, the snakeskin's ability

to reanimate at the mere touch of a sensitive means that no CMES member would dare approach it, for they would know of its dangerous proclivities. Thus, this aftereffect, if you will, targeted us.

"How does that make you feel, *Monsieur*? Manipulated perhaps?"

CHAPTER 7
The Weasel

It had been eighteen years since Presto had cut the hit contract on the First Soul with Shapiro. When the news of his demise in a car crash first reached the Roman, he had not thought much about it as the churning wheels of CMES' politics had already made their choice. The attempted hit job lost all importance to the newly-elected chairman, who had much more important things to occupy his mind.

However, his family's treaty-bound oracle, Valeria Costa, had not forgotten, and had, on countless occasions, reminded him of the fact in private. Specifically, Valeria stressed the threat that the First Soul could represent to both the future of the Roman family and CMES in general. To all of this Presto himself just laughed, and relegated the issue of Shapiro's failure to the status of a bad and tired joke.

Because of this cavalier attitude on the part of the headstrong Presto, Valeria threatened to sever her treaty-bond with his family. This, and with the pressure of other family members, finally goaded Presto into action after the eighteen year hiatus.

Swallowing his ego, Presto contracted a well-respected operative within the Gathering who went by the uncommon name, the Weasel. The moniker referred to his uncanny ability to make awful things happen, in tight situations, while always getting away scot-free, and not any resemblance to the carnivorous mammal.

*   *   *

Having studied the situation, the Weasel decided to strike during a social event, the target's senior prom, where alcohol surely would be present and could be attributed to a vehicular crash. The brand new Ford pickup he would render a catastrophe happened to be a close friend's high school graduation present.

Conveniently jacked up to the sky, access to its inner right front wheel became a simple matter. The Weasel positioned the primer cord loop along the entire inner circumference of the wheel's huge barrel. The tiny remote ignition device removed all chance of premature detonation. The Weasel would follow the truck at a reasonable distance and remotely ignite the primer cord.

The fact the prom revelers had been drinking when they climbed aboard only made the "accident" appear all the more believable. The truck made a right turn from the high school gym's parking lot onto a two-lane rural road.

At a place of the Weasel's choosing, he pressed the remote's button and the pickup truck's right front wheel exploded from its hub, wrenching the vehicle right and into the neighboring ditch, where it rolled over four times in a spectacular fashion. After what seemed an eternity, the Ford came to a rest upright and in a freshly plowed cotton field. Its cab's roof flattened to the door sills. Driving by the crash scene, the Weasel judged by the look of things that the truck's occupants had died and his job was complete.

Now he had to wait for confirmation. The Weasel, bored silly while staying in a downtown Denton hotel, finally got his proof two days later. With newspaper in hand, he discovered that one of the four had somehow survived, specifically his target.

"Huh. That doesn't happen too often," he remarked after reading the newspaper column. "I'm going to have to think about this." And with that, the Weasel began to plan anew.

CHAPTER 8
Surrender

While the town of Denton came to grips with the tragic prom disaster, two of Denton's finest had their doubts if it was indeed an accident at all. In fact, Troopers Scott and Rollins, both Army veterans, suspected foul play. They based that assessment on the oddly bent remains of the pickup's wheel and the residue that coated it. So they carted over the remains of the pickup truck's right front wheel to the local university's Archaeometry Laboratory for a chemical analysis. Given the local notoriety of the event, the needed resources made themselves available.

"Doc, this is the wheel I told you about." Officer Rollins said to Professor James Greer of forensics.

"If you'll notice, the entire inside of this rim is coated with a greasy, almost paraffin-like substance under the coating of dirt and grit. Its feel and burnt smell kinda reminds me of a plastic explosive."

Professor Greer, a former Navy frogman and demolitions expert, grunted at the trooper's assessment, held out his gloved hands, and said, "Let me take a look at that, son."

Working from his lab bench, Greer took two samples, which his assistant processed.

Fifteen minutes later, he pronounced, "Officers, it sure looks like you have a multiple homicide on your hands. And Officer Rollins," nodding in his direction, "you're damn close in your gut assessment. The explosive agent sleuthed out as pentaerythritol tetranitrate, PETN, better known as primer cord.

Someone rigged that wheel to catastrophically collapse, and then probably detonated it by remote control."

*   *   *

The funerals came and went as heart-rending and painful blurs. As I witnessed Grace's casket lowered into the ground, a big part of me went in with it never to return. I stood there, tears streaming, and feeling guilty as hell I should have been the one and not her.

Through it all, mom and dad were always there.

*   *   *

"Our son looks haunted," Constance said.

"He is," A. R. replied. "I've seen that look in Vietnam. He's damn near suicidal. He needs a change of scenery right quick, Honey Bee."

"What do you have in mind, A. R.?"

*   *   *

That very evening I had a serious talk with dad. He made a suggestion that made a whole lot of sense.

"Whatever you decide to do, J. J., will be fine with your mom and me. Always know that we love you and are always here for you."

The next day I enlisted in the United States Marines. When I announced this personal decision at the dinner table that evening, my parents shared a meaningful look.

My father said, "Well, son, that is an honorable thing you did. I know your mother and I will support you on this one hundred percent."

Then he uncharacteristically fiddled with his glass of water, while mother did the same with her napkin.

"Tell him, A. R.," My mother prodded.

My father sighed. "You're right, Honey Bee. He should know."

Know what? I wondered.

My father got up from the table. He went into his office and came back with a large white envelope. Opening it, he took out its contents.

"J. J., I hold here your baptismal certificate. Our family minister, Reverend Paul Roberts, baptized you. He conducted all of our family weddings, baptisms, and funeral ceremonies. A good man, some even say, gifted in some special way. This I firmly believe.

"J. J., you might not believe this, but Reverend Roberts said that you didn't need baptizing."

Now that got my attention.

"The reason why is because you are special, as in divinely special. He even had a term for you, 'a golden child.'

"J. J., every father thinks their sons are special. But what the good reverend told me about was your golden glow, your golden aura. We have often remarked around here about your charmed life. The way you never ever got stung by any bees, never got sick, never broke nothing. Now, given what you have experienced, I would say you must have a whole squad of guardian angels hovering about you.

"But there is one thing more Reverend Roberts drilled into me son, and now I am going to do the same to you. J. J., you might not realize it, but you are very important to the whole of humanity. That humanity is depending on you. Why? I don't know. But someone, somewhere, must know that you have a remarkable destiny before you. Try to find them."

*   *   *

The Weasel had failed before, but never twice. This time he decided to drop his target and witness it with his own eyes. A good rifle can provide both. That decision settled, the hit man made a visit to a local sporting goods store.

*   *   *

Because of this homicide case's explosive lethality and the implied sophistication involved, the local Denton police jurisdiction alerted the FBI in Dallas/Fort Worth. They in turn rummaged through their criminal databases and came up with seven similar cases, all still open, that had occurred over the past four years.

The course of a homicide investigation can turn on a dime's worth of information. In this instance the Denton Police Department received a tip from the owner of a local sporting goods store.

"This is Officer Rollins. How can I help you?"

"Office Rollins, this is Bobby Johnson," which the officer wrote down. "I don't usually call like this, but I just sold a bunch of items to a man that caused me to think twice after I made the sale."

"So, Mr. Johnson, what caused you 'to think twice' about that sale?"

"Well officer, just so you understand, I'm a life-member of the NRA and a staunch supporter of the Second Amendment. But in walks this long-haired city-boy in a fancy suit looking to buy a deer rifle and scope. First off, it's not deer season. Second off, he doesn't ask about purchasing a hunting license. He's not interested in a gun case or cleaning kit neither.

"Then right before my very eyes he tears down this sweet Browning BAR .30-06 rifle to its stock, peeks through the barrel, asks about its twist, smiles, and reassembles it in the blink of an eye, like he's done it a million times. He shoulders the gun, tests its balance, and wraps the webbing around his shooting arm like it was meant to be there. Then, without a thought, he says, 'I'll take this.'

"Then he wanders over to one of my counters, points to a pretty illuminated Zeiss scope with 2.8 x 20 x 56 power. He asks if the mounting rings are included. I say yes. He says he'll take it, too.

"While still at the case, I tell him the Nikon scopes are pretty good, and cheaper. He just shakes his head and says, 'The Germans know their shit about what they're doing.' Then he points to a sweet set of Zeiss binoculars, big ones with 10 x 42 power. Says 'they'll do nicely' as well.

"But officer, he ain't finished. He buys five boxes of Horady 178 grain, ELD-X, boat-tailed ammo.

"Then he asks me for directions to the nearest rifle range.

"Officer. When was the last time you used a 178 grain boat-tailed sniper round on a white-tailed deer?"

"Mr. Johnson, I can see your point. Can you describe the man?"

"Yes, I can. He's a Caucasian, five ten, about a hundred and seventy pounds, with long brown hair and eyes. He's a city-boy, from Florida, because that's what his driver's license said."

"Sir, do you have a copy of his driver's license?"

"Yes, sir, and I have his credit card information as well."

"Mr. Johnson, what was the total on the man's purchases?"

"$7550 before the governor's share. And the man didn't blink at it twice, neither."

A whistle emanated from the Officer Rollins. "Mr. Johnson, you really saw that man coming."

"Man's got to make a living, officer. But what got my antennae twitchin' on this city slicker was an off-hand comment that he made."

"Which was?"

"Something about what a shame it was about the recent high school pickup crash. Officer, it wasn't his words that upset me. It was the fact an out-of-towner knew about the crash. But the real clincher was the look on his face, like he had just been cheated out of something."

"Well, thank you, Mr. Johnson. I'll send someone over right away for driver's license and credit card information. In the meantime, try to think of anything else you might have forgotten to tell me. If something pops into your mind, call me."

"Will do, officer."

"Here's my direct desk number."

The fact of the matter remained that Mr. Bobby Johnson couldn't tell the officer why he called. Bobby, the grandson of Denton's late Reverend Paul Roberts, had inherited the old man's ability to assess a person's character, an important talent when running a gun shop. To Bobby, everything about that Florida city-boy named Sikes had screamed pure, unadulterated trouble.

*   *   *

Thirty minutes later, an FBI agent from the Dallas/Fort Worth office arrived at Mr. Johnson's sporting goods store. The owner had indeed forgotten something–he had taken down his customer's license plate number and noted the make of his car, complete with its Hertz Rent-A-Car sticker on the bumper.

After that, wheels began to furiously turn. The FBI sent an agent over to the Dallas/Fort Worth airport, searched the rental car agency's paper files, and confirmed the Florida man who rented the car also had made the purchases in the Denton sporting goods store.

The FBI, who now considered Geoff W. Sikes a suspect, uncovered some further curiosities. As in Mr. Sikes' credit card had been used only a handful of times, and only during the past three weeks. His Florida drivers license, when checked by the Tampa, Florida, FBI office, came up as bogus. More ominous, his very name, Geoff W. Sikes, matched a similarly named man who died four years prior. Even the address associated with the credit card tallied the same as the deceased. This last caused an all-points-bulletin to be declared on Sikes and his Ford rental car.

Officer Rollins and his fellow officers, now with a vehicle description, tag number, and the suspects name, checked out the local gun range and found out that a polite, thirty-something, white Caucasian, medium build, with long brown hair had indeed spent a hour or so using their facilities. The staff said the man sighted in a brand new hunting rifle, a real beauty.

*   *   *

Around noon two days after Mr. Johnson's phone call to the Denton Police Department, the local police found Sike's empty rental car on a dirt road. The fact it flanked the backside of the Flying Wedge Ranch perked up lots of people's interest, especially Officer Rollins', who alerted the FBI and had the car impounded. But where was Sikes?

*　　*　　*

For the first time, the Weasel felt trapped. Laying down in a homemade ghillie suit below the brow of a little rise of the Flying Wedge's inner pasture, the hit man watched as first a local squad car showed up, then an unmarked car, followed by a flatbed that loaded up his rental car.

Where did I go wrong? he wondered. *Must have been that guy at the sporting goods store. I knew I should have hit him with a forgetfulness spell!*

Why didn't I? the assassin continued with his critical self analysis.

Because, dickhead, you got so excited to sight-in your new toy. You fucking idiot. He could have kicked himself.

*　　*　　*

Officer Scott and FBI Detective Gregg stood chatting beside their vehicles as the loaded flatbed vanished down the road behind a tan cloud of dust.

"So where do you suppose the owner of the rental car is?" Agent Gregg wondered aloud.

"Well," Officer Scott offered, "right there is the Flying Wedge Ranch, the home of the lone survivor of that terrible pickup crash that turned out to be a multiple homicide. So my guess is he's somewhere about, with that fancy rifle of his, waiting to shoot the Stone boy."

"So you think the pickup crash actually was a failed hit job, where the target didn't get nailed?" Agent Gregg opined with a raised right eyebrow.

"You got a better theory?"

"Guess not."

"Well, Agent Gregg, if we surround this pasture, and set it afire, I'll bet we'd flush out this Sikes fella right quick. Wanna' call in that idea, agent? I won't mind, but I sure as hell want to be in on the round up."

*   *   *

The Stone's inner pasture that Officer Scott and Agent Gregg surveyed amounted to a square-shaped six by six acre piece of land covered with tall volunteer wheat and barley. Nonetheless, Agent Gregg's superior thought the idea of a controlled brush fire a thing of beauty, called up the Denton Fire Department, and had them empty their barns of all their available fire-fighting equipment. A mixture of FBI, county, and state police cars arrayed themselves alongside them.

*   *   *

It sure didn't look good from the Weasel's point-of-view. As far as he could see, multiple fire trucks and law enforcement elements had positioned themselves all around the pasture. The closest fire truck idled no more than three hundred yards away.

In a moment well-reasoned logic, the man removed

the bolt from his rifle, dropped it in the dirt, wriggled out of his ghillie suit, and stood up with his empty hands raised high above his head. As he walked over to the nearest clump of idling vehicles, the Weasel had already figured the potential criminal charges and weighed them against any circumstantial evidence.

* * *

While the news of Sike's surrender caused a buzz throughout Denton County, Presto's U.S. contacts created a blizzard of legal motions on the man's behalf. As for Valeria Costa, she told Presto over lunch, in no uncertain terms this *l'uomo potente*, this 'powerful man,' will soon become dangerous and has to be dealt with, the sooner the better. With this potential problem a world away, Presto remained more fixated on his F1 team's upcoming race in Spain.

CHAPTER 9
Melaina

In 1970, a baby girl arrived to an Alexandrian upper middle class Egyptian family with a Greek surname–Makris. Her late father, Ahmed, who had been a government functionary during the regimes of Sadat and Mubarak, had done very well for himself and his family. Because of her father, Melaina had met the international archaeological community that worked in her city. The fact the girl spoke fluent English and French made her presence at their various dig sites a delightful commonplace, and her ability to date ceramics developed as did her curiosity in all things ancient. As one archaeologist from the French mission had told her father, "Melaina is such a bright and precocious scamp. She should be rushed off to the Sorbonne *tout de suite*."

Melaina's initial demeanor could be described as understated, but not shy. She liked to fly under the radar, observe, and "take a pulse" until she understood someone. Only then would she open up and reveal her infectiously broad smile. Her face glowed with olive-colored skin and a flawless complexion. Her dominant features included a narrow and long nose, a triangular face and full lips. Her jet black and shiny hair hid her large-lobbed ears and framed her brown intelligent eyes. Lean of build, Melaina stood five-foot something, with tiny feet and delicate hands notable for their long, artistic, almost spidery fingers.

Her surviving parent, Fatima, an extreme sensitive and empath, had, unknown to Melaina, guided many of the family decisions through Egypt's turbulent political times. Again unknown to Melaina, she had received her mother's psychic heritage, an attuned sensitive with empathic traits.

Her family, old and Coptic Christian, active in its religious community, gave freely when it came to the care of those in need. This is where young Melaina first came into contact with the poor; she assisted her mother by making bread or passing it out.

At eighteen, Melaina's mother, Fatima, passed due to a botched medical procedure, made by an uncaring Moslem doctor, who made no secret of his dislike of the Copts. Without her influential father and now without her mother, Melaina, on her own and without recourse, could not lash out at the travesty. She did, however, possess a memory and she vowed never to forget.

Now nineteen, Melaina, a mature-thinker, had done well in school. Her parents had left her a considerable bank account, so the young woman applied to Oxford on the advice and encouragement of a family friend, a professor of classics at the University of Alexandria. There, Melaina would study Egyptian archaeology, history, and linguistics because she wished to become an archaeologist. Oxford represented a big step, but one she accepted with open eyes.

*   *   *

"*The Book of the Dead*," her first year lecturer began in An Introduction to Ancient Egypt, "is a handy and popular misnomer attached to an entire class of funerary documents. More properly, these documents should be referred to as *The Book of Going Forth by*

Day, as that is how the ancient Egyptians referred to it, a title which emphasizes the deceased soul's longing to go back and visit the familiar daytime scenes of everyday life."

So droned on the lecturer, an advanced graduate student.

"What is so fascinating about *The Book of Going Forth by Day*, an Eighteenth Dynasty creation, is that as a class of funerary documents, they represent a compilation of known Egyptian spells, which themselves are based upon hymns, prayers, myths, guidebooks, incantations, and even outright threats to the gods.

"Allow me to be clear," he said, "this class of funerary documents in no respect represents the entire corpus of ancient Egyptian magic. Rather, it's the tip of a vast iceberg, itself a commercial collection, fashioned by temple priests to appease a need. Think of it like automobile insurance, but for the afterlife.

"So, when did the Egyptians begin building their corpus of magical spells? The earliest preserved examples date back to Egypt's Old Kingdom, its Fifth Dynasty. Called the *Pyramid Texts*, the Egyptians carved these exclusively royal spells, as you might expect, inside pyramids and sarcophagi of pharaohs.

"But within the *Pyramid Texts* themselves, are clues, hints, and references to things that are much older than the Fifth Dynasty. References that reach back into ancient Egypt's Predynastic history, whispers of ritual cannibalism, human sacrifice, and star worship. My point here is that the practice of magic, manifested through oral and written spells, goes way back before Egypt, the unified civilization, came to being.

"So, what is Egyptian magic? Put simply, magic purportedly can manipulate the natural world through unnatural means, or, find knowledge about the natural world that is otherwise not obtainable.

"Great, wonderful. But how is it done? First off, you need to somehow acquire its secret knowledge or participate in a tradition or belief system that accepts such notions. So, right from the start, magic requires a cognitive component.

"Next, for magic to exist it requires an act of faith that the supernatural indeed exists. In short, another cognitive component. But for magic to exist, faith alone is not sufficient, for the emotional desire to influence must also be acknowledged.

"So, only with secret knowledge," the lecturer began to tick off with his fingers, "a belief system, faith, and desire, can rituals and objects be empowered by spells or incantations. That makes Egyptian spells, a faith-based, emotionally charged, verbalization of sheer desire. In essence, such visceral energy imparted by the magician energizes, empowers, and makes effective a ritual or object, be it a mask, amulet, staff, or even a common *ushabti* figurine."

Suddenly, this lecturer's message had meaning. His words spoke to the first year student. For empathically, it all made sense.

"For example, Spell Number Six, of *The Book of Going Forth by Day*, is a command that empowers a *ushabti* figurine to labor for its owner in the afterlife. What kinds of labors are depicted on the figurine, be it a farmer, a baker, or a brewer of beer. However, this is all possible because the *ushabti* originated from a priestly source, which manufactured the figurine and then sold it, no doubt, at a significant price. In essence, that purchase transferred the control of a semi-sentient magical being from its manufacturer over to its purchaser. And, human nature being what it is, there must have been a black market for such figurines. A market where the form and decoration of the *ushabti* figurine lacked the standardized quality of the mass produced temple-controlled versions. On the other hand, the black market perhaps manufactured figurines more specialized, maybe even more formidable. Which begs the question–did the ancient Egyptians use *ushabtis* only for assistance in the afterlife, or, did they employ them during life as well?"

For Melaina that lecture made an impact, as it put into perspective many things she had seen her mother doing as a child. Things hidden, secret things. Perhaps things that she would have passed on when her daughter had come of age.

Then, Melaina remembered mother's leather bound book—something she had forgotten about in the midst of all the turmoil of her mother's burial, the sealing up of the parent's flat, and the preparations for Oxford. Fortunately, Melaina knew where mother had hidden that book, having seen her returning it to its hidden sanctuary many times. Her mother had consulted it quite often, and almost always before something noteworthy had happened.

* * *

The next break between semesters, the first year returned to Alexandria, opened her parent's sealed flat, and retrieved the leather-covered book from the kitchen. The first time Melaina held it, the book opened naturally once on her lap, its format being wider than tall. Its discolored and blank cover looked sad and forgotten. Its brittle animal skin pages had yellowed with age. The writing faded and inscrutable. But while being held, Melaina smelled the lingering scent of her mother's favorite perfume, and in a sudden rush of emotion, cried over their memories forever past and future ones together never enjoyed. All of those had been so suddenly stolen away.

With tears flowing, several of them managed to land on the open pages of the ancient book. Brushing them aside so as to not further damage it, the pages before Melaina's eyes lost their yellowed patina and transformed themselves from brittle planes into soft and supple sheets. But most telling the cursive writing on their pages became darker, clearer, as if the ink had been applied that very day. She gasped at the miracle and almost dropped the old artifact. Then Melaina saw the book's cover. No longer blank, it now possessed a single line of large yellow characters. What they said, she didn't have a clue, but had a strong suspicion.

As Melaina ruffled through its pages she noted a different hand had written each page. Some wrote with an open and florid style, others small, tight, and cramped, and the rest, every style in between. At this point, for some reason, Melaina suspected the language was Egyptian Demotic, a language mixture of Egyptian and Greek, a precursor to medieval Coptic. If she wanted to know what mother's precious book said, what secrets it contained, she had to learn this ancient language, the very successor of the ancient Egyptian tongue. With that goal in mind, Melaina now knew what the focus of her studies would be at the university.

*   *   *

One semester later, Melaina had figured it all out. The book constituted a collection of useful and clever spells, along with some of a far darker purpose. In all, it contained one hundred and seventy-nine spells, all penned in black ink, divided with titles inked in red. Even the places for the insertion of a person's name, also indicated in red, paralleled in an uncanny way the form and vocabulary of known pharaonic magical spells. The only thing lacking to complete the parallel would be illustrations, those ever-so-poignant vignettes of the last judgment of the soul and the presentation of the justified deceased before the god of the Underworld–Osiris.

No. This book of spells could not be compared with a commercial production like *The Book of Going Forth by Day*. Quite the opposite. This was a private compilation, a book created to be read, and read aloud, by psychic individuals, who with their oral recitations "made effective" their desires. But no known magic spell from pharaonic times—preserved or published— had ever covered such topics as "The Blessing of an Infant's Bedding," "Causing Thread to Heal Itself," or "Pleading for a Hateful Neighbor's Death."

In the back of the book Melaina noted several leaves covered with what appeared to be a list, also written in Demotic, in all some sixty-seven items. To her everlasting shock, she noted that her mother's name appeared as the penultimate, with her grandmother's before hers, and her own name was the last, written in her mother's own hand. Perhaps this is how the book had recognized her. Tears had resurrected it from its own self-destruction triggered by Melaina's mother's death, a process explained at the book's beginning. Such a safeguard seemed wise given the book's varied content. All in all, this book carried the markings of an heirloom passed down from mother to first daughter. If correct, that meant Melaina's blood represented the last of a long line of pagan witches.

Also, that meant this list of names represented an unbroken line reaching back at least 1675 years, if one calculates a generation at twenty-five. Given the present year of 1992, that calculates out to the year AD 317, and the reign of the Roman Emperor Constantine the Great. Christianity had been decriminalized just four years prior with the Edict of Milan. In short, AD 317 fell within that gray transitionary period between the ascendency of Christianity and decline of paganism. Christian monasticism in Egypt had yet to begin. The last pious pagan Egyptian hieroglyphic inscription had yet to be cut. Melaina's book of spells originated from a profoundly pagan environment– Egyptian, Greek, Roman, Persian, and who knows what else, yet tinged with early Christian beliefs. In sum, the book constituted a marvelous collection of magical confections. Now Melaina was its caretaker.

*   *   *

At the end of Melaina's first year at Oxford, she again returned to Alexandria and her parent's flat, but this time a smell of disagreeable air and a thick layer of dust greeted her. The kitchen, painted and tiled in white, now knowing what she had learned from the leather book of spells, no longer resembled a once favorite childhood place of memory. Instead, as Melaina stood in its center, the kitchen had taken on a strangeness. So she went into the dining room and placed the leather spell book in the very center of its table, orienting it in such a way as to imitate the cramped rectangle of the kitchen's layout. Then, the young witch began searching for what she did not know, but was quite certain she would find.

Melaina began, why she did not know, at the kitchen's eastern side, with its narrow counter, shelving above and drawers below. It didn't take long before she came upon a small brown paper bag. Within Melaina discovered a tiny mouse encased in a rectangular block of yellowed wax, with its head and bound feet with string extending out of the block. Oriented inward towards the kitchen, its head faced west. Removing this odd artifact, she placed it on the dining room table in its proper orientation. Melaina then began looking for other such tiny paper bags of waxed encased mice and soon did, finding three more, one for each cardinal direction, all facing inward.

Kitchen drawers are fascinating places where items, sometimes needed, sometimes not, find their place. In the drawers along the eastern side Melaina discovered a bound bunch of papyrus reed stems, all sharpened at one end, twelve in all. These too she transferred to the dining room table and arranged in their proper place.

Then, in the same drawer, she came across a crudely handmade wooden spoon with a round hole in the center of its shallow bowl. For whatever reason, Melaina held the spoon's concave bowl to her right eye and peered through it. Nothing. So she tried her left, dominant eye, and her world changed into an outline of detail suffused by grayish mist, but populated with glowing green objects scattered all about.

Removing the spoon, the normal world reappeared. Shocked, Melaina examined the counter's salt shaker that had glowed such a beautiful green. It looked normal, but upon opening it, it contained not salt, but something else, something unidentifiable, without smell, a grayish powder. So she moved it to the dining room table, placing it just so.

In a southern drawer, she discovered a small bag of wooden golf tees, all glowing green. Right next to them, sat a small ball of string. After unraveling a length, Melaina noted the presence of colorful knots made of yarn along its length.

What was their purpose? She thought.

After easily another thirty minutes of examining the kitchen through the magic "seeing" spoon, the dining room table began to fill up with items, most common-looking, but all anything but, because of their special greenish glow.

Then, for whatever reason, Melaina reversed the "seeing" spoon, and tested it first before her right eye and then again before her dominant left. Once again she beheld objects, but now with a marvelous golden color, against the grayish outline of the kitchen. While not many, she transferred them too to the dining room table.

One, however, requires mention. A common silver fork uncommonly formed. Made with four tongs, someone had bent back the outer ones onto themselves to form perfect circles as if to hold a soda straw or reed. Without question, the former utensil had been fashioned for some purpose. But what was it?

Finally, at long last and after a half a day's poking around, Melaina judged the kitchen clear of her mother's magical paraphernalia. But to make sure, she made another sweep. This time she reached out with her will and emotion and received a surprise. It turned out that four family pictures, which like the mice located on the four sides of the kitchen, emanated a strong pull, an irresistible tingling draw.

Again beginning with the eastern wall, Melaina removed the black and white still, this one of her youth, covered in flour, "helping" mother make bread. A tide of memories issued forth just gazing at it. The laughter of the moment, a mother's disapproving stare as she struggled not to laugh, and a smiling father who had captured the moment with an old Leica camera. Turning over that vivid memory with a smile, Melaina's eyes widened when she discovered on its back a small envelope sealed with a large red wax seal impression. Somehow resisting to open it, the picture went to its proper place in the dining room. And in mere moments, all four pictures, each with their wax-sealed envelopes, adorned the dining room table on its four sides.

Now, sure she had emptied the kitchen, Melaina stood before the dining room table, a mini facsimile of it, and attempted to take it all in. She tried to divine some rhyme or reason for it all. Then, it hit her. The envelopes!

*　　*　　*

Indeed, the envelopes, for they explained so very much. Written on rose-colored paper, scented with her mother's perfume, and with a subtle Demotic watermark, the contents of the four envelopes went into excruciating detail as they explained the entire kitchen's arrangement of magical protections, the many implements, and various ingredients. But not all, for when viewed through the "seeing" spoon, the golden-colored objects turned out to be those of her father! Melaina ever-adoring and industrious bureaucratic father had been a witch as well, or perhaps, maybe even a wizard!

CHAPTER 10
Alexandria, Egypt, 1991

THE FIFTH LESSON

The Creator allowed both good demons and bad demons. Both, if carelessly left unattended, produce mischief and disaster. To conjurer forth such beings without proper preparation or plan, are the actions of a witless fool. Only those practiced in such dealings should do so, and, only for the most honorable of reasons.

The Knot of Eternity. (trans.) G. L. Love. 2nd. edition with T. Good. (Old Oaks Academy Press, 1960), vol. I.1, 16.

Melaina well recognized honest mistakes happen within all professions, even medicine. But when harm is done, and its correction is either by intent or through malice, ignored, then such action, or in this case inaction, constituted an egregious violation of the Hippocratic Oath. However, this animal, who so harmed her trusting mother in her time of medical distress, needed due punishment. The only question in Melaina's mind was how. In time, however, an appropriate solution made itself known. She would send him a gift, a word that means "poison" in the German language.

*   *   *

The DHL delivery truck pulled up to the women's medical clinic on Amin Fekry Street near Alexandria's El Gamaa Hospital. This is where Melaina's mother

79

had been allowed to bleed out due to sloppy procedure—a careless nick of an artery, and thereafter sheer indifference. The young witch addressed the package, a shoebox, to the senior physician of the clinic, the animal who had committed this atrocity. Within the package, she sent the physician a green faience mummiform figurine, shaped in the ancient manner with its arms crossed on the chest and its length covered with the black hieroglyphs of its "awakening" spell. Patient like a spider, Melaina watched as the delivery man performed his task and waited for him to depart the clinic.

From within the book of spells she selected a nasty one. Curious as to how it worked, Melaina invoked this spell and its associated demon upon a dressed chicken purchased in the marketplace. That experiment had not worked. Undeterred, she next bought a live chicken, brought it home, tried again, and the spell worked its horrible deed while the chicken screamed in agony until it expired.

Sitting outside the clinic on the bus stop's bench, Melaina closed her eyes, gathered herself, and began to mouth the necessary words, lips moving soundlessly, as she chanted in the ancient Demotic tongue:

I invoke you today, Syrokkata.

You who dissolve the sinews and the ligaments and the joints, you are to dissolve the sinews of Dr. Hisham Ibrahim Matraway for all time.

Once your dreadful task is completed, banish yourself to back from which you came.

This she repeated four times, once each in deference to the cardinal points of the compass. Again she waited, but this time not for long. Shrieks and cries for help began emanating from the clinic's second floor, from the physician's office. Several moments later an emergency ambulance appeared from the hospital nearby. Several medics rushed their gurney into the clinic, pushing aside many in the process.

Again, she waited with a brief smile of satisfaction. From the noise and commotion coming from the ground floor, Melaina reasoned something unusual was going on. Then out came the gurney, this time occupied by the most horrible sight she had ever witnessed. The man on it, still in his white examination coat, had his chest exposed and an oxygen mask in place. The bluish hue of his skin didn't look good, nor did his labored breathing, his face contorted in agony. His entire form appeared disjointed, unarticulated, and limp-looking, like a bowl of well-cooked noodles.

At first Melaina felt a moment of conscience for the unfortunate animal, experienced a pang of guilt for what she had done. But then the young witch remembered what her mother had gone through, recalled the ignored calls for help, the screams of pain, all because her mother was a Copt and her physician a follower of Allah.

As the wail of the ambulance's siren faded off in the distance, Melaina looked down at hands that shook with fear for what she had done. She had murdered a man with her very first act of magic. Then and there, Melaina vowed not to take a life again. Then and there, the young witch prayed that she would never have to break that vow.

*   *   *

The Egyptian detective shook his gray and thinning head of hair in shock and disbelief as he read the summary of the autopsy report.

> Subject died from asphyxiation due to the sudden loss of the diaphragm's structural integrity. Death was secondarily caused by multiple constrictions of the aortic network as the subject's skeletal structure had failed.

How did this happen?
Did someone do this to him?
If so, how?
And more importantly, why? The homicide detective wondered.
Is there a connection between his recently received parcel and his sudden death?
Having never seen anything like these contents before, and not knowing what they might mean, the detective continued to speculate in ever-widening circles of fantastic possibilities. His innate instincts told him nothing seemed right. Then a thought occurred to him, considering the odd contents of the man's parcel, he reached for his desk phone.

After five rings, the perplexed detective reached his party.

*   *   *

The Egyptian detective paced in his office before his visitor arrived from the Antiquities Bureau of Alexandria. He seemed to be the best one to identify the object found in the unfortunate gynecologist's DHL parcel.

The French antiquity's expert, while wearing a pair of protective Latex gloves, lifted out the greenish-colored object from its tan-colored seltzer swaddling. The man squinted as he held it up to the light, turning it.

"Detective, it is good that you did not disturb this ancient artifact, that is, *if* it even is one." The man said with a knowing smile. "I suspect it is a copy of an Eighteenth Dynasty *ushabti*, or burial figurine, meant to assist its owner in the afterlife. Typically, these represented magical laborers, farmers, weavers, and the like. But since I do not read hieroglyphs, may I borrow this," and then he made a rude sound with his lips, "this artifact for a professional translation?"

While the detective didn't want to do so, he also wanted to get to the bottom of this grisly case, and so relented.

Seeing the detective's face, the antiquity's expert assured, "Have not a care, *Monsieur*, I will return this to you within three days' time, without damage, and with a complete translation of what these symbols say."

*   *   *

"*Monsieur*, thank you for bringing to me this extraordinary *objet d'art* to examine. As you rightly surmised, it isn't ancient at all, but it is an extremely fine copy. I would judge it to be in the style of the Eighteenth Dynasty. As for its inscription, I know as well as I its meaning."

Also wearing Latex gloves, the heavy-set CMES head of the Security and Communications of Alexandria turned the object in his massive hands while reading its message to himself. After all, both men realized that you never, ever, verbalize an unknown magical spell unless you know its content and purpose.

"*Monsieur*," the CMES security expert said, "this inscription is as straightforward in its meaning as it is harmless. It merely awakens the *ushabti*." As he replaced it back within its seltzer-filled box.

"*Monsieur*. Did you happen to notice these hieroglyphs written on the interior of this parcel?"

"*Quoi?*" the French antiquity's expert exclaimed.

Looking up into his face, the CMES security official then said, "The act of opening the parcel triggered the *ushabti*, allowing the sender to project a spell through the lips of the figurine, as if they stood face-to-face with the victim."

By the look on the Frenchman's face, the CMES security and communications official could tell he hadn't grasped the significance of his words.

"*Monsieur*, the clever conjurer who sent this object is very dangerous. Because once this *ushabti* awoke, it acted like the phone on your desk. It could project sound, words, a voice, music, and yes, even a dangerous spell that breaks down the bone and cartilage of a human being. Think of the awakened *ushabti* as a magical radio speaker."

Now understanding what his colleague wished to impart, the Frenchman blurted out, "I cannot tell that to the homicide detective! He'd have me committed!"

"*Non Monsieur*, you cannot tell the inspector the sad truth. But you can honesty tell him the hieroglyphs on his figurine have no significance to his case. In short, they are a dead end.

"But, *Monsieur*," the CMES security and

communications head said with a raised eyebrow, "we know differently, don't we? We know definitively the that magic caused the physician's death and magic alone. We must alert our Gathering that a formidable rogue practitioner is abroad. Even more importantly, that practitioner killed one of our own."

*   *   *

Murder, and in particular the murder of one of their own, CMES does not take lightly. Needless to say, the report of Alexandria's CMES head of security and communications got the immediate attention of his superior, The Dark One, who in turn contacted Rome about the case and made a very pointed request. That very evening, a spell whisperer contracted from a non-aligned organization flew to Alexandria to examine the *ushabti*.

*   *   *

"This is an odd case," the spell whisperer, who wished to remain anonymous, stated for the record.

"How so?" The Dark One replied from behind his massive desk.

"Well, first off, the paint used on both the figurine and parcel's interior for this simple awakening spell is itself spell-bound. Whoever mixed the paint in essence encrypted the identity of its maker. That in my experience is quite unique. The implication is the spell is either ancient and obscure, or the conjurer created it *de novo*. Either way, we are up against something brand new, and as you are well aware, that in itself is *extremely* rare.

"Secondly, the actual spell which claimed your unfortunate member, cannot be recovered nor tracked back to its conjurer as the figurine itself acted as a secondary, filtering medium. In short, the Egyptian figurine served as a magically-empowered, one-way, sound device, much like a common electronic speaker.

"So, in conclusion," the man shrugged, "I cannot be of any help whatsoever in identifying who performed this quite uncommon conjuring."

"I see," The Dark One quipped. "However, if this murder had happened to one of your enclave, what would you do?"

At this direct question, the spell whisperer thought, shook his head, and took his time before he replied.

"I am at a loss. But I will discuss the matter confidentially with several members. If there is a breakthrough, I promise you will be the first to know. On that you have my word.

"Sir, I cannot stress this point enough. What your Gathering has experienced with this murder is unique. Uniqueness in the paranormal community is not a good thing, as there always has to be a balancing factor. Some sort of a corrective. But this mode of conjuring represents a dangerous escalation, an open license to kill without any possible recourse."

CHAPTER 11
Battle of Nasiryiah, Iraq, 2003

THE SIXTH LESSON

The mortal world provides the battlefield upon which good and evil compete. Here souls have a choice. Either to better themselves through acts of charity, mercy, and love, or to wrongly bond themselves to the spearhead of hatred, prejudice, and utter inhumanity. The mortal world is an unforgiving place, often referred to as the crucible, the flame, or the balance.

The Knot of Eternity. (trans.) G. L. Love. 2nd. edition with T. Good. (Old Oaks Academy Press, 1960), vol. I.1, 14.

When I entered the U.S. Marines, my world as seen through people's auras changed a whole bunch. I discovered what serious stress could do. One guy in the platoon wanted to do well, and in the main, he did fine. But for him to get there, his usual light pastel yellow-green aura under stress would brightened like a light bulb ready to explode. That is what stress does to you. You have to manage it, otherwise, it will consume you.

To this very day, I still do not know why a particular drill sergeant derived such pleasure from his unnecessary brow-beating ways. Nonetheless, there are many ways to reach a goal, to make a point, I didn't buy this joker's approach, and so I gutted through the experience as a lesson in how *not* to do things.

After all, what is the point of tearing apart an inspected barracks needlessly, pilfering parts from dissembled rifles during timed maintenance drills, and removing toilet paper from the heads? When all that time could have been better spent on the firing range or with defensive skills classes? Normally, and I'm not naming names, but this sergeant displayed a deep red aura that underlined his grounded, strong-willed, and realistic world view. Fine. But when he went on an angry tear, his red aura would muddy up. That's when I first encountered my first military nut-case.

*   *   *

Somalia and all the U.N. efforts surrounding that theater brought into stark relief what happens when people's auras are amped up in battlefield conditions. Hate, courage, raw fear, pain, stress, and helplessness added unmistakable qualities to auras. But by far the creepiest auras I saw had to be the browns, muddied browns, dark colors, and blacks, which marked someone as a dangerous threat.

At times, these ghastly-looking auras even seemed to take on a life of their own, hideously writhing around their host like slimy eels. I saw such an individual at our base camp in Qatar before the First Iraqi War. He looked like an everyday Joe except he wore his personal body armor right in the middle of our bivouac. That in itself didn't make sense, especially in such heat. But when he walked into our NCO Club, all hell broke loose. He killed almost twenty of my fellow Marines. His personal armor was a bomb vest.

Ever since that horrific experience, as soon as I saw a black writhing aura, I would apprehend or stop them any way I could. As a consequence, my auraic sight kept my squad alive. I uncovered dozens of ambushes, picked out suicide bombers from within a crowd, and spotted bad guys. I found them so easily that my squad called me a witch. Maybe they're right.

*   *   *

> The bloodiest day of operations for the Marines was 23 March, 2003, when eighteen men of Charlie Company, 1st Battalion, 2nd Marines, were killed, and eight Amphibious Assault Vehicles were disabled in heavy fighting with Iraqi forces. The Marines were engaged by RPGs, mortar, and artillery fire, as well as by Iraqi tanks hidden behind buildings. In addition, a friendly-fire incident occurred when two A-10s strafed the Marine vehicles of Charlie Company by mistake, killing at least one Marine and wounding perhaps as many as seventeen.

> ("Battle of Nasiriyah", *Official Regimental History of the First Iraq War,* Washington, D.C., 2009, p. 43).

I, Sergeant Jonathan Joseph Stone, 1st Battalion, 2nd Marines Expeditionary Brigade, Alpha Company, 1st Rifle platoon, 1st Squad, fought the acrid, choking smoke. Soot floated suspended in the air like fluffy feathers. Sand and grit found its way into every nook and cranny. The rank, sweet stink of rotting corpses permeated everything. But some of those poor devils hadn't died yet. Their bodies torn asunder, somehow they managed to yell their heads off. Their continuous screaming lent an eerie and surreal soundtrack to the battlefield. You couldn't listen to it or it would drive you crazy. Somehow, you had to learn to block it out.

The air buzzed with ordnance, the kind of stuff that can kill you in a heartbeat. Pure, sheer death. With so much of it in the air you couldn't do the merciful thing, and put an end to some crying guy's misery. Yeah, the Battle of Nasiriyah was a real slice.

Even today I struggle with the memory of that battle, much less how I managed to get my twelve guys through it. One would have thought I had seen it all after twelve years in this man's corps. Well, guess what? I sure as hell hadn't. Nasiriyah dished out to us grunts an epic, professional-grade shit storm.

Our mission profile told us to take and hold a highway cloverleaf, so our mobile forces could roll on toward Baghdad. Our mission' challenge, however, involved the occupiers of the immediate buildings surrounding the cloverleaf, who needed to be cleared.

The Opposition Forces, or OpFor, turned out to be a smorgasbord of fanatical terrorists, disaffected religious extremists, criminal gangs released by Sadam "Insane," all too sneaky guerrilla Republican Guard elements, not to mention some international anarchists who joined in for fun.

OpFor of every type I could identify, by their auras. Normal pastels and solids got jacked up with battlefield emotion. Fear and stress rendered an aura bright, blurred, and fuzzy. Occasionally, I'd run into these odd-ball auras, muddied, darkened colors, ranging even to deep, jet black. I identified those as the true bad guys, versus an enemy combatant scared out of his wits. These individuals needed to get zapped, like right quick.

Regardless of which OpFor flavor, all dug themselves in as deep as a Louisiana tick, and these motherfuckers lobbed everything they could at my rifle squad. As a result, we spread out in six teams of two, grabbing whatever cover available, with me running around checking on my guys, while trying to make sense of the situation.

As for the Opfor, they hid out there, somewhere, sure as shit in all that urban rubble, shielded by smoke, no doubt itching to ambush us first thing. Damn motherfuckers.

Proof of that happened while I shuttled between Team Two and Three.

Twap!

Twap!

Twap!

Twap!

Grunt.

The bullet impacts took my breath away. Each gasp laced with knife-like pain. My heart wanted to explode. I looked down and saw no blood.

That was close, I thought, curled over my knees in excruciating agony.

Then a thought screamed into my ear.

J. J., get up off of your fucking knees! Move to cover, Marine.

My eyes widened.

And while you're at it, keep your men moving, too!

I staggered to my feet and began scrambling, jinking and juking, directing my rifle squad to better cover and keeping us alive.

Twap!

Twap!

Grunt.

*   *   *

Private First Class Homer Johnson saw his sergeant go down and didn't think twice. He leapt from his cover and started dragging his commander over to a pile of rocks by his collar strap.

"Sarg! Are you okay?"

Groan.

"Got hit in the back. See if I'm bleeding."

A quick look.

"Nope. You're dry, sir."

Relief passed through J. J. like a tidal wave.

"Damn. I thought that one split me in two. Thanks, Homer, you saved my bacon."

He earned a big dusty and sweaty grin.

Pause.

"Now stay put here, Homer. Where's your buddy, Peters?"

"Over there, behind that wrecked pickup, Sarg."

"Good. Okay. Be sure to hook back up with him. Remember we're all buddies. Got that, Mister?"

"Yes, sir."

"Does he know you're here, Homer?"

"Yeah. I drew the short straw." Johnson said, again with that big grin of his.

*   *   *

With my act together, I took off to check on the rest of my team.

At that very moment, my men had scattered themselves along our sector, forming a ragged line facing the OpFor in the buildings beyond the cloverleaf. We took advantage of every square inch of available cover, be it a wrecked vehicle, the concrete abutments of the cloverleaf, or in my case, a shell crater. With all the burning tires, diesel, cordite, dust, and what-have-you in the air, visibility sucked. Breathing in all that shit sucked worse.

On top of that, it was high noon, and hotter than hell. With our poor visibility, the heat, and the uncertain location of the OpFor, I wasn't very happy. No, sir. Not one bit.

As I peeked over the forward rim of my crater, I heavy fire greeted me that kicked up a rock and dust sandwich. I ducked and got a stony shower.

Then, for some dumb-ass reason, I peeked again.
TWANG!

*   *   *

Private Johnson saw his sergeant's head snap backwards.
Holy shit! Sarg bought it!

CHAPTER 12
Melaina's New Life

Three days after her mother's murderer met his end, Melaina departed Alexandria for the United States. Armed with an Oxford degree, she had been accepted by the University of Chicago's graduate program in ancient Near Eastern languages. Melaina didn't know what excited her more–starting her life anew or becoming part of that department's ambitious Demotic Dictionary Project.

Upon her arrival, she discovered that her three large parcel post boxes had preceded her and had arrived unscathed to an office space on the second floor. Within these Melaina had packed her life's possessions, which included all of her mother's magical paraphernalia. As for the book of spells, that she had kept on her person out of a paranoid fear of somehow losing it.

*   *   *

Four years later in 1996 Melaina matriculated with a PhD in ancient Near Eastern Languages. Time had flown by. Her thesis, no surprise, dealt with the magical language and vocabulary of the Demotic and Coptic languages. While a broad topic, the young witch ended up learning quite a bit about her mother's special book and uncovered in the process three hidden spells to boot.

Three months after her graduation, Melaina published her thesis and thereafter secured a tenure-track assistant professorship at Berkeley in their department of Near Eastern Studies.

Life once again changed. While her Midwestern colleagues had voiced their warnings, the entire California scene overwhelmed the Egyptian. She felt more than once as if her feet floated across the ground.

By the fall semester of 2004 and eight years of scholarly pursuit, Melaina became part of the department. Already promoted twice, now a full professor, she had found her academic niche within a tight circle of international scholars devoted to the magic of the ancient Near East.

A brilliant scholar named Peter Glass at the University of Pennsylvania led this obscure movement. He asked Melaina to read a paper at the next archaeological convention being held in San Francisco. While she demurred to Peter's offer, Melaina did promise to would attend and join him and several others for dinner that evening.

However, Melaina didn't want to present a paper. To Peter's objection she pointed out it didn't seem fair to take up time that a hungry and more deserving graduate student could put to good use. While Peter didn't like that answer, he did say he would reserve a slot if she changed her mind.

As it turned out, Peter gave away Melaina's slot to a military-type who wasn't even in college. In fact, Peter later explained that the fellow had applied to his department on the recommendation of a colleague. On the basis of this man's presentation on a topic already accepted by a professional journal, Peter thought of it as a final interview. That impressed Melaina and here this fellow had not even entered college. Never in Melaina's wildest imaginings did she realize how that session would change her life, for his presentation rocked her world.

CHAPTER 13
USNS Comfort

Oh shit!

The round's impact caused me to tumble down to the bottom of the crater. My ears peeled in my helmet like a church bell. With the left side of my head numbed stupid, it felt like a blindside hit from a linebacker. Reflexively I reached up and felt a ragged gash across my helmet's left temple.

I kept shaking my head in an effort to clear all the ringing.

Then, I looked down and stopped breathing, because between my knees, sticking out of the ground, lay a tan hexagonal shape.

"Oh God no! Please, God no! Don't be a chemical munitions!" I moaned as I needed to get my shit together right quick.

"Okay, J. J. Calm down. Remember bomb school. Bomb school. First. Access the threat," I babbled as I dug out the longish, handmade object from the crater's wall, using the two fingers of my right hand.

"Okay, J. J., it's not manufactured, not made of metal. That's good...I think," I tried to reassure myself. "It's made of that stuff you make bricks out of... mud, clay." I murmured as my racing pulse began its fall from the heights of Mount Everest. In fact, each of its six sides seemed to be impressed with tiny little wedge-like markings.

With the object almost revealed, I grabbed the hexagon with both hands and pulled it out of the earth. It weighed only about a pound or two. I rocked the object in my hands, noting a subtle shift in its weight.

I turned it upright to examine it. For some odd reason my right index finger traced along the top edge of one of its flat surfaces from left to right. I sensed a snag on my index finger's pad. So I mindlessly performed the action once again. To this day, I don't know why, but boy what a game-changer.

At the completion of my finger's second pass, the surface of the ceramic container glowed blue, a color that spread wave-like up my fingers, arms, and covered my entire body. I didn't feel any fear or pain. In fact, I sat there at the crater's bottom, dumbfounded, while the battle beyond seemed a million miles away. I heard in my head a deep, resonant, male voice.

"I am so very happy you have found me! Now, place this container carefully amidst your belongings and protect it so it might not be lost. Once so secured, then sleep my soul carrier…sleep."

Tearing off my backpack, I clawed at its main pouch and made room for the object by flinging thoughtlessly over my shoulder my last four pairs of clean socks. Then I inserted the object, zipped up the flap, put my pack back on, cinched it snug, and passed out.

*   *   *

I woke up with painful beams of light shining into my eyes. Like persistent fireflies that I couldn't swat, they would not leave me be. My ears felt assaulted by a loud beeping. I almost levitated off the bed at the sound of a beeping bedside monitor.

"Well, hello there, Sergeant Stone!" the doctor holding the offending pen light said while smiling down at me. His name plate said BLAKE. His rank said lieutenant.

"What…where am I? Where're my men? Are they okay?" I managed to croak out.

"Easy Marine! Easy now! Get a hold of yourself," the doc said as he restrained me from getting up.

"Your men are *all* safe, Marine. In fact, they're all on leave in Qatar. As for you, you're aboard a hospital ship, the U.S.N.S. *Comfort*. We're anchored off the Saudi coast." The doctor narrated as he poked me here and there, his forehead creased in interest as his fingers traced some old scars on my forearms.

"What about my M4? My backpack?"

"Your weapon and battle gear are in inspection, and after that, they'll be stowed in a secured locker.

"As for you, sergeant, you've been through a lot, and had us worried. You came in with six deep thoracic bruises. You sustained three cracked ribs and your kidneys took a beating. The left one has me worried. You might have a laceration. As to how bad it is, I won't know until I get the blood work back," he said as he continued checking all the monitors hooked up to me.

He checked my eyes again with that damn pen light.

What a multi-tasker this guy is.

"As for that crease you got across your helmet. Now that was a real doozy." The doc concluded.

Crease?

That detail jogged loose a memory or two, because I reached up to feel my left temple.

"Yes, sergeant, that's correct," said the pleased doctor. "That hit your left temple.

"In short, Marine, you got e-vaced out of a real hornet's nest. Do you remember anything about it?"

I tried to answer the doc, but my dry throat wouldn't let me.

"Sorry about that soldier. Where's my manners?" he said while extending a large plastic water bottle and a bendy straw.

"Here, drink up. But drink *slowly*. It'll wash out some of that crud in your throat."

Now crouching down in a squat next to my bed, Lt. Blake looked me in the eye.

"So you know, sergeant, if your blood work is clear, I'm going to transfer you over to psychiatric observation because of that ding to your head. Your eyes are still dilated from a concussion. Once there, you will be asked a bunch of questions. My advice? Answer them. Trust me, I'm doing this for your own good. Just roll with it. Got that sergeant?"

I nodded like a bobble-head doll.

*   *   *

Finding patient J. J. Stone aboard the U.S.N.S. *Comfort* didn't faze Gunny Sergeant Mason Grant, as he knew the ship stem to stern.

He located his quarry in the Recovery Ward.

As Gunny Sgt. Mason approached the bed, he saw a torso bruised black, blue, and yellow in spite of the extensive bandaging. The injuries looked bad, as in painful to breathe. Mason watched the nurse as she removed an IV drip from Stone's right hand.

Walking up to the bed, Mason said, "You must be First Sergeant J. J. Stone. It looks like you're being transferred out of sick bay."

"Yo, Gunny. That's me. And yes, sir, I passed my blood work," Stone replied, assessing the stocky and well turned out non-commissioned officer.

"I have some souvenirs for you, sir," Gunny Mason continued as he turned over a weighed down baggie.

"You came out of a real shit storm by the looks of your gear. I found these six bullet fragments in your armor. They're all .762s."

The gunny looked the soldier in the eye.

"Rest assured. All your gear and weapons have been inspected, cleaned, repaired as needed, and placed in stores. God speed, son."

"Thank you, gunny."

The men shook hands.

When the gunny turned to walk away, he sensed out of the corner of his eye a warm glow. Stopping in his tracks, he turned on a heel, and glanced back over at Stone. For all the world, he swore that Stone was bathed in a golden light.

*　　*　　*

Eventually, Nature called. The first time I tried to get up from my hospital bed, my knees buckled. Fortunately, my nurse caught me.

"Easy there, sergeant. You can't jump up like that and expect your body to respond after what you have been through. Go slow, or I'll get the piss bottle."

So I did, like baby steps, as I shuffled my way toward the head, needing to pee. By the way, I hate those piss bottles. I entered the head and got lost as if I had never been on a Navy ship before, worse, the reflected image in the mirror shocked me and caused me to stagger back.

Jesus, J. J.! What made you to stagger like that? I know my bell was rung, but to stumble, too?

Holy shit!

Maybe the doc's right.

Maybe my head is messed up.

CHAPTER 14
Nergal

I am Nergal, son of Hanal, of the city of Ur. What an odd sensation. So this is what merging with my soul carrier is like. The pleasure of feeling once again the rhythmic staccato of a heartbeat, the swell of a chest after so long. The tactile chill of goose bumps across the hair of my soul carrier's arm tickle me. My soul carrier begins to stir and even the subtlest of body movements are quite novel, filling my mind with glorious sensations. The incantation worked!

As a test, I make an exploratory brush of the tongue against my soul carrier's teeth and am rewarded with feeling their slickness. So indeed I do possess some control.

Suddenly, a cacophonous sound assaults my ears. Several people are speaking, but their language is unintelligible. So many guttural grunts and strange intonations.

Smells, yes, strange odors assail my nostrils, and for the life of me, I cannot begin to identify any of them.

Then my eyes flutter open. The images are outlandish and disorienting. There must be something wrong. Everything is a blur. Does my soul carrier have poor eyesight? Then, they clear.

Truth be told, I am quite frightened. In many ways I feel much like a new born babe, except that I possess a mature consciousness and a full set of memories. This new world is very different from my homeland. I have to learn to understand it. But before I can begin to do that, I am confronted with complexity everywhere. This new place is overwhelming. The spoken language I cannot directly understand. Instead, I must "listen" to my soul carrier's conscious thoughts to better understand their meaning. That process isn't easy, as his thoughts are made and discarded so fast, while my understanding of them is so slow, second-hand, and inexact. In addition, this language they are speaking is layered with strange emotional flavorings and meanings that I can only hope to decipher with time, experience, and context.

*   *   *

I find this new world to be both wondrous and frightening. As a young boy I often heard traders in the marketplace describe the vastness of the Great Southern Sea, but now I can see those waters through my soul carrier's eyes. To my surprise, the open sea smells like a typical salt water marsh from my homeland, but only much fresher and sweeter.

The small island we stand upon, called the Comfort, *is not an island, but instead a metal boat of unimaginable size.*

*   *   *

I find my soul carrier obsesses with personal hygiene and grooming. Regarding bodily elimination, while I recognize the need and bodily parts involved, their custom of standing above a clean water container I think is a wasteful practice. The sudden disappearance of the befouled water, once my soul carrier finished urinating, I again find to be a mystery. Where did the befouled water go?

Next, we stand before a walled area with a shiny

metal offering bowl. Then I received the surprise of my life! For arranged above the offering bowl is a reflective metal or stone, and in it, I see for the first time the visage of my soul carrier. I jerk back in surprise. My soul carrier, however, seems confused, and discomforted. Why? I do not know.

We are naked from the waist up wearing a tawny, sand-colored covering around our girdle. Our skin is pale, yet our forearms, hands, neck and face are dark and tanned. Our eyes are the blue of the sky, a thing I had never before seen, but heard whispered about in the marketplace. Our hair is the color of ripe wheat and is cut very close. Why does he not shave his head altogether, as I always did? But the greatest shock is that we are beardless, like the rest of the men we encountered. How can a man exhibit his manhood without a beard?

Before I had time to consider this last detail, my soul carrier moves again, and this time he begins another ritual, which takes place before the shiny metal offering bowl. From a small leather bag, my soul carrier takes out a colorful stick with stiff white fur at one end. Upon the stiff bristles of the stick, he squeezes from what looks like a goat intestine a greenish substance. The stick and substance then go into our mouth, while moving the stick back and forth across our teeth. This process creates foam in our mouth, and drips out, much like a maddened dog. The greenish substance tastes like a fresh mint salad. Our gums tingle, which I find pleasurable. My soul carrier spits out the foam into the stone offer bowl and then turns the right hand shiny metal fixture. When he does so, clear and cold water issues forth from the center fixture like a rushing mountain stream. Where does that come from? And to whence does it go? Overall, the brushing of the teeth ritual cleans our teeth no better than the application of fine sea salt to one's finger.

The day's marvels, however, are not over. My soul carrier next produces another stick from his leather bag, but this one is black with an odd attachment at one end, which he places in the bottom of the offering bowl. Is he preparing a sacrifice? He turns the left hand shiny metal fixture and again water issues forth from the central fixture, but this time the clear water is hot. How does that come to pass? Where is the smoke from the cooking fire to produce it?

My soul carrier grasps another goat intestine from his leather bag and he squeezes out another green material. This he wets in the offering bowl with the warmed water and then rubs it all over our face, creating a great foaming reaction. This tickles the skin wherever it is applied. Looking into the polished surface, my soul carrier appears to possess the short beard of an adolescent, except it is white. He grasps the oddly shaped stick and begins to remove the white foam from our face with short, purposeful strokes.

Unfortunately, I am so fascinated by this process that I interfered, causing several bleeding cuts on my soul carrier's face. With embarrassment, I back away as he finishes the process, swearing at what he thinks is his own clumsiness. Then, my soul carrier touches to the three bleeding cuts yet another stick from his magical bag. This stick is small and thin, but stings our face wherever he touches an open wound. Ah ha, *I* conclude, practical medicine at work. *But I do not understand the process. So I search my soul carrier's memories and find that this ritual is called "shaving."*

It must be clear to anyone even with a donkey's brain that one's facial hair grows quickly. So why remove it? My own luxuriant beard I found to be quite practical and handsome. So, in this culture, is this ritual of shaving a daily process? What a waste of time. And water.

To complete my soul carrier's morning ablutions, he steps into a narrow, shiny metal niche in a wall, which on one side wall again are three shiny fixtures, but the central one in this case is placed high above the other two. Upon seeing them, I have my suspicions based upon the small offering bowl. After he turns both of the lower fixtures, that action produces a warming cascade of clear water upon our head. After he wets down our body, a roundish soft stone is rubbed all around, and it too creates a foaming reaction, is pleasantly scented, and again delights the skin. This ritual, called "showering," is brief, much to my relief, as it too is wasteful of water. Do these people perform this every day? Do they not revel in nature's own bodily aromas? Afterwards, he dries us off with several white linens. That process I understand.

As for my soul carrier's physical state, ours is a large body that seems to be always hungry. Granted his choice of food is unrecognizable, but it is palatable. As for his drink of choice, called Diet Coke, I find it to be refreshing. I especially like all the bubbles, but it is so cold, for mixed in within the liquid are clear-looking nuggets, something called "ice." Is there no end to these curious marvels?

The answer to that question is no, for by far my greatest shock occurred during our preparations for the long journey back to a place called the "States." I searched through my soul carrier's vivid memories to get a sense for this place he calls home, but none of it makes any sense. The journey itself, and especially the views out of the windows of the metal flying bird, causes me to shrink back in utter horror at the blasphemy. Only the gods traverse the sky. And yet, here I am, doing so.

*   *   *

In my attempts to understand my soul carrier's life, I probe his memories while he sleeps. I am curious about who my soul carrier is. What I discover is a strong family background, a warrior's son, and a ingrained sense of discipline. In some ways my soul carrier could almost be my brother. Searching further, I find a powerful sense of loyalty, place, community, and an emotional love affair. But my soul carrier also suffers from a tragic loss, like I did. Excruciating emotional pain, bitter sorrow, and personal guilt! All so unnecessary. He didn't even have command of the conveyance.

This grotesque memory that my soul carrier harbors deep in his heart, the beautiful girl Grace, the imbibing of too much drink, his inability to protect his love, all bind my soul carrier's inner-most thoughts into knots of pain.

After I lost my Erish, oh, how I grieved, and yes, I cursed the very ground upon which Nippur stood. But never had I internalized the anguish so! Then I decided to do something that I dared not to do before, until now. I spoke to my soul carrier's subconscious, sleeping self.

"What happened to you is not your fault. You shouldn't persecute yourself. It is not fair, either to you, or to the memory of Grace. Your grief is destructive, and is something that is most unnecessary. Instead, my soul carrier, consider this. Your love for Grace, your purest love, will endure. It is eternal. It is something that must be remembered and revered. But there will be another. Be at peace and grieve no more."

CHAPTER 15
The Raid

God-awful screams that wrench the soul. Frantic
cries for assistance. The dreadful moans of the
lingering. A black smudge of stifling smoke filled
the air and burned the lungs as entire
neighborhoods burned, horribly. Cruel soldiers,
moving about like ghostly wraiths, blundered
about pillaging. Males of all ages were slaughtered
like cattle. As for any women and girls so
unfortunate to be found, well, imagine their plight!

(W. Pohl, *Sumerische Keilschriftentexte. Erlauter-
ungen und Überstetzungen.* Band I. Berlin. Nr. 35:
Spalten 1-6)

Thus an ancient cuneiform tablet described the raid on
the Sumerian city of Ur, by its northern neighbor
Nippur, over 4,000 years ago.

*   *   *

*I am Nergal, son of Hanal, of the city of Ur, I survived
that raid, but my wife did not as a raiding party took
her. Looking back on this horrific event, I had
descended from our temple's observation tower at
dawn's first light, for I saw the fire and smelled the
smoke.*

*I, Nergal, am a scribe and the second temple
astronomer of the god Nanna. I remember walking
through the temple's library and scribal archive. In the
courtyard, the lightening sky had already blackened*

with smoke. *I panicked, and ran as fast as I could all the way to my household. Along the way, I saw many places burning. Several bloodied bodies lay in the streets. Those not injured ran about, not stopping to help the fallen. I didn't either. I needed to get home.*

What is going on?

Who has done this?

By the time I reached my household, I found it ablaze. Heedlessly, I entered in search of my young bride, Erish. I did not find her. The frame of her vertical loom that she loved and labored over, had been knocked askew and her fine work lay torn to pieces smoldering on the ground. That one detail alone had almost stopped my heart from beating.

I emerged from my household batting at a spark in my singed beard. My white robe and arms were streaked with soot. Frantic beyond all imagination, looking from side to side, I screamed my beloved's name.

"Erish! Erish! Erish!"

Moments passed like hours, and nowhere could I find my wife. I did not find Erish at her parent's household, which had been spared from the flames. The wounded had not seen her. Thank the gods she could not be found among the rows of the gathered dead.

I slowed down and forced myself to think. Clues began to materialize all around me. Most of the dead had been slashed. While many households burned, the granaries did not. The temple and its treasury remained untouched. Whoever had done this, their numbers could not have been great. It all seemed so senseless.

"Where is she?" I hoarsely screamed.

"Probably taken by those soldiers," a bedraggled

elderly man said. "Must have been a small raiding party, as they acted like blundering oxen, taking little, but burning much."

"What? Where?"

"Through the northern gate." He pointed with a bloodied hand. "They broke in before dawn and overpowered our guards."

I ran to the northern gate. It stood wide open. Its timbers pushed in, shattered, white with sharp splinters. Amid this wreckage, the mangled bodies of our soldiers littered the area. Stepping over them, I reached the gate's threshold, and in the distance saw the dust cloud of the retreating raiders. I pulled at my beard in anguish. Erish had been carried off, captured as war booty to be sold, or worse. I fell to my knees. The blood-soaked earth stained my white robes. Tears ran down my cheeks in hot torrents. I knew I would never see her again.

*   *   *

For me, everything changed after the raid, after Erish disappeared. While I set to rebuilding my household, my skills centered on the stars, mathematics, and writing, not with the saw and adz. Nonetheless, its excursions helped numb the pain. I hung the singed and crumpled piece of tapestry that Erish had been working on over the top of her repaired loom. It's intricate design and interplay of colors constantly reminded me of her.

In the weeks that followed, I vowed not to give myself to another, as no one could fill my heart as had my Erish. My arms ached to hold her close again. My beard grew long and became ill-kept. My clothing became dirty and tattered. My neighbors thought me mad, as I so often cried out during my sleep. I turned inward and became solitary, cynical, and filled with doubt. Even so, I prayed to the all-powerful god Nanna for guidance. Why? Because if a man is to turn his back upon that which is known, he must first have an alternative. I didn't.

So I prayed.

Oh he who is Nanna.

The self-existent one, who is and exists by himself and that he is the self-perpetuating one, who is able to, and did, beget offspring out of his own nature.

Oh he who is Nanna.

Source of everything that belonged in the heavens above or the earth beneath, of the gods, of the world, of the macrocosm, and microcosm.

I, Nergal, entreat you to hear my plea and settle my mind and heal my soul.

Never once did my entreaties receive a reply. I prayed again and again. I began to contemplate on how could my all-powerful city-god allow such monstrous things to occur to his people? How could Nanna sanction it?

All my prayers came to naught. My will to live ebbed from my bones. I was a broken man. A sense of abandonment flowed in my veins. I felt adrift as in a river, snapped in half as if an unwanted reed. Yet the story of the reed reminded me there is a reason and a purpose for everything. I thought perhaps my prayers insufficient. Perhaps I had to do something more to attract the attention of my god.

In the months that followed, I took to searching the sacred archives of the temple for guidance. I looked for a means to sooth the eternal burning within my heart, a way to restore my confidence in my god.

Our city's temple housed an archive, a library, and a repository of administrative, literary, religious, and texts devoted to medicine, astronomy, architecture. They all survived the fire, which had been contained to the neighborhood nearest to the northern gate.

Some of the texts I found suggested the value of fasting, the purging of the body, to achieve renewal. This I did until I looked like a walking skeleton. Others recommended prayer and deep meditation in order to find a peace. These I also performed, but in their many chants and verses, I found no peace, only hollowness.

Each tablet held another suggestion or opinion. None of them worked. I could not get a restful night's sleep, free from the nightmares, the self-doubt, the outright guilt, the awful loss.

I overheard hushed conversation among my priestly brethren. They thought me insane. They were correct.

On the third anniversary of Erish's abduction, I stumbled across an ancient group of texts in the archives. These I discovered within a shuttered niche, in a seldom-used chamber. This cache, stored apart and covered with dust, contained treatises about strange and macabre rituals, unheard of tales and legends, which named profane divinities, and described incantations of dark purpose.

Why my interest in arcane tablets with texts

containing forbidden subjects? I knew then I had crossed a spiritual river and had turned my back upon my impotent god. In his failure to console me, I sought out solace in darker and more forbidden realms. With my scribal training, a new world opened to me. One filled with esoteric and cabalistic passages of hidden knowledge. In my desperate despair, I hoped that these could offer me the peace that Nanna had not.

The fragile tablets themselves had to be handled with care, as one of their kind had already been shattered. As for their message, that could only be divined after several readings and even then, perhaps a fourth, to grasp their hidden intent.

Three months into my studies of this niche's texts, I came upon several clay incantation tablets, unlike the others, which had been hidden in the wall behind a wooden panel. While not originals, these copies claimed the original author had been the demigod Gilgamesh himself. Within their cramped lines, I found a remarkable spell, which whispered to me of a meager chance to reunite with my beloved Erish in the afterlife. I believed my Erish was dead. Yes, there, I said it. After all, I reasoned, what else did I have to lose?

Whoever composed the instructions for this spell did so in an archaic form of writing, which helped to obscure their meaning. Taken together, they outlined a terrible, unbelievable course of action. If I understood their words, their instructions ran against everything that I considered to be sane. But then again, was I?

The spell described the securing of a personal item once owned by the lost one: a locket of hair, a favorite piece of jewelry. This memento I prepared as a magical guide—a thing that would help find my lost one's remains. However, a great sacrifice was needed to empower the container's spell and this magical guide. I had to bathe the talisman in my own blood. Once so crafted, I placed the magical guide within a six-sided vessel inscribed with the spell on each side. I empowered the whole, "made them effective," with my ultimate sacrifice–the forfeiture of my very life.

The final portion of the enchantment involved a stranger to set the spell in motion. Once a stranger found the six-sided vessel, they would have to touch the opening phrase of the spell that I applied to each of the vessel's six sides. If I could provide these conditions, then the spell would activate, I would spiritually possess the stranger, and my search for Erish's remains would begin. Hopefully, once I found her, our blissful spiritual reunification would take place.

Yes, this scheme revealed my utter desperation. This I acknowledge. Since I believed my Erish dead, this spell represented my only recourse. It offered me hope, no matter how slender the chances for success.

*   *   *

The psychic shock of my death far outweighed the more measured physical response. As the blood drained from my wounded body, leaving it feeble and limp, my soul filled the six-sided vessel like water poured from a jug. Having discarded my empty physical husk, I became elated and bursting with energy at my successful transmigration. Safely within the container, my essence found rest. I waited for that "other" to find and release me, so I could begin the search for my beloved Erish's remains. Little did I realize that my wait would last so long.

CHAPTER 16
The Diagnosis

"Next case," the head of the medical department said, as she placed a medical file in the outbox and reached for the next.

"This one is a real doozy, commander," announced the red-eyed emergency intake physician named Blake.

"How so lieutenant?"

"Because, on the basis of his global thoracic bruising alone, he should be dead as a doornail. Yet, he presents only six god-awful bruises, three broken ribs, and a bruised kidney. He should have been cut in half."

"So you're a ballistics expert as well as an internist?" the commander quipped.

"No ma'am. That assessment Gunny Sergeant Mason Grant laid on me."

"Anything else?"

"Yes, ma'am. Sergeant Stone received a terrific blow with no tissue damage to his left frontal lobe as the result of a bullet graze. He manifested confusion when he tried to perform common tasks, showing clumsiness, and difficulties with his concentration."

"Sounds to me like classic symptoms of traumatic brain injury. Route him through psych. I'll authorize a full workup on him. We'll get to the bottom of his troubles."

"Next case," the commander said, after she had made several notations in Stone's medical file.

* * *

Without question I am responsible for my soul carrier's mental and physical difficulties. I attempted to do things in a strange body. My curiosity and interference caught the notice of his physicians, who rightly thought that something troubled my soul carrier. They were correct. That something was me.

*　　*　　*

"Sergeant Stone, my name is Dr. Parker. Do you know why you are here?"

"Yes, sir. Dr. Blake wants you to follow up on my occasional clumsiness."

"That's correct, sergeant. But the duty nurse also observed confusion, and sometimes even you struggling with basic motor skills, like shaving. Is that correct?"

"Yes, sir. That is correct, but I only cut myself once while shaving. As for the confusion, I passed out on the battlefield and woke up on a hospital ship with a doc shining a light in my eyes. I didn't know what happened to my rifle squad, my rifle, helmet, or gear. Yeah, I was pretty confused."

Smiling and nodding with appreciation, Parker liked what he heard so far, but for some reason, he asked, "So, sergeant, tell me about your head injury."

And the patient did, to the best of his ability.

"On the battlefield. Sergeant, did you see anything that you would consider out of the ordinary?"

To this question, the clinical psychologist saw a furrowed brow followed by a negative head shake.

"Nope, doc, not a thing."

*　　*　　*

"Sergeant Jonathan Joseph Stone, for outstanding leadership and extraordinary heroism, while under enemy fire at the Battle of Nasiriyah, Iraq, this proud nation has awarded you a Bronze Star with Combat V for Valor, and, a Purple Heart for injuries sustained in the field," recited my battalion commander.

Reality blurred: my brief hospital ship stay, my flight back to the States, this award ceremony at Camp Lejeune, everything. I knew what I had done, but still didn't know why or what I'd done to deserve these much-coveted honors.

Mom and dad had flew in for the ceremony, both proud as punch. Bless them. Only my Grace would have made it better.

I stood there, rigid at attention, as my turn came for the battalion commander to pin on my ribbons. Then unbidden, for some reason, I remembered that vibrant blue glow back in the shell crater at Nasiriyah.

Did that really happen?

* * *

After my discharge from the U.S.N.S. *Comfort*, and even before I arrived Stateside, my entire mental outlook began to change. For the first time in my life I became a voracious reader, one with focus, purpose, and drive. This from a former high school jock who struggled to maintain a C-average.

This sudden studiousness caught the attention of my superiors. In their eyes I appeared withdrawn, introspective, and insular, instead of the explosive, gun-ho extrovert, gym rat, and leader of men they had come to know and love. Before I knew it, I received orders to report to the base hospital for a full physical checkup and a battery of neurological tests.

My workup from the U.S.N.S. *Comfort* they resurrected. In short order they diagnosed me *again* with a traumatic brain injury, or TBI, which I declared to be pure bullshit. The shrinks, being shrinks, overruled me and ordered me to participate in a ten-week hybrid physiological and neurological regime. Oh what fun.

Well, I *had* been experiencing some rather odd sensations, and I did need to brush up on some basic motor skills like shaving, polishing my boots, and my penmanship. Hence my ten-week pleasure cruise through the Land of Oz.

*   *   *

I admit responsibility for my soul carrier's reading enthusiasm. In order to better understand this new world, I wanted to learn all I could as quickly as possible. This benefitted not only me, but also my soul carrier, who for the first time in his life took an interest in things other than hiding within his warrior culture.

*   *   *

From the beginning of my "intellectual growth spurt," as the physicians referred to it, I sensed that I read for two individuals. An odd concept, one hard to explain, but one the experts wanted to chalk up to some kind of schizophrenia. I didn't blame them. But whenever I reported feeling that sensation, they all took notes, no doubt figuring the blow to my helmet as the cause.

The special sensation felt like someone looking over my shoulder with immense curiosity. The feeling did not trouble me in any way. Instead, the sensation seemed to enhance my appreciation of those commonplace things folks take for granted, those everyday modern miracles of life.

This feeling of duality nonetheless *was* weird. I could pretend I was getting used to it, but in reality it sometimes pissed me off. Sometimes, when I closed my eyes to rest them, I felt something driving me onward, pushing my limits, and tickling my curiosity.

About halfway through my ten-week session, I became a big fan of Tylenol that numbed the headaches and relieved my eye strain. Lesson learned–the brain is a muscle, muscles require exercise. Over-exercise causes stress, stress relief comes in the form of a little pill. End of story.

Early on, the medical people had tested my IQ, probably to establish some sort of a baseline. Before I was discharged Stateside, they did it again and boy did they get a surprise. They found it had jumped thirty-six points.

The funny thing about all of this is they never told me. Instead, I overheard them arguing over how "the grunt," me, had done it. One even opined the initial test results had to be thrown out. Another figured that my test results had been misfiled with another patient's. Well, screw that.

Over time I found I could cope with this weird sense of duality, and reconciled myself to this second consciousness that never seemed to go away. It was like thinking through a second filter, one that was insistent and demanding son-of-a-bitch. With many subjects, the sensation would almost, but not quite, fade away into the background like the hum of a noisy air duct. With other subjects, however, this sensation would weigh on me, to the point I felt like the word I read repeated itself, not as an acoustic echo, but internally, rolling around on a phantom tongue.

A positive consequence of this second-self–it enriched my vocabulary and improved my reading retention. My memory has become almost eidetic. That's a fancy word I picked up that means–"recalling sights, sounds, and memories with exceptional vividness and detail." See what I mean?

On average I read two books a day, sometimes more. Compulsive? Addictive? Call it what you want. Overdrive? I kinda liked it. I finished books left and right. I pancaked them like defensive linemen.

All of this drove the medical experts nuts. So I grinned a lot.

*   *   *

During the last third of my neurological sessions, I realized my career in the military had begun to lose all meaning. I didn't need it anymore to run from my guilt concerning Grace's death. I no longer needed to hide within the Marine fraternity. In fact, I came to the conclusion I hadn't done anything wrong at all. So before the sessions concluded, and finding myself no longer needing the military for an emotional crutch, I applied for an Honorable Discharge, much to the surprise of my commander, colleagues, friends, and family. As for my medical staff, they all went bat-shit because they had just lost an interesting lab rat, so I grinned some more.

*   *   *

One might think I influenced my soul carrier to leaving his beloved warrior's band. Nothing could be further from the truth. I only helped him get past his guilt about Grace. He realized why he joined his warrior band in the first place–to escape, to forget, and possibly find death. I am quite proud of his decision.

* * *

To prepare myself for my future, I memorized all the pertinent parts of the G.I. Bill as it pertained to the funding of higher education. Going to college didn't scare me anymore. Instead, it had become a very attainable goal. My goal.

The modest base library carried an interesting mix of publications. Every week new magazines and newspapers flooded in and I eagerly devoured their contents. All too soon, however, I returned to a holding pattern waiting for the next infusion of magazines.

* * *

When my discharge paperwork came through, I signed and handed them off for final processing. Next, without blinking an eye, I applied for the fall semester at North Texas State University, in my hometown of Denton, Texas. That act alone I found liberating and satisfying. Why? Because for the first time in a long time, I stood on my own two feet and planned my future without a military safety net.

Up to that point, everyone had considered my snap decision to leave the Corps as a knee-jerk overreaction and even said so to my face. Mom and dad couldn't believe it. My base commander didn't either. They all blamed it on Nasiriyah and a traumatic brain injury. They hoped it would pass, given enough time, psychiatric therapy, and further reflection. My medical experts didn't have a clue. So guess what? I grinned some more. This ranch hand from North Texas discovered he had a brain and had found it wanting, seriously wanting. Intellectual achievement became my goal and I had twelve years of catching up to do.

*   *   *

With my discharge finalized, I moved back home. Just me, two stuffed duffle bags, and a Greyhound bus ticket. When I arrived, Dad and I went out and opened a civilian bank account, into which I transferred my sizable military account balance. That squared away, the two of us rooted around until I settled on a used truck–a bright red Chevy Colorado. I then rented my own furnished apartment, much to my mother's displeasure and my father's satisfaction.

Once settled, I started a routine of a three-mile morning run, breakfast, and then a visit to the reference section of the Fowler Public Library on Oakland Street. Fowler's Reference Librarian, a middle-aged woman called Mrs. Lilly Nelson, helped me a bunch. In fact, she even remembered once helping out my father with a research topic, but she couldn't remember what, just our family name. Yep, I became a library rat. A serious dude preparing for college in the fall.

Two months later, having exhausted the Fowler Public Library, I moved on to the Willis Library at North Texas State University. I started with the Willis' far better stocked reference section, where I stumbled upon a collection devoted to ancient history.

Fourteen massive and hefty volumes, all bound in handsome maroon covers with fancy gold lettering, took up almost ten feet of shelf space. Entitled *The Cambridge Ancient History*, I started reading the first volume. Called *Prolegomena and Prehistory*, I found myself a cozy spot, sat down, and began to devour its 758 pages.

A day later, I had reached the chapter about Sumerian Iraq. I noticed my reading rate slowed to a crawl. Each word weighed not twice, but thrice. Finishing the last chapter, I slapped the book closed, and went on to the next volume of the series.

* * *

There it is! My proof! I have been waiting for my soul carrier for FOUR THOUSAND YEARS! This is unthinkable, but this book proved it. I, Nergal, found it difficult to even imagine such a vast expanse in time. A far greater shock, however, was the realization that I might not be able to find my Erish's remains.

* * *

In volume two I focused on those chapters devoted to the ancient Near East and skipped the rest. I found myself homing in on Mesopotamia, a Greek word that means "the land between the two rivers," the Tigris and Euphrates, the territory of modern-day Iraq. My experiences in the region caused me to note how many ancient cities I had been near, and in some cases, practically on top of. Places with weird names like– Larsa, Uruk, Lagash, Nippur, and Ur. I continued reading.

During this time, while I read the history encyclopedia, I began to have frequent, startling dreams. The visions of foreign landscapes, people, and events that caused me to toss and turn.

One theme reoccurred with gut-wrenching clarity–scenes associated with the brutal sacking of a city. When I reviewed their grim detail the next morning, I couldn't tell what time period these dreams represented, modern or ancient history. They always took place in a desert environment, obscured by smoke and fire, overlaid with an all too real sound-track of the harrowing cries of the injured and dying.

*   *   *

When I finished the ancient history reference section of the Willis, I embarked on the exploration of the graduate DT-stacks. There, surrounded by history books of the ancient Near East, I found a slim book by Samuel Noah Kramer entitled, *History Begins at Sumer: Thirty-Nine Firsts in Man's Recorded History*. Despite its diminutive size, the book contained a wealth of information. Part of me enjoyed Kramer's engaging narrative. The other part scoffed at almost every sentence. This doubting side of my intellect, which became so vocal, made me again question my sanity.

Where did those thoughts and opinions come from? Maybe those damn Marine shrinks were right all along. Perhaps I am suffering from a brain injury that keeps causing this firestorm in my head.

One night, my dreams became more disturbing. Interwoven with the usual imagery of a sacked city, came forth a continuous narrative commentary which sometimes agreed, but more often than not, disputed whatever Kramer's Sumerian book had said. I sat in the stands while an intellectual tennis match took place. In no way did this contest present disjointed images, but vibrant pictures and well-organized arguments that possessed a surety, spoken with authority, that felt rock solid.

*   *   *

I believe it's time. The shock of how many years have passed is behind me. I have located where we need to go–Nippur. I also believe I understand my soul carrier well enough. The time nears when my soul carrier must learn of my quest–the search for my Erish's remains.

CHAPTER 17
First Contact

I read somewhere that dreams contain tidbits of wisdom and truth, that they reveal our greatest fears, deepest anxieties, and most cherished hopes. It is said dreams coincide with rapid eye movement, or REM sleep. In a deep dream state, color, sound, touch, and even smell can all come together to make a dream come alive.

In my case, my most recent dream began with me standing bare foot in my desert tan boxer shorts. Opposite me stood this short, lean, bald, and bearded man who looked a whole lot like Ben Kingsley. This man wore a white tasseled, toga-like garment over the shoulder. He stood before me with his hands clasped together in a curious manner, and looked up at me with deep, dark, and inquiring eyes surrounded by heavy thick lines of black paint.

"No, soul carrier," the man corrects, "that is eye kohl, not paint. It is applied around our eyes to lessen the glare of the sun, and has become a mode of accepted decoration among the men of my city."

Shocked at the voice, its clarity. I blurted out, "And who are you?"

The man smiled, revealing a fine set of whitish, even teeth.

"I am Nergal, son of Hanal, of the city of Ur. A scribe and astronomer. So, who are you?" The bearded man invited with an encouraging slight tilt of his head.

"I'm J. J.! Who else would I be?" I said with exasperation. "And why am I dreaming this anyway?"

Ignoring my demeanor, the man bowed low, and in

a deep, sonorous voice that I recognized from somewhere, he said, "It is a great honor to meet the man who found my *nam-šub im-habannatu*, the man who freed me, and the man who will assist me in my quest."

"What's a namshub imhabannatoo?" I mouthed as best I could.

"Why, it is an incantation container. It once housed my spirit. But once you set me free, J. J., my soul, now, resides within you. You, J. J., are my soul carrier."

"What?"

"There is nothing to fear, J. J.," the man reassured. "I am not an evil demon or a demigod. I am a *gidim*, a spirit, who is seeking the lost remains of his beloved wife."

"So you're in my head?"

Again with that tilting gesture of his head, "Yes, J. J., in a sense. My conscience, all of my memories, everything that is me, is accessible to you. This is a gift I wish to share with you."

"So what's your name again?"

The man looked down, sighed, and repeated.

"I am Nergal, son of Hanal, of the city of Ur. Scribe and astronomer..."

"I've got to be dreaming!"

"If you wish to believe that, than do so. I, however, will remain. And when you are better prepared to converse, I will do so, J. J."

Pausing for a moment, I said, "So Nergal, son of Hanal, of the city of Ur, how do you plan to find your wife's remains?"

The wide-eyed man answered, "J. J., you indeed listened to me after all. I see in your memories you once lived on a ranch, played a martial game, and became a warrior leader. Is that not so?"

I nodded.

"Even among my people it is well understood that many times a hunter or a warrior needed something, some object, with which to find their prey. We possess such a thing, J. J."

I furrowed my brow. "You mean bait?"

"No, J. J. Do you remember shaking the *nam-šub im-habannatu*?"

"Yeah, I do. I remember sensing its hollowness. I felt something rattling around inside it."

A brief chuckle.

"Indeed J. J. Something did rattle around inside the *nam-šub im-habannatu*, a wax encased braid of hair from my wife. With this vital talisman, we will be able to locate my wife's remains. It will be our guide."

"What is so important about you finding your lost wife's final remains?"

"J. J., when we find her final remains, then I will be able to find her spirit. J. J., I wish to reunite with my wife beyond the grave. Is that so selfish an act?" He said with outstretched hands in supplication. "That is why I built the *nam-šub im-habannatu*. That is why I sacrificed myself and placed my *gidim*, my spirit within it. To be found by you. All to be with my wife once again."

I didn't quite follow everything this Nergal had dumped on me, but I could see the intense love this man had for his wife. I could also feel his determination to find her remains. So I asked, frowning in disbelief, "Okay, tell me again about this namshub imhabannatoo thing."

Gesturing with open arms, Nergal said, "So many questions J. J. That is good, very good. A *nam-šub im-habannatu* is the clay incantation container that holds my wife's braid of hair. But in this particular case, it also became my soul's container.

"When your fingers found the triggering spell, you freed me. Do you not remember the blue light?

"Yes, I do." I said frowning.

"I think we have spoken enough this night. But before we part, I know that your personality and culture requires absolute proof of my existence. This I will provide, but only after you learn to read my language and translate the spell upon the *nam-šub im-habannatu.* Only then will you know my words ring true. For now, sleep J. J. We will have more than ample time later to consider the question of *how* we will find my beloved Erish."

The dream ended. I jerked wide awake in a pool of nervous sweat.

"Jesus. That one felt real," I panted. Then I looked over at what time–1:23 a.m.

I spent several moments in confused and disbelieving review.

"Am I going nuts?" I asked myself. But with that thought my eyes fluttered into a deep and restorative sleep.

*   *   *

I am optimistic. I believe our first conversation went reasonably well. My soul carrier is physically capable, intelligent, and now emotionally strong. He is also inquisitive, which is good. In time, I am confident his rational nature will eventually be won over to my side, once he himself translates the spell on the nam-šub im-habannatu. *That way, he, and only he, will believe everything I have told him. So the first step is to help him with my language. A clear enough task for a once temple scribe.*

I will find the location of my wife's remains. While I do not wish to force J. J.'s cooperation, I must get him to cooperate for I cannot do it alone. Especially given my clear limits in controlling his dexterity in this complex world. I need him to comply, as I would never be able to even drive a car.

Gaining J. J.'s cooperation, I sense will be an uphill struggle. His culture is so driven by what they call qualitative data, proof, and evidence. What nonsense. Have they no trust or sense of belief? I will assist him in learning to read my language. That way he will better understand what is at stake, and at the same time prove I am real and not some bad dream.

* * *

The next morning I jumped out of bed with this annoying itch at the back of my head. It bugged me during my morning run and didn't let up until I began scouring the Willis Library. Kramer's book got me hunting for a Sumerian grammar of all things. The impulse demanded that I translate the strange artifact that I had brought back from Iraq. I knew that doing so would answer an important question about my sanity.

When my eyes fell upon a slim paperback written by Dietz Otto Edzard called, *Sumerian Grammar*, I sat down at an open study desk, and began to read its 191 pages.

The book's introduction stated that Sumerian was

the first and oldest language expressed in the cuneiform script and that it, as a script, enjoyed tremendous staying power. From 2500 BC to AD 75 it expressed a variety of ancient languages. Just as a modern keyboard today can transcribe English, German, French, Spanish and Italian, so also could cuneiform transcribe Sumerian, Akkadian, Assyrian and Persian.

*   *   *

My soul carrier found a grammar book about my language. Unbelievable. The real question is—how good is it?

CHAPTER 18
Professor Gibson

When I read Edzard's *Sumerian Grammar*, it was like running into an old friend. The book's linguistic concepts seemed familiar, logical, and understandable. Even the odd twists and turns that all languages have, came naturally to me.

As with any kindergartener new to their letters, my first wedge-shaped glyphs sucked, but after a bit of practice, I got the knack.

By the time that I had gotten halfway through the Edzard text the second time, this time doing the grammar exercises, my stomach growled in protest. Looking down at my wristwatch, it said early afternoon. No wonder. Essentially, I had been studying five hours straight. Fortunately, the basement of the university's library had a decent cafeteria. So I left my stuff on the study desk–Edzard's book, my pen, notebook of cuneiform "scribbles," and went to feed my face.

*   *   *

I am pleased at J. J.'s progress. As for the grammar book itself, I am impressed. Many of the lessons are ones I recognize, and even remember, as being the classics of my time.

*   *   *

Back from the cafeteria, I got back to the rest of those Sumerian glyph exercises.

As I approached my study table, an older

gentlemen had taken a seat kitty-corner from mine. He had a book and occasionally made a note on a yellow legal pad. Without another thought, I returned to my exercises.

After a couple of minutes, I got a distinct feeling that the man really was watching me, which I found rude and distracting.

I stopped, looked up over his book to his eyes, and pointedly asked, "Can I help you?"

The older man replied, "Ah, well no." Then with embarrassment, "Well, perhaps yes, since you asked. You'll have to forgive me, but it is not often that I see students working on their cuneiform drills in the library."

"How would you know that?"

"Well, for one, because I am the only one at this school who teaches cuneiform. And two, my students do so in the language lab. In fact, I use Edzard's textbook in my classes. How do you like it?"

"I just started it. It seems okay," I admitted.

The older man cocked his head, amazed. "You don't say…"

Then the man continued, "I am so very sorry. Where are my manners?" Extending his hand across the desk, he said to me, "I am Adam Gibson. I'm a professor in the History Department."

"A pleasure to meet you, sir. My name's J. J. Stone."

"Ah, Mr. Stone, it's a pleasure to meet you as well. By the look of your haircut, are you in the military, or a veteran?"

"Veteran, sir. U.S. Marines. One tour in Somalia and one in Iraq. Have you ever been there?"

"Oh, my word, yes, Mr. Stone. Many times. I'm a dirt archaeologist as well as a student of ancient history and its languages. But did I hear you correctly; you began your cuneiform studies—*just* this morning?'"

"Yes sir. Edzard's book practically jumped off the shelf at me."

"You don't say," Gibson said again as he leaned forward putting his book down. "Well, Sumerian is a difficult language to grasp, much less on your first day."

Rubbing his jaw, the academic then asked, "May I have a look at your work there?"

Spinning my notebook, I slid it over and said, "Sure. Have at it."

After a few moments of reading my scribbles, he said, "Mr. Stone, your glyphs are well written and legible. They're all properly proportioned, arranged, and placed." Gibson remarked as he sat back, and crossed his arms.

"What I find most remarkable is your use of the *boustrophedon* style. In other words, the way your writing begins on the right, progresses to the left, and then, reverses its course from left to right. Do you realize this style of composition originated as a cultural imitation of the way farmers once plowed their fields?"

Gibson, catching himself, pushed back from the table and said, "I'm sorry. I'm babbling. But I am curious nonetheless, why did you choose to compose your sentences in this overlapping, right to left, left to right style?"

This has to be Nergal's doing, just like the selection of the grammar book, I thought.

"Well sir, it is far quicker and more efficient to do

so. I barely have to raise my pen from the paper and I'm on to the next line."

"You realize, Mr. Stone, the *boustrophedon* style of writing is nowhere mentioned in Edzard's text."

I blushed.

Heck, it damn ought to be. It makes things so much easier. That's probably why Nergal taught it to me.

Pinching his lower lip between his thumb and forefinger Gibson looked down again at my notebook.

But his question left me at a loss for words. I couldn't answer him by saying that I intuitively invented that style of writing.

Yes, J. J. I indeed taught you that.

Well, I must have blinked hard when I heard Nergal speaking to me directly and not through the usual nighttime filter of a dream.

My reaction Gibson saw. "Are you all right, son? You just turned as white as a sheet."

Recovering, I said, "I'm fine, sir."

*   *   *

The professor noticed that the soldier sitting across from him possessed a glowing golden aura. Hiding his complete surprise, Gibson made a mental note to inform a certain paranormal society about this extraordinary "find."

*   *   *

After about forty minutes of gabbing about the Willis Library, my experiences in Iraq, and my new-found interest in that country's ancient past, Professor Gibson invited me over to visit his office. He used his cooler of beer as bait. Besides, I liked his ready and genuine smile, but the beer offer sealed the deal.

Gibson closed his office door, cracked open two frosty longnecks, we each took a swig, and he got down to business.

"Mr. Stone, do you have any college behind you?"

"No, sir."

"Have you ever considered using your G.I. benefits to attend college?"

"Yes, sir. I did, in fact."

I paused to again quench my thirst. As for Professor Gibson, he sat back patient and silent as a church mouse.

"I started my prep for college at the base library. Then, after my discharge from the Corps, I moved on to the local public library here in Denton, and now the Willis. Professor, you might not believe this," I admitted with shame, "but I barely got through high school with a C-average." I then looked him in the eye before continuing. "But now, I've gotten serious and I'm looking forward to college. What I've discovered is that I've a whole lot of catching up to do."

"So," Gibson asked, "What subject interests you?"

Looking down at my hands, I knew what I wanted. Expressing that desire, however, challenged me. Something deep inside, nonetheless, egged me on. I had more than a half notion about who that might be.

Go ahead! Nergal urged.

With a furrowed brow, I said, "Professor, I know I need a practical education. Fine, I can live with that. But what drives me is the other Iraq, the one that is thousands of years old. I feel a special kindred with that ancient land, its culture, its history. What I need is some advice as to where I can go to accomplish that."

Professor Gibson leaned back into his office chair, and said. "You know, Mr. Stone, this university can supply you with a fine education. But you will probably get bored with it and its ways.

Pursing my lips, I didn't want to answer out of fear that it might bring up a whole bunch of uncomfortable questions.

J. J., go ahead. Nergal encouraged. *Speak up. Here's your chance to prove to yourself that you're not crazy. Find out what my incantation container says.*

"Well Professor, it's like this. In Iraq I found this object covered with cuneiform writing. I need to know what all that writing says. That's why I worked so hard on Edzard's Sumerian grammar today. I need to know what that artifact is all about."

Gibson, suddenly silent, pondered my quest.

"You have this ancient Iraqi artifact, here, in Denton, Texas?"

"Yes, sir, I do. I knowingly smuggled it out of that country among my personal effects. I know it's against the military regs and all, even international treaties, but I didn't steal it from their national museum either. I found it in the wall of a shell crater during a battle. So I brought it back home."

"I see," the archaeologist said. Getting up from his desk, Gibson went over to one of his cluttered book shelves, retrieved an old and battered twelve by twelve cardboard box, and placed it at one end of his desk. Sitting down, he sighed, and said, "Mr. Stone, I want to show you something."

From the box Gibson pulled out several white

plastic bags, from which he removed handfuls of broken pottery that he began to arrange before him.

"Mr. Stone, what you see before you are what I consider teaching tools. These broken bits of pottery are considered worthless by the Iraqi government. But if I ever got caught with them in customs, either theirs or ours, there would be hell to pay. Now go ahead and look at them. Touch them."

So I did, but very carefully. First lifting this one, and then that, I noticed that each one left its own bit of fragile dust on my fingertips. When in country, the very same "moon dust" invaded every crack and crevasse, making a thorough gun cleaning a mealtime necessity.

Gibson, noticing me staring at my fingertips, said, "Mr. Stone, you have now touched thousands years of history. Each fragment before you is at least four thousand years old."

Nodding in reply, "I can believe it, sir."

"So, Marine, you have a choice. Currently you are in possession of a stolen artifact. An artifact that you knowingly smuggled from its country of origin. To fix this mess, you would have to return it and that process would have to be a very delicate one, one no doubt fraught with all sorts of ramifications.

"On the other hand, you could lie to yourself and consider your illegal artifact so much worthless junk like what's spread out before you.

"Or, you could go ahead and translate what's on the artifact, and then at some later date return it, give it to an Iraqi museum, and leave it at that. It's your call."

I thought hard about what the professor had said and it made sense. It removed a guilty burden from my mind.

Nodding, I said, "That makes sense. I choose to translate it now and return it later."

"Good decision. So when are you going back?"

"As soon as the translation is complete."

Now leaning forward with his chin in his palm, the academic continued. "Okay. Fine. Now I understand your interest in Sumerian—a practical application, to fulfill a natural desire *and* your curiosity. So, I propose that we, as a team, work together on the translation of this artifact. And, if its text is unique, significant, or noteworthy in some way, shape, or other, then we'll try to publish its text, transliteration, and translation in a professional journal. But we do that only after you return it. That way we can say that it's in such and such museum with such and such a catalogue number. We might even offer a brief commentary of sorts. What do you think?"

Do it J. J. a celebratory Nergal chortled. *You won't regret it.*

The opportunity to finally figure out what the artifact said hit me hard. I needed to know what it said. Doing so with an expert to check my six, so to speak, provided an ideal opportunity. What sold me on the notion was the implied teamwork behind the endeavor, something that I had missed since leaving the Corps.

"Professor Gibson," I said, extending my hand across the academic's desk, "you've got yourself a deal."

*   *   *

That evening Adam Gibson composed and then rewrote three times an e-mail to the president of TIIIS. In Gibson's experience, he had never before used the noun "prodigy" to describe an individual. That evening, he had used the word, along with a detailed description of the individual's background, intellectual capacity, and his rare aura.

*   *   *

At nine o'clock the following morning I returned to Professor Gibson's office. This time I came with the artifact tucked under my left arm like a football in my faded light blue Nike gym bag.

As I entered, I saw that Gibson had cleared off his desk. In its center lay a mass of cotton batting.

Gibson greeted me, got up, and closed his office door behind me. "Mr. Stone," he announced. "Let's get something straight right from the start. Henceforth, I am not Professor Gibson. I'm Adam. You got that, Mister?" He finished with a big broad grin while extending his open hand.

I cocked my head in amusement, and quickly replied, "Yes, sir, 'Professor' Adam. I read you loud and clear. And by the way, I'm J. J."

Adam, pointing to the cotton mound, said. "Okay, J. J., let's see what you've got squirreled away in that gym bag."

When I took the object out, Adam, looking thoughtful, put on a pair of thin, white muslin gloves that he took out of his desk's side drawer.

"You know J. J., the last time I held something like this I was a grad student at the Oriental Institute in Chicago. They have a museum copy of Hammurabi's *Law Code* in their Near Eastern collection, constructed the same way–as a six-sided ceramic box. But if this is of Sumerian date, then it's much older."

Adam searched through his desk drawer again and pulled out a small tape measure.

My tawny colored ceramic artifact measured sixteen by six inches wide. Adam took some notes. Then, he measured each of its six panels.

"You know J. J.," Adam said without looking up, "as I look at this artifact, it appears that each of these six vertical sides have pretty much the same cuneiform inscription."

They are the same inscription! Nergal said.

In silent response to Nergal's outburst, I pretended to wring out my left ear.

Gibson continued. "That tells me that someone tried really hard to get the message out. The question before us is–what's the message? That, my dear friend, we will discover together."

Adam gave the artifact a gentle shake. He felt the jangle inside, as I had, that the hollow artifact contained something.

"Jackpot, J. J. Something's inside. I just felt it. It could well be another inscribed artifact. The ancient's sent important or sensitive documents back and forth inside primitive clay envelopes to prevent their tampering. The question is–which is more important? The outer casing or its protected contents? We'll have to wait and see."

At this point, Adam bubbled with excitement.

"Let's finish our physical measurements, take some photographs, and then make a careful transcription of the texts on the artifact's six sides. When we are done, we'll take it over the Archaeometry Lab for some tests. What do you say?"

Gibson's enthusiasm and his list of things to do did

not reassure me. Here he wants to submit my artifact to a lab for tests. In near panic mode as things had begun to move way too fast for my taste, Gibson then read the concern on my face. I wanted to call a halt on the whole deal, until my little internal tenant again spoke up.

J. J., Nergal entreated, *this is an unprecedented opportunity for you to translate the soul container's inscription with someone other than myself. Then you will have your proof of my existence. Also, these tests will show how old my incantation container is. Most importantly, you will confirm what is contained within.*

"J. J.," said Adam, registering my look, "I know that all of this might seem like overkill, but aren't you even a little bit curious about it?"

Snapping to, I admitted, nodding, "Adam, you're right. We have to figure out what this thing is all about. Let's do this."

With great care, we worked up the artifact's particulars–its re-measurement to the millimeter, digital photographs of all eight of its surfaces, and only then did we begin the transcription process.

Gibson pulled out of one of his file cabinets lighted magnifiers on stands and set them up around the artifact on the table.

We assigned the six sides of the tablet with letters A through F. Sitting opposite from one another, with the text illuminated, we hand-copied what we saw unto centimeter graph paper as precisely as possible. We had to do this to establish whether all six sides indeed said the same thing.

We worked straight through lunch and into the late afternoon. Finished, we compared our copy sheets up against Adam's desk lamp. In fact, we only found four minor inconsistencies between the six sides—a feat that we both agreed seemed remarkable.

"J. J., look at these texts. The same hand produced them. There's no question about it. Whoever produced these texts, six times, must have been one hell of a scribe. Then consider this. He did it on a slowly drying medium. He had to hurry, but not so fast as to make any mistakes. That's quite a feat if you ask me!"

Finally, Nergal sighed, *someone appreciates my labors. And, J. J., I went through this process four times. Four times before I got it right.*

With my eyes fried and Adam declaring his shot as well, we agreed to call it a day, and take the artifact over to the lab the next day. Victorious, we established the base text. The next step toward its translation–its transliteration.

*   *   *

I went home with the artifact and fed the beast that is my stomach, but I couldn't resist beginning the text's transliteration. Sumerian, an agglutinative tongue, required the painstaking assignment of Latin characters to specific cuneiform symbols. Why do this? Because this is how modern dictionaries, like the *Pennsylvania Sumerian Dictionary* are organized. Besides, the sooner we completed the base text's transliteration, the quicker the translation process would begin.

*   *   *

The following day on the way over to the Archaeometry Lab, both of us admitted that we had been up late the previous evening.

"J. J., you wouldn't believe it. Last night I went into overdrive on the transliteration. My wife hit the ceiling, but I finished it," he said with satisfaction.

"Guest what, Adam, so did I," I responded with considerable pride and a big, broad grin.

"That's great. We'll have to compare our efforts, but first things first."

Adam then began to tell me all about the Archaeometry Lab as we walked over, no doubt to calm my nerves regarding the artifact's safety.

"You know J. J., this fellow Paul Jacobs is a well-respected archaeological lab tech. When the university approached him, they had to pay him big time to snag him away from those Austin, Texas boys." Adam remarked as we walked along one of the many footpaths that interconnected the campus. "I talked to him yesterday to set up today's meeting. We're in luck. Things are slow at the lab, so we should get back some quick results."

That sounded good to me, but how much would all of this fancy lab work cost me, and said so.

"Not to worry, J. J.," Adam said with a dismissive wave of his hand. "I have a research account with the lab. Besides, we're a team. Remember? If we're going to publish this properly, then guess what? We need those lab results."

"You're sure?"

"You bet."

CHAPTER 19
The Rent

The Creator found itself in a difficult situation. A mortal, Nergal of Ur, had died, but his *gidim* had never arrived to the Underworld. Once there, the souls chose which path to follow–to rise toward the light and the soul's fulfillment or to remain in the darkness and sink into eternal depravity and hopelessness. Lacking Nergal's soul and its subsequent choice of path, the Creator's conceived Cosmic Order had veered off toward chaos, and as a consequence, a noisome vibration began to make itself known.

At its onset, the cosmic imbalance began as a slight unnatural vibration, barely noticeable, but detectable. This unfamiliar oscillation affected the cosmic fabric that made up the boundary of the dark realm. Given sufficient time, this vibration would begin to stress, flex, and with time create a tear. In many respects, the process could be explained as nothing more than the pure physics behind material's fatigue. The dire result would be the formation of an illicit portal through which the damned of the dark realm would have direct access to the mortal realm—an unthinkable situation. In addition, the Creator noted a change in the behavior of his dark primordial minions as well. The noisome vibration of imbalance vexed them, made them restless.

Far worse would be the passage of the dark realm's primordial overseer, The Devourer of Souls. If it traversed into the mortal world, that would signal universal obliteration. The end of time. Despite all of the Creator's best efforts and those of its primordial minions, they could not find this lone discrepancy. A missing soul had occurred once before, but the situation had been righted before the vibration of disequilibrium had any opportunity to cause harm. That first instance involved a demigod named Gilgamesh, who the gods punished for his attempt to harness eternal life. This judgment summarily stripped him of his godhead, and reduced him to a mere mortal. Problem solved.

But the Creator puzzled over this particular inconsistency, this blot upon an otherwise perfectly maintained ledger of souls, because a demigod had not perpetrated this, but a mere mortal. That suggested to the Creator and his minions that this heinous act against the Cosmic Order, had to have been accomplished by some wholly unnatural means.

Through the passage of years, the much-concerned Creator had searched for this lost soul, and to its utter amazement, still could not locate it. Thus, rightly reasoned the Creator, if one *gidim* could escape the primordial cycle of life, death, and rebirth, then, why not more? Nergal's missing soul had endangered the very makeup of the Cosmic Order.

* * *

If the Creator had hands to wring, it would have had stumps for arms. Nergal's wretched soul had indeed gone missing for far too long. The first rent in the dark realm's boundary broke with a psychic shriek. With that event, sensitives throughout the mortal world sought relief from this overpressure, sensing that something terrible had occurred, but what?

Helpless, the Creator witnessed the first escape through the rent by a demented *gidim* some 3,480 years after Nergal's death. In the year AD 1431, the birth of a babe occurred, to a certain Wallachian nobleman. Called Wladislaus Dragwlya, he is better known by his posthumous appellation: Vlad the Impaler. Only that one had passed through the rent, the Creator noted.

Many centuries passed before the next *gidimr* stumbled upon the rent. But in this instance, not one, but many of its cohorts made their way into the mortal world. These demented ones chose to be born during the early twentieth century in Germany. These same wayward and fervent souls believed that their national birthright had been denied, their country traitorously deceived, and as one, espoused the superheated hate and excesses of the *Nationalsozialistische Deutsche Arbeiterpartei*. As a consequence, they bathed Central and Eastern Europe in the blood of innocents.

After another hiatus, the Creator saw that another clutch of *gidimr* broke loose on the mortal world in 1948. This time many chose to be born in and near the lands of sand and wind. Raised in an atmosphere of perceived cultural disrespect, fanned by intense religious fervor, and ignited by impassioned clerics, these *gidimr* found their gruesome purpose in the rigid and wrongful interpretation of a book. While called by many names, all knew by instinct what to do. So the bloodletting began anew, their insanity total and complete.

The level of savagery that they embraced went against every known modern moral code. Their keystone–the total acceptance of self-immolation as an acceptable means of advancing their cause. These *gidimr* did so, because the dark realm had been so perforated, that they could quickly return to infect the next generation, and thus continue the cycle of carnage and atrocity.

Also during that post-World War II generation more *gidimr* escaped and chose to return to their beloved Central and Eastern Europe and several even ventured to North America. Their Central European kin formed the backbone of terrorism within those regions, notably the Baader Meinhof Gang, the *Rote Armee Fraktion,* and several other splinter groups. Meanwhile further to the east, amid several socially fractionalized nations of the former Eastern Bloc, they had their heyday in gruesome massacres of innocents that rivaled the Nazis in scale. Whole village populations disappeared overnight. Meanwhile, in Indonesia Pol Pot and his Khmer Rouge wrecked their human havoc. Across the Atlantic, the Ku Klux Klan and several white supremacy movements enjoyed an uptick and several serial killers and bombers terrorized in spectacular ways the open society of the United States.

The Creator knew that the finding of Nergal's soul provided the only solution for these dreadful events. Short of that, the First Soul would have to act as appropriate, hence why it was created.

*   *   *

The mass defections into the mortal world angered the Devourer of Souls. The troublesome vibrations of the imbalance irritated it. But worse than that, the most insane and demented fled before it could dine upon them. Its hunger grew insatiable. It began hunting for where its prey had gone.

*   *   *

Then, once released from its magical container, and after the passage of over 4,000 years, the Creator became aware of the lost soul of Nergal.

"It is about time," it rumbled with displeasure. "Where does it reside?"

The Creator then realized with confusion and alarm Nergal's location. "No! This cannot be! Nergal resides among the living! And blasphemies of blasphemies, resides within another mortal's form! How can that be?" it asked in complete frustration. "How could a mortal carry two souls?"

After the Creator's consternation abated, it then realized, "Now that I found that most troublesome soul, I must get it back before more chaos is wrought upon the Cosmic Order."

CHAPTER 20
The Emissary

"I must find a way to bring Nergal's soul back into the natural way of things," The Creator ruminated. "But how?" This desire the Creator shared with its far more single-minded, but self-aware subordinate, the Ledger Keeper, the actual accountant of the Ledger of Souls.

Bowing before his creator, the primordial entity said, "Allow me to create an emissary that can be sent to the mortal world. Once there, I will find this wayward soul and bring it back to where it belongs. Thus returning everything to balance."

"And how would you identify this most wayward of souls?" the Creator countered.

"Once my emissary is within the mortal realm, by its aura. That would be the sign."

Perturbed by the prospect of one of its primeval entities sending an emissary into the mortal world, the Creator then stopped and considered the solution.

"By its aura," the Creator thought. *What a novel idea. Every living thing and creature has its own unique signature. Perhaps,* the Creator considered.

*   *   *

As the peril warranted drastic measures, the Creator made a quick decision.

Forthwith, the Creator commanded the Ledger Keeper to pluck a portion of its essence for the perceived greater good. The portion, a mere fraction of the Ledger Keeper's primeval energy, once so removed, slightly diminished the Keeper's state of being. Energy is energy. The Keeper formed a fictional construct with it, a pseudo-soul bereft of an aura, that could pass into the realm of the light. Once there, the pseudo-soul would strengthen, would pass into the mortal world, and seek out a mortal carrier through which it would find the soul of Nergal. This Emissary of the Keeper would explain to that wayward soul its egregious error and return it to where it belonged, by force if necessary.

The Creator believed this strategy sound, since this manufactured construct existed apart from the usual manner of things, and so, did not make worse the current imbalance. Upon the Emissary's return, the Ledger Keeper would welcome it back and enfold it within itself once again. In this way, the totality of its very essence would be restored.

*   *   *

After months in a coma, the body of "Terrible Tess" McGonagall had deteriorated. Her slack face created shadows across sunken cheeks. As she lay in her hospital bed, the nurses had taken care that her red hair had been brushed, her freckled complexion kept flawless. The star soccer player, reduced to an eighty-three pound bag of bones and functioning organs, had attempted to score, but instead she had rammed her head against the side of a goal post. That fleeting moment earned her this new state of being with only oxygen and fluids as her companions. While indeed alive, her brain waves no longer registered.

Her family, wealthy Boston suburbanites, refused to give up on her. Their strong Roman Catholic roots supported them and the belief that Theresa Ann would pull through. After all, they all agreed "Terrible Tess" McGonagall was a real fighter.

*   *   *

The Emissary entered the mortal world through the light realm's portal, strengthened by its brief sojourn and the guiding love of the Teacher of the Way, another self-aware primordial subordinate of the Creator.

Self-guided by its innate intellect, bequeathed by the essence of the Ledger Keeper, the Emissary glided like a wind-blown leaf across the world as it sought out a mortal to merge with. In moments, it sensed a weakened mortal called Theresa Ann.

Here, the Emissary thought, *is someone of promise. This candidate would be suitable for my purposes.*

*   *   *

At 11:03 in the morning, Terrible Tess' brain wave monitor sprang to life. Donna McGonagall, Tess' mother, started at the sudden beeping.

Looking up from her knitting, Donna shrieked, "My Tess is back! My Tess is back!"

*   *   *

Such noise! the Emissary realized in shock.

What's that repetitive and piercing scream?

How can I escape it?

I can't...I'm trapped within this weakened body.

I opened my eyes to a world of confusion. Mastering their movement and focus would take effort.

What's going on around me?

CHAPTER 21
The Archaeometry Lab

As we entered the modest two-story building that housed the Archaeometry Laboratory at the university, Adam told me to say nothing about the artifact or how it came into my possession. "J. J., you don't need to concern yourself about that subject. We've discussed it. You've made your promise to return it and that's good enough for me. So I'll handle it."

Entering through a heavy maple door, the institutional kind with a wire-meshed window pane, sharp chemical smells filled my nose. Microscopes and other apparatus littered every flat surface. Several people bustled around wearing white lab coats. Our presence remained ignored, until Adam rang the bell on the counter.

A middle-aged man, who had been peering into one of the microscopes, looked up, smiled, and said, "Hey Doc. I'll be right over. Give me a moment to stabilize this specimen."

Moments later, Paul Jacobs stood before us, a lean and hungry-looking guy with a ready smile. "So Doc. What do you have for me this time?" he said rubbing his hands together.

"Well," Gibson began, "we need a full lab work up on a ceramic artifact. That means a fabric analysis and a thermal luminescence test. On top of that, the artifact is hollow and has something in it. So it needs to be opened up. Whatever is inside might need analysis as well."

While listening, Jacobs looked back and forth

between us, his eyes settling on my Nike bag.

Turning to me, Gibson put out his hands, and I handed over my bag with reluctance. Seeing my haircut and generally sizing me up, Jacobs quipped with a nod in my direction.

"Okay Doc, since when did you need a security guard?"

"Oh, I'm sorry Paul. This is Mr. Stone, a promising graduate student of mine."

I smiled and shook hands with the man.

"Oh," Jacobs said.

"So," Gibson asked, "when do we begin?"

"Right now. Follow me."

After a brief, wordless, snaking tour of the lab's facilities, we found ourselves before a large stainless steel lab table.

"We will need some padding, Paul," Gibson quickly noted.

"Not a problem. I'll be right back." Paul returned with about three feet of heavy-duty bubble wrap.

"That big enough?"

"That'll do fine." Gibson replied.

Adam opened my gym bag, slipped on his cotton gloves, and made his presentation. At seeing the artifact, Jacob whistled.

"Well preserved. What is it?"

"We don't know yet. We're still working on its inscriptions." Gibson said.

The lab tech approached the object, snapped on a pair of Latex gloves, and hefted it. Jacob, then said, "Bet you a quarter that it weighs less than two pounds. And, you're right. There is something inside. But before we crack open this sucker, let's weigh it."

"You're on," Gibson responded.

A digital lab scale appeared from a shelf below the table's surface. "Yep. You owe me, Doc. Pay up."

A shiny quarter flipped through the air that Jacobs deftly caught and thrust into a pocket. He then made a note on a nearby pad recording the precise weight. The scale disappeared and a cordless Dremel tool with a box of attachments took its place.

Selecting a round, carbon fiber cutting wheel, Jacobs, pulled out of his lab coat pocket another pair of latex gloves.

Handing them to me, he said, "They should fit those big mitts of yours."

"Excuse me," I said, "but shouldn't we scan this before we open it up?"

"Scan, as in X-ray or MRI?" Jacobs asked.

"I don't know. Do you want to take that chance?" I countered. "We don't know what's inside, or whether your drilling will damage anything."

Pause.

"Mr. Stone," Gibson said. "A scan would be an unnecessary step. What are you concerned about? This isn't a mummy, just a ceramic container."

Jacobs watched with interest our exchange.

I could only shrug in ignorance. "Just a thought," I offered.

Once I struggled into the gloves, Jacobs said, "Okay, Mr. Stone, I want you to hold this steady, while I cut into one of its ends."

Turning again to Gibson, Jacobs said, "Okay Doc, it's your call, which end do you want me to hack into?"

Turning his head to ascertain where the text began,

Adam indicated the opposite end, where the text ended, as the preferred point of entry.

Nodding, Jacobs said, "Okay, Mr. Stone, hold it real steady now."

"Roger," I replied.

With the drill a buzzing, the lab tech applied the spinning cutting wheel and began to create an ever-enlarging pile of pumice-fine tan dust in the bubble wrap. Moments later, having carved six neat incisions along the artifact's bottom, it fell away.

"Perfect. Absolutely perfect, if I do say so myself," Jacobs remarked.

"Doc, this small section that I cut off we'll sacrifice for the TL analysis. As for all of this cutting dust, I'll gather that up for the fabric analysis. As my mother always used to say, 'Waste not; want not.'"

Putting away the drill, he next bagged and tagged the hexagonal base of the container and collected the ceramic dust in a test tube with a brush. Without skipping a beat, Jacobs said, "Now, let's find out what's in this thing."

He produced a small probe with a light source from his lab coat's breast pocket and peered inside.

"Well gentlemen, this is indeed interesting. This artifact was not thrown on a potter's wheel, as the interior is not circular, but instead consists of six flat sides. Most unusual."

"Okay, but what's been rattling around in there?" Gibson said insistently.

Jacobs took out a long pair of tweezers from his lab coat's breast pocket. He probed inside, chased something around, and snagged it.

With a victorious grin, Jacobs teased out an ugly

little thing. About four inches long, the blackened object came out and went immediately into its own sterile baggie. Once sealed, we each examined it, turning it this way and that, trying to understand it.

"Looks like it was burned," I offered.

"No, I don't think so," Jacobs countered, "it looks like it is coated with something. I'm sure glad that I didn't come into direct contact with it. You never know with unknowns. I'll have to put in some lab time on this one, Doc. Sorry."

*　　*　　*

Since the lab traffic had been so slow, Jacobs had jumped on the preparation of my artifact's analysis that same day. He performed a basic flotation and microscopic analysis on the gram or so of the object's powered fabric, in order to determine its chemical makeup, and hence its possible place of manufacture. With that done, he prepped the ceramic hexagon for the TL analysis, which would produce a date for the firing of the ceramic material. As for that mysterious black mass, well, this is where Jacob's formidable forensics background came into play. The man loved challenges, and any opportunity to determine an unknown, fit that bill.

CHAPTER 22
Kirlian Devices, 2004

> Fingerprints, biometrics, and database's filled with names aren't going to tell you what is in somebody's head, unless somewhere they have already tipped their hand.
>
> (Internal memo: CIA Special Operations. July 14, 2003.)

Most people can tell you the "where" and "what" questions following 9/11. Because of it, the U.S. homeland changed forever. In many ways, America became a box turtle. With every possible way to protect the country considered, no matter how expensive, bizarre, or over-the-top the concept–X-ray, electro-magnetism, bottled liquids scanners, explosive detection scanners, advanced imaging technologies, sniffer dogs, explosive trace detectors, biometrics, pat-downs, visual profiling, even the reading of body language. However, none could ensure absolute security, much less predict an individual's intent.

Buried deep within a government agency, an imaginative group of researchers tried to figure out how to detect just that–an individual's intent. They had an idea. Best of all, they judged the required technology simple, deployable, and inexpensive.

*   *   *

Jeremy Clark, the head researcher, preferred simplicity. As a consequence, his team sought to take advantage of a phenomenon called the Kirlian Effect. Discovered by the Russian, Semyon Kirlian in 1939, Kirlian found that all objects, both animate and inanimate, when excited by a pulsed or pulsing electrical field, gave off a detectable glow. This technique, called perturbation, the scientific community knew quite well. Less understood remained the significance of the colorful electrophotonic images that surrounded the perturbed objects within the electrical field. These images Clark and his team decided to investigate.

They focused on the fact that inanimate objects possessed colorful glows particular to it and it alone. Meanwhile, the radiance of animate objects changed over time, potentially reflecting the object's physical vigor, health, and emotional state. Clark hoped that these colors could serve as a way to estimate the potential threat of an individual.

So Clark's team set out to determine whether the Kirlian Effect might be used to detect certain human tendencies. To do so, they researched how to interpret the colors represented by any one individual's aura. To tackle this challenge, the team split into two groups.

Team One investigated the traditional paranormal interpretations of an aura's color. This led them on a subjective multi-cultural examination of the phenomenon, both ancient and modern. They wanted to create a color wheel that matched hues to emotional tendencies.

Meanwhile, Team Two took a far more qualitative approach by going into the field to gather their own interpretation of an aura's color. First, they visited two college campuses and randomly performed the Kirlian test on one hundred students. An individual's current major marked the only discriminator. The researchers did not accept double majors or undecideds in their survey. Then, using the college data as a baseline, they visited two high-security prisons. As with the college students, they collected one hundred samples.

When Clark's two teams completed their research, they met to compare their data and found congruence. The color of an individual's aura could be used to indicate intent, *if* interpreted correctly. Several colors and their hues earned sufficient attention to be deemed outright warnings. They discovered that muddied reds signaled deep and barely controllable anger; dark greens a mixture of resentment, hostility, and jealousy; dirty browns deep-seated insecurity, emotional instability, and violence; and black as the absence of humanity. Hardened criminals and international terrorists ranged from dark muddy browns to jet blacks. The team could not address the possibility of an aura's change over time. They dealt only with snapshots in time.

On the other hand, Clark and his teams identified colors across the entire color spectrum which denoted individuals with healthy psychological profiles. Of these, one aura stood out from the rest. Team One logged it as a possibility, but Team Two failed to record any individuals with it–a clear, shiny bright, golden metallic aura. This color Team One's color wheel interpreted as a spiritually powerful, inspired, and enlightened individual. Moreover, the aura implied divine qualities of uncertain nature. When Team Two hypothesized why they had not encountered this rare aura, they shrugged their shoulders and blamed it on poor sample size.

*　　*　　*

Two months after the conclusion of Clark's research, no fewer than three hundred and seventy-six airports throughout the United States, all which provide scheduled airline service, had Kirlian Effect devices installed. Soon after, all major U.S. international hubs added the simple device to their passport control procedures.

The results staggered the security community. Now with a far greater sample size, these data substantially refined the interpretations based upon the initial color wheel. With a frequency of occurrence algorithm established, secondary security screenings became far fewer and more effective.

After its first twelve months of deployment, the frequency of secondary screenings had fallen to an unheard of 4%. Of that percentage, three fourths either had no business using public air transport or represented *bona fide* bad actors. During those secondary screenings, alcoholism, drug use or addiction, anger management issues, and recent emotional stress–like divorce, explained away the most common reasons for someone's disturbed aura. Mental health issues came next.

As for the bad actors, the 1%, these individuals identified by the Kirlian devices turned out to be the malevolent. Bent on chaos and mayhem, their muddied colors and black auras tagged them. They hadn't a clue as to how they had been detected, and no level of guile or disguise could fool the Kirlian devices.

After their first year of Kirlian detectors deployment, individuals found with muddied or black auras had a 98% chance of having an established criminal record or an international agency alert associated with them. Separated out and sequestered in a secured room or office, a special airport functionary would begin by asking their full name. Typically, their answer did not match the database. Whereupon, airport security removed the individual under heavy guard, processed them, and then sent them either to a domestic facility where they awaited a court hearing, or in the case of foreign nationals, to a temporary holding facility where they awaited extradition.

Airline travel within the U.S. became a far safer experience. No longer did people hear the incessant repetition of color threats over airport loudspeakers. Security lines moved briskly. While the TSA would change up its security processing and procedures, such measures proved to serve as purposeful mind-games and window dressing. Never once did the agency ever mess with the use of the Kirlian devices.

As a consequence, without fanfare, the airport security of the United States became the gold standard. So much so that the airport security of Ben Gurion Airport in Tel Aviv requested, through the U.S. State Department, to speak to the TSA about their procedures. Specifically, the Israelis wanted to know how the U.S. had come to manage its security so well. When told, they shook their heads in disbelief and instituted their own Kirlian procedures.

*   *   *

Three administrators in McLean, Virginia, poured over a spreadsheet in a windowless and tamperproof conference room.

"This data is incredible." The first said.

Her two colleagues nodded in agreement with deep concern reflecting on their faces.

"What we are experiencing," the first continued, "if I'm reading this spreadsheet correctly, is an exponential uptick in the arrest of individual's with 'forbidden' color hues attempting to board our commercial aircraft. On top of that, the results of their secondary screenings only confirm it. This figure here, of all the unprovoked physical confrontations during those secondary screenings, is the one that concerns me. Where are all of these individuals coming from? That's what I'd like to know."

Number three, the wizened veteran of the group, offered, "Administrator, the majority are domestic criminals, who have done prison time. How they got loose on the world is anyone's guess.

"Huh. Domestic criminals you say." The first administrator said.

Administrator three continued.

"Then, note with this last group, we come to the foreign nationals, who include criminals involved in the drug trade, those on the run, and terrorists who no country wants within their borders. Among this terrorist subgroup are radical extremists, the worst of the worst. Many of their crimes and atrocities are well documented–beheadings, bombings, the whole gamut."

"That's a rather sweeping judgment, wouldn't you say?" administrator two said with indigence and distain.

Unfazed, administrator three answered, "Well, have you done your homework and reviewed this subgroup's personnel jackets?"

Administrator two bristled at the implication.

"If you had, you would have seen in those jackets the stuff of nightmares, pure and simple. That subgroup contains outright monsters with blood on their hands."

Administrator one waited a moment for the exchange to ebb before saying, "So where are we putting these well documented foreign nationals?"

"We are temporarily 'housing' them in the Nevada desert, because Guantanamo is in the process of being shut down. They live in tents, behind electrified wire, while their extradition paperwork is processed by the State Department. We have a holding camp for men, another for women, and we took a page out of the Arizona Maricopa jail manual." The third administrator added, "Pink tents, pink uniforms, pink blankets, and pink boxers."

Administrator one then asked, "How vigorously is the extradition paperwork being processed on these documented foreign nationals?"

"Actually, quite briskly," offered administrator three. "The problem is that no one wants them. Close to two-thirds have been identified as radical elements, if not leadership. Getting these individuals off the street has been a real godsend. I don't know where we would be today without the Kirlian devices."

The second administrator then asked. "Is there any danger of them escaping?"

"To where?" answered the third. "They would have to cross over fifty miles of desert terrain. Facilities N and M officially don't exist, don't have guards to take as hostages, much less vehicles to steal. They're holding pens, pure and simple. They're provisioned by helicopter drops courtesy of the Air Force. Bottom line: it's up to the detainees to care for themselves, or not, while their paperwork is being processed. We are not part of the detainees' landscape at all."

CHAPTER 23
The Afghan

Ahmed Ali-Hassan had never before seen such a diabolically conceived place matched with such flawless simplicity of purpose. Its entire setting dared him to challenge it. But to what purpose? To initiate an agonizing and lingering death in the open desert?

The camp's design maddened the sane with its sameness. A huge square area, fenced in, with a tall, continuous earthen berm bulldozed all around it without an entrance. This blocked off any view of whatever existed beyond the tall multi-layered electric fences. A small array of solar panels powered the four water well pumps within the camp. To cannibalize or damage them meant suicide. As for the outer fences, Ali-Hassan speculated that there must be another solar array beyond the high berms.

Each pink wall tent held eight cots. Each pink cot had two pink woolen blankets. Skids made of a black plastic composite material floored the tents. Ali-Hassan didn't dare investigate what lived under them. His two-piece pink uniform included only one pair of boxers, dyed in that same blindingly pink color.

The detainees heated their food on sixteen solar ovens scattered around the camp. To Ali-Hassan, they reminded him of the barbecue grills found in any U.S. national park. With no refrigeration, all sustenance arrived via the U.S.A.F., which airlifted in out-of-date military ready-to-eat (MREs) rations. Unfortunately, a good portion of the MREs the Moslem population could not eat, due to their pork content. It became maddeningly difficult for the true believers to turn away good food and face hunger, while the infidels, who numbered over half the camp, gorged themselves. This place, Ali-Hassan saw, focused on one's personal choice, which only added to its diabolical nature.

In this sunny paradise or hell, the days blended together into one constant mirage of time. The daily rising of the sun and consistent blue sky made it difficult to separate one day from the next. Again, that theme of maddening sameness. A timeless torpor plagued the general population. Fierce arguments ignited between the faithful and infidels over even what day it was.

Fortunately, the sunrise established the camp's perfectly diagonal orientation. When Ali-Hassan and his brothers realized that, the true direction toward Mecca ceased to be a problem.

Ah, the sun, that ever-present and oppressive orb. The daily source of blinding radiant heat by day. By night, the cold bit hard. Fights broke out between the faithful and infidels, but this time over the ownership of some disgustingly pink blanket.

The wells provided sufficient water to stave off thirst and dehydration, but the quantity did not allow for daily ablutions, much less a cleansing for each of the five cycles of prayer. Clothing became rank. The latrines did not flush, being simple chemical honey pots buried in the ground with covered ports.

Ali-Hassan, a law student at the University of Minnesota and a veteran of the latest Afghan conflict, had made his mark as an effective interrogator. Sure that no one in the camp knew their location, Ali-Hassan suspected that the camp's very existence and their presence within it, without any sort of legal representation, constituted an affront to the U.S. Constitution. But even he knew that hollow argument had no teeth, for all here, faithful or not, were hardened foreign criminals of one sort or another.

With nothing to read, the detainees resorted to memorizing the moronic preparation directions from the MRE wrappers. Never before had any of the detainees experienced such a stark and sequestered existence, and it showed in their ever fluctuating behavior. Even those that hailed from the sands of Saudi Arabia, the mountains of Afghanistan, or the wastes of Syria, Iraq, Yemen, and Iran, shook their collective heads in desultory defeatism. The non-believers suffered the worst, for none of them had ever tasted true personal sacrifice.

*   *   *

"So how does it look down there, in that god-forsaken shit hole?" the U.S.A.F. captain asked the drone operator.

"Over Facility N, pretty much the usual. Last night's food drop produced several fights. One might even have been fatal. His IR image faded out quickly. Other than that, they're all still there. All one hundred and three, now one hundred and two. As for Facility M, that hasn't been populated yet."

"Any evidence of tunnel digging?"

"Not yet. But it's only been a month. Someone is bound to try that scam sometime."

"Not likely. I'm told that the top soil of that salt pan is only inches deep, then it's all bedrock.

"Look over and monitor the perimeter fencing.

That's where I expect them to do some digging."

"Roger that, sir."

Pause.

"Ah, sir. Why is it called Facility N? What's the 'N' stand for?"

"That's easy Lieutenant. That's clever bureaucratic-speak for 'Nowhere.'"

*   *   *

Ali-Hassan harbored a great distrust for Americans, America, and everything that they stood for. Most of all, he despised their confidence, their attitude of superiority, and their endless ingenuity and resources. Without question, the Great Satan had devised the most diabolical psychological rat experiment imaginable, out in the middle of a desert wilderness.

The Afghan even noticed that their food deliveries occurred on a random schedule. It came sometimes days early, sometimes a day late, but always in the early morning hours during REM sleep. It riled up both Ali-Hassan's Moslem brothers and the non-believers, causing fights, dissention, and general mayhem.

The Minnesota law graduate didn't have to be a clinical psychologist to see that the population teetered on the brink of tearing itself apart. This concerned Ali-Hassan, a natural born leader, who realized that the population needed something to focus upon. Needed something to do. Without some project, the camp would soon devolve into a pack of animals.

*   *   *

By his best reckoning, they had been there for over two

months. During that time, there had been only two prisoner deliveries, both by helicopter, and during the early morning hours. Of them, only the strongest nine had survived, after being grilled for news and information.

That information told Ali-Hassan that everyone in the camp shared one thing in common–all had been identified and apprehended in American airports. How? He did not know. But a tantalizing nugget of information did surface. One said his handlers referred to the camp as a temporary holding facility until their extradition paperwork could be completed.

Ali-Hassan didn't believe one word it. He took this hard-line position because he himself had been taken into custody while en-route to an academic conference. No one had even bothered to ask him a single question. One moment he stood in the security line at MSP. Then, poof, the next he found himself hooded, transported, stripped down and clothed in pink, and deposited here, wherever "here" might be. A rational, educated man, Ali-Hassan knew that he had been abducted.

*   *   *

Since their numbers had not yet reached the camp's maximum capacity, an entire tent had been commandeered for the camp's leadership, where they passed judgment on the unruly, summoned the faithful to prayer, and considered their community's general situation for both the faithful and not. Within, five men listened with interest to Ali-Hassan's proposal.

"As I figure it," Ali-Hassan began, "we use the floors of several tents to create a barrier that we lean against the first electric fence. We push it over. Then we repeat the process on the next two barriers. That done, we climb over the earthen berm and discover where we are. I expect to find at least one road, after all this place had to have been constructed with heavy machinery. Then, we follow it to civilization."

"Ali-Hassan, you make many assumptions," said a willowy Afghani veteran named Yosef, a man whose claim to fame involved the leveling of sixteen Christian villages.

"If we penetrate the fences, the authorities will be notified. If we climb the berm, what guarantee can you offer that there is indeed a road for us to follow? The heavy machinery that you refer to could have been transported here by helicopter. This I have myself witnessed in our homeland. The Russians loved their tractors. But most foolish, if we attempt to walk out of this god forsaken hell, we will need water. How do we do that?"

Having anticipated all of these objections, since he had heard them all before, Ali-Hassan, nonetheless listened to them in polite silence, pretending to measure their words.

Then he answered, "Water, without question, means life. I propose that we fashion water carriers from the plastic wrapping of our next food drop. We should be able to make sufficient for all."

"And how do you propose to do that?" Sneered one of the infidel leaders.

"In two days' time, I will show you."

*   *   *

Seventy-four days since their incarceration, in the early evening, Ali-Hassan witnessed the first electrical fence fall, its metal posts shrieking in protest before they gave way. Apparently the camp's designers had not planned on the will and ingenuity of twenty men.

Now standing atop the berm, Ali-Hassan saw that Yosef had been right. There wasn't a construction road in sight to follow back to civilization.

The Afghan grunted to himself, "Well, we'll use Plan B."

*   *   *

"ALERT! ALERT! PERIMETER FAILURE!" the overhead speaker in the drone command center blared.

Turning off its repetitive message, Lieutenant Joshua Park looked at his watch and barked out to his staff of four.

"Breakout at FACILITY N. Call the U.S.A.F. to cancel the next food drop. Flash alert our Blackhawks. Deploy in twenty. THIS IS NOT A DRILL."

Park shook his head in sad disbelief.

All they have to do is to stay put. Let the government suits find them a new home. The sad thing is that no one wants any part of them.

Now, they have to get creative.

*   *   *

Ali-Hassan couldn't believe how easy it had been. The fences toppled quickly. Plan B organized the camp's population into four teams. The entire camp, faithful and not, spilled out with each man shouldering blankets and a water supply of about a gallon and half. Each team went off toward its own quadrant, ignorant of where their feet might be taking them. They knew only that they were doing so as free men, wearing pink.

*   *   *

When Ali-Hassan left the prison camp dressed in his pinks, he fell in with the third group that headed in a northerly direction toward the North Star. The others followed their own quadrants. With the aid of a bright half-moon, his team struggled across the uneven and prickly terrain, which made for a treacherous journey in their pink flip flops. But they were free. Even the desert air seemed to smell fresher outside the camp. Chests again swelled with purpose. The men held their own destinies once again. After over two months of incarceration, that's all that mattered.

Ali-Hassan never heard them coming.

Barely thirty minutes into their daring and ambitious adventure, Ali-Hassan's team, faithful and infidel alike, fell.

*   *   *

One Blackhawk helicopter, designated Sleepy Two, with its wing-like rotors and muffled exhausts, swooped in like a silent great horned owl pouncing on field mice. The chopper, tasked by an overlooking sentry aircraft, vectored in toward a specific huddled group. To the co-pilot and gunner, they looked like an amoeba-like blob in their helmets' IR targeting visors.

Given the compact nature of the target, the co-pilot elected to fire his rockets from about a half mile away.

CHAPTER 24
Theresa Ann McGonagall

"There Are Never Too Many Miracles."

(Boston) Miracles keep happening at Massachusetts General Hospital. Theresa Ann McGonagall, a Wellesley College senior, is living proof. In a coma for over ten months following a serious sports head injury, Ms. McGonagall can once again be counted as among the living.

Speaking for her daughter, Donna M. McGonagall said, "Once Theresa gets this behind her, she'll need several months of rehabilitation before she can care for herself, much less continue her education and graduate. We certainly hope that Tess will be able to finish her education. But having her back is all that our family could ask for. We've missed her dearly. We're so very blessed."

An honors student in American History, McGonagall, Wellesley College's star soccer striker, had injured herself in a hotly contested match against Smith College.

(*Boston Globe, Health & Wellness. Section,* D1-2, Tuesday, August 5, 2005)

Donna McGonagall's estimate of only "several months" for her daughter's recovery turned out to be optimistic. Given her near-death state, the extreme atrophy of her muscles, and above all the precarious state of her cognitive faculties, that she breathed unassisted remained miracle enough.

Theresa Ann, however, fought her way back. She

began by relearning the simple things, like how to smile, button a button, and control her bladder and bowels. A long and arduous road, but day by day, Theresa Ann became stronger, more aware of her surroundings. Nonetheless, her inability to speak troubled the medical professionals. This suggested a deeply rooted cerebral problem, yet a problem MRIs could not pin point or explain.

*   *   *

For the Emissary learning to control a near-invalid's body represented a considerable challenge. The body, while intact, needed strengthening. Theresa Ann's conscious mind, diminished, could be impressed with a new set of learned responses, habits, and even memories added to those few that remained. The five physical senses functioned, but speech would require considerable work. After all, the Emissary had to learn firsthand what speech meant, much less which set of organs made it possible, and how.

Many mortals cared for the person called Theresa Ann. The Emissary could easily discern this fact from the color and texture of their auras, which displayed the full power and force of human emotion. Its raw impact staggered the Emissary, as did an amazing intellectual warmth and sense of wellbeing. That something it would come to know as love.

*   *   *

Six months passed before Theresa Ann could dress herself, perform on her own all the necessary hygienic functions, and speak her first words. After that last accomplishment, rapid progress followed, leading to a torrent of emotion-filled and impassioned utterances of sheer joy at the accomplishment.

Finally, I can speak, rejoiced the Emissary. *Finally, I can express myself. Finally, I can begin my search for the soul of Nergal. I hope that I am not too late,* the Emissary fretted.

*   *   *

The McGonagall family expected it would take time for Theresa Ann to recover, but they hadn't anticipated any changes to her personality. The doctors warned them of this potentiality, but the stark reality nonetheless hit them hard. Neither parent could voice the next unspoken question, "How 'different' would our Theresa Ann be?"

By her seventh month of recovery, Theresa Ann could walk, jog, run, and even ride a bike after a fashion, but she didn't have her old confident and sassy gait. Her lope lacked its old natural fluidity and her balance seemed sketchy at best. Her hand, eye, and foot coordination rated as nothing special. Theresa Ann 2.0 was average, instead of physically gifted.

"Where has my little girl gone?" lamented Mrs. McGonagall. "All those years of piano lessons. And now, what's this love affair with New Country music?" Her father could not express his distress verbally. Instead, his endless and unbidden tears told a grim story of precious memories with *his* little girl forever lost.

As a consequence, both parents came to the independent conclusion that their Theresa Ann indeed was a different person. Not that they liked it. Yes, some flickers of the past remained, but down deep she was another person who lacked Theresa Ann 1.0's soul.

Theresa Ann's personality changes ran the gamut. Her smile looked genuine enough, but not sufficiently lop-sided and purposely goofy. The voice sounded similar enough, but the choice of vocabulary, intonation, and delivery differed. Theresa Ann struggled to translate her thoughts into English. She acquired facial expressions that manifested themselves in odd ways, some even appearing to be nothing more than imitated than genuine.

"Yes," her parents would say to their friends, "we are blessed to have our Theresa Ann back." But in private, they wondered about Theresa Ann. At times they would catch her vacant looks staring off into the distance, with a frown on her face, as if in some sort of silent conversation, or, when Theresa Ann thought she sat alone, while her eyes blazed. During those times, her parents saw something else. Something foreign. Something not their Theresa Ann.

As for her overall demeanor, gone forever was the ebullient and confident school girl. In her place stood an observant figure, who furtively looked about, scanning her environment for threats.

*　　*　　*

"Emissary," the Ledger Keeper encouraged, "it is time you begin looking for the wayward one."

"But how will I find the wayward one?"

"I will provide you with guidance. That is all you require."

*　　*　　*

At the end of Theresa Ann's eighth month of recovery, a stranger would not have been able to tell the sheer hell the young woman had been through. The endless hours of physical therapy, speech training, and coordination drills had worked. Theresa Ann had made a reasonable recovery. Ready for prime time, Theresa Ann, for her part, did not disappoint, because soon after she announced she wanted to complete her college degree.

This brought great tears of joy to her parents. That is, until she made it clear she didn't wish to return to Wellesley. Instead, she would complete her studies at some cowboy school called North Texas State University.

Aghast at her defection from her mother's alma mater, so began the first family argument since before the coma. Donna and Gregg were adamant that she complete her degree at Wellesley, Theresa Ann stubbornly defied them. On top of that, her parents didn't know, but their daughter had already bought an airline ticket for Dallas the very next morning.

CHAPTER 25
The Hunt for Nergal

The Emissary's taxi ride to Boston's Logan International Airport had been uneventful. Having passed through the airport's security, and traveling light with a small wheeled travel-case, the Emissary found the appropriate gate, and then waited for the flight's departure to Dallas/Fort Worth.

*   *   *

Jenny Smith worked hard to get her job. After having applied to the TSA over a year before, they had e-mailed her with a date, time, and place for a series of computerized tests. After that, and another wait for a full month, then came another notice for her to report for a face-to-face interview, which turned out to be three separate ones. Then, two weeks later, she reported to a specific building at Logan airport to pick up her TSA uniform, fill out even more paperwork, have her security badge photo taken, and swear an oath to defend the United States of America.

Two years later, Jenny operated a new security device. While the job bored her to death, Jenny remained grateful as she had a union job with benefits.

Waist high, Jenny's security post consisted of a small, shiny, stainless steel table. Each passenger pressed the lone button in the table's center and held it for a count of five until the little yellow light came on. Finished, Jenny then wiped off the button and the table with a moistened sterile pad after each use. Her supervisor said she prevented the spread of harmful germs.

Whenever folks asked what the button test did, she said it checked fingerprints. Jenny didn't know her table energized the Kirlian effect, and the pressing of its slotted button revealed a passenger's aura. The actual reading of the excited aura fell to another TSA employee. That person spent their entire shift sitting before a large flat screen in full view of Jenny's table, and the passengers who passed through her station.

The flat screen of the second TSA agent displayed a row of forbidden color hues along its bottom border– muddy to dark to black colors. The operator pressed either the DELETE key to clear the screen for the next passenger, or the ENTER key, if the aura displayed a forbidden color.

Joe, a lanky fellow who struggled with acne, had felt somewhat of an expert on the flat screen after a full week. In his brief experience with the new security scanning device, he had only had to press the ENTER key twice, and when he did, two TSA security agents stopped the individuals and shuttled them away for additional screening.

Joe sat at his station as the passengers queued pass him. Light green, yellow, light green...

"What the hell?" he whispered to himself. No color registered for the pretty little redhead.

He scratched his head in thought.

What did I do wrong? Did I forget to refresh to the screen? Or did something break?

Then he quickly consulted his manual and scanned its contents for "no color." It was not mentioned among any of the forbidden dark or muddy hues. Nope. It said nothing about anyone without a color. So he moved on and hit the DELETE button.

*   *   *

The Emissary found flying an unending source of excitement. Sitting at a window seat, the Emissary pasted its nose to the portal the entire time and took it all in.

Upon arrival, the Emissary located the cab stand and jumped into one.

"1524 Union Circle, Denton," the Emissary announced, settled in for the fifty-odd minute ride, and positioned its head to gaze out the window and marvel as the world passed by.

Off and on snow flurries had chilled the Boston area, but here, in bright and sunny Dallas, the temperatures rose into the fifties. In comparison, it felt almost balmy. The Emissary judged this to be a good omen as it took off its down overcoat. Besides, to be free and out from under the continuous and smothering scrutiny of Donna and Gregg, felt liberating.

That feeling soared when the taxi stopped at the curb on Union Circle, in the heart of the North Texas State University campus. Here, life flourished everywhere. Rows of beautiful trees stood all decked out in their fall colors. Students either milled about, or strode on toward their classes. The entire tableaux exuded an atmosphere of youthful vitality.

A huge flat-roofed edifice of tan brick and white stone accents loomed before the Emissary. The signage said University Union. The Emissary felt the distinct tugging of the Ledger Keeper's guidance toward, and yet beyond, the structure, toward the west, and away from all of the busy construction activity.

So the Emissary made off in that direction and soon encountered another large flat roofed building called the Willis Library. Somewhere within it knew it would find the wayward soul.

CHAPTER 26
Highway 6

Ali-Hassan survived the night's aerial barrage, because of the lawyer's battlefield experience. When the attack hit his team, he instincts took over as he buried his face into one of his blankets. Simultaneously, he shielded himself beneath two of his compatriots, who had toppled over on top of him. Their still and warm bodies masked him from the American's IR targeting system.

Breathing became difficult through his blanket, but he dared not remove it. Ali-Hassan could not risk movement or discovery. Staying still, however, proved not to be a good option, because the combined weight of the two men pushed his lungs flat and empty. He began to panic.

Calming himself, Ali-Hassan then did what any other frightened human would do. He waited. Time would tell if the helicopter would land and deploy any infantry. To his surprise, the helicopter did not. Instead, it left as silently as it appeared. Still, he didn't dare move a muscle for some time. His lungs ached.

With his body contorted, his muscles cramping, and the chill of the evening setting in, Ali-Hassan finally levered his lanky frame out from under. He grabbed two nearby blankets and, wrapping himself up, collapsed against a small boulder. Shudders followed. At least he now had some cover.

"Allah loves me," he whispered when he later found three unspilled water carriers. Shouldering them, he staggered on in the direction of the North Star.

"I must find shoes, clothing, and a highway," he

whispered to himself. "I must act as if I am once again in my homeland. Hiding from the Great Satan."

So he did, choosing to travel only on the rock shelves and the compacted sand of the narrow and winding arroyos. These provided easy passage with concealment, and minimized his flip-flops' tracks.

By his own reckoning, Ali-Hassan made good time. Adrenaline can do that. Two hours into his desperate trek, he consumed his first water carrier, but he estimated that he had covered nearly seven miles. So he pressed on, fearing dawn's first light. Further, he knew that the farther he distanced himself from what he thought of as "the kill site," the better.

I need to find a road.

Two hours later and another seven miles more, the first signs of civilization appeared in the distance as a lighted cluster of buildings next to an airstrip on his left, maybe five miles away. Suddenly, a car pulled out with its head lights beaming bright. Ali-Hassan noted the direction where the car headed as it left the area.

"There must be a highway up ahead," he said with satisfaction as he redoubled his efforts.

*   *   *

"This is Rescue One to base. Over."

"This is base, Rescue One. What's your status? Over."

"We're at the third gas site, base. Permission to land. Over."

"Permission granted, Rescue One. Over."

A skin-tight Air Force green flight glove toggled the radio to that of the helicopter's internal communications system.

"Listen up everyone. We have gas victims down there. Do not, I repeat, do not forget your side arms. It might look quiet, but don't be fooled. Some of those bad guys might be playing possum."

The chopper pilot, a veteran of God only knows how many black op insertions and recoveries, looked over to his right, and said. "Jonesy. I don't know about you, but I haven't cleaned up a mess like this since Kosovo."

"No shit," said his co-pilot as their medical team of eight, clothed in hazmat suits, disembarked down the ramp, each with their own collapsed stretcher.

Each medic carried their full kit. The chopper's interior looked like a bakery truck with all of its racking. About twenty minutes later, the medical racking now filled with sleeping detainees, the chopper took off for Facility N, while leaving behind the eight medics who readied the next load.

Meanwhile at Facility N, several engineering crews repaired the collapsed fencing with sturdier posts, re-established their conductivity, and repositioned the tent floors to where they belonged. The worst job involved refreshing the camp's honey pots with fresh chemicals.

They finished in under three hours. An engineering officer made a cursory sweep of the camp and judged ready it for its population, and the next batch of twenty-two detainees, who that very night, would arrive.

On the opposite side of the camp, the still sedated detainees had been arranged in neat rows covered in fresh, pink blankets. Of this adventurous group, three didn't survive their exploratory excursion. Two succumbed to heart attack and one fell breaking his neck in the dark.

As the sun rose that morning, the gassed detainees began to stir and discovered that they had company. Grouped on one side of the compound, the detainees found themselves surrounded by heavily armed and armored soldiers looking like black insects. No one wore any insignia. They remained silent ciphers, that is until the air horn sounded off, followed by a bullhorn announcement:

ATTENTION ALL DETAINEES.

YOU ARE THE GUESTS OF THE UNITED STATES GOVERNMENT.

YOU ARE BEING HELD HERE WHILE YOUR DEPORTATION PAPERWORK IS BEING PROCESSED.

ONCE YOUR DEPORTATION PAPERWORK IS COMPLETE, YOU WILL BE TRANSFERRED TO THE NATION THAT HAS ACCEPTED YOU.

ON YOUR RIGHT ANKLE IS A PLASTIC BRACELET. IT IS A TRACKING DEVICE. DO NOT REMOVE IT. TAMPERING WITH IT WILL CAUSE IT TO EXPLODE.

This message blared out three times, in English, Arabic, Farsi, Spanish, German, French, and Russian.

Not three hours after the helicopters departed, a detainee managed to somehow detonate his ankle bracelet, removing several fingers and his right foot in the process. He died of shock and blood loss.

*   *   *

"I cannot believe my good fortune! Allah wishes for me to succeed, and to bear witness to the cowardly massacre of my brothers by the Americans!" Ali-Hassan said with fervent passion.

It took the Afghan two days to get this far. During that time, after skirting the airport, he encountered a large farm with an elevated irrigation system. There, he showered for the first time in months. The cascading water felt wonderful as he stumbled along following beneath the spray of the overhead sprinkler's path.

In the sprinklers' maintenance shed, Ali-Hassan found a pair of rubber work boots, bib overalls, a windbreaker, and a worn and sweat-stained Broncos cap. Needless to say, he praised Allah again for his generosity, took them all, and discarded all of his pinks, laughing like an insane man while he buried them in the farm's muddy soil.

The Afghan felt somewhat presentable in his borrowed garments, even with his shaggy hair and beard. However, he could not hide his cracked and weathered lips. Nonetheless, this misplaced lawyer and mountain fighter, having drunk his fill of water, headed north again, but this time in the daylight.

When the sun neared its height, he reached the glorious pavement of an east-west two-lane road. Never before had a lined straightaway of black top meant so much to him. While it represented his best hope for escape, he had to choose which way to go. So Ali-Hassan turned right, toward the east, toward Allah's Mecca, and began walking along the pavement's runoff with the sun at his back. After all his days of struggling through brush and cactus, walking along the roadside, unhindered, felt like flying. Not long into his eastbound journey, he encountered his first road sign. The white shield with black borders said:

NEVADA
HWY 6

Up until that moment, Ali-Hassan hadn't a clue where he had been held. By the terrain alone, he had guessed Utah or maybe New Mexico, but never as far west as Nevada. The revelation shocked him. It also went a long way in explaining why he had yet to encounter anyone.

Walking next to the shimmering road in the afternoon sun turned out to be brutal, mesmerizing, and brain-numbing. Looking ahead, mirages would form in any depression. It all seemed so endless. Then the lawyer noticed something. He felt, more than heard, the approach of a vehicle.

Startled by the change in air pressure as the tractor trailer neared, the lawyer stuck out the thumb of his left hand. As the sixteen wheeler roared past, its draft shook his slim frame and threatened to blow him off the road and into the nearby stunted cactus.

Dust and sand filled Ali-Hassan's nose and stung his eyes. He swore a choice curse. Then, to his amazement, he saw the red glare of brake lights and smelled the sharp stink of overtaxed brake pads.

It took the Afghan almost three minutes to get even to the passenger side door of the massive Kenworth's green cab, where a voice greeted him from out of the open window.

"Where's you headed?"

Remembering his plan, the roadside refugee said, "Salt Lake City, Utah."

"Damn, that's almost three hundred miles away. But I'll make you a deal. Hop in and I'll git' you as far as Ely. That's my best offer."

"Deal," He called back with a cracked and unfamiliar sounding voice.

In reply, the cab's door popped open and Ali-Hassan climbed in total acceptance of Allah's will.

*   *   *

The cab's air conditioned interior proved to be quite a shock to Ali-Hassan, and he shivered. It also smelled like home, as the driver smoked a pleasant aromatic pipe tobacco. Mounting the passenger's seat, he found it to be comfortable and springy.

The Afghan smiled and said, "Thank you for your kindness. I know I look like a total wreck, but I have been on a Mormon mission that went terribly wrong."

The driver, a hefty middle-aged guy, himself with a full brown beard, eyed Al-Hassan appraisingly.

"I'll bet you have," The driver said as he began getting the big rig up and moving again, passing through its many gears. Before Ali-Hassan knew it, they reached eighty-five miles an hour.

"Sorry about dusting you back there, but as you can probably imagine, old Betsy here cannot stop on a dime. "My name's Pete Campbell. What's yours?"

"Al Hass. Thank you again for the lift. I know my family in Salt Lake are worried about me."

"So what happened with your mission, son?"

"Well, as you can see by my clothes, I worked a farm," Ali-Hassan improvised. "The family who owned the farm had some rather strange ideas about farming and who did what. So, I up and left."

"So how's you working on a State-side farm on your mission?"

"I worked on a farm owned by Korean immigrants in northern California. I did so because I wanted to learn their language. That way I could complete my mission overseas," the Afghan embellished yet again.

"Damnation. That's bad luck, son. I'm sorry you went through that wringer."

Not understanding what the man meant, Al-Hassan thought it best to just nod in affirmation.

"Korean immigrants, you say. What kind of farming?"

"Rice, cabbage, and hot peppers."

"Did they physically harm you in any way? Now tell me true, son."

This time the Afghan said, "No, sir."

"Well, at least that's good. By the way, if you're tired, that seat there can recline back real nice. I'll take no offence ifn' you choose to nod off."

Al-Hassan fumbled with the many seat controls, but eventually he got into a comfortable position. Mr. Campbell had been right. Then he chance to ask, "Is there a bus station in Ely?"

"Yes, I do believe there is." Campbell said, again looking over at his passenger, again with an appraising eye.

"Mr. Campbell, is it possible you could spare the money for a bus ticket to Salt Lake?"

"You're that broke?

"Yes, sir. I am."

The driver grunted and drove on. The gentle swaying of the vehicle hit the escapee like a narcotic and soon his eyes began to flutter. Sitting back into the seat, he sighed, contented, but with a lot on his mind.

Meanwhile, the driver too must have been doing a lot of thinking as well, for he reached into his shirt pocket and drew out a tight wad of bills. He extended them to his passenger and said, "Here, son, take this. It isn't much, but it'll git' ya' a bus ticket, some food, and maybe even a shave and a haircut. I can't have you frightening the wits out of your kin folk back home."

Looking down at the wad in his trembling hands, Ali-Hassan, amazed, counted out six twenties.

"I can't take this. It's too much."

"Yes, you can. Besides, that's my gambling money. And I shouldn't be doing that anymore. Now settle back and grab yourself some shut eye. You look like hell. I'll wake you up when we git' to Ely."

CHAPTER 27
The Confrontation

I sat at my favorite study desk in the graduate section, amidst the PJ stacks, reading Huehnergard's book about the Akkadian language. Per the usual, I read in deep dive mode, oblivious to my immediate surroundings, when Nergal startled me.

J. J. Something has entered the library and it is coming near. Something most terrifying!

I looked up to a row of empty study desks and endless lines of stacks. No one here, no one coming, no one browsing the book shelves, nothing. Zero. Zip. Nada. That morning the aisles of the graduate library remained quiet as a church on an early Monday morning.

"Whadda ya' mean Nergal?" I whispered. "There's no one else here except us."

No, J. J. it's not here yet. Trust me, I can feel its approach. Watch in the directions of the stairs before you!

The words "it" and "feel its approach" resonated within me, or should I say, they communicated a far better sense of Nergal's absolute terror.

Then I heard the distinct click-clack of woman's shoes coming up the stone staircase.

J. J. It's here!

My military training took over. I closed Huehnergard's book, pushed back my chair, went on full alert, and braced myself.

Then, two crazy things happened at once.

Nergal started screaming in abject fear at the top of

his psychic lungs when this "it" with long red hair appeared at the top of the stairs pulling behind her a small wheelie garment bag. Her head swiveled only once and the red-head's eyes locked on me. Then she headed my way with a brisk, purposeful stride. I don't know what disturbed me more, Nergal's nonstop wailing or how much she reminded me of my Grace.

J. J.!

RUN! Nergal pleaded.

I ignored him and stood up from behind my study desk. With my feet planted and armed with a 660 page book in my right hand, I judged myself ready to engage the enemy. Yes sir, I was packing and dangerous.

My resolute stance seemed to startle the approaching woman in the gray pin-striped pant suit, since she stopped in the middle of the aisle about ten feet away. She had left her wheelie behind her, freeing both hands.

"Mortal, please do not interfere. I wish to speak with Nergal, immediately," she said with firmness and piercing eyes that bore right through me as if visualizing something within.

Nergal?

She knows about Nergal?

How?

"What do you wish to say to this...Nergal?" I countered.

"That he has jeopardized the Cosmic Order and has caused a serious imbalance within it. I am here to accompany him back to where he belongs."

Me? Nergal gasped in disbelief. *I did what to the Cosmic Order?*

"Yes, you, Nergal. Your sojourn has ended. It is

time for you to go back where you belong."

J. J. How did she hear me?

"Apparently, Nergal, she can quite well." I replied.

Nergal! Come to me! She commanded with her arms outstretched in...greeting?

"COME TO ME, NOW!"

The sheer force of her psychic command staggered me.

NO! Nergal shrieked in defiance. *I have sacrificed so much, come so far. I will complete my quest first! I will not abandon my Erish!*

The force of Nergal's rejection caused the brow to furrow on the young woman's unhappy face.

J. J.! Do something! Nergal pleaded.

"Do not interfere, mortal," she gritted out with her shoulders tense and arms held rigidly at the sides. "This issue is between the Ledger Keeper and Nergal, alone."

"Interfere with what?" I said, while I swiped my free left hand through the air like I had swatted a fly.

J. J., this thing is extraordinarily dangerous! Nergal entreated.

Now with mounting exasperation the woman said, "Do not interfere with *me* mortal! For I am the Emissary of the Ledger Keeper, sent by the Creator. Surrender Nergal to me. *NOW*." Her right hand pointed to the floor before her in emphasis.

Nergal couldn't speak, even if he wanted to. This woman had reduced him to a quivering mass of jelly.

Now pointing her right arm at me like the barrel of a rifle, the green-eyed emissary commanded. "My business is with Nergal, and Nergal alone."

"Oh really," I blurted out.

J. J.! Nergal moaned in fear. *Don't play with it.*

At my insolence, her green eyes widened, and she repeated as if to a child.

"I have warned you, mortal. *STEP ASIDE.*"

Then the hair on the back of my neck rose as she moved forward and made a grab for my chest with her outstretched hands. Her fingers forming like claws clutched only air. The woman had run into an invisible wall. She bounced back, gasping, her fingers flexing and unflexing as if numbed by an electrical shock.

So violent had Nergal reacted at the woman's attempt to grab my chest that I should have staggered back, but didn't, because I had planted myself so firmly.

Shock painted the Emissary's face. "How dare you resist mortal! I'll have you...a golden aura!" The woman exclaimed with considerable wonder. Her head tilted to one side, while her green eyes regarded me.

"No. It's *the* golden aura! So," the woman concluded with her hands on her hips, "the soul of Nergal hides within the *su.mannu.uzuzzu.eli,* the one who carries the First Soul of Creation."

J. J.? Nergal said with surprise mixed with awe. *What is it talking about? Were you not aware of this?*

At this point everything weirded out for me. First, a woman resembling my Grace made a move to do some sort of harm to my chest, like that crazed East Indian priest in the Indiana Jones movie. Second, for some amazing reason, when she went for Nergal, something stopped her. And now she's talking about, my golden aura and the First Soul of Creation. I had no idea what she was talking about so I asked.

"Okay, what is this First Soul of Creation?" I said while putting down my book.

J. J.? Nergal wondered.

"Why you, mortal soul carrier, your very soul," the Emissary reverently stated, "is the first, the oldest, of Creation. You are the embodiment of balance…the one who ensures the stability of the Cosmic Order."

At that formal pronouncement, the red haired woman bowed her head in my direction. "It is an honor to stand in your presence."

I didn't know what to say. Flabbergasted came to mind. I carried the First Soul...

J. J.? Is this true? Nergal gasped.

Then I remembered. Golden aura? Heck, my dad told me I was a golden child. I needed to figure all of this out. So I did the logical thing, I asked, "Emissary. Let's talk this out. Please, take a chair." As I gestured for her to sit opposite me at my study desk.

"Please tell me all about what Nergal has done to the Cosmic Order and how the First Soul of Creation fits into the picture."

The Emissary sat, folded her hands before her. Her eyes took on a dreamy aspect and then she spoke in a wooden manner as if channeling some ancient text.

"First Soul, Nergal has placed into serious jeopardy the original plan of the Cosmic Order, as established by the Creator."

What! What did I do? Nergal protested.

Plenty, apparently. I snapped. *Now listen up.*

"Either purposefully or through ignorance, the soul called Nergal, caused a serious imbalance within the Cosmic Order. He accomplished this by sequestering his soul through the artifice of magic at his mortal death. At his death, his soul should have arrived in the dark realm, but it did not. This discrepancy in where

Nergal's soul resided caused a dangerous imbalance within the Cosmic Order, and tore an opening in the border of the dark realm. As I recount this mischief, countless depraved souls from the dark realm have, and are entering, the mortal world at will."

By the gods what have I done? Nergal prayed. *What a disaster I have created. Who knows how many innocents have been harmed because of my selfish deeds?*

His single-minded purpose now placed into question.

How dare I place into jeopardy the entire Cosmic Order?

"Thank you, Emissary. However, I am ignorant of the details of the Cosmic Order. Can you describe them for me?"

Again with a slight bow in my direction, she began, again in that spooky, detached voice.

"In the beginning there was a profound inky blackness, a gloom so old that the first mote of sunlight had yet to be created. Within that darkness lurked swirling, unseen energies, which existed as things psychically felt, like the oppressive weight of a wet garment.

"This total darkness waited, eternally patient, for the coming of light, and with light, begat the realms, immortal creation, the first souls, and then mortal creation. So the eternal cosmic cycle began."

Okay...so this creation sounds like the Big Bang. I surmised in an attempt to get a grasp of the magnitude of her words.

The emissary paused to entertain my thoughts, and then continued.

"The Creator fashioned the dark, light, and mortal realms as distinct and separate. At a mortal's passing, its soul, first arrived in the dark realm. There the soul chose whether to rise toward the light and pass into it, or to remain unperfected and sink ever deeper into the endless darkness.

"Souls that do not rise toward the light do so because they are bereft of hope and love. They choose misery, become demented, twisted, and vengeful. Souls, so doomed, as their depravity mounts, descend until they meet utter destruction. This journey is called damnation."

"Excuse me, Emissary. But is there no hope for the damned?"

"Yes, but it is all too infrequently pursued."

"Please continue, Emissary." I encouraged with fascination mixed with abject horror.

"Those souls that rise up through the dark and enter the light do so based upon their innate sense of contrition, hope, and capacity for love. From the light realm a soul continues its progress through a portal, provided for the purpose, to the mortal world. This journey is called incarnation."

Huh! So that's how it works...

Once again the emissary paused, listened, and continued on. Thereafter, I made a point not to be so disruptive with my thoughts.

"Coincident in time with the creation of these realms, the Creator caused energies to form into several immortal entities. One is called the Ledger Keeper. It records the presence of every soul and tracks their comings and goings.

So this is what I'm talking to...

"The Ledger Keeper maintains the ledger in order to ensure the balance of souls, the equilibrium. For to allow an imbalance to occur, disequilibrium would portend disaster and usher in the end times."

At this gloomy note, the emissary paused. As for me, I held my head in my hands in astonishment.

"Emissary. Please tell me about the First Soul."

"Gladly. The Creator fashioned the First Soul, which you carry," she said with a respectful nod of her head, "an artifice made from the energies of the light. This First Soul, by its very nature, embodies balance itself. As it incarnates, it learns and gains wisdom. All that it lacks is the ability to transcend, for to do so would remove it from its primary purpose–the preservation of balance. The First Soul was called by the ancients 'it which stands apart.'"

Nergal gasped in recognition as he translated the phrase into his native Sumerian–*su.mannu.uzuzzu.eli.*

"Fundamentally, the First Soul prevents the end times from occurring. While a heavy burden, this responsibility focuses the actions of the First Soul so it will be ready when the need is most dire. During trying times, it is said, the First Soul is capable of anything.

"Regarding the mortal vessels who carry the First Soul of Creation, they are considered cursed by great loneliness as no individual or thing can stand in the way of its first duty: the preservation of balance.

"The unscrupulous have long realized that the First Soul's life partners, family, and friends, can be used as a means of leverage to influence the First Soul.

"Mortal carriers of the First Soul are born without fear. Some are protective of the weak, infirm, or persecuted; others not. Some developed a powerful sense of altruism, which became their weakness, as such qualities collided with its primary purpose. Meanwhile others, because of their station, championed their pride of place overly, sometimes causing its mortal vessel pain and injury. In outright defiance, these mortal vessels often carry proud scars of battle. Such is their lot."

At this point, I got this funny feeling in the pit of my stomach. For this humble Baptist from North Texas, all of this ran far afield of my upbringing. What the Emissary said, however, did explain my charmed life and my many run-ins with death and danger along life's path. Maybe, just maybe...

*   *   *

When the Emissary finished, my head continued to spin. Her narration so unbelievable, and yet...

"Emissary, can you prove anything that you have just told me?" I countered.

"No, First Soul. I cannot within the mortal realm," the Emissary stated with finality. "Do you believe the soul of Nergal does not reside within you?"

"Yes, Nergal resides within me, and yes, I will protect him until he completes his quest. And here's why. He is seeking the lost remains of his beloved wife, Erish. In this, I will help him. And once he finds her, then you can have back your lost soul."

*   *   *

"So, who are you? I mean, the woman sitting before me," I probed.

"She is merely a means to an end," stated the

Ledger Keeper, Emissary, woman, whatever, whichever.

"How so?" I prodded some more.

"My Emissary resides within this mortal form," said the Ledger Keeper. "We found this mortal in a terminal physical state. She for all practical purposes neared physical death and had been in that state for quite some time. In fact, her soul had already passed. It took many, many months to rehabilitate this body."

That reply confounded me as way too much information. No matter how much Nergal had helped my intellectual capacity over the past year. So I focused on things that I could grasp.

"So, does this woman have a name?"

"Theresa Ann McGonagall."

"Does Theresa Ann have a family, parents, brothers and sisters?"

"Yes. A family. Her parents are Donna and Gregg McGonagall."

"Once your Emissary has completed its task, what will happen to the person called Theresa Ann McGonagall?"

"She will die."

"How is that possible? According to you, she is already dead. That means you have already recorded her passing. Wouldn't her second death cause another imbalance to the Cosmic Order?"

"No," the Emissary replied, "that which causes this mortal's animation originated as a portion of my essence, which is not the same as a mortal soul. Thus, the physical body is forfeit and of no consequence."

Was I the only one in the room who felt a distinct chill with that answer? I noted an eye twitch on Theresa

Ann's face, and it prompted me to push the issue.

"I have another question, Emissary. Does the essence that animates the Emissary wish to rejoin with the Ledger Keeper?"

"Its purpose is to do so."

"Yes, that's its *original* purpose. Its *planned* purpose. But hasn't the Emissary's contact with the light realm and mortal kind changed it? Isn't it possible the Emissary has grown apart from the Ledger Keeper?"

A deep furrow crossed her smooth brow. At least from my perspective, a serious conversation was taking place between the Ledger Keeper and its Emissary.

Tears formed in the corners of Theresa Ann's green eyes, and several moments passed in silence. So I pressed on.

"And, if the more experienced essence of the Emissary rejoined with you, would you not be changed as well? Perhaps even, not for the better?"

"I cannot prevent the Emissary from standing apart. Ultimately, the Emissary must decide. After all, it is self-aware, as am I. Regardless, its decision will not affect the counting of souls."

As its lips moved, I sensed a difference between when the Ledger Keeper spoke and when the mortal named Theresa Ann did.

"But as for the soul of Nergal," the Ledger Keeper decreed, "it must be returned now, because its actions have caused sufficient mischief."

Nergal cringed at this flat pronouncement.

"Yes," I said. "You've said that before and I have told you Nergal's quest comes first. And, once it is completed, he will freely return to you.

"Now, may I speak to Theresa Ann?"

A single head nod.

"Theresa Ann. When did you last eat?"

"This morning, at breakfast."

"Well, it's three-thirty in the afternoon, Central Daylight Time. When did you leave Boston?"

"Eleven in the morning."

"Did they feed you on the plane?"

"No."

"Are you hungry?"

"Yes, come to think about it. I'm famished."

"Well, let's fix that, like right now."

*   *   *

By this time Nergal had been reduced to one very nervous Sumerian. He did not like my idea of taking Theresa Ann to an early dinner, the very one who held his one-way ticket back to the hereafter.

Trust me, I told him.

I took Theresa Ann to my favorite country steakhouse for some dinner and drinks. We talked a whole bunch about Nergal, his wife, and how much they loved each other, and how critical Nergal found his wife's remains. The entire time, I pretended that the Ledger Keeper sat in the empty chair next to me.

"Well," Theresa Ann said with a wistful smile and shoulder shrug, "I now appreciate Nergal's predicament much better. While in the hospital, I felt love. So many wonderful strangers cared about my wellbeing. Little things, like playing happy music, are my first memories of love as a mortal. That's not to say I didn't feel the same about Donna and Gregg, but believe it or not, they felt far more distant than the doctors and nurses."

Theresa Ann's vivid revelations about experiencing emotion, for the first time, I knew that had to have had an impact on the Ledger Keeper.

"Could it be the care of total strangers impressed you more than that of your own kin?" I asked.

"Yeah. I see your point. That could be, because the doctors and nurses didn't know me before the coma, whereas Donna and Gregg had their expectations. And from what I could feel, I hadn't lived up to them."

"It can be a real pain, Theresa Ann, trying to fulfill another's expectations instead of accepting you for what you are. In many ways, the very same thing can be said about your relationship with the Ledger Keeper."

"We are confused," Theresa Ann's said, speaking for the Ledger Keeper, Emissary, and Theresa Ann, as she looked down into her lap. "What is your purpose, First Soul, in promoting this turmoil?"

Shrugging, I said, "Well, from where I'm sitting, I see a worthy goal, namely, the finding and accounting of Nergal's soul. Fine. But I also see the creation of something unique, the Emissary, who is in possession of Theresa Ann's mortal form. Surely you broke some rules of the Cosmic Order in doing so. Am I correct?"

Once again that furrowed brow appeared across Theresa Ann's brow.

"Strictly speaking, First Soul, we broke no rules of the Cosmic Order in fashioning the Emissary. However, the possession of a mortal's form by a primordial's essence, the Creator had not envisioned. As you yourself have pointed out to us, the pristine essence of the Emissary has indeed been changed, modified by its passage through the light realm, and its exposure to mortal experience."

Again, Theresa Ann looked down into her lap. Then, to my surprise, she said, "What do you propose?"

"A truce and an experiment. That the accounting of Nergal's soul is postponed until he finds his wife's remains. And, that the mortal Theresa Ann can live out the rest of her natural life. That is my proposal."

"We can agree to the first, only if it is accomplished with all due speed. As for the second, there is nothing preventing the Emissary from continuing on in this mortal's body."

"So, do we have an agreement?"

"Yes." the Ledger Keeper replied. "We have an accord."

*   *   *

To say I didn't like the smell of this entire agreement would have been an understatement. Whenever a primordial being is ordered by the Creator to pinch off a portion of itself to animate a near-dead human being, it's hard to believe they rolled over that easy.

Then, all of a sudden, it occurred to me.

"Theresa Ann, what kind of 'happy music' did those kind folks back at the hospital play for you?"

"New Country," and her eyes lit up.

"Really," I deadpanned.

"Yes. I learned a lot about mortal life from the lyrics, and about something wonderful called God."

At this outstanding news, I got up and chucked a fiver into the juke box. I selected several different songs. Returning to our table, I put out my hand. At the gesture, I got an inquisitive look, so I said, "Take my hand."

I led Theresa Ann over to the dance floor as the

catchy electric music began.

She asked, "What are we doing?"

"Dancing."

"But I don't know how."

"Then I'll teach ya."

Well, I'm here to tell you this North Texas boy can two-step, cha-cha, and slow dance with the best of 'em. So I led and she followed.

At first, she was kinda' clumsy, so I started her out on two moves, and kept repeating them. It's no secret she struggled some, so I had her slip off her shoes and ride barefoot on the tops of my boots. That worked like a charm, which earned me a dazzling smile.

The second song, she knew the words to, and so while we danced she sang along. What a wicked voice. Adding more moves, and now with her shoes back on, here and there, we commenced to some serious dancing. She kept smiling, and even laughing at some of the spins, dips, and gyrations I put her through.

By the time we got to a slow dance, which I had to teach her as well, things began to get kinda' blurry for me. She looked so much like my Grace it hurt. Then, the dance floor filled with several other couples.

During the fourth dance, I slipped, "Damn girl, you're beautiful."

"Why thank you, J. J. You're the first one to notice." Her arms squeezed my waist a little more.

"I don't believe that for a minute."

She grinned up at me, "And you have the softest touch," she said with a whisper. "You must be a very gentle man."

"Why thank you. I certainly try. But there are times, well, that's not always possible."

"That I can well imagine for the First Soul."

Hearing that I missed a step and almost smashed her dainty foot.

"What's wrong, J. J.?"

"I forgot about who you are, that's all."

She leaned in conspiratorially. "You know, J. J., the time I have spent with you has been a lot of fun. I have truly enjoyed it. I am new to all of this emotional mortal stuff, but you have helped tremendously."

"You don't say."

"J. J.! Don't you dare freeze up on me! This entire concept of 'fun' is new to me. And, you're a great dancing teacher, too."

I smiled back, felt embarrassed, goofy, and exposed all at the same time.

*   *   *

After several more dances, Theresa Ann said, "J. J. Remember, I'm new at this mortal stuff. But you are the first to understand me. I can be myself around you."

"Well, that's nice, but when did you last hug your parents? Not that you would tell them you are a supernatural representative of a primordial being, but let them into your heart. You might be surprised."

"You know J. J., for a big brute you can be quite a philosopher. But you're right, my parents right now are probably in a panic, wondering where I am."

"No 'probably' about it. I'm sure they have the police out looking for you. So give them a call. Put them at ease. Settle things out. See where that takes you."

Well, that evening I put Theresa Ann on a red-eye back to Boston, along with several heartfelt promises.

As it turned out, I was dead right. Her folks were worried sick about her.

Driving away from the airport, yes, I was an emotional mess, but I couldn't remember the last time I felt more alive.

CHAPTER 28
Conflicted Feelings

Ali-Hassan had to admit Mr. Campbell's kind generosity made him stop and reconsider his deep-seated suspicion of all things American. While he could intellectually acknowledge the vast divide between a country's leadership and its population, this stood as the first time the Afghan tangibly experienced that chasm. The lawyer in him could not find one shred of difference between the Koranic rule of hospitality offered to those in need and what Mr. Campbell had done.

Ever true to his word, Mr. Campbell dropped his passenger off at the bus station on Campton Street in Ely, Nevada. There, Ali-Hassan purchased a ticket to Salt Lake. While waiting for his ticket to process, he overheard someone referring to him as "Grizzly Adams." The Afghan didn't know this Grizzly Adams, but he understood what grizzly meant and took that observation to heart. So he next made a visit to a local barber shop.

When he entered the empty barber shop, its barber, who had been engrossed in an old copy of *Motor Trend* magazine, smiled and took him on.

After some thirty minutes of buzzing this, clipping that, a shave, and even a shampoo, Ali-Hassan had been transformed. The barber charged him five bucks.

When Ali-Hassan tried to tip the man for all his hard work, he said, "Son, without a doubt you were a real project, that's for sure. But keep the money for a hamburger. It sure looks like you could use one."

At the nearby restaurant, the Afghan ordered that hamburger, but when his order arrived it included two hamburgers, a mound of French fries, and some cold slaw.

"There must be some kind of mistake," the lawyer said to the waitress. "I didn't order all of this food."

"Don't worry, son. The cook took one look at you and decided you needed some serious fattening up. Five dollars and we're all square."

Somehow he finished it all. Ali-Hassan guessed he must have been hungry after all. When he got up to leave, he left a dollar tip.

With two hours to kill before his three and a half hour bus ride to Salt Lake City, Ali-Hassan went exploring. He walked across Court House Park toward the town's center. He found a secondhand clothing store and bought some white socks, underwear, a pair of blue jeans, a gray felt cowboy hat, and a yellow shirt, all for seven dollars. That left the Afghan with almost fifty dollars still in his pocket, so he splurged and bought a pair of boots for another ten.

Despite all he had eaten, Ali-Hassan's stomach voiced its need again after all the shopping. Who knew buying clothing could be so taxing on the body? So he stopped at another restaurant in town and devoured another burger and fries. At this point, the Afghan began to feel whole again. With another good hour before the bus' departure, he visited the public library, which he had passed by earlier in Court House Park. Once again, Ali-Hassan encountered the most helpful people. While pretending to read a newspaper, Ali-Hassan asked himself: *What is America?* It seemed one portion had denied him his basic freedoms, tried to kill him, while the other cared about him like extended family.

*　　*　　*

When the U.S. Coachways bus left for Salt Lake City, the transformed and well fed Afghan on the lam had a seat on it. The bus, only a third full, Ali-Hassan chose to sit in the back near the bathroom. From there he could watch whoever got on or off the bus. Comfortably situated in his place of observation, the lawyer sat back and again began to collect his thoughts on this place called America. While not convinced, Ali-Hassan's recent experiences began blending with his fond memories of living in Minneapolis, the university's law school, its friendly student population, and now this brush with Mr. Campbell and the people of Ely, Nevada. For the first time since leaving Afghanistan, the Ali-Hassan started to question his motives.

Yes, the U.S. and Afghanistan differed greatly, but Ali-Hassan asked himself, why? The people of Ely did not tear themselves apart over tribal allegiances. There, native Americans, Whites, and Hispanics all got along peacefully. The same thing occurred in Minneapolis, a far larger and more ethically complex city than Ely. America had obvious racial issues, but somehow they managed not to exacerbate the situation with religious strife. While pondering all of this, Ali-Hassan fell sound asleep.

*　　*　　*

Salt Lake City, the headquarters of the Mormon

religion, but Ali-Hassan found its bus station like any other. People came and went with the same purposeful looks on their faces that could be found in anywhere throughout the world. Meanwhile, others sat, slept, read, and killed time, waiting. He headed to an unused bank of pay phones, searched through its many hinged phone books, and found the number for the local university's main operator. After several calls, he reached the appropriate individual, who agreed to pick him up within the next thirty minutes.

Standing outside in the waning sunshine, Ali-Hassan looked at his reflection in the building's plate glass. For all practical purposes, there stood a clean-shaven American cowboy. The reflection affected him and he couldn't refute it with an easy philosophical or religious argument. Mr. Campbell's generosity made it all happen. That simple gift, given to the Afghan in time of great need, had made all the difference. *Would Mr. Campbell even recognize me now?*

* * *

While the escaped detainee stood there gazing at his reflection, a late model BMW pulled up to the curb, the kind with blue and white racing stripes and big, fat Pirelli tires. With its rumbling engine still running, the driver got out and looked around for someone, but he didn't see him. Just some hayseed cowboy, busy admiring himself in the bus station's windows. Disgusted, the driver got back into his car, killed the motor, got out of the vehicle, and locked it with a frustrated wrist flick of his key fob.

* * *

At the sound of the car's door slamming and its locking mechanism honking in confirmation, Ali-Hassan saw in the window's reflection a man in a three-piece, gray pin-striped suit, wearing *keffiyeh*, a Palestinian scarf.

That must be my contact, he thought.
Who else could it be?

But for some reason, the Afghan froze in place, as the academic had already dismissed him as he entered the bus terminal's entrance.

He had distinctly said on the phone he would be wearing a keffiyeh. But he looks like he walked out of a damn country club, or some Hollywood movie set, complete down to the vehicle. What academic drives a gas-guzzling BMW with racing stripes?

So Ali-Hassan decide to wait for him to return to his car, and perhaps, teach this academic something about camouflage.

* * *

Lieutenant Joshua Park had developed an itch he couldn't scratch. The medical recovery out near Facility N had gone well enough. What bugged him, however, was the final body count. After going through a double-check, he had twice come up missing one detainee.

Given the detainees involved, he preferred to be sure, as in absolutely sure. Consulting a topographical map, he made several mental calculations: *There are too many roads nearby.*

And then concluded. *Christ almighty! One of them somehow has escaped.*

"Corporal, I want you to contact the Nevada State Highway Patrol. Tell them we're missing a dangerous middle-aged Afghani detainee. They'll understand. Ask them to interview any truckers or civi's at the truck stops, who might have picked up a hitchhiker over the past three days."

*   *   *

When Ali-Hassan's ride returned, the contact found him waiting, leaning against a precious, custom flared fender. With arms and ankles crossed, his head down, the Afghan hid his face and eyes.

"Hey you drunk, get off my car! And if you scratched it, you'll..."

Ali-Hassan looked up and greeted him in Arabic– "*As-salaam alaykum.*"

At hearing the Afghan's solicitous words, the academic's mouth hung open like a gasping fish. To his credit, the lawyer's ride then caught himself, transforming his face in a remarkable way, as if the two of them were long lost brothers. As he approached, he opened wide his arms expecting the usual embrace, but Ali-Hassan stopped him with an extended, open palm, and said in English.

"Let us leave this place."

Sputtering, confused, and still in shock at the cowboy appearance, he said, "Absolutely!" He tried to open the door, but again the Afghan stopped him with an open palm.

The contact drove in silence. Then, needing to fill the void, he began to babble. Throughout all of his attempts at ingratiation, Ali-Hassan remained silent. This technique he knew well. People under stress will say just about anything to fill the silence.

Upon arriving at the university, the contact pulled into a reserved faculty parking place.

The lawyer maintained his silence until within the academic's office. Then, in hushed tones. "Professor Azziz, I presume?"

A nod in confirmation.

"I wish to thank you for fetching me from the bus station. However, may I ask, when did you last check your car or office for..." Ali-Hassan then mouthed the word "bugs."

A look of horror stared back.

"I thought so." So the Afghan took from the top of the academic's desk a legal pad and a pen.

He wrote, "Do you have fresh identification papers for me?"

Azziz nodded.

Ali-Hassan returned a smile. "Are there any reports in the press about anything odd in the Nevada desert?" his next note asked.

Negative head shake with widening eyes.

Interesting, the Afghan thought.

Again he wrote, "How long have you been with the university? Fingers only."

Seven fingers displayed.

He then wrote, "Professor Azziz, you have much to learn about survival. Academic camouflage," as Ali-Hassan indicated outside to the parking lot, "and keeping a low profile."

The escapee paused for a moment thinking about his next question, while inspecting his dirty finger nails, wanting his message to sink in.

The lawyer wrote, "How long have you owned the BMW? Fingers only."

Two fingers.

Again he wrote, "Did you purchase it new?"

Affirmative head shake.

"How many of your academic colleagues drive BMWs?"

A negative head shake.

None. Azziz probably owns the only BMW racer on campus.

He paused with the pen suspended above the pad.

Ali-Hassan wrote: "Are the ID papers accessible?"

A vigorous nod with a mouthed, "Bank."

He wrote, "Let's get them now. Do you have cash?"

Two affirmative head shakes.

He wrote, "After the bank, take me to the bus station."

Two wide-eyed head nods, but with questioning eyes and hands palms up that screamed–*why the bus station?*

The lawyer wrote, "Airport is NOT safe. The U.S. authorities captured me in one."

Again, that wide-eyed look.

At this point in the conversation, Ali-Hassan rose in his chair and they left for his ostentatious car. Once moving, the Afghan rolled down his window and spoke over the buffeting in Arabic.

"Professor Azizz, thank you for your kind assistance. I do not know how, but I was detected at the airport. After that they sent me to an awful internment camp, located in Nevada, two and a half days hard march south of Highway 6."

*   *   *

The next day Professor Azziz sold his BMW and bought a Prius.

*   *   *

Through hard-earned experience the Afghan had read his contact as helpful but inexperienced, and that's why he chose to be dropped off back at the bus station. A short taxi ride later, he stepped into the Amtrak station. Here the Afghan's instincts told him that trains did not represent secure transportation, at least nowhere near that of airline travel, hence the whole point behind his decision to head south by train to the Mexican frontier. From there he booked a flight for his first destination–Madrid.

Ali-Hassan thought of trains as marvelous things. The never ending scenery streaking by mesmerized the mind. If on the rails for any length of time, good-natured conversations inevitably started, and sometimes, friendships begun. Trains invited stopovers at interesting sights that highways and airplanes bypassed. Trains therefore became time machines. If Ali-Hassan planned a route, he could get off at any time, and enjoy an unexpected overnight stay. Then, the following day, he knew he could grab the same train and continue on his way.

Once he arrived in Madrid, Ali-Hassan purchased a Eurail Pass and took full advantage of it. Along the way, he stopped at each and every one of the major cities en route to Istanbul–Barcelona, Marseille, Milan, Venice, Zagreb, Beograd, and finally, Sofia.

This tour of Western Civilization from west to east, again, and for a constellation of reasons, resonated within the lawyer. Everywhere he went, he encountered good people, regardless of national flag, language, or creed. It tore at him. Made him think. Never before had he considered the word regret and the weight it could bring to bear. Now, he did. In city after city, he encountered another Ely, Nevada, experience, only with a different language and currency. People cared.

*   *   *

The Afghan dared the short flight from Istanbul to Baghdad, for during his transcontinental train journey never once had he detected a tail. One flight later, dozens of time zones to the east, Ali-Hassan made it back to his home in Kabul.

CHAPTER 29
The Translation

While the transliteration process of the cuneiform texts had gone well, their translation proved to be otherwise, which took us a full two weeks to accomplish.

I read somewhere to be a good philologist one must provide a sound translation. That simple goal described one bitch of a job. The reason why revolved around the fact that for any given transliteration, multiple citations existed in the *Pennsylvania Sumerian Dictionary*, many of which had different meanings, like a word in English can have more than one meaning. For example, the Sumerian word for "milk," could also mean "suckling." Similarly, the Sumerian word for "advice," or "counsel," could also signify "resolution," "intelligence," or a "reed bundle."

This meant that the selection of the correct translation depended upon context. Trial and error came into play like filling in crossword puzzles. A well-worn, laborious method, but one well understood by a language expert or philologist.

After some work we could now refer to my artifact by its Sumerian name, *nam-šub im-habannatu*, or "incantation container." That discovery alone reassured me, for Nergal had used that term many times in my dreams. I began to feel saner and saner by the moment.

After many discussions and false starts, we agreed to break the text down into three basic stanzas.

Stanza 1

> He who reads this instruction releases the spirit-seeker contained within;

> He who utters this instruction releases the spirit-seeker contained within;

> He who touches this instruction releases the spirit-seeker contained within;

Stanza 2

> Only chance will provide.

> He who does so is bound to the will of the spirit-seeker contained within.

> As in heaven a wind arose, on earth dust swirled;

> South wind rose, north wind rose;

> Gale and dust storm arose;

> So will the spirit-seeker Nergal contained within arise.

> He who is bound to the spirit-seeker contained within must find the spirit of another until death;

> He who is bound to the spirit-seeker contained within must use the talisman contained within to find the spirit of the other;

> The spirit of the other is named Erish;

> She is the spirit who must be found.

Stanza 3

> He who is bound to the spirit-seeker contained within must search despite south wind, north

wind, gale, and dust storm, to find the spirit of the other.

Once the spirit of the other is found, he who is bound is released from this task.

This is the Incantation of Nergal, whose spirit-seeker is contained within.

This is the Incantation of Gilgamesh, which Nergal has employed.

Holy Inanna has blessed this incantation.

"You know J. J., this spell alludes to some serious stuff," Adam said. "This Nergal fellow must have been one desperate guy. I'll bet that this Erish woman was a family member. Maybe even his wife."

Of course, Erish is my wife! Nergal railed in my consciousness.

"Yep. It sure does," I said as dispassionately as I could. "As for this Nergal, I have to agree. He must have been quite driven."

Deep down inside, I exploded with emotion as the translation proved I hadn't gone nuts. That I hadn't suffered a brain injury of some kind. And yes, that Nergal and his quest were the real deal.

* * *

I went to bed that night feeling relieved, but the perplexing flip side meant I carried an ancient Sumerian soul.

Just before I dozed off, Nergal piped up.

So J. J., you see. Everything I have told you is the truth.

"Yeah, Nergal, you did, but you also royally

screwed up the Cosmic Order in the process and that's something that must be fixed up too. So, buddy, we have a lot to do in a short amount of time."

*　　*　　*

The next morning I arose as a man with a purpose. Not only had Nergal helped me get over my guilt-ridden nightmares about Grace, he had driven me to learn his language to prove his very existence. He hadn't taken over. No, he just needed my help in finding the remains of his beloved.

I concluded that without question, Nergal was a very driven and desperate man. If I helped him, he promised he would release me from his influence. But there remained one nagging thought–could I trust him?

While shaving I decided to make a leap of faith. Laying down my razor and looking into my reflection, I decided to trust Nergal, and believe, that once I found his wife's remains, I would be myself again.

So I started with a simple leap of faith. It also turned out to be the start of something unimaginable.

*　　*　　*

I knocked on Adam's office door.

"Damn J. J., you're up early."

"Yes, sir," I said.

"Well, so which journal are we going to publish your artifact in?" Adam asked.

"I'm very sorry Adam, but we're going to have to put this project on hold for a while."

"Whadda' mean, 'on hold'?"

"Last night I got word that I'm due to return to

Iraq," I invented. "How about we let the lab do its thing, and when I get back, we'll publish this."

"Iraq? Are you nuts? That place is death."

"Yes, it is, and the pay is outstanding. Do we have a deal?"

With a sour look on his face, Adam nodded, and said, "I suppose so. But do me one very big favor."

"What's that?"

"Come home safe."

*   *   *

During that night's dream sequence, I confronted my Sumerian tenant.

"Nergal, I think it is time that we prepared ourselves for that long journey you have been pining about for so long. So while Iraq is still quite a mess, I have an idea on how to get us in the country.

Nergal, weeping in relief, said, *Oh J. J.! You do not know how long I have been waiting to hear those words. How long I have been hoping you would freely say them.*

Then I continued, "But before we begin on those plans, you must tell me how this talisman works. How will it help us find your wife, Erish? And if we find her, what will happen then?"

J. J., the talisman first must be suspended around your neck, in a pouch, in a way it can easily move on its own.

"You said 'move on its own' didn't you?"

Nergal frowned.

Yes, he said, *'move on its own,' because as we near the place of my Erish's remains, the talisman will indeed move, indicating which way for us to go, much like a water diviner seeks out a new well. At first, its tug will be lightly made, but as we near the correct location, it will pull harder. Finally, the talisman will feel as though it is a great weight. That is when we will know we have found the location of her remains.*

"And then, Nergal. What will happen once we're at the location?" I pressed.

I will release you as I have promised you so many times.

*   *   *

Two days before I left for Iraq, the laboratory results on my artifact came in. Adam called me and suggested that I get my butt over to his office.

"J. J., your artifact is indeed ancient. The thermal luminescence read, drum roll please, Old Sumerian. J. J., it's Old Sumerian! The TL test came up with an Early Dynastic IIIb horizon of 2420 BC ± 47 years. That's over 4,400 hundred years old!

"The petrological analysis of the artifact's fabric composition didn't contain any organics. Paul thinks the clay probably originated from the industrial clay pits of Ur. That means fine-grained, sandy clay. Clearly, no expense was spared." Adam stood up.

"When Paul began investigating that curious looking black blob, then things got interesting." The professor's said with pleasure.

"His analysis judged the object to be a braided lock of hair, encased in pure bee's wax, and then coated in a thick layer of blood. Both the hair and blood tested out as human, the hair female because of the presence of nuclear DNA, and as for the blood, that came out as male. Weird huh?"

"Adam, where is this lock of hair now?"

"Right here, old buddy." Adam passed me the blackened mass inside a labeled, heavy-duty lab baggie, the kind with a milky panel for scribbling an easy identification.

"Paul said he didn't need very much of that thing to get a positive analysis. Straightforward forensics he said. By the way, do you want this back as well?" Adam said as he hefted the incantation container out of his left side desk drawer.

"Yes, Adam. The container and talisman I'm taking back to Iraq, as promised, now that its translation is completed."

CHAPTER 30
A Dark Influencer

The Devourer of Souls twitched with restlessness, for while noting the progress of its master's emissary, it had found a possibility for mischief it couldn't pass up– a mortal with a rare golden aura. It wanted it dead. The thought of consuming this soul caused the Devourer to tremor in ecstasy. It believed that after devouring such a powerful soul it could challenge its master, the Ledger Keeper, maybe even granting it the ability to ignore its master's commands. The Devourer even knew of a useful tool to make its desires become reality. So it planted a seed.

*　*　*

Ali-Hassan knew Ali Mohammed bin Ali El-Joorie. While born to a wealthy Saudi family, El-Joorie always found himself the butt of jokes because of his short stature and slight build. This abuse fed his classic Napoleonic complex, which explained his tendencies of excessive behavior and violent mood swings.

As a young adult, El-Joorie would not allow himself to be slighted, nor would he tolerate criticism of any kind. Then, he fell under the influence of a radical Egyptian Wahhabi cleric, who managed to somehow channel, and then enthrall, the errant youth.

El-Joorie's lavish hedonism attracted many to his circle, as his "private affairs" eclipsed the imagination, and so overshadowed his perceived shortcomings. Some of his followers included anti-Western anarchists or radical fundamentalists interested only in El-Joorie as a pure funding source for their causes. Others, however, tended to focus on satisfying his monumental ego, again for a price. To this latter group, a much younger Ali-Hassan had lobbied for the funds for his legal education in the States. But, as with all expressions of largess, there remained the tacit understanding of personal indebtedness, which could be called in at any time.

*   *   *

"May I speak with my U.S.-trained barrister?" the voice said over the cell phone.

Ali-Hassan froze at the sound of those heavily coded words.

How the hell did he find my cell number? I've only been in Kabul a week.

"May peace be on you, my most generous brother," said Ali-Hassan.

"Enough pompous nonsense. I have need of your talents."

"Indeed, my brother, as always, it is most pleasant to hear from you. How might I be of service?"

"You are still the ever impudent one," El-Joorie breathed over the receiver.

"In one month's time, there will be an American in Iraq. I believe the term most appropriate for this task is 'wet work.' I desire him to be killed.

"As events draw near, I will inform you of further details. Prepare, my impudent brother. Do not disappoint me. Remember–procuring your cell number is one easy thing," he hissed, "finding the address of your dear and loving parents is another."

*   *   *

So Ali-Hassan, a man with a heavy personal debt, became a guided missile, a cheap contract killer. At least the latter description fit, in a perverse sort of way, to his legal training.

So the Afghan prepared for his adventure into that god-forsaken place known as Iraq. He needed to arrange for tools, specific ones. With the task once complete, perhaps the lawyer would be a free man. If so, then he would open a law office in Kabul. Become domesticated, settle down, and start a family. Wouldn't that be grand?

*   *   *

The Devourer loved its mischief. It found pleasure in making the arrangements, influencing the ignorant, and taking advantage of that most marvelous of human weaknesses–the lust for power. The demon, ever patient, knew if El-Joorie failed, others would do its bidding.

For its entertainment, the primordial contacted another mortal of weak character, who in turn contacted others in search of gainful opportunities involving questionable adventure. Fed all the pertinent particulars on the American's whereabouts, his vehicle, and his description, the Devourer smiled with satisfaction. These prescient details the Devourer of Souls knew, while hardly foolproof, represented only the best that it could divine. Nonetheless, it believed them to be sufficient.

CHAPTER 31
The Green Zone

Somewhere during my reading, I noticed a reoccurring theme. In times of upheaval, while the powerful take every opportunity to add to their coffers, great fortune can be a liability. So entered the mercenary to safeguard those ill-gotten gains.

As soon as I told the Ledger Keeper through his Emissary about us going ahead full-blast on Nergal's quest, I put out some feelers for a contract job as a security specialist. Being located in northern Texas helped in my job search because many firms in the area dealt with security. In no more time than it took to place several telephone calls and conduct two face-to-face interviews, I had a six month contract in hand, tasked with security arrangements in Baghdad's Green Zone.

* * *

My flight over took a very circuitous path: Dallas, Atlanta, London, Frankfurt, Dubai, and finally Baghdad. While the trip cost me almost three days' time, I knew the grind.

* * *

The Green Zone amounted to a bunkered up and paranoid existence. You had to keep your head on a swivel twenty-four seven, but I acclimated as my old Marine ways took hold.

After a few days of settling in, I began sending out

feelers through the security company's contacts that I wished to speak with an Iraqi archaeologist. After only two weeks of looking, I hit gold.

*   *   *

The Iraqi contact listened to me patiently. First, he would pretend to listen, but in actual fact, he sized you up as either an easy mark or not. This I expected from this individual because of the scuttlebutt I had heard on this particular intel source.

The contact said, "It is said this man knows every archaeological site, in the whole of the country, like the back of his hand. In fact, he's the best archaeologist in the region. If you wish to find what you are looking for, then tomorrow go to the old souk, seek him out, and offer to buy him some tea. He will be waiting for you in the silver souk sometime after ten. Here is his photo."

"Jeez, a lot of Iraqis look like this," I said. "How will I know I am talking to the right guy?"

"Ah, Mr. Stone. I have already told him about you, complete with your description. Remember: he always selects the *chai hamuth*, the 'bitter tea' that is made from dried and crushed Basra limes. And notice how much sugar he puts in his *istakhan* glass! Two spoonfuls at least! That will be your proof."

*   *   *

A visit to the souk must be slowly savored as one of the few remaining pleasures of Baghdad, otherwise the senses will be overcome by the overload. Like many old European cities, the alleyways of this vast marketplace separate the many product and trade specialties. Sadly, after all the war, with its civil and religious strife, the entire marketplace is no longer intact. In fact, as of April 2005, the entire *Shorjah*, or spice bazaar, came to an end because of a fire. Fortunately, the rest has survived.

Threading my way through the vast marketplace, with my head unconsciously on a swivel, I located the silver souk. As I walked in, the gentle taps of the silver smiths' small mallets filled the air. What a perfect place for a private conversation.

I arrived an hour early to reconnoiter the area. So I took a small unoccupied table off to the side of this hive of activity, sat down, and opened a fresh pack of Dunhill cigarettes. The deep blue and gold hard pack stood on its own, displaying its contents seductively. I personally don't smoke, but its damn good bait in this part of the world. I slid a cigarette out, lit it up, stifled a cough, and returned the distinctive blue and gold box to the table's center, open and inviting. I leaned back in my chair and crossed my legs.

Here we go, I thought. *Bait in place.*

The local tea waiter who catered to the silver souk appeared, and said in Arabic.

"Sir. Some tea perhaps?"

Nodding, I smiled back and replied, in accented Egyptian Arabic, "Yes, please. *Chai hamuth*. And light on the sugar."

Blinking in surprise at both my ability to understand *and* speak Arabic, the young man, smiled, stiffly nodded back, and disappeared.

"You speak Arabic quite well," a British voice sounded behind me, "but it is the Arabic of an Egyptian."

I swiveled around to greet my guest, annoyed at being outflanked. There stood a short man with wavy steel gray hair, a florid salt and pepper moustache, and a paunch that probably came about because of too many honeyed sweets. His face matched the one in the photograph.

"So, you are Stone. Am I correct?"

A single nod.

"I am Mohammed. Let's leave it at that." The Iraqi archaeologist said as he sat down at my table, and quite naturally, helped himself to one of the available Dunhill's.

He took a deep draw and let the smoke escape his lips with obvious pleasure. "You probably don't realize this, but Dunhill's are, how do you American's say it? As rare as hen's teeth in this part of the world, especially in this god-forsaken day and age. You should offer our tea waiter several. It might prevent him from pissing in your tea."

The waiter arrived moments later with my tea. I reached over and offered him the entire pack of cigarettes.

I said, "For you, if you promise to get me a fresh pot." Conflict burned in his dark eyes, but he snatched the entire hard pack.

I turned to Mohammed, "What are you having?"

"Oh, I will have a regular *chai hamuth,* with extra sugar on the side."

Right answer, friend.

As the waiter scurried away, we sat in silence regarding each other.

In what seemed mere moments, the waiter returned with a new tea service. Mohammed looked at me straight in the face. His lips cracked into a smile.

"Good move. Tea?" He poured me a glass.

"I suppose so," I admitted, "but are you as knowledgeable of this country's ancient monuments as you are of its tea preparation?"

The Iraqi sat back in his chair and held his smoldering cigarette out dramatically between his thumb and forefinger. He opened his mouth to expose his teeth and exhaled his cigarette smoke through them. His eyes transformed from amused to a cool, snake-like hardness.

"My dear, Mr. Stone, or whoever you are, our tea is safe. And yet, I have already done you a favor, while you insult me in return. Why is that?"

A tense silence followed as two pairs of eyes locked as one.

J. J., Nergal prompted, *he has what we need. Give in to his ego.*

I sighed theatrically in resignation.

"Mr. Mohammed, you are quite right. I apologize. I am not a natural-born negotiator. In fact, I should fine myself." And with that, I reached into my thigh pocket and pulled out a fat money clip of c-notes. Peeling off the outer one, I returned the clip to my pocket, straightened out the bill, put a crease into it, and placed it next to the Dunhills. "Peace?"

Mohammed looked down at the bill, cocked his head to the left, and said. "How do I know that it is not counterfeit?"

"'In God We Trust,' Mr. Mohammed. Besides, it's my best work yet," I said. I could not contain the toothy grin that split my face.

At this snarky response, the Iraqi's eyes relaxed

and turned playful again.

"That's only for the insult," as he placed his hand over the bill and palmed it.

"I understand."

"So, Mr. Stone, what do you want to know about my country's ancient monuments?"

I leaned forward over the tiny table, "Mr. Mohammed, I am a linguist; a specialist in ancient Sumerian."

Mohammed snorted in mild derision.

I ignored it, and pressed on.

"What I need to know about is the city of Nippur. How big did it get during the Old Sumerian period? Did it have any outer, subsidiary temples?"

Mohammed gave me a look as if I had revealed some top secret information, so I elaborated.

"I have been working on an inscription that mentions them, and I want to see them for myself," I improvised.

With a face of intense interest, Mohammed leaned forward. "Mr. Stone, Nippur's main temple covered an immense area during the period you mentioned. I estimate about 32,000 square meters, give or take. As for the rest of the city state, we're talking about an area within the city's walls of about one kilometer by two." He spread his arms wide as he continued, "But I do know of some very suspicious Old Sumerian religious remains that seem to fit your description. These can be accessed rather easily, as they are in a small town to the north of Nippur proper, far outside of the archaeological preserve. The town is called Afak. The remains you seek are located beneath a ruined mosque.

When I was a young man, the Oriental Institute

spent some weeks excavating there. The local inhabitants, scandalized by all the Americans grubbing about, built a mosque upon the mud brick foundations of an Old Sumerian temple. Did it pissed off those archaeologists! Find that old mosque, Mr. Stone, and I think you will find what you are looking for."

I made to leave, ready to settle up with the waiter and archaeologist.

"One word of caution," Mohammed said as he reached out and beckoned me to sit down. "Afak is not a good place for Americans. There are still elements living there that fought savagely against your military."

The man paused while he took his last drag on his cigarette, before he stabbed it out in the cheap aluminum tray.

"While you're at it, Mr. Stone, grow a damn moustache. You'll fit in better. And besides, with it, everyone will think that you are full of wisdom, instead of shit."

CHAPTER 32
The Assassin's Arrival

A former U.S. soldier; highly decorated; responsible for the murder of many Iraqi freedom fighters; responsible for the rape of countless Islamic maidens, while their mothers were forced to look on; a noted defiler of men, and collector of penises.

Kill him in the basement of the old mosque of Afak. Then butcher him and leave his parts to be eaten by the local dogs.

(Message from El-Joorie to Ahmed Ali-Hassan, July 14, 2004)

Three weeks later Ali-Hassan landed in Baghdad and still did not know why this American had attracted El-Joorie's attention. For whatever reason, he had vexed that vicious Saudi in some way.

When the Afghan arrived at his hotel, an envelope waited for him. His instructions from El-Joorie, complete down to a physical description of the target and an accompanying narrative were filled with invective that reached legendary, if not mythic, proportions. That El-Joorie had composed it, there could be no question.

As the lawyer read, and then reread this gruesome list of wrong doing, a thought came to mind.

Is this real? Or better, the conjured fantasies of a sick man?

By the beard of a dear and merciful Allah! The

man's a decorated soldier, so he must have killed Iraqis. What of it? The Americans invaded bringing their own brand of total war. That's what Americans do. Impose their crushing will, kill, and break things. Most of Iraq's military forces deserved to be put in the ground. Their numbers were bloated by anything and everything that could carry a rifle. This I knew from personal experience. But freedom fighters? That's pure delusion.

After the American invasion and Baghdad's fall, one must not forget those dark times for Iraq. Banks repeatedly robbed. By whom? Museums plundered. By whom? Expensive hotels ransacked down to the carpeting on their concrete floors. By whom? The freedom fighters? No, by the Iraqi population themselves.

As for the rest of El-Joorie's rant about the rape of women and girls and the defilement of men, Abu Ghraib prison represented the only outright, publicized Western atrocity. I am not so naive as to think that's all, however. But the West has always held women and girls in a sacred place, given them unimaginable freedoms, even allowed them access to politics, while Islam does not. Hence, more El-Joorie embroidery.

As the Afghan sat there in his hotel, he asked himself again, *What had this American done to El-Joorie to attract his ire?*

* * *

Assassins need reliable firearms and ammunition. The Afghan's favorite arms contact had set up shop within the vast warrens of the Baghdad Souk. Here, in this place within a place within another place, the lawyer knew that anything could be purchased for a price. He once even heard an outlandish rumor of a Saudi sheik who wanted to get his hands on an American F-16 fighter jet for his personal use, and, then had the balls to have it delivered to his private airport near Jeddah. Supposedly, that blockbuster deal had been cut and concluded here. That's the kind of place the Baghdad Souk is. In fact, the Americans have an appropriate expression for a place like this: "What happens in Vegas, stays in Vegas." So also with the dealings that occurred within the Baghdad Souk.

Ali-Hassan preferred an old AK-47 as his weapon of choice. Anonymous and untraceable, easy to clear, its ammunition plentiful, and best of all, it had a terrific rate of fire. In short, Ali-Hassan judged it the perfect weapon for an ambush at close range. Besides, long rifles and their ammunition could not purchased on such short notice.

Next, the Afghan looked for and found a set of infrared goggles. At first glance, Ali-Hassan could not believe how ungainly the apparatus appeared. Attached to a headband, the weighty monocular lens, if worn too long could become a burden. But he wished to be prepared for all eventualities, and the goggles would provide him with a narrow, but useful, field of vision, so he bought them as well.

As for transportation, the Afghan wanted to rent a car at the airport, but none could be had. So after another negotiation with his arm's contact, he ended up renting a private vehicle. While the Toyota Corolla had seen better days, Ali-Hassan thought it perfect for his purposes, being non-descript in every way–dirty white, with no side windows, and brakes that squealed.

Ali-Hassan now armed, loaded down with the night vision goggles, sufficient ammunition, a gun cleaning kit, and a vehicle, returned to his hotel room. There, he field stripped the rifle, inspected its internals, receiver, barrel, thirty-round clip, and removed its wooden stock and discarded it. Again assembled, the lawyer safed the weapon and loaded it into a cloth bag that he could carry over one shoulder.

Next, he opened up his laptop computer, found the hotel's Wi-Fi-signal, and called up Google Earth. Ali-Hassan then plotted out his route to the ambush site and planned two escape routes. One can never be careful enough, or over prepared, in this sort of work.

That settled, Ali-Hassan tested the night vision goggles, since the evening's darkness had arrived. Peering out his window, the world turned green with various hues. People walking about showed up as black shadows against the lighter outlines of the neighborhood's buildings.

Perfect, he concluded, and then went out for dinner at a local family restaurant. He returned early to his hotel, as tomorrow, he knew, would be a long one.

CHAPTER 33
An Archaeological Tour

Three weeks after I met with Mohammed, I sported a full mustache that itched like the devil in the Iraqi heat.

Have no cares, friend J. J. Imagine growing a full beard. By the way, you would probably fit in easier if you did! Nergal teased.

After I cleared my "archaeological adventure" with my boss at the security firm, I borrowed a rust-bucket Toyota pickup from the security detachment's motor pool. Once upon a time it had been white, though it still ran great. My planned route would take me from Baghdad's Green Zone, south toward Diwaniyah, a dicey drive of one hundred miles. From there I drove another seven more to Afak.

I packed light for the trip. Under my cotton windbreaker I wore an armored vest and a shoulder holster packing my trusty 9mm S&W M&P. In one pocket I had several ammo clips. In the other a suppressor. My combat knife I wore on my web belt along with a personal GPS unit. First aid items and four energy bars I stuffed in my thigh pouches. In a small zippered pouch, I carried a borrowed set of AN/PVS-7s night vision goggles, and a small halogen flashlight.

I left the security compound in Baghdad at two in the afternoon, banking on the sheer heat of a July day to protect me. I sweltered in the vest. Life's full of tradeoffs. I also figured fewer of the bad guys would be active then, something about being British and mad dogs sort of thing. Believe me when I say there roamed a bunch of bad guys out there, who ranged from released criminals, ex-Republican Guard, Iraqi unit members, and lest I forget, radical elements and terrorists. With all of these bad actors on the loose, daily ambushes happened daily, not to mention the roadside bombs. While the mid-day heat did improve my chances, I made sure I had a full case of water sitting next to me in the truck. Gotta stay hydrated in this hell hole.

I took it real slow getting out of Baghdad, driving with my head covered in a *keffiyeh* and sunglasses off; Iraqis are very big on eye contact. No eye contact, no trust, which equals big trouble. In short, my drive involved lots of squinting through the truck's cracked and sand-pitted windshield.

For all appearances, as I scanned myself in the rear view mirror, I looked native enough with my dark tan and moustache. Before I knew it, I had reached the southern limits of the city.

At this point in the journey, Nergal decided to pipe in. *J. J., I still think you should have grown a beard. I think you would look most distinguished.*

What a nut case.

*   *   *

Of all the possible virtues, Ali-Hassan possessed patience, which had prepared him well, for he had been waiting in the mosque's basement for over three hours. Sitting in the corner with his rifle supported by his left knee along the wall, the Afghan sat in relative comfort, ready, and in position.

Now, where's the American?

*   *   *

I headed south on Highway 8 and after some driving made a left onto Highway 1. I wanted to stay on Highway 1 all the way to the Al-Qasisiyyah province, in the south central part of the country. Once there, I'd then grab Highway 17 at the Diwaniyah clover leaf, and head east to Afak.

But it's never that easy, for each and every clover leaf that you encounter can be a real adventure. The natives consider it sport to hide on overpasses and randomly drop cinder blocks on cars that pass under them. You can somewhat prepare yourself for that trick if you can see any block fragments ahead of you on the road. The only real defense is a lightning quick lane change.

The real pucker factor kicks in whenever there is some odd object lying beside or near the pavement. It can be anything: a wheel, a tire, a box, or even a pile of trash. These things scream "road side bomb," and I have been in country long enough to sense them. It's like the feeling you get when you know a cop is lurking over a hill or around the next bend. The hair on the back of your neck starts tingling. Whenever I see or sense something suspicious, I drive on the opposite side of the road. Period.

Today even that common sense strategy didn't work. Eight figures sprung an ambush at the next clover leaf, about two hundred yards ahead. They appeared from behind the viaduct's concrete supports, all carrying AK-47s and wearing black hoods. Real subtle.

This is not a good thing anytime, but then these guys started in on the white Toyota pickup ahead of me. The driver didn't have a chance as the concentrated crossfire ripped through the pickup's paper thin sheet metal, killing him. The vehicle turned violently to the right, flipped over several times, and threw gasoline and debris all over the highway.

Traffic slammed to a halt, while the eight encircled the burning vehicle and continued to shoot it to hell. That's when I ducked down under the dash and grabbed the M4 rifle there. I threaded on its thick suppressor.

Pissed off at this act of lawlessness, I got out of my truck, hunkered down low against its left front tire, and began dropping the ambushers with double taps either to the head or upper torso. As my weapon coughed away, their nonstop weapons fire smothered its sound. Only the last three realized the tables had been turned on them, when they saw the shattered and bleeding out remains of their comrades on the concrete pavement. Their confusion lasted but a moment as each succumbed to "the red mist."

All told, the engagement lasted less than two minutes, but it felt like an eternity. Engagements always do. Not wishing to attract any further attention, I jumped back into my truck, and sped off. Thereafter, and to my complete surprise, the rest of my journey along Highway 1 turned out to be a Sunday drive in light traffic. Not even a stray donkey or camel wandered onto the roadway.

I'm so excited, J. J.! We're nearing my Erish. I can feel it! Nergal enthused.

Once safely past the Highway 1 and 17 clover leaf, I saw that the fuel gauge had gone down a third, and, the talisman around my neck had made a sudden, nervous twitch. Both worried me. Nergal, thinking himself a gymnast, did several mental cartwheels in his excitement.

*   *   *

The Devourer, while very disappointed at the outcome of the ambush, did enjoy the sudden arrival of eight demented souls to its dark pit. All trigger-happy fools, they had attacked the wrong white pickup truck. Unfazed, the Devourer knew another opportunity would soon present itself.

*   *   *

After about four miles, I encountered a fuel stop on the south side of the road. Little more than a concrete awning supported by three poured columns, I figured that you can never have enough gas, especially in this hostile environment. I pulled in and told the attendant to "fill 'er up" with high test in my best Iraqi accent. At twelve cents a gallon, I felt like a real high-roller. Meanwhile, the folks back home get socked $2.05 or worse. Go figure.

Now topped off, I tipped the attendant and continued east on Highway 17. Next stop, the garden paradise of Afak.

Truth be told, Afak, a small town of maybe 20,000, resembled a billiard table. Surrounded by agricultural fields, the town itself consisted of low, flat roofed structures of concrete and mud brick that rarely went beyond two stories. Greenery, flowering bushes, and date palm trees filled in the gaps. The town's curbing was painted in yellow and white stripes indicating where not to park, which seemed to be everywhere. All over bullet holes, RPG craters, the works, pock-marked the environment. For such a small town, it sure looked like a real shit storm had rolled through.

I arrived around six in the evening, right before sunset. The evening call to prayer commenced. So being the good Southern Baptist I am, I pulled over, parked, and pulled out my own prayer rug. And right there and then, I began doing my best imitation "of the bob" right there on the sidewalk next to a curb painted in yellow and white stripes. I became invisible. I became part of the landscape. That's what Marines do.

By the time the *adhan* finished, a moonless night had fallen. That meant I had to get to work and begin circling the town to see what the talisman around my neck would pick up.

*   *   *

The Ledger Keeper, while impatient with its Emissary, watched with even more impatience as the First Soul and Nergal's wayward soul progressed in their search. While its Emissary had located Nergal's wayward soul, it had done little about returning it to the dark realm. When the First Soul co-opted the Emissary and argued for its independence, that forever changed the Keeper's own issue with mortal emotion. The Keeper found it distasteful.

More worrisome, however, the wayward one in the company of the First Soul had been provided sanctuary within its mortal shell. Yet, the Keeper noted the First Soul in fact moved toward his promised goal of uniting the wayward one with its mate's remains.

The significance of this act remained lost on the Ledger Keeper, for it had far more important considerations to confront than its willful Emissary. Unwittingly, its precarious relationship with its subordinate, the Devourer of Souls, had now been put to a test. When it diminished itself to create the Emissary, that act had weakened it, and the Devourer sensed it.

The subservient demon began to brazenly act inappropriately. The Ledger Keeper had noted with dismay the Devourer's meddling with the narcissistic El-Jorrie and its machinations behind the failed ambush on the highway. Already frustrated by the ever-diminishing losses of the damned through the rent in the border of the dark realm, the Devourer became ever more restive.

The Cosmic Order depended upon equilibrium. Two related events had caused the exact opposite. The question remained whether the First Soul would provide a solution to both, and if he could, do it in time. Or, would the Devourer of Souls exploit the fissure in its realm's boundary and burst forth unleashed upon the mortal world?

CHAPTER 34
The Mosque

The dark is my friend. That moonless night I began circling around the outskirts of Afak, trying to coax a spooky twitch out of the talisman. On my second orbit, the tugging began, which led me toward the town's old center.

Parking the pickup, I decided to let my feet do the talking. It didn't take very long. As I neared this one habitation block, the talisman stirred big time. So I circled the entire block, all the while the talisman around my neck squirmed, urging me on toward its center.

Nergal, as we neared the location of Erish's remains, went bonkers.

Going by dead reckoning, the talisman pointed to a location within a narrow block of buildings. Slipping into an alley, I got a stronger pull from the magical device, but found the passage blocked. I backtracked to the street and re-entered the block the next street over. This one I could see ran all the way through. A ramshackle structure with a destroyed minaret stood midway on the left. The talisman responded in that direction, toward these near-ruins.

Mohammed had been right. My only question–*how would I get in?*

Like any good Marine, I improvised, and began nosing about. With the front entrance blocked and boarded up, I probed around the rectangular structure's sides. The narrow gangway on the left produced nada. So I poked around to the right, passed the trash heaps left by the neighbors, rank piles long discarded against the abandoned structure. Nope, nothing there either. I ended up crawling in through the broken glass of a ground-level window. Fortunately, I had my tactical gloves on.

Once in, I put on the night-vision goggles and pulled out my suppressed 9mm. I waited in a tight crouch against the wall, while the goggles acclimated to the gloom.

With my goggles powered up, they illuminated the interior with a bright and greenish light. The first floor plan included two large rooms joined by an arched doorway. Wide open and stripped to its bare walls, that room had been long plundered of anything of value. I nonetheless glanced about looking for any threats.

Not seeing anyone, I looked down and checked my footing, noted some fallen plaster, avoided it, and began my stalk, sensing through the talisman that I had to descend.

I need to get to the basement.

Halfway across the first room, the second room became visible through the adjoining archway. It too lay barren except for a short flight of stone steps that led to a small sermon platform—the room's *minbar*.

Another passageway on the right led down into a darkness beyond belief, where even my night vision goggles proved to be useless. I pushed them back atop my head since in that gloom they displayed more electronic noise than meaningful imagery. I felt my way down each of the stone steps, pressing my back against the right side of the passageway's slowly curving wall. The talisman twitched like crazy, insistently pulling me hard to continue the descent.

As I continued, the air became noticeably cooler, musty, and stale. Stopping about ten steps down, I reached out with my senses and listened. I met only a smothering silence, but the talisman continued to pull, urgently, ever downward.

*   *   *

A patient Ali-Hassan glanced at his watch, sighed, and continued to await his prey in the basement's darkness. Then he stiffened when his senses went on high alert.

The sound of cloth rasping against a wall. There is indeed someone slowly coming down the cellar's steps.

Out of habit, the lawyer fingered the safety on his weapon. Still on SAFE as it had been since he had cleaned it at the hotel. With the tip of his finger, he flipped the setting to AUTO.

*   *   *

As I descended further, my skin crawled. My antennae twitched as I approached a darkness like none that I had never encountered before.

Pure evil? Or was it my imagination?

I had this creepy feeling. The pucker factor was sky high. Then, I heard something. It sounded like a well-oiled mechanical snick. The kind you hear all the time when a weapon is being prepared to fire. I froze in place, feeling exposed, in the pitch blackness.

*   *   *

The Devourer of Souls not only predicted where the First Soul would appear, it had also found a worthy opponent for it. So worthy, in fact, it figuratively licked its jaws in gluttonous anticipation. Yes, the Devour preferred to gorge on only the most demented and insane souls, but the enticing opportunity to rend such a powerful one, like the First Soul, caused a Pavlovian-like reaction like no other. But at the moment, the demon did not know which soul it would devour first—the wayward Sumerian or the golden one. Both would do nicely.

* * *

In all, I figured that I'd so far descended some twenty-odd steps.

My back touched the wall as I tried to move as silently as I could. Then I encountered an unexpectedly soft surface under my boots. The steps crumbled under my weight with an unwanted and noisy crunch.

* * *

I am the hunter, who is in control of his prey. He is now on the crumbling steps. This I clearly heard. There's only a few more left before I can claim him.

* * *

Halting somewhere near the bottom of the stairs, I listened real hard. Complete silence. Holding my breath, I leaned far forward and felt with my right hand for the basement wall's edge, and found it.

I'm close to the bottom of these stairs. Maybe only one or two steps left, max.

I closed my dominant left eye, and figured my only

chance would be surprise. Prepared to take that risk, I held my silenced automatic in my left hand, and then stuck my halogen flashlight around the wall edge on the right.

Confronting the darkness and whatever else, I turned the flashlight on.

The intense glare of its sudden radiance caused me to gasp. Fortunately, I had closed my left-dominant eye beforehand. A dark figure, caught dead center in the flashlight's beam, I saw crouched down low along the wall. My automatic coughed six times center mass.

*   *   *

The sudden light from the flashlight caused an excruciating surprise through the IR goggles, but Ali-Hassan's trigger finger responded instantly to it, firing at least four or five rounds. Then, for some reason, he couldn't hold his rifle any longer.

Looking down, the lawyer could see in the light's blue glare that his chest had been torn open. Blood splattered everywhere.

The Afghan could not feel his legs.

Then the American's beam of light shifted away, scanned the entire basement, and then came back. His target staggered toward him.

Ali-Hassan felt himself bleeding out, could sense his life draining away. With an unsteady head, he glanced up at his prey in time to see a most marvelous sight. The man standing over him in silhouette had the most beautiful seven rings of gold surrounding him.

Then, the lawyer's fading and befuddled mind screamed out.

You idiot! You tried to assassinate an angel.

*   *   *

Trained to expect the unexpected, I wheeled about, flicking the halogen beam around, looking for another assailant. Nothing. Breathing heavy, partly from the adrenaline rush, partly from shock, my mind recorded a bare rectangular room with two empty racks of shelving to my immediate left a forgotten stub of a candle. The floor, littered with aged, yellowed paper, suggested the basement once served as the mosque's administrative archive or maybe even a school room.

My opponent had figured me to be a righty, and so laid in wait along the right wall. That makes him a professional, especially with the IR goggles. Only then did I notice my left thigh had been hit, twice. Structurally iffy, I bled like a stuck pig. My boot started to fill with blood.

Him? Well, six sub-sonic,147 grain hollow points will ruin your day. Kicking away his abbreviated AK-47, he sat there an absolute bloody mess. I took off his goggles and his dead eyes stared back at me. I closed them with a light brush of my right hand and said a silent prayer for him.

Then it hit me. How many rounds did he fire at me anyways? So I did a quick inventory and discovered my cotton windbreaker had been scored black three times by glancing blows, which left ugly black streaks across my chest. As for my left thigh, what a mess.

*   *   *

From the absolute depths of the dark realm the Devourer of Souls unleashed a psychic scream that reverberated through time and space. Even the Ledger

Keeper noticed, wondered why, and then returned to its accounts as another soul needed recording.

*　　*　　*

Staggering and unsteady in shock from my wounds, the talisman goaded me forward. Its pull dragged me to the far right corner of the basement, but stopped about five feet from it. Then, with a force like several gravities, it dragged me down. I resisted, as I continued to shine my light around. Absentmindedly, I noticed the lower courses of the basement wall had not been constructed of stone or concrete, but of a brownish mud brick. I could see here and there, straw poking out in the brick's matrix.

My God. I realized. *This mosque is indeed founded upon an ancient structure. Mohammed, you magnificent bastard.*

The urge to sit down overpowered me. I did so with a gentle plop, which sent nasty stabs of pain from my thigh.

We have arrived, most brave J. J., Nergal said. *We have arrived at the place of Erish's final rest.* He sighed with deep emotion. *J. J., remain still while I join with my beloved Erish.*

"How do you plan to do that?" I whispered.

J. J., strange as this must seem to you, your open wound will allow my passage.

"Damn it, Nergal," I said with considerable frustration. "How?"

Nergal let out another deep and heavy internal sigh.

J. J., bleed unto the floor beneath you.

"Oh! That's all?" I said. "My thigh's bleeding all over the place. Is that good enough?"

Like a man possessed, I began cutting away at the left thigh of my fatigues with my combat knife, exposing my bloody leg. A steady stream of blood poured out, transforming the dusty, mud brick flooring of the basement into a bloody pool.

Morbidly fascinated by its quick formation, I wondered how much it would take to "release" Nergal. To this internalized query, I got a quick response.

J. J. I want you to close your eyes and slowly count to five. Then, and only then, can you tend to your most generous wounds—true warrior wounds.

I followed Nergal's instructions. At the end of my count, I bound myself up.

Tied off, I took several deep breaths, wished for a bottle of water, and then noticed something truly odd. The pool of my precious blood had disappeared and the basement floor once again had become dirty and dusty. Absolutely no trace of my blood could be seen anywhere on the floor.

Very weird.

One other thing, I noted the absence of an all too familiar sensation–Nergal. While his memories, his many talents still resided, my bearded and bald Sumerian with the odd eye shadow had flown the coop. In my personal silence, I felt a deep sense of loss, although I tried hard not to admit it. Instead, tears fell in gratitude that I been freed, but what of Nergal and his quest?

Did you find your dear Erish? I reached out.

Then, quite suddenly, the wick of the old and discarded candle across the room snapped into a bright blue flame. Seeing this theatrical display, I grinned.

Yes, Nergal, you did find her, didn't you!

*　　*　　*

Warmth. Soothing, blissful warmth followed by the soft delirium that comes only from relaxed, loving companionship.

After the initial electric charge occurred at the touching of their souls, Erish and Nergal, reunited, nourished one another.

Together, the two *gidimr* began their ascent out of the dark abyss toward the light—two souls, a husband and wife.

Spiritually, their foreheads touched, nose to nose, eyes melting into each other.

I waited so long, Erish whispered, *but I knew, I knew that you would come for me. I heard your many prayers.*

With a slow blink of his eyes, *I came as soon as I could, my love.*

A smile of sheer joy, endless pleasure. *Yes, I know my love, as I also know of your soul-carrier, this...J. J. How brave a man for us. How sad it is about his first love. He, too, has suffered much. What can we do for this selfless warrior?*

Beloved flower, he already possesses all of my memories and skills, and, do not forget, he carries the primeval soul, su.mannu.uzuzzu.eli. *What else can we possibly bestow upon him?*

Our watchfulness over this old soul, my dearest, would be advised. He is a mortal, who does stumble about so, much like a blind one blundering in a strange marketplace, what harm would it be? Is he not deserving?

Indeed my flower. My dear friend J. J. is indeed

deserving of our continued watchfulness.

* * *

Equilibrium, at long last, had been gloriously achieved. The lost *gidim* had been accounted for. With that crucial addition to the Ledger Keeper's accounts, the fissure between the dark and mortal realms sealed.

* * *

I am satisfied. The First Soul, my creation, performed well. The Cosmic Order is once again as it should be.

* * *

As for the Devourer of Souls, it raged, screamed, and all to no advantage. With the boundary of its dark realm once again made whole, all hope of escape vanished. The supreme feast of the soul of golden one had been denied. But the worst form of torment now faced it– eternal mediocrity. With ready and plentiful prey, it would survive, but not thrive. It would only perform its primeval directives and appointed tasks. While it's mischief-making had been curtailed, the Devourer nonetheless held close the fact its master remained weakened, and therefore remained open to a future opportunity.

* * *

The *gidim* that once had been housed in the mortal form of Ahmed Ali-Hassan, struggled to maintain its sanity. Surrounded by the demonic horrors of the dark realm, it had not yet understood, or perhaps learned, how to survive.

Yet, a glimmer of hope existed for this pitiful soul, and in fact, for all souls. For whenever it reflected upon the selfless generosity that had been extended to it, and by so many, sheer joy filled it. As a consequence, the *gidim* rose toward the light. And whenever the *gidim* thought about the golden American who had forgiven it, the utter and crushing anguish and regret the *gidim* felt for its actions against the golden angel, it rose even more.

The *gidim* of Ali-Hassan realized these lessons had to be learned, realized, and embraced. So it began to focus upon the positive and good, instead of the negative and hateful.

*   *   *

As any soldier will attest, an infiltration is far easier than an exfiltration. The enemy does not necessarily know you're coming, but they sure as hell know when you're leaving, especially after the shit storm you kicked up. In my case, however, I had no clue whether the multiple reports of the AK-47 in the mosque's basement had been noticed.

My thigh, it hurt like hell. The four Tylenol I gulped down had yet to take effect. Wounded, shocky, and thirsty, I somehow had to get my ass out of this hostile situation in one piece.

I crawled out the dilapidated window I had used to enter the old mosque. That simple task turned excruciating. As I limped away back to my truck, a real joy, I felt hostile eyes on me from the buildings around me. Yeah, in my condition I knew that I looked like easy pickings, but the talisman around my neck suddenly jerked me painfully to the ground, rolling me into the gutter.

Remain vigilant dear friend, J. J. I heard in my head...*Nergal?*

At the fall I did not cry out in pain, because not fifty feet away stood three armed men smoking cigarettes in a dark alcove of a building. They hadn't seen me, probably because of the glow of their cigarettes. Laying in the gutter between two vehicles I had decisions to make. Either stay put and bleed out or chance a belly crawl passed them, and on to my truck parked around the corner.

I started crawling, using only my right leg for a push off, while my left scrapped along. That crawl etched itself into my brain, as I zoned in and out of the pain. Only twenty feet from the shadow of my truck, I passed out. I regained consciousness only because Nergal screamed into my ear. After that, I pushed on.

Getting into and sitting in my truck, I gutted out as equally memorable and painful moments, but not as much as trying to get my left leg to operate the clutch. Somehow, someway, I did it anyway, with a lot of teeth-gritting and grunting.

Afak at that time of night, or early morning, remained a quiet, dead zone. It seemed its sidewalks had been rolled up, even its striped curbing. So I made my escape and headed back toward Baghdad.

During the long drive, the Tylenol kicked in, making the occasional gear shifts tolerable. I thanked God I had filled my tank. I do not know how many bottles of water I guzzled, but I seemed to go through them every couple of minutes. I could not get enough of the stuff. Despite all the clotting powder I had applied, my seat had a damp spot as my damn leg kept on weeping.

By the time I pulled up to my security firm's stockade, dawn broke. After one look from the guard on post, he called the infirmary. I never caught his name, but I'm sure his swift action saved my life.

*   *   *

Three weeks later, walking with a slight limp, I now had a cultural mission to complete. Through a company contact I received permission to visit the Iraq National Museum. Once there, I waited in a small conference room for the museum's representative to arrive. Several minutes passed before a well-dressed man with a very familiar face entered the room and greeted me like a long lost colleague.

"Ah, so we meet again, Mr. Stone," the man said effusively with his arms held wide. "And I see you took my advice. Nice moustache. It suits you."

There stood Mohammed, my archaeologist contact that I had met in the silver souk of the bazaar.

Smiling, I said, "I am afraid I am at a disadvantage...Mohammed?" I replied with my head cocked in question.

"Mr. Stone, my real name is Dr. Abdulamir al-Hamdi. I understand you wish to make a gift to the Iraqi nation, is that not so?" he said eyeing the package under my arm.

"Indeed, Dr. al-Hamdi. Indeed I do."

"Wonderful," he said with a single clap of his hands. "But perhaps first, some tea?"

"Yes, Dr. al-Hamdi, that would be wonderful.

261

Perhaps a regular *chai hamuth,* with extra sugar on the side."

*   *   *

Four and a half months after my archaeological adventure, my security firm offered to re-up my contract. But after a few moments of consideration, I thanked them for their generous offer, the opportunity for employment, and turned them down flat.

I wanted to get back home to Denton, Texas, check in on my folks, get serious again about my college education, and figure out my place within this continuously evolving paranormal world. Besides, without Nergal, I had gotten sort of lonely.

CHAPTER 35
2005

On my way back to Texas, I had plenty of time to think about things, and in particular my future. Post-Nergal, I missed him rattling around in my head with all of his weird ideas, and even weirder interpretations about our culture. I also found myself trying to understand what happened in the basement of that mosque. Things had happened around me I didn't understand.

Without question that conversation with the Emissary of the Ledger Keeper troubled me to the quick. It downright spooked me, but also gave me a clue as to who J. J. Stone, the golden child, might be–the carrier of the First Soul of Creation. Not exactly what you would call the norm. Another world out there needed to be explored–the paranormal. How would I find it? And when I did, what then?

After dinner at mom and dad's, I made it back to my old apartment to find it in need of a serious dusting. While dad had made sure the mail, rent, and utilities had been all taken care of, I forgot in my haste about the interior of my fridge. Call in the HAZMAT.

* * *

When Adam first saw me at his office's open doorway, he said, "Step inside young man and close the door. You look parched!"

While only ten in the morning, who am I to argue with a full professor? Per our usual ritual, two long necks clinked together, a deep swig, and the good professor got down to brass tacks, as always.

"So how's Iraq?"

"Dusty, dirty, and hot."

He chuckled.

"Well, J. J., I'm happy you're back in one piece. And now that you are back, I think it's high time that you figured out where you're going to college."

"I already have, Adam. I've already spoken with the admissions people and I'm starting here in the fall."

Pause.

"J. J., as I have said before, you'll outgrow this provincial frontier school within a month's time. You'll be bored silly. No, Marine, you need continuous stimulation, challenge, and resources that will ensure your academic growth. This place is not for you. No how, no way."

Surprised at Adam's pronouncement, I piped in. "Okay, I'm up for a challenge, a change. Do you have any suggestions?"

"I've got three: Brown University, The University of Pennsylvania, and the Oriental Institute in Chicago."

"Why those three?"

"They are all blessed with excellent faculty that will challenge and push you until you bleed, unbelievable resources, and dynamite connections. Now get out of here and look into these institutions. When you've made your choice, come back and we'll make a plan for your application. Got that?"

"Loud and clear, sir."

*   *   *

Four days later and a whole bunch smarter, I

knocked on Adam's door.

"I know where I want to go."

"Where?"

"The University of Pennsylvania."

"Why?"

"I liked their emphasis on ancient Mesopotamia, their museum collection, and a hunch."

"How interesting. You're dead right about the first two. As for that hunch, I just so happen to know the chairman of their Ancient Near Eastern Languages and Cultures Department. As for their museum collection, well son, they have unbelievable resources."

"What do you mean by 'unbelievable resources'?"

"The university museum has its own cuneiform collection. Many of their tablets haven't even been catalogued, much less read, or published. And that means prime research material."

"Wow. That's something."

"Yep, the chairman and I are good colleagues."

"Okay, you sold me. The G.I. Bill pays for my tuition. And I have a nice nest-egg in the bank for incidentals. So how do I convince them to accept me? I'm only a veteran grunt."

Shaking his head in disbelief, Adam scolded, "J. J., you are not 'only' some veteran grunt. Never have been. Never will be. You're a decorated Marine officer. Never, ever, forget that son. You read me?

"Now as for how to apply, I have a plan you might like. We go on the offensive. We make them want you. And guess what, you don't come cheap. Yes, we'll use your G.I. Bill for the tuition costs, which will be astronomical. But your housing, books, and meals, you negotiate. In return, you become a departmental assistant. Yes, that means you become a grunt again, but you're a highly paid grunt. And you don't say a word about your nest-egg." Adam walked around his desk and put his hand on my shoulder.

"Now, how do we get 'em to want you? Well, we need to set you apart. And that first taste will be your artifact's publication we will co-author. Believe you me, very few prospective undergrad applicants have behind their name a published article, in a peer-reviewed journal, much less on a topic as unique as yours."

"Huh." I said, as I sat there dumbfounded thinking about what Adam had said.

"But a publication takes time to appear in print and we're willing to wait for that, so what you're going to do is read a paper summarizing your forthcoming article at the next national archaeological conference. In other words, you get your face out there. And knowing you, you'll blow their minds."

Sneaky, I thought. *Pure marketing, complete with a tease.*

"So what do you think of my plan?"

"I've never given a lecture."

"You mean you never gave a briefing? Never delivered an intelligence assessment?

Silence.

He had a point.

"Yeah, I thought so, you've given plenty of 'em. By the way, what are you doing in late December?"

"Adam, I haven't a clue. But usually, the family gets together over the Christmas holidays–church, dinner, relatives, watching football, catching up around the kitchen table and such. Why do you ask?"

"Because this year's conference is being held in San Francisco. You'd be in and out in one day and home before Christmas Eve. Whadda ya say Marine? Are you up to the challenge?"

*   *   *

Later that week, Adam asked me again to stop by his office.

"Where in God's name are we going to publish that artifact of yours?"

Unsure, I responded with the one name I had remembered seeing the most in all of my readings, the *Journal of Ancient Near Eastern Studies,* or *JANES.*

"That journal is the big time, my friend. But what the hell! What can they do to us? They'll either reject us with some worthwhile comments, or accept our submission. Either way, we win. By the way, J. J., have you ever written an article before?"

"No, sir, not by a long shot, but I have written plenty of mission contact reports and intelligence assessments."

"Well, J. J., that being the case, what I want you to do is go over to the library, visit the serials section, and take a long look at the *JANES* volumes on the shelf. There's a bunch of them. While you're there, note what their article submission rules are. That should be in the latest volume. Then, find an article that is similar to what we're doing here. We'll use it as a template." He waved his hand.

"Now get out of here. I have a class in five."

*   *   *

The *JANES* series dated all the way back to 1942. Removing the most recent volume, I sat down, scanned it, and even found an article that would be perfect for our template. Meanwhile the variety of the articles and their subjects, blew my mind. Right there and then, I made a mental note to spend some serious time in the serials section. I know that good old Nergal would have approved. Then I remembered to look for the author submission guidelines, found them, and began to take some notes.

*   *   *

Two weeks before I boarded the plane to San Francisco, Adam told me he had received an e-mail from the editor of *JANES*, who accepted, on a provisional basis, the first draft of our joint article.

Adam grinned at the news, as in, "Somehow, we survived a double-blind review. And with our first draft no less. Hot damn!"

After a furious week, we finished our second draft, and in the process accommodated most of the reviewer's comments. When Adam hit the SEND button, I could not believe the pride I felt. My heart soared.

With my very first article now a reality, I felt that I had a good chance of getting into the University of Pennsylvania. But now I had to sell them face-to-face. Little did I know.

*   *   *

I had never been to San Francisco, so I treated it like a mission deployment. In other words, an opportunity to see new things, meet new people, and conquer stuff.

I found directions to the site of the convention from the airport, but before I entered the hotel complex, I stopped to get my shoes shined near the subway.

"Damnation son," the elderly man said, "those are a fine pair of cappers. Where'd you git 'em?"

"Nordstrom's, sir."

"Sir? You military?"

"Not anymore. Going for a job interview."

"Well then, by the look of you, you's still look real military. But ifin' you's going to an interview, den dis one's on me!"

Well, he did two passes over my shoes, and I tipped him a ten for his time and care, as not one bit of polish had touched either my laces or socks.

"Best of luck son. Now knock der socks off."

With my lecture in a manila folder under my arm, I walked into this big fancy hotel wearing my Brooks Brothers suit. I went to the hotel's check-in counter and asked where I should go, since I could already tell this place had multiple layers to it, and a huge atrium that could break your neck looking up into it. A nice lady produced a map and drew on it with a yellow marker the route I should take.

After following the map, I approached the archaeological conference's registration table, with my shiny shoes glowing like patent leather. Since childhood, well turned out grooming had been the norm. I stood out with my knife-edged creases, starched white button-down collared dress shirt, red power tie, and my hair high and tight.

Meanwhile, the milling academic crowd surrounding me wore a hodge-podge of ill-pressed corduroy jackets with leather elbow patches, Birkenstock foot coverings with and without socks, profuse and errantly contrived head and facial hair, and cotton, floor-length dresses topped with a variety of multi-colored shawls and scarves.

Mr. J. J. Stone of North Texas State University, as my conference name tag declared, made a subliminal impression on this crowd, who seemed to make a point of giving me plenty of space, like a great white shark swimming within a school of mackerel. But that feeling reminded me of Adam's sage advice.

"J. J., I'm gonna warn you. San Fran is not Denton. There are folks out there that are, well, out there. Way out there, if you get my meaning. Whatever you do, even if provoked, you must remain in control at all times. You got that Marine?"

"Yes, sir."

"Good. Now I'm talking no emotion, no matter how provoked. Be like Spock."

"Adam, I read you loud and clear. 'Live long and prosper.'"

*　　*　　*

I saw my session, entitled "Ancient Near Eastern Magic," posted on the appropriate salon door. To my chagrin, of the session's five papers, mine appeared last.

Damn, I thought, *I hate being last in anything.*

So I decided to kill some time and try to relax. Yes, I admit it, I had butterflies. Who wouldn't before their academic debut? Especially as so much rode on it– college admission, funding, future career, the whole shebang. So I burned off some energy by pacing, race track fashion, the long corridor as I went over the paper in my head for the millionth time.

Midway during my second lap, the double doors to the Livingston room burst open, as a human wave from the previous session's audience dashed out to the john, other lectures, the bar, or to escape outside to light up. As the river of humanity receded, I entered the still warm and humid chamber. Several stragglers remained engrossed in a discussion around the podium.

I took a seat in the front row to wait it out. I had done this a million times before in the military. Eventually, the hangers-on left and the room filled with new people. Then five minutes before our start time, the session's chair, a jaunty individual in a garish navy blue, double-breasted jacket, complete with shiny gold buttons, arrived.

Moments later, he cleared his throat into the microphone, and called the session to order.

"Ladies and gentlemen. Welcome to our session on 'Ancient Near Eastern Magic.' I am Professor Peter Glass, of the Department of Near Eastern Languages and Cultures, at the University of Pennsylvania."

So this is Adam's colleague...

"This afternoon, we have five papers. Each will be limited to ten minutes and not one second more. Thereafter, questions will be entertained. So without further ado, our first paper is by..."

I tuned out the rest, as the chair's accent intrigued me. To my ears it sounded like a blend of German and something else, something exotic. I also acknowledged that I had been presented with a personal challenge–to beat the ten-minute limit. Smiling, I thought, *Piece of cake.*

*   *   *

I sat in the last row of the session, being the shy Alexandrian witch that I am. While I didn't take Peter up on his generous offer to make a presentation, I, Professor Melaina Makris, attended his session nonetheless, as did several others of his research circle.

Peter, ever-looking like a dapper cruise director in his blue double-breasted jacket and white slacks, chaired the session crisply and fairly. Only once had he found it necessary to shut down a loquacious speaker who had managed to blather away her extra four minutes of grace time.

Oddly, from where I sat in the back, I do remember sensing one figure who appeared to be sitting in the very first row. Broad shouldered, erect, and with a short haircut that almost hid his sandy blond hair, he stuck out from the rest of the academic crowd like a tiger among sheep. *Who is this guy?* I wondered. Well, I soon found out when Peter introduced the last speaker.

"The last paper of this session, with the intriguing title, *A Sumerian Incantation Container*, I saved for last, as I am quite sure it will leave all of you buzzing. So without any further ado, Mr. Stone, the podium is yours."

A giant of a man, this Mr. Stone, presented himself as a confident, no nonsense double-A personality. He looked up while he took off his wrist watch, and then delivered the most succinct and to the point presentation I had ever heard within academe.

His topic, fascinating and unique, presented in a riveting, staccato-like style of enumerated bullet points left everyone breathless. All easily digestible, yet all leading his audience to the inevitable thesis that the Sumerians believed in the survival of the soul, that they considered it a tangible thing, and that it could be preserved within a magical construct. Before I knew it, he listed his conclusions in a logical progression that only underscored his command of the topic.

Then he said, as he put his wrist watch back on with a secret smile, "Are there any questions?" That simple statement he delivered as an outright challenge, a gauntlet thrown down at the audience, almost a dare. I found myself smiling as I thoroughly loved his moxie.

When the question and answer period finished, I felt embarrassed for my kind. Not one questioner could challenge this intellectual juggernaut, although some tried with their usual petty sniping. Throughout, he endured, so sure, so positive, and so very refreshing to listen to. I could tell several became peeved by his innate dynamism, mistaken for arrogance. But as I best remember, this Mr. Stone hadn't once resorted to the use of the subjunctive and never waffled, not once. Only later did a quiet concern sink in–the very real and distinct possibility that he knew his subject first hand.

With considerable regret, I missed Mr. Stone following his presentation. He got up and left. But later that evening, during our circle's dinner soiree, I got an earful, for Stone and his presentation topic dominated everyone's conversation, as Peter had predicted. Throughout it all, Peter remained curiously mum, almost as though he knew something germane to the discussion, but remained unwilling to share it. Could it be that I only noticed this uncommon reserve on Peter's part? I think so. After all, I am my father's and mother's daughter.

*   *   *

Following my presentation, Professor Glass surprised me when he asked me to join him in the hotel's bar. We sat down and Glass flagged down the bartender. "Two Anchor Steams, if you please."

Turning to me, Professor Glass began without preamble. "Mr. Stone, regarding your paper, I found it philologically sound, convincing, not to mention that it was a unique topic. As for your paper, the last time I heard one delivered in such a forthright manner occurred at the Pentagon prior to the First Iraq War. As for the question and answer period, you competently handled that, even though it contained a complete falsehood, the location of the artifacts."

He took a long pull from his beer.

"Professor Glass," I said while returning a steady gaze, "you are mistaken about the whereabouts of those two artifacts. Both are in the Iraq National Museum, unless Dr. al-Hamdi did not place them there."

The academic leaned away from me as he digested what I had said. "You know Dr. al-Hamdi?"

"Yes. I personally entrusted those artifacts to him."

"I'm pleased to hear that, Mr. Stone. I owe you a sincere apology. Nonetheless, I believe your mentor, Professor Gibson, has indeed found himself a diamond in the rough. You came highly recommended. I can say, without reservation, I now can see why."

Pause.

"So, would you be interested in applying to my department? I am quite sure we could put your philological talents to good use. What do you think?"

"First off, sir, thank you for all those kind words.

As for your department, sir, I am very interested, Professor Glass. I will apply, but I do have some financial questions that need clarification."

Nodding with understanding, Glass said, "Yes, I'm quite sure you do."

* * *

"Adam, this is Peter. How are you, old friend?"

Pause.

"Well, I just finished listening to Mr. Stone's presentation, and he proved to be everything you said he would be."

Pause.

"Yes! I saw that, too. That's quite an aura he has. I've never seen one like that before. Most striking."

Pause.

"You bet I did. And my word, he does strike a hard bargain. He had me on my heels most of the time."

Pause.

"I agree. Do you want to alert our society about him, or should I?"

Pause.

"Oh, you already have. Well, then, I will send in a report as well. Adam, he would make a fine addition."

Pause.

"Yes, I agree as well."

CHAPTER 36
University of Pennsylvania, 2006

I have always liked to drive to wherever I'm going. It gives me an opportunity to see stuff I never would have from an airplane seat. It also gives me lots of time to think. And for methodical me, that's important. So are maps.

Well, at this point it's pretty obvious Adam's plan for getting me into the right school had worked like a charm. I loaded up my pickup truck, the red Colorado crew-cab, and commenced to driving it all the way from Denton, Texas, to the East Coast. Since I've never done that before, I started my journey early so I could make it a full out, wide-eyed, adventure.

Without a doubt, I had to visit Washington, D.C., so I took a more southerly route through Little Rock, Memphis, Nashville, Knoxville, and Harrisburg. Then, from the capital, I breezed through Baltimore to Philadelphia. In all, I drove nearly sixteen hundred miles, counting all the historical side trips, and took a leisurely four days to do it.

Damn, I love this country.

*   *   *

My negotiations with Professor Glass went reasonably well, as he got me room and board in a dorm and a research assistantship with their museum. Luckily, the G.I. Bill would pay for the sky-high tuition and fees. The monthly check from the research assistantship did pay for my books and some incidentals.

I didn't realize that research assistants had access to the business side of the museum practically year-round. I also could use its research archives. In my case, Professor Glass had even arranged for me a personal carrel within it. In short, my very own reading table, cubby hole, and Fortress of Solitude. It had its own reading lamp, two electrical connections, and Internet port.

Now a word about the museum at the University of Pennsylvania. This rambling brown-bricked structure holds over one million artifacts of all sorts representing the cultures of the Mediterranean, Asia, the Near East, Europe, Africa, Oceania and America. When Adam mentioned "resources," I had no idea.

*　　*　　*

Given my life experiences, age, and other tangible qualifications, the University of Pennsylvania waved a whole bunch of college credits up front, so I started out as a second semester sophomore. That meant I got credit for a boat load of required freshman classes. That pretty much left the required classes from the physical world, natural sciences, and mathematics. Then came my obligations to my major in Ancient Near Eastern Studies. While I had a jump on the ancient language, Sumerian, I also saw coming down the pike the need for reading comprehension in German and French. Then came the looming challenge of a senior thesis. Technically, with a co-authored article to my credit, I could have pushed this issue aside, but chose not to. Besides, this is probably why Professor Glass had me familiarizing myself with all the Sumerian material, so I could write another article, this time on my own.

Ah, dorm life. I had thought I had it bad in the military, which enforced rigorous hygiene. The dorms bred every disease known to man. Fortunately, because of my "advanced age," I got a single in the graduate dorms–a Spartan place to crash, sleep, and store my stuff.

Dorm food. As I had been granted both room *and* board, I found myself at the mercy of the cafeteria staff for my breakfasts and dinners. A minefield of starches, care had to be taken at all times as proteins tended to be camouflaged or flat out non-existent.

My neighbors, serious bookers, who never seemed to open their doors, could have been vampires. After three weeks of this, isolation and loneliness hit. I even missed Nergal.

As a consequence, the museum became the focus of my life. Per Professor Glass' direction, I had to familiarize myself with its cuneiform collection. Never mind that most of it had been digitized. I liked examining the tablets themselves. Professor Glass had me working with the Sumerian material.

So here I sat, wearing thin cotton gloves, attempting to read these fragile clay tablets no bigger than the palm of my hand. Their writing, tiny and cramped, took some time getting used to.

After my third week, I had gotten familiar enough with the tablets' format that I began seeing letters, words, phrases, and even dates. I began to appreciate the method behind Professor Glass' madness.

* * *

There is a crude expression that says something to the effect while everyone has a backside, just don't be one.

Well, there's this research assistant at the museum, who fit that description to a tee. Why Lloyd hated my guts, I could easily figure out. Here's this hick with a Texas accent, an old fart too, who waltzed in and scored his own research area in the museum. Pure, competitive jealously. When he saw my truck's license plates, those big white Texas ones, my name became "Tex" at the museum. "Tex" this and "Tex" that. That didn't sit well with me.

Then in mid-October, right at dusk, I had just left the museum to grab some dinner at the dorm, when I found Lloyd getting hassled by three gang bangers. Shoving him around between them like a pinball, I could see Lloyd needed help before things got ugly fast. So I walked up and grabbed him away from the thugs. They had never seen an audacious move like that before, and for a moment, I had caught them flat-footed.

With Lloyd out of immediate danger, I put him behind me and faced the punks.

"Okay you fucking assholes," I said, "whose man enough to take me on?"

Well, they reverted to their neighborhood pack-instincts. Big mistake, because I took out the nearest one's knee with one kick, and splattered the second square on the bridge of his nose with the open palm of my left hand. Both went down, hard. The last one decided a moment too late to run for it, so about twelve feet later I tackled him, smearing him into the concrete sidewalk with little old me on top. Pancaked and definitely broken. At that point campus security arrived. Someone had called them, and after showing them my student ID and with Lloyd explaining the entire situation, I left the remains for them to clean up.

Thereafter, Lloyd never hassled me again. In fact, he turned out to be a regular sort of guy.

*　　*　　*

Somehow, someway word of Lloyd's rescue got back to Professor Glass.

"Mr. Stone, I know you were once in the United States Marines, but I cannot allow you to endanger yourself on this campus. Furthermore, I also cannot allow any smirch or hint of thuggery whatsoever to devolve upon my department. Therefore, I have decided that it would be best if you received some, let us say, special training."

Then the man handed me an airline envelope.

"Mr. Stone, you have been working hard. Now, I want you to go to Santa Fe, New Mexico, for a week. This coming week to be precise. You will be met at the airport. All meals and accommodations have been arranged for. And, Mr. Stone, this trip is not optional. Am I clear?"

"Yes sir," I responded, but wondered why.

CHAPTER 37
Santa Fe

I'd never been to Santa Fe, but I found its crisp and clean high-altitude air and robin's egg blue sky breathtaking. But I am getting a bit ahead of myself.

When I landed, an odd quiver of excitement hit me. It felt like I had arrived at my second home, one that I had never been to before, but one that had a strong emotional pull. As I walked through the jet way the feeling continued to build. As I passed through its doorway and entered the airport that quivering became an eel-like electrical pulse. Then I ran into a smiling Native American.

"You must be J. J.," he announced. "You look just like Professor Glass described you." He emoted with his arms held out wide in greeting. And then the man, maybe all of five four of him, gave me a great hug of kinship around my waist.

Then in a low voice. "But that golden cloud that surrounds you is indescribably beautiful. Like a heroic sunset in the desert."

Huh? I thought. *He can see auras, too?*

"Yes." Running Deer grinned with mirth. "Peter did say you had promise."

Did this guy just read my mind?

"You don't say," I replied with a raised eyebrow, Spock-like. Then I caught myself, "Do you mean Professor Glass?"

"Who else?" his crisp reply said.

Releasing me, he said, "Welcome to Santa Fe, J. J. I'm John Running Deer. Do you have anything in baggage?" His well-creased smile burbled wide and infectious.

Stunned, I stepped back, but the man took me by my arm and guided me away from the flood of deplaning passengers. His movements flowed so naturally, so smoothly, it was like he slid on tracks. As for me, next to him, I felt like a crude, mechanical, and oversized thing lumbering along. I couldn't break my focus on this man. He had filled the terminal with his presence.

At this point, in full-on recording mode, I took a real good look at this dude. Male, fortyish, deeply tanned, pale gray eyes, worn blue jeans, leather cowboy boots, yellow plaid shirt open at the neck, and flowing black and gray hair that broke like a wave on each shoulder.

Noting my appraising eye, Running Deer quipped, "Ah, a man of few words." Then he repeated, "Nothing in baggage?"

Shaking the cobwebs out of my head, "Nope. Just my carryon."

"Great! Then let's go." And off we went. I continued to watch this force of nature, and couldn't help but notice his aura–a shimmering silver, burnished with tiny flecks of a rich blue.

"By the way, are you hungry?"

"Sure am."

"Great. I know this wonderful piece of heaven called the Pantry on Cerrillos Road. They serve up food the way mom used to."

"I'm sold. What's taking you so long getting us there?"

*　　*　　*

Once underway to the restaurant our conversation shifted in a manner I had only done with Nergal, directly, and wordlessly. It shocked me, but, the progression seemed so natural with Running Deer.

I see J. J. you don't have a clue as to why Peter sent you to me. The answer is simple. You have gifts. Now's the time to do something with them.

For instance, J. J., you are accomplished at the wordless tongue. That's a gift, a most precious one. You should try to use it more. The ability is like a muscle. Exercise it, and it becomes stronger. If you don't use it, it atrophies and fades away.

I don't know if you realize this, J. J., but you represent a virtually untapped well of potential. In fact, I'm willing to bet that up to now, you have been bashing your way through adversity, instead of finessing the desired outcome.

The memory of dealing with the three gang bangers in Philadelphia came to mind. Running Deer saw it.

Precisely, that situation, J. J., could have been handled far more deftly, without any contact, or possibility of injury. This is why Peter contacted me. This is why you are here—to learn.

"Peter?" I said.

Yeah, Peter. You mean he didn't tell you about his own gifts?

*　　*　　*

John Running Deer, my personal training instructor, nice guy that he seemed to be, undertook my training seriously, which suited me just fine. On our first day, he picked me up from my hotel and took me to a local dojo in Old Santa Fe. There he began helping me to survive the big, bad land of magic. The place turned out to be a converted gas station, and where the lifts had once been, a vast expanse of training mats lay.

We began by assessing my natural offensive weapons, which included physical strength, average flexibility, Marine-bred hand-to-hand combat skills, and extensive training with a Bush knife, 9mm handgun, and M4 carbine. Then Running Deer inquired about my skills with the wordless tongue and mind reading. These I admitted needed work.

As for physical defensive skills, the Marines had taught me plenty, but with anything more serious, my divine protections kicked in, which while protecting me, hardly prevented me from scars or injuries.

Nodding with understanding to what I had imparted, Running Deer said, "Then let's begin with some basic mat work, Grasshopper. Later, we will transition into some other things."

"Sounds like a plan."

*   *   *

"Basic mat work" translated into the most grueling hour I can remember in recent history. In spite of the low humidity, I emerged slick with sweat after Running Deer finished schooling me. While a smaller guy, he's quicker than a rattlesnake, and just as deadly.

Stopping for a much needed breather, Running Deer inquired. "How often do you run, J. J.?"

"At least four times a week; most times I go every day for at least three miles. Why'd you ask?"

"Well, it shows. You have excellent endurance for a big man. But did you notice anything particular during that workout?"

"Yeah. I'm always a step slower than you. You move like grease lightning. No matter how hard I tried, I could never get out of defensive mode. How'd you do that?"

Grinning from ear to ear, Running Deer sheepishly admitted. "I, unlike you, Grasshopper, can multi-task."

Grrrr...

"What'd ya' mean by 'multi-task'?"

"I allowed my head to guide my body. In other words, I reacted in my mind before my body moved. So, your reactions must become faster. Right now, they are barely adequate.

"You did, however, manage to block and avoid *some* of my blows. In fact, toward the end of the exercise, I noticed you began to unconsciously read my mind, and that is the key. We must train you to do that all the time. It must become instinctive."

"Huh. My guesses, my intuition. I never considered that before."

"Yes, J. J., and when you do, I will have my hands full. But, dude, you have a long way to go before that will happen."

*　　　*　　　*

For the next three days, Running Deer busted my tail at the dojo. Ever the sneaky guy, he mixed up the training. Then, in mid-motion, as I found myself reacting in my mind to his movements, and I accidently cold-cocked him.

When he came around, he said, "J. J., I deserved

that. No harm, no foul. As far as I'm concerned, you're close to being certifiably deadly."

Then he shifted gears on me.

"I think it's high time we move on from the physical and begin to focus on your mental skills. Believe it or not, because of the merging of your mind and body at the dojo, you're already half way there toward your goal of mindreading.

"Telepathy, or the silent tongue, call it what you will, operates differently with every individual. For me, I learned early on that focusing upon someone consciously didn't work, but unconsciously focusing on them sideways, at an angle, indirectly, always worked.

"But before we get into that, I want to show you today how to block your own mind, and, how to penetrate someone's mind who is consciously blocking out their thoughts. So, imagine for a moment in your mind as an impregnable wall..."

*   *   *

During another grueling couple of days, and a whole bottle of aspirin, Running Deer introduced me to the art of mental shielding. To block one's thoughts, a mental construct must first be created in order to do so. This construct, image, whatever, has to be something unforgettable, personal, and unique, much like a computer password. The construct must, in some "tangible" way represent an impassable barrier that can be incrementally bolstered if need be.

For me that construct represented a barbwire fence I took from a childhood memory. That damn thing had scratched and scarred up my little legs when I crawled through it while running away from an angry bull. In my mind I enlarged the fence's barbs to the point it looked like a dense briar thicket.

Running Deer would then try to penetrate that thicket, probing here and there, all the while I countered as best I could. As with everything, time, practice, and experience made my fence a formidable barrier.

I didn't like penetrating someone else's mental shielding. To me it felt all wrong, a violation of personal space. But to his credit, Running Deer wouldn't hear any of that. So I grudgingly learned how to invade a person's mind. And once in I learned that, I then had to figure out where I wanted to go.

Like I said, I didn't like the entire notion or process, so I figured out what I did like. I called it "listening in." It's a more passive method than Running Deer's battering ram approach to reading other people's minds. I must admit that I'm pretty proud of my ability to unobtrusively "listen in."

Privately, I was relieved to finish this brief boot camp. All the mental stuff gave me the creeps.

*　　*　　*

At week's end I went back to Philly with my head in a whirl. New offensive and defensive tactics, wordless speech, and psychic game playing. What more in the way of surprises could there be?

*　　*　　*

The Native American punched in a local phone number within the 505 exchange. Running Deer didn't even have to look up the number.

"Betsy, it's John. Got a minute?"

"Sure. What's up?"

Then Running Deer began his blow-by-blow account of a man called J. J. Stone.

Hanging up the phone, Betsy breathed, "I just have to meet this guy."

CHAPTER 38
Philadelphia

I must admit I'm very inquisitive. Twelve years in the military does that to you, where you learn early not to believe in coincidence. So I began digging into the background of my benefactor and boss, Professor Peter Glass, who, by the way, knew both Adam Gibson and Running Deer on a first name basis. After all, Professor Glass not only interviewed me for admission to his university, he had helped me out with my financial arrangements, and then set me up within the museum. So I asked myself, why did he do all this?

I called up Adam and asked. I read a bunch of literature that listed Professor Glass' biography, his parents, and several other scholars who played important roles in his development. In the course of all this, Professor Glass earned my respect as a scholar of some renown. Here's what I found out.

Peter Martin Glass, for all practical purposes, spent his childhood on an archaeological excavation amid floored wall tents and communal showers. His archaeologist father, Hans Manfred Glass, worked in the Egyptian Delta on several sites believed to be Hyksos in origin. Hans died in his mid-forties because of a nasty parasitic disease. His mother Miriam, an Akkadian cuneiform expert, thereafter raised Glass in Israel from the age of fourteen on. Upon entering the University of Tel Aviv, Glass transitioned to cuneiform, his mother's own subject, where he too embraced Akkadian, as a student of none other than the famous philologist Anson Rainey.

Rainey had sponsored Glass to join him at the Tel Beer Sheva excavation, and that's where young Glass first came into collegial contact with Yohanan Aharoni, Israel's foremost historical geographer. The impact of this dynamic pair influenced Glass in ways that probably cannot be calculated. Not surprisingly, Glass' future dissertation came from that excavation–the publication of over fifty curse or execration texts, spells painted on pots and ritualistically smashed. Once the magician painted the pots, their smashing launched the curses affixed to them. For ever more, Glass and the magical world of the ancient Near East became one.

Rapidly, Glass climbed within the academic world, with many research invitations, which became a series of short-term lectureship positions at several prestigious East Coast universities. Not long after that, the University of Pennsylvania offered a heavily credentialed Glass a tenured professorship. Throughout, Glass became the academic darling and advocate for the study of magic and magical practices in the ancient cultures of the Fertile Crescent.

The Professor Glass that I know, carried two very distinctive auras, light blue overlapped with light yellow. These, not surprisingly, fit him to a tee, as the blue indicated creative and scientific intellect with a penchant for detail verging on perfection. On the other hand, his light yellow band revealed natural strengths toward the spiritual, coupled with powerful psychic abilities.

As one might suspect, with this kind of insight on Professor Glass, I pegged him as a very specific kind of manager. One that I wanted to please. So I made damn sure that I completed all of my assignments on time and as well as I could possibly make them. He knew I doing well in my ancient language classes, thanks in part to good old Nergal's memories. But I had been studying hard on them anyways. I had found my stride.

Truth be told, in opposition to my philological studies, I didn't give a rat's ass about my math requirements. Their presentation of the stuff bored me as too abstract. Give me something practical, like plain geometry and a range and windage calculation.

Well, it worked. By the end of my second semester, Professor Glass had granted me access to a restricted and unpublished collection within the museum's archives. Most of this dusty stuff came packaged in dense raw cotton within wooden crates. Come to think about it, they reminded me a lot of old rifle crates. I inspected one and discovered what they used to be–German rifle crates.

Back to the restricted tablets. These artifacts, while assigned an acquisition number, had not been categorized as to what they contained, hence my job. So I got down to it, but I had barely started getting my fingers dusty and filling in a logging spreadsheet, before the semester ended. Summer break ensued and I needed to find a job right quick.

Before I could get going on finding a job, on the last day of my second semester, the Professor Glass called me into his office, for a performance review.

"Mr. Stone," he said with his very measured and distinctive accent, "you have done well. Yes, you came to this department with a unique set of qualifications, but you adapted and integrated in well with the faculty and staff. So, I have renewed your room and board in full for next year, which is technically the beginning of your junior year. In fact, you do not have to move out for the summer if you don't wish to. Further, I similarly renewed your museum assistantship for next year, your carrel, and I have seen to it your monthly stipend has been raised. Now, Mr. Stone, please continue, and don't disappoint either me or Professor Gibson, who, incidentally, sends his best regards."

*   *   *

I had heard stories about summer break for most of my life, and yet to experience one ever, because I had always worked on the family ranch. So I got a job working nights in Philly, at a local university dive bar, as a bouncer, of all things.

The pay was decent. The occasional tips from management made it even better. The hours allowed me to work out, spend some time on my Sumerian tablets—must always exercise the language muscle—and enjoy the city. This job also gave me the genuine opportunity to practice reading auras as Running Deer had counseled, sometimes even seeing them subtly change over the course of a patron's evening of drinking. For the inebriated, I learned to identify the telltale signs needed to preempt those so inclined to wreak havoc. This management much appreciated.

I practiced wordless tongue exercises, another Running Deer imperative. These came in handy as I eavesdropped on flammable social situations. Running Deer also taught me how to plant images in susceptible minds. Things like giant hairy spiders on a robber's gun arm worked well, because they almost always threw their weapon away. My visits to the zoo, to improve my imagery, had made these a specialty.

During those eight weeks while I worked at The Greasy Onion, I single-handedly stopped who knows how many drunken and disorderly patrons. After a while, you lose count.

Needless to say, the local men in blue and I became fast friends, as several of them were ex-Marines. One week into the job, the owner thought he had some kind of a heaven-sent guardian angel. So much that after the first two incidents I broke up, he began stuffing stray Benjamins and Grants in my breast pocket.

Cha-ching!

*   *   *

Even though Nergal no longer resided between my ears, I still found myself thinking about him, and this wife Erish. Quite a bit, in fact, to the point I suspected that they were watching my back like two guardian angels during some of those hot summer nights at the bar.

One time I distinctly remember something tickling my right ear. Unconsciously bringing up my hand to swat at it, I blocked a flying beer bottle directed at my cranium. Heck, I can think of several more instances, but I knew those two spirits were about, and I pray for their everlasting happiness as a consequence.

*   *   *

I visited mom and dad twice during that summer. Proud of their college man, mom, whenever we went out for dinner (almost every evening), would introduce me to all these folks. It got to be embarrassing, as there seemed to be more folks to meet. I began to grouse about it, until Dad told me each and every one of those women had a right pretty daughter, who dreamed of being wed to a college-educated man.

While I appreciated their concern for my social well-being, I began to ask myself some serious questions as to why I remained so socially elusive. Who after all was I saving myself for? Then it hit me. The Emissary had said that whoever carries the First Soul was a lonesome, 24/7 warrior, always on call to ensure the Cosmic Order. "A curse" the Emissary had called being a carrier of the First Soul, where family and friends became leverage. That sobering detail kept me on the straight and narrow.

*   *   *

With the summer over, on my second day back at school, I got an e-mail from Professor Glass to meet him in his office. A couple of hours later, after my last class of the day, Calculus 101, I knocked on his door.

"Thank you for stopping by, Mr. Stone," he said into his cluttered desktop. I must admit, the current state of the good professor's office and hair could be best described as random.

"Mr. Stone, it is time for you to consider your senior thesis. And for you, that means not some half-hearted term paper, but rather a project that is ready for the press. This is why I have put you in contact with unpublished, restricted material. I want you to find something within that dust-bin worthy of publication. Is that understood?"

"Yes, sir. How long is this ready-for-press project supposed to be?" I asked.

"Whatever it takes, Mr. Stone. Your first article with Professor Gibson broke new ground in the discipline. I want you to come up with something similar, but this time on your own." He rose from his desk.

"Now, you're probably wondering why I am so demanding with you. It's because you have the right stuff, Mr. Stone. Your grades are excellent, that's rare enough. But your natural gift for languages must be exercised, pushed, and polished. And I intend to do just that." He rummaged around in the upper drawer of a nearby filing cabinet. Looking up, he continued.

"I also wish to make clear that if you encounter any issues with this project, do not sit on them, trying to figure them out on your own. My door is open to you. Consider me your resource. The first and biggest flaw with a senior thesis is to try and do it all on your own. To surprise me with it, so to speak. So, to initiate this collaboration, I want on my desk, in two weeks' time, a topic, title, and preliminary project outline. Is that understood?"

"Yes, sir," I said with a smirk.

"Have I said something funny, Mr. Stone?"

Shaking my head, I backpedaled, "Oh, no, sir. It's just I do better whenever I'm presented with a challenge. That's all."

* * *

With my hands on hips, standing before some shelves in the museum's basement, I stared at six wooden rifle cases. There, somewhere, I would find my senior thesis. The first case, which I had only briefly examined at the end of Spring semester, looked to contain about twenty broken tablets, if I interpreted the crate's internal wooden dividers correctly. Within each divided section

I found a tablet wrapped in its own cotton nest.

Wearing a pair of thin cotton gloves, I began the laborious process of unwrapping and examining each tablet, noting on my laptop its acquisition number, and then attempting to make a meaningful comment as to what it recorded. I didn't know where these tablets came from nor their time period. I had to establish that information from the tablets themselves.

In all, it took me the better part of four solid days to plow through the six rifle cases. But now, at least, I had my very own inventory list of one hundred and fifteen tablet fragments. In almost every case, I could see an opportunity for joins and mends and made careful notes recording that fact. But to do that, I would need the space to arrange them all on an open table. Professor Glass could arrange for that, so I popped by his office unannounced and found the man at his desk, elbow deep in paperwork.

"Excuse me, Professor Glass, may I have a moment of your time?"

Looking up with glazed eyes, the academic waved me in. Standing before his desk, I explained the situation and my needs. When I scanned his aura, I saw that he strained being analytical to the point of fatigue.

With a tired reply, he said, "Sounds to me you should give up your museum carrel and move into the vacant office next door."

Picking up his desk phone, he punched out several numbers from memory, listened for the other end to pick up, and announced. "Henry, this is Professor Glass over at the Carlton Building. How are you today?"

Pause.

"Good. Well, the reason I am calling is that I have

a favor to ask. Could you stop by and open up Office 302, and have a six-by-three foot table set up in it?"

Pause.

"No. The office is already furnished, complete with a phone. We need some additional work space."

Pause.

"Yes, I will be needing a set of keys for the room. I am temporarily assigning it to one of my students for his senior thesis."

Pause.

"Yes, I know, all the other lab rooms at the museum are occupied. And one other thing, if you don't mind. Move all of Mr. Stone's books from his research carrel to 302 as well."

Pause.

"Yes, the name is S-T-O-N-E, and kindly authorize 302's keys under Mr. Stone's name."

Pause.

"Henry, you're indispensable to this university and my department. Never forget it."

Hanging up the phone, he looked up at me and said, "Will that do?"

Speechless that I had been assigned my very own office, I dumbly nodded my head in the affirmative.

Then Glass added. "Wait around, for about fifteen minutes. Henry will be up by then with your stuff, the table, and set of keys. You will have to sign for them.

"And," he pointed toward the ceiling, "be sure to give Henry something. That will ensure he's on your side, and believe you me, you want Henry on your side around this place!" And with that Glass returned to shuffling through his papers.

"Now, if you will excuse me, Mr. Stone, I am

currently doing battle with next year's budget. Someone seems to think that I have oracular powers." With that, I left, as his head bowed low over a much-scribbled upon spreadsheet.

*   *   *

About twelve minutes later, the floor's elevator bell rang and out rolled a teetering four-wheeled trolley that carried a banquet table and the books and gear from my museum carrel. A wizened man , about five foot two, pushed the whole, while wearing starched white bib overalls, with chest pockets brimming with pencils, pens, and fine tools. Underneath, he wore a starched white dress shirt with the arms rolled up over his forearms. That revealed an old blue tattoo on his left arm. His boots were spit polished. His neatly trimmed shock of white hair completed the look of spotlessness, like someone almost laboratory-ready, just minus the latex gloves and face mask.

He stopped, looked me up and down, and surmised, "You must be Stone," in the thickest Philly accent that I had ever heard.

"And you must be, Mr. Henry," I answered.

Eyeing me suspiciously, he then turned around to his trolley, produced a clip-board, and a pen.

"Sign at the two X's, Mr. Stone."

This I did, and in return received a small manila key envelope. Looking inside, I saw the two keys that I signed away my life for, pulled one out, and opened the door to 302, while the custodian tinkered with his cart. Then he turned around.

"Okay," he began, "so where do you...?"

I already had the banquet table up and in my mitts.

"Well, how about here against the bare wall, Mr. Henry."

Taken aback, he instead quipped in Yoda's choice of grammatical proclivity, "Helpful, you are."

Together, we opened up its legs, and placed it against the wall in one fluid motion.

Looking down, I commented.

"That's a professional polish on your boots, Mr. Henry. Which service?" I asked.

Looking down, his look dismissed them as filthy. Then, "US Marine Corps."

"You don't say," I said as I extended my hand, which he took with a firm and callused grip, all the time looking me in the eye, measuring me. As he withdrew his hand, he had palmed the folded twenty and put it into his bib's side pocket as smoothly as a pickpocket.

"Will that be all, sir?" he inquired.

"No, Mr. Henry," I replied. "Don't be a stranger. You have friends."

That brought a wry smile to his face as he turned to leave. His aura: bright yellow, soft blue, and red, which indicated at this moment he felt grounded, realistic, truthful, and yet somehow, someway fearful of losing his respect and prestige.

How sad, I thought.

"Do you have a card with your number on it, sir?"

"Nope." He snorted over his shoulder. "Just call 7878."

*   *   *

Professor Glass, back to his god-awful departmental paperwork, found where he had left off on the budget's spreadsheet. As he wrapped his head around a particularly knotty issue, the phone rang.

Another distraction! What now?

"Peter. Is that you? It's Melaina Makris calling from Berkeley. Have I caught you at a good time?"

Peter always found it amazing how Makris' musical voice always seemed to cut through anything.

"Mel! How wonderful! You rescued me from next year's budget projection. What's up?"

"I'm going to be in New York next week, and I hoped to catch up with you sometime. Perhaps you and Georgia for one of those epic Philly Italian dinners? My treat."

Peter's stomach rumbled its approval.

"That sounds wonderful. Why don't you take the train down and we'll make a day of it? You can stay with us and the kids for the night and return the following morning. What day were you thinking about?"

"A Wednesday."

"Great. Just come on down to my office and we'll roll from there."

"Wonderful, Peter. I'll e-mail you the particulars. See you soon."

* * *

While having my very own office stunned me, having Professor Glass as my next door neighbor made my eyes go wide.

Glass has put all of his chips in my pot. I have to deliver.

Well, by the end of the day, again with Professor Glass' permission, I had signed the paperwork with the museum's security staff to move the six rifle cases of artifacts to Carlton 302, and had begun arranging the tablet fragments on the banquet table and bare book shelves which covered two of the office's walls. This simple process made it rather easy to cluster likes with likes–by their color, size, and fabric textures. Within the hour, I clustered them into eight provisional groups of one hundred and fifteen fragments, while three breaks remained incomplete orphans. Then, I began to assign each cluster a Roman letter designation complete with individual card tents.

I was making tangible progress toward my senior thesis. I had my inventory spreadsheet and potential joins. Now I needed to examine each cluster to understand them.

* * *

The next day I noticed something very odd. Whenever I placed the broken fragments of any of the tablets within close proximity of each other, I sensed an overall change in them. Not that they glowed, but as the fragments neared one another, they acquired a sort of electricity to them. On top of that the air felt thicker, denser somehow.

At first I blew this off as my imagination. But when I moved the smallest cluster of the collection, labeled Tablet C to my desk, and began to move the fragments closer together to the point of almost touching, then I saw its aura–a muddy brown to black color. Not a good omen.

Experimentally, I separated the Tablet C fragments out a bit and their aura faded as did the tablet's quite depressing dynamism. This phenomenon got me to thinking about the use of curse texts in the ancient Near

East, and Professor Glass' experience with them. The logical assumption became that if a clay tablet had power associated with it, then breaking it up, would thereby diminish its magical potential.

I thought. *Is their current broken state deliberate to prevent their use?*

But before I approached Professor Glass about this assumption, I needed more data. I needed to first divine Tablet C's content.

So I began, looking for what, I did not know.

Out came my trusty yellow legal pad and pencil. I first transcribed Tablet C's text, and then transliterated the cuneiform wedges into Latin characters. As I did so, stock words and phrases started to jump out at me. In all, this tablet broken into eight pieces, contained twenty-two lines, and seemed to be a formidable conjuring that named a demon of the Underworld and then instructions for sending it back from whence it came.

For me, this rough estimate of Tablet C's content went a long way in explaining its dark aura and the thickening of my office's atmosphere. In many ways, I found my little discovery exciting and the potential content engrossing stuff. The next day, I did one of my classic deep dives and roughed out a transcription and transliteration of all eight tablet clusters and the three orphans.

All eight of the tablet clusters displayed dark to muddy auras when arranged in close proximity. The three orphaned fragments did not. In the end, I identified five curses, while three summoned a demon by name. As for the three orphans, far too damaged to assess, what did remain suggested sheer evil intent. As a consequence, I judged them all to be extremely dangerous. Why? I don't know. Just plain old intuition.

I worked into the night and made a point of separating the fragments apart farther still, occupying several more wall shelves, all in the hope of lessening the psychic thickness of the office's atmosphere. In case the cleaning staff appeared, I left neat little tent signs all over the place, which said, "Do Not Touch!"

Bushed, I went to dinner to mull over my outline for Professor Glass. It seemed clear enough. The eight tablets had been broken on purpose in ancient times for a reason–because their content was so damn dangerous.

* * *

The next day I had a class entitled "Physics for the Humanities," in other words, "physics for poets." The pleasant course passed on basic physical concepts to those mathematically challenged, using more practical and mechanical examples, than theoretical models. The instructor, an absolute hoot and an avowed *Star Trek* fan, loved to use the science fiction series for many of his examples.

Today, however, something he said resonated. He talked about the impossibility of an anti-matter warp drive engine within which the annihilation of matter and anti-matter would take place. To me, this sounded a lot like the Emissary' description of Creation, and what it had described as the vast differences between the several realms, and what would happen if the boundary between the two ever collapsed. The words "annihilation" and "end times" began to look very similar, and all of a sudden basic physics had gained practical meaning with this ex-Marine. Then, I wondered if laws governed magic like they did for physics, with basic cause and effect. This led me to contemplate what constituted magic, and from whose perspective.

On my way back from my "physics for poets" class, I passed by Professor Glass' office, en route to mine, and saw him speaking with a dark-haired woman. Not thinking much of it, I got to my office, sat down, and got to work on my tablets.

About ten minutes later, I heard a knock on my door frame.

"Mr. Stone, I'd like to introduce you to Professor Melaina Makris. She's in for the week from Berkeley, California."

Unbidden, I took in this exceptional looking woman with dark hair, skin the color of darkened honey, a striking triangular face, and eyes like almonds.

Very exotic, summed up my first impression.

"It's a pleasure to meet you, ma'am," I said standing up from behind my desk.

"And I, you, Mr. Stone. Your paper made quite an impression in San Francisco," she said, as she took in my office cluttered with labeled cotton nests of broken cuneiform tablets, including the Tablet C spread out on my desk. "In fact, I thought perhaps we could spend some time discussing it."

"Professor Makris," Peter offered in explanation, "is part of a specialized cadre of experts in ancient Near Eastern magic."

"Oh," I managed. "Sure, Professor Makris. I'd be happy to."

"Wonderful. What's your availability tomorrow?"

Glancing down at my schedule I said, "I'm free for

lunch. Anytime between ten and two in the afternoon would be fine."

"Splendid. I'll stop by your office at eleven. And oh, it's my treat."

*　*　*

"President Smithers," Geoffrey began, "I wish to inform you about something that has been on my mind for some time." The personal assistant formally stated to the president of TIIIS.

"Is this good or bad news, Geoffrey?"

"Well, sir, I am not sure. Several of our members, notables from the United States no less, have been submitting a stream of reports about a potential membership candidate named Jonathan Joseph Stone."

"And Geoffrey, what do these reports say about this Mr. Stone?"

"Well, sir, an exceptional academic mind, a golden aura, ex-military officer, who received a recent week's worth of physical and psychic combat training."

"And?"

"Well, sir, some time ago we established a file on an individual by the same name."

"And?"

"The individual's birth notice had an extremely high psychic index, *and*, a Soul Numeral of one."

"Why yes, I do remember that report. It had come from the central U.S. as I recall."

"The very same, sir. And as I well know, sir, you have been looking for someone to relieve you as the Lictor of Magic. This might be that individual."

"Send me everything that you have on him, Geoffrey. And thank you for the heads up."

CHAPTER 39
The Twins, 1948

Twins are special for a whole host of reasons. Some say they share an uncommon bond that transcends the normal. Others that they stand at the brink of the paranormal, where all that it is needed is just one gentle push, or perhaps a situation that they together have to overcome.

When Peter and Charles arrived into the mortal world, Peter, breached first and became nominally the elder, much to his brother Charles' eternal vexation. So the die had been cast.

$*$ $*$ $*$

We grew up needing little. Our parents, well-to-do and educated, had professional university careers, which neither wished to relinquish. Consequently, a series of nannies cared for us.

This parental distance and coolness left us largely on our own. For amusement, we babbled and goo-gooed like any other babies. But little did our nannies know that we held sophisticated telepathic conversations. Ones that sometimes referred back to our time together in the womb. For Peter and I "silent talking" represented a norm as natural as breathing.

To be certain, neither our nannies nor parents knew about our silent conversations that often included them.

Why does that one always look the same?

or,

Why does this one tickle us under the chin?

or,

Why does that one always smell funny?

or,

How come we can't hear them? Don't they know how to say anything?

We found it far more natural to use our silent talking than to master the complexities of spoken language. So much so, that the our parents thought we needed speech therapy. After only several dreadful sessions, we came to a decision.

Yes, we would have to communicate orally with the outside world. But as for our silent talking, that is to be our little secret.

Prior to our third birthday, my brother Peter, who needed glasses, became self-conscious about them as well as their fragility. He always tried to be careful with them while we played, and as a result, he developed a cautious temperament. Meanwhile, I had perfect eyesight and could see a mile, well, sort of. Unlike my older brother Peter, I didn't have to be careful. If anything, I reveled as the family daredevil, the dashing charmer with an electric smile.

Between ourselves, we competed over everything imaginable, be it wooden building blocks, running, drawing on the blackboard, who got the last muffin, crisp or sweet. You name it. We battled for each and every one.

On our third birthday, something happened that had a lasting effect on me, almost as much as Peter's early birth. We had to share, as we had in the past, a birthday cake. But frankly, I wanted my very own, and said so.

"I want my own birthday cake," I announced with

my arms crossed upon my puffed up chest, "and I want it bigger than my older brother's, too!"

Taken aback by my most reasonable request, my father, Alec, apparently didn't quite see it that way.

"Charles," he said, "clearly, you have a high opinion of your importance within this family. In case you haven't noticed, we *share* things here, equally. Same cake, same number of presents. Am I clear on this? Or, should we have a private talk?"

I couldn't believe it. So I shook my head in silent negation all the while my thoughts betrayed me.

Father! It isn't fair. Why must we share *a cake?* I blared out in silent talk.

Because, Charles, sharing is better. My prim brother Peter diplomatically responded. *I like sharing things with you, Charles. I'll even let you cut the cake. You cut and I'll choose.*

"NO!" I shouted at Peter with my arms held at my sides. My hands formed fists held tight and bloodless.

Father, witless and oblivious to our silent conversation said to me. "Charles, are you sure you want your own cake?"

I spun back to face father and said, "Yes, sir. I do!" Then came out a pouting lower lip for emphasis, something I unconsciously did.

"I see. Well then, young Master Charles, you leave me no recourse..." as he glanced at mother for support. "No birthday cake for you. No supper, either. And, no presents. In fact, your mother and I will return them all on the morrow."

I couldn't believe father's verdict to the point my eye's moistened.

But Father! That isn't fair! I screamed in the silent

talk with my hands clenched tight at my sides.

"And, don't you even try to pull that weepy look on me and your mother, young man. Overdone theatrics! That's not how we Smithers act around here! Now, without further delay, get yourself up to your room, while your mother and I decide what to do with you."

With that, what could I do? So I stomped up the old flight of wooden stairs to my room, booming my displeasure ever upward step by step. My feet tingled.

They just don't understand! I screamed back in my mind. *Peter and I are old enough to have our own cakes!*

So had been established the keystone block of our brotherly schism, and all because of biological timing and a damn birthday cake.

*   *   *

I never forgot the birthday cake incident, ever. It represented the first time I had tried to exert my will with father and failed. So, during grade school, I took to the football pitch with a vengeance, determined to establish myself as better. Meanwhile, Peter, himself no slouch, set upon being the class's number one student. Our contest disregarded the crass issue of brawn versus brain, for us it became more a matter of emphasis, of spear-won territory. That we both understood.

In spite of our natural competitiveness, we stood back-to-back willing to take on any and all comers, using our silent talking to our best advantage. We were twins, through and through, and our sense of brotherly loyalty never left us. But we each wished to set out on his own way.

"Charles," Remy, my boyhood crony, would ask, "why do you always back up your brainiac brother?"

"Because Remy, he's my brother. So don't get it in your head to mess with him, or else!" I emphasized with gritted teeth and my clenched fist in Remy's face.

His was the first time that I read another's mind, I saw what good old Remy had in store for my brother, and I didn't like it. So out-of-the-blue, I decided to make a point and cold-cocked Remy, taunted him unmercifully while he lay on the ground, and then kicked him several times to make sure he gotten the drift. In my mind Remy deserved it, and I enjoyed letting him know.

On another level, I must admit I had been shook up by "hearing" Remy's hostile thoughts about my brother. So much so that evening, after supper, I had to tell Peter about it.

Peter! You know how I beat up Remy today? Well, guess what! I accidently read his mind. I heard what Remy wanted to do to you and I got really pissed. I think high emotions may have something to do with it, but I'm not sure. Has that ever happened to you?

Blushing, my brother admitted, *yes, Charles, I read another person's thoughts about a month ago, but for me it had absolutely nothing with being pissed.*

Peter paused for a moment and then confided.

Charles, you know those quiet times in the school library, when you're trying to study. For the past week I have been fighting off all of these random thoughts of others that come crashing down on me. It feels like drowning, Charles. Trust me. It's not pleasant.

*　　*　　*

Come university, we entered Cambridge, following in our proud parents' footsteps. And, per the usual, we did it our own way, with Peter earning an academic scholarship and me one in athletics. This pleased our parents as we had been admitted on merit alone, and not as legacies. Both of us took pride in that.

Ever true to form, we also chose to follow different courses of study. Peter, ever the empirical one, went with physics and mathematics, while I selected anthropology and ancient history. In a sense both of us gravitated toward a language–the one of science, the other of culture.

But as my older brother Peter developed more and more as a serious investigator of the physical realm, bent on deciphering the universe's many secrets, I approached the question differently. I felt the need to go to the basics. What did a culture believe and why? How did a culture come to grips with unknown phenomena? With childlike wonder or heart-stopping fear? Not surprisingly, my course of inquiry led me away from the hard sciences into the paranormal, which I erroneously believed to be an adjunct to them.

"So Peter," I asked over a pint of bitters at our favorite local pub, The Eagle, "what's your take on creation?"

With a furrowed brow, Peter looked at me and must have seen the earnest passion in my gray eyes. Looking down into his pint, Peter said so that the rest of the patrons could not hear.

"Don't you think we should be cool about this subject?" Which for us signaled our shift to silent talking.

"Sure, no problem." I said.

Creation is serious business, Charles. It's serious to science. It's serious to every religion I have ever heard of. So what are you asking me? Quit being so cryptic.

Sure, I began. *If we suppose that at creation good was created, should there not be evil as well? Wouldn't the creation equation require balance to it, like the balancing of a chemical reaction? Like positive and negative numbers in mathematics? After all, how can you measure goodness if not against its opposite?*

Several moments passed before my brother responded. During that time, I couldn't help but grin at the pretty girl at the neighboring table.

The Big Bang Theory supports an ever-expanding model for the universe, which explains the observed red shifts in spiral nebulae. The problem with the Big Bang, philosophically, is how did it begin? What triggered that event? The Belgian priest, who first proposed this theory, himself remained mum about the "first mover who itself remained unmoved." What Aristotle, and later Thomas Aquinas, defined as God. Nowhere is there any mention of a balancing act between good and evil.

I downed my pint and replied. *Peter, do you think your beloved science has become too secular even to consider the possibility of the creation of good and evil? To the point that a Catholic priest can choose to ignore Aquinas?*

Peter stalled to think while looking into his half-finished pint. *Yes, Charles, I see your point. From a purely philosophical standpoint somehow good and evil must have been created. The real question is when. Put another way, in atomic theory there are lots of protons, electrons, and other sub-atomic particles floating around. Particles must appropriately arrange themselves to become stable atoms. So, it might be said, philosophically, that at creation, or when the Big Bang occurred, when these particles were created, so too were created particles called good and evil. But science cannot support such a thing.*

So, to summarize, I postulated, the creation of matter is the preserve of atomic theory and hard science, while the creation of good and evil is the stuff of philosophy, religion, and magic.

Charles, how can you place magic on a par with philosophy, much less religion?

Dear brother, isn't one the reflection of the other? Let me read something to you.

I put aside my pint, reached into my briefcase, and took out a thick book. Opening it, I quickly found the page.

"Peter, listen to this. This is what an Egyptologist thinks about the subject."

> From the Egyptian point of view we may say that there is no such thing as 'religion;' there was only 'heka,' the nearest English equivalent of which is magical power.

Smiling and simultaneously slamming the book closed, I put it away in triumph and continued my thought.

Isn't religion the theory, and magic the practical application of it? In many ways, Peter, we are pursuing the same goal. We're trying to make heads or tails out of our environment. You with physics and me with anthropology.

After another thoughtful pause between us, Peter drained his glass, which our waitress noted.

"Would you fine gentlemen like another round?"

Peter replied, "Yes, please! How did you know?"

"Two things. Your pints are bone dry and I could smell the wood burning." She cleverly quipped and turned to fetch our pints.

Then Peter challenged. *Charles if you wish to equate philosophy and religion with magic, then you have to define what you mean when you use those terms.*

Leaning my chin on my fist, I replied, *That's simple, Peter. To the ancients, magic represented an extension of religion, a practical tool used for good or evil, which in itself is a philosophical choice. In this definition of mine, I do not follow the time-honored dictates of Frazer or Malinowski, where magic is seen as separate from religion, something threatening, limited, and focused upon an individual's desires. To this opinion, no, I say. Magic, above all, is an activity that binds the tenets of religion.*

Peter, have you ever considered what the difference is between the words spoken in pious prayer or a magical spell? Well, there isn't one wit of difference. The problem is not with the word 'magic,' but instead with the interpretation of it.

That's quite profound, Charles. So, in your mind, magic is the tool that empowers religion. Have I got that right?

Exactly dear brother!

So, to extrapolate you believe that magic, as a tool, should have tangible characteristics, rules, and perhaps even laws by which one might wield it.

Now I beamed back at my brother with full enthusiasm, *Precisely again.*

But Charles, how are you going to investigate these characteristics, rules, and laws?

Through thorough and careful research.

Research on what?

Ancient texts that purport to be magical tools.

So where are you going to begin?

I already have. The Egyptians were well known for their magical texts. But I think the most fertile ground will be with the Sumerians. They were a prolific bunch who have some wicked curse texts.

At this point we paused while our refreshed pints appeared. Peter, ever the proper gentleman, slapped down a ten quid note.

Charles, in your studies have you come across any good magic?

Yes. Mostly love potions, healing spells, and the like. Amulets to protect children from harmful stings and bites. Poultices for ensuring an easy birth. Ancient medical documents are full of positive magic.

But Charles, which side of the magical coin attracts you the most? Good or evil?

CHAPTER 40
Cambridge, 1968

THE SEVENTH LESSON

The Creator granted the Second Soul free will, freed it of all responsibility, and allowed it to evolve through incarnation. Thusly, the Creator caused a vast proliferation of such souls, as these were all destined for perfection, something only attainable through myriads of incarnations wherein the soul, like beaten iron, slowly perfected itself through the hard experience of mortal existence.

The Knot of Eternity. (trans.) G. L. Love. 2nd. edition with T. Good. (Old Oaks Academy Press, 1960), vol. I.1, 14.

Throughout our Cambridge University days, we continued to discuss the place of magic and its relationship to science and religion. For the most part, our *tête-à têtes* remained civil, good natured, and we conducted these contests using our silent speech. Any meal presented a perfect cover, with our mouths preoccupied, our minds raged unheard. But not this time.

During one of our many brazen luncheon discussions, which took place in the central dining room of our college, another person followed our hidden conversation with great interest. This interloper observed us, for several members of his society had become aware of our unique mode of communicating with each other.

After some digging after the fact, I discovered that

Jeremy Stokes' family had been members of The International Integrated Interface Society for over four generations. Like many of its membership, the Stokes' hereditary line possessed a genetic propensity for telepathy and Jeremy carried the gene.

Stokes took full advantage of the fact that we thought ourselves secure, when he placed his food tray down on the unoccupied table next to us. What made Jeremy so good at what he did, telepathic eavesdropping, was that he could simultaneously block his own thoughts while he listened in. In short, Jeremy thought of himself as a perfect fly on the wall.

*   *   *

Charles, Peter argued, *I will grant you magic is part of the paranormal landscape, but what then are its rules? And if you can assert it does have rules, then does it also have limitations? Does, for instance, magical energy, whatever that is, follow physical laws? Like the conservation of energy? Newtonian physics? Can the casting of a spell exhaust the conjurer? Do magical devices or props help focus a spell? Or enhance the power of one? Must one be some sort of sensitive or adept to use it? Or, can one be trained to use it?*

On the face of it, I cannot accept that magic is on a par with science. Science and magic do not operate in the same space, they are not comparable. Science theorizes, gathers data, measures it, and then verifies whether a theory is correct. Dear brother, have you even considered magic might be willfully arbitrary?

*   *   *

When Jeremy sat down to address his lunch of fish and chips, that's what he first "heard." The clarity, logic, composition, and subject matter caused him to swamp his chips with vinegar. The transmission flowed so naturally he rated their talent as excellent.

Daring to glance about he saw that the two students at the neighboring table looked for all the world engrossed in their lunches, eating with both hands, and sipping on their beverages as well. Neither seemed stressed or preoccupied. Quite the contrary, they multi-tasked at a furious rate and only occasionally raised their eyes to emphasize a given point.

*　　*　　*

Peter, if we both believe magic exists, then there must also be people who are very good at it. Can you accept that?

Actually, brother, I can, and it troubles me.

Why?

Because if I do accept there are practicing witches and wizards out there, then where did they learn their craft and from whom? Did they have textbooks? But even more crucial, are they practicing their magic blindly, haphazardly? That, to me, sounds like a very dangerous course. Which leads me back to the entire question of rules.

*　　*　　*

At that last statement Jeremy choked on his food. Having made a mess of his lunch, Stokes cleaned up after himself, glanced at his watch, and left the college cafeteria in a hurry, as if late for a forgotten appointment. He had heard more than enough to fill out a report to his local chapter of the society. Besides, he had serious doubts whether his psychic block would have even worked against these two if they had detected him.

*　　*　　*

The Membership Committee of The International Integrated Interface Society studied Jeremy Stokes' report on the Smithers twins.

"The candidates under review must be interviewed before we can recommend any other action. Given both young men are consenting adults, I suggest that they be approached directly and without subterfuge," stated the middle-aged chairman of the committee, as he closed the two personal files.

"How should we do this? By a posted invitation?" the gray-haired woman to his left suggested.

"Yes, I believe that should be sufficient with these two," the middle-aged man said. "Charles, by his own nature, will respond on his own. But as for Peter, that might be more of a challenge. He seems to be the more skeptical of the two. Regardless, Millie, kindly send out the invitations and let's see what falls out."

*　　*　　*

Three days later, again during lunch, we discussed a most curious development: a dinner invitation from an organization called The International Integrated Interface Society.

What sort of name is that for an organization? I scoffed. *Peter, have you ever heard of it before?*

No, and I haven't the faintest idea what it stands for either. I've checked, but it seems they delve to paranormal research of some kind. It's an international organization, and an old one, too. Seems that it's gone through several name iterations over the years. Other than that, there's not much to go on, shrugged Peter.

Paranormal research, dear brother?

Indeed. And that troubles me. How did they single us out for their invitation? Peter frowned.

Could they have detected us somehow?

That would imply that they themselves are telepathic, Peter thought with widened eyes. *There are others...literally in our midst?*

Perhaps those others could answer some of our questions about magic, science and religion. Wouldn't that be grand. So are you going, Peter?

Another shrug.

Can't hurt. I agree the possibility of getting some questions answered appeals to me. A free dinner at a reputable address on High Street. Right next to old Trinity Church. That means five stars and coat and tie, Charles. And no jeans, either.

Peter, is that restaurant housed in the old Bottisham Church School?

Seems to be the place. Why?

Because its located adjacent to hallowed ground. Right next to Trinity. That's all.

Charles. Peter allowed a frown. *Are you getting all weird on me about this 'hallowed ground' thing?*

No...just teasing.

*   *   *

For a change, that evening shaped up to be clear and

crisp, instead of rainy. So we decided to walk and arrived at the restaurant five minutes early. That gave us the opportunity to take in the old school's rough limestone blocking, steeply pitched gray slate roof, and high arched windows, which let out a warm, mellow, yellow glow of greeting. As we neared the arched entrance and its twin wooden doors, we noticed affixed to the right jam a small, tasteful notice that read.

CLOSED THIS EVENING
PRIVATE PARTY
BY INVITATION ONLY

Peter said, "Shit. I forgot to bring my invitation."

"Don't worry. They'll have a list inside. They always do. Let's go," I said impulsively as I wrenched open the massive right door. "Follow me and act like you're supposed to be here."

When we entered soft candlelight, and the glorious smells of fresh baked bread enveloped us. A long table, set with plates and silverware for twelve stretched out before us. The lighted candle flames danced across and reflected through the fine stemware.

"Wow. Nice," I whispered.

The door closed with a thud behind us and a tallish middle-aged man, in a tailored dark wool suit, appeared from around the corner.

"Ah, splendid," he said rubbing his hands together, "our guests have arrived."

As it turned out, we were the only guests for this soiree. Quite by design, each of us sat toward the opposite ends of the table. Once so ensconced, ten pairs of eyes took us in. We, as one, noted that no matter whether male or female, young or old, all of our hosts possessed penetrating eyes that seemed to look into our souls and we found the intense scrutiny unnerving.

I blundered and first made mention of it, when I shared my first impressions with Peter.

Peter. This dinner gathering is strange.

This comment caused the most curious reaction, as all ten of our hosts stopped and turned to look at me.

Seeing this, we threw up our mental shields, and in essence, zipped our minds closed. For Peter, the image he liked to use consisted of a painted, box turtle. A fond memory from his childhood investigating the neighborhood streams and ponds. For me, I dropped my iron portcullis gate with an authoritative boom.

"Mr. Charles Smithers," the gray-haired woman named Millie, who sat across from me, stated with considerable gravity, "while we accept and applaud your casual use of telepathy with your twin brother, have you ever considered its use to be impolite around others of similar skill? Or even worse, around those without it? You never know, we might be listening in, in spite of your rudimentary blocking. So, if you gentlemen don't mind, would you please use your young vocal cords?"

At this revelation, we shared a quick look.

At this juncture the middle-aged man in the custom-tailored suit began the proceedings.

"Gentlemen, welcome to our little dinner party. My name is Henry Crows and I'm the reason you are here. I am the head of our local chapter of The International Integrated Interface Society. You no doubt wonder what we do, what we stand for, and why you have been invited to dine with us. Firstly, to enjoy a fine meal among equals. Secondly, to discover how able you are.

You see, Peter and Charles," he said nodded to each of us, "we know about your well-developed telepathy. What we want to know is whether you share any other forms of psychic or paranormal abilities."

The appearance of six waiters suddenly interrupted him, each carrying two bowls of soup, the first course. After the waiters withdrew, he continued.

"As for our organization, the T, triple-I, S is a paranormal research organization. Our members display a wide variety of abilities ranging from sensitive clairvoyants to telekinetic adepts. We provide training and instruction. We support what is referred to as white magic. We combat the opposite. And trust me when I say this–evil is quite real. We feel our organization is a bulwark against the darkness, and we are ever on the lookout for new members to join us in our quest to defeat it.

"From your faces, I can see that you, Charles, are fascinated and excited at the prospect of joining us. But as for you Peter, you are a man that demands something more substantial, our society's mission statement perhaps...But first, let us attend to the first course before it chills."

* * *

As we walked back to our dormitories later that evening, we both admitted our mental exhaustion. Never before had either of us been so intensely quizzed, while maintaining our "rudimentary" mental shields.

Finally, Peter summed up the evening best, "Now I know what a PhD oral exam must be like."

* * *

"Well, well. We now have the final tally as to who we should extend a membership to," Crows stated. "The results I find surprising, but a vote is a vote, and I am not one to challenge the collective wisdom of the chapter.

"Mr. Peter Smithers will be extended an invitation, while his brother, Charles, will not."

Millie cocked her head and asked, "How close was it? I mean, the vote on Charles. I thought the lad was the more gifted of the pair."

"Not close at all, Millie. Seven against and only two for."

"Who didn't vote?"

"I didn't."

"Why, Henry?"

"I found his aura all wrong."

"Really. What did you see?"

"Muddied greens, yellows with a hint of brown. Not a pastel hue to be found. His brother Peter, on the other hand, displayed one of the brightest silver-blues I have ever seen. Simply breathtaking."

"Are Charles' muddied hues in any way redeemable?" Millie inquired. "He seemed so promising, so hopeful."

"There is always hope. People do change. But in my experience, someone as old as Charles would be a difficult one to turn. He's far more set in his ways than he perhaps realizes. He carries some significant baggage and there's something else that I couldn't put my finger on. Well, that is why I abstained from voting on him. I didn't think my qualms should be counted. But just wait, Millie. He could indeed change *if* he wished to."

*   *   *

Three days later, Peter received in the post his invitation, while I did not.

In my mind, this disappointment reminded me of the birthday cake slight all over again, only this time, far, far worse. After all, I had been the one searching for just such an organization, and now that I had found it, the bastards had rejected me. As for my stiff, empirical brother, he joined forthwith, and became in my eyes something less of a brother for it.

How could they turn their backs on me? That wasn't fair! I raged and raged and all for naught.

There and then, I planted my first handful of seeds, seeds of pure, virulent hate for TIIIS, and all that it stood for.

They will suffer this slight against me.

CHAPTER 41
Parting Ways, 1969

When we graduated from Cambridge in 1969, we did so with honors. Peter pursued the sciences, while I earned degrees in the humanities and made my own plans.

Four years later, I learned that my brother Peter earned his hood with a PhD in theoretical physics from his alma mater and found employment within the British military establishment. Always curious about everything, I knew that Peter's inquisitive mind would led him far and wide. In fact, I remember thinking at the time how I very much doubted that he would be happy at his first post. So when I found out the he had later secured a post within TIIIS, and as a researcher, I jumped for joy for him.

Little did I know, however, where he would be located, deep in a Pennsylvania wood, at the Old Oaks Academy campus, TIIIS's center of research and training. Yes, I remained jealous and hurt, but for Peter, I continued to only wish him well. I suspected that much which lay before him he and I had long discussed. On more than one occasion, I felt him thinking about me and me of him. Even of the possibility of me being examined again, and perhaps, just perhaps, of the two of us working side by side.

Peter didn't know where I had gone following university. We had split up rather abruptly, and for that I own the guilt. Soon afterwards, rumors abounded about a young adept, who once even defaced the exterior of the Cambridge-based TIIIS enclave's meeting place.

*   *   *

"Yes! I did that! I admit I indeed defaced the meeting place of those weak-minded pretenders!" Raged a wide-eyed Charles Smithers, more than drunk, to a group of entertained pub listeners.

"They had their opportunity and they blew it!" Charles concluded with a swing of his empty tankard as he fell back into his seat.

"So, Charles, what is it you're looking for?" came the reasonable question from a pretty face.

"A paranormal community that can teach me new skills, hone my native ones, and not preach to me about ethical standards all day long," he slurred.

"Well, Charles, it seems to me being a punk graffiti artist is not far from pure vandalism. Is that how you truly wish to make yourself attractive to them?" She purred. "You'll have to do something more, Charles. Do some traveling, perhaps learn some skills on your own first. Then try to find them."

The very next day, Charles made up his mind and impulsively left Cambridge for the Continent without so much as a goodbye to Peter.

*   *   *

Once on the Continent, I made advances in my unorthodox investigations into the paranormal, but I struggled with some issues. The biggest was rejection, which outright fueled my personal quest to make TIIIS eat crow. Perhaps irrationally, I wanted to make them pay. Their rejection of my membership had hurt deeply. But worse, TIIIS had denied me, of all people, the opportunity to be trained in the magical arts.

With my family's inheritance behind me, I toured the Continent, and during a chance visit in Munich, this restless and wandering soul came upon an odd leather bound notebook in an antiquarian's bookshop. The patina of it suggested a long and varied past. The yellowed outer margins of its heavy paper leaves only reinforced that impression. At first glance, it appeared to be filled with nothing but column after column of cuneiform characters. Then, I noticed here and there the minuscule and crabbed penmanship of a German writer, which seemed to be commenting upon the wedge-shaped figures.

The notebook originated from the Nazi Era, or so said the book seller. The personal inscription on the inside cover indicated its original owner as Professor Dr. Berthold Thaddeus, assistant director of the *Reichsministerium für Volksaufklärung und Propaganda* and lecturer of ancient Near Eastern Languages at the University of Berlin. In my eyes that made the slim tome interesting, a collectable, a must-have. After all, that made Thaddeus part of the Nazi fascination for magical artifacts, led by Joseph Goebbels. As one might expect, that fact made its price steep, but I paid it anyway.

With the notebook in my possession, I applied myself to translate the German portion, as I had no training in how to read the *Keilschriften*. That deficiency I would address in due time. The German commentary spoke of a special set of clay tablets, housed in the *Vorderasiatische Museum*, trapped behind The Wall in East Berlin. Their purported content claimed to include magic, curses, and the summoning of demons by name.

I sensed a defining moment and began studying anything and everything I could find about the magical world of the ancient Near East. Along the way, I made a point to visit East Berlin, passed myself off as a graduate student in ancient history, and gained access to the museum's *Keilschrift Sammlung.* Guided by the inventory numbers mentioned in my notebook, I stole one hundred and fifteen tablet fragments from the museum's collection over the period of some two weeks. I just had to have them.

In the storage trays of the originals, I inserted cuneiform tablet paperweights–tourist kitsch. The originals I smuggled from East to West Berlin on a daily basis, walking them across the checkpoint in the false bottom of my briefcase while en route to my West German hotel. These became my crown jewels, my tickets into the shadowy world of the paranormal. I cared for them in every way and commissioned the customization of six West German rifle cases to store them.

With my rifle cases in tow, I returned to Munich and enrolled in its fine university. There I concentrated on the ancient Near East, where in the course of four semesters I became proficient in the Sumerian tongue, the language of my tablets. With both the tablets and the notebook's commentary, this unconventional rogue thinker crafted his translations.

Once satisfied with my translations, I rationalized that the stolen tablets had become a physical and psychic burden. Being around them caused intense negativity and depression that affected my thinking. After all, I had the notebook, its commentary, and my own handwritten transcriptions of the tablet fragments, and their translation, which included several additional spells. So in one swift move, I dumped them on a Munich antiquity's dealer for a pittance along with all the legal and psychic liabilities they represented.

*   *   *

A West German Egyptologist by the name of Hans Manfred Glass soon was contacted by the same Munich antiquity's dealer, who claimed he had in his possession a cache of East German relics, complete with what appeared to be museum cataloging numbers. Intrigued, Glass visited the modest shop on Amalienstraβe located near the university. Once there, Glass for the first time gazed upon no fewer than six wooden rifle crates, each with interiors subdivided into neat, square spaces, filled broken clay tablets, all nested in their own cotton batting.

While Glass recognized them, he himself could not read the documents. Nor did he recognize their affixed numbers, but he knew of a colleague who could, and so promised to return the next day.

Two weeks later, Glass did return with his colleague in tow. However, the antiquities dealer no longer had the collection. Three days before, an American from Philadelphia had bought all six rifle crates for cash.

CHAPTER 42
The Conjurer

Every army has a core of willing recruits, led by committed veterans. The problem, as the radical religious leadership saw it, stemmed from the pervasive technical influence of the West, which often stole willing recruits. The technology of the Great Satan, above all being the Internet, sapped away their recruiting source–the young, idealistic, and gullible. Religious zealots, who twisted the Koranic teachings into a modern-day call for radical *jihad*, could have their lies backchecked in mere moments. In short, the Internet questioned the *imams'* dogmatic control. Never mind the Internet provided to the entire world the latest beheading of a Westerner in vivid detail, or promulgated their latest radical message of medieval hate.

The movement needed an infusion of easily radicalized and energetic youths–those yet to finish their secondary education.

*　　*　　*

After Charles Smithers' acquisition of the Berlin notebook of Sumerian spells, a colleague at Munich University introduced him to others also interested in investigating the more esoteric side of ancient religions. While the Brit at first hesitated to join their circle, he nonetheless learned a sufficient amount of esoteric knowledge, which launched him further along on his quest.

Charles stopped next in Rome, where he briefly fell under the allure of a shadowy organization referred to as The Gathering. There he studied under their *veneficas imperium*, "imperial witches." For a time, the Cambridge man found himself in his element. But as the months passed, the wandering adept learned, grew, and then outgrew his smothering, narrow-minded, and insular teachers. And once again, Charles moved on, this time to study in Central Asia.

After brief visits with several East Indian religious sects, and the monks of the Hindu Kush, Charles turned around and settled in with an obscure aesthetic Aryan enclave in northern-most India. There he immersed himself in Sanskrit texts that offered much in the way of personal protections, spell casting, and astral projection, many of which he had affixed to his body in the form of tattoos.

While Charles did not realize it, his personal journey paralleled that of his estranged brother Peter, who at the age of thirty-seven had become the TIIIS Lictor of Magic. In typical dualistic twin style, Charles had become an anti-lictor of magic, all on his own.

By 2005, Charles had aged. While clean-shaven, he chose to wear his long white hair across his shoulders. He possessed a constitution that seemed to rebel against any infirmity. His stride remained as brisk as his mind, his body well-toned, like a taunt bow string. When Charles walked into a room, people naturally turned to him. Needless to say, he enjoyed the attention, played up to it, and basked in its emotional warmth, like a lizard on a rock at high noon.

Once a British citizen, Charles had acclimated, as an expatriate, to the wilds of Pakistan. Looking back, he smiled, whenever he recollected his youth during the experimental and turbulent sixties, the London scene, and of course, the Beatles and the Rolling Stones, before they had made it big.

Now advanced in years, Charles became quite set in his ways. He despised modern technology. An avowed Luddite, he instead embraced magic as the basis for a new, more naturalistic science. Since the West invented, promoted, and evangelized technology in all of its forms, Charles found himself quite sympathetic to any cause that would bring about the West's destabilization and eventual fall from grace.

With a mindset and magical reputation established among the frontier peoples of northeastern Pakistan, Charles found kindred spirits, not many, but enough to satisfy the ego of this self-proclaimed, self-made adept and holy man.

They came to him for simple, small things. A love potion, a reading of a palm, the determination of the sex of an unborn child, the blessing of a household, the blessing of their goats—in short, the usual sorts of things that concerned mountain folk. Charles in turn provided his followers harmless parlor tricks that provided hope and peace of mind.

However, rumors circulated that other magical acts could be performed, but of a far darker variety. Such services came at a steep price, made known through whispers, by those who had requested such godless assistance.

During times of regional civil war, business boomed for Charles. Internecine tribal conflicts, that pivoted upon personal power and standing, often sought him out in search of an unfair advantage. More often, tribal hatreds, which ran high, employed his talents. Death curses always remained in high demand, while other, far more heinous magical spells, could be acquired.

*   *   *

One evening, a rolling junkyard of a car drove up and parked in front of Charles' modest household on the outskirts of Taxilia, a town located west of Islamabad. From it, three men exited, who trudged their way through the open gate of the forecourt and along the flagstone path to its main entrance.

One of them, with considerable trepidation, knocked on the door frame. When the door grate opened, he inquired, "We seek an audience with The Conjurer. May we do so at this time?"

The young boy nodded, opened the door, bowed deeply to the trio, and said in their native Pashto tongue. "We have been expecting you. It will be but a moment. The man you seek is mediating. In the meantime, may I offer you some refreshment after your long journey? Clear water, tea, or juice perhaps?"

At this statement, the three men shared quick glances with one another, for all found themselves disturbed that the Conjurer had expected them. But to his offer of hospitality, they decided as one.

"No, thank you."

"Then, may I suggest that you make yourselves comfortable in the receiving room. I have dusted and fluffed the pillows. Please be at ease," gestured the boy, who guided them to their places, and then disappeared around the corner.

Five minutes later, an old man, clean-shaven, bare foot, and dressed in white robes, appeared before them. The lack of a beard disturbed them. Nonetheless, out of respect, the three rose.

With a raised open hand, the old man said in their native Pashto, "Be at ease, my brothers. You are my guests, and all rules of hospitality must be met."

The three, wide-eyed and confused, glanced between themselves. The old man read their minds easily.

Rules of hospitality? And how did he and the boy know we only spoke Pashto?

"You are perhaps disturbed by my appearance?" the old man asked with his arms open and palms facing them. "It is true, I am not a believer of Allah. But I have memorized the Koran and can argue any stanza or verse with you, or with any *imam,* for that matter. Are you prepared to do so? No? Forgive me if I am not surprised. After all, you are men of great responsibility and courage. Is that not so?"

The old man paused for effect while his guests all bowed their heads in reflexive acknowledgment.

"Yet, here you are, having traveled so far, and through hostile territory as well. That means your purpose is a serious one. Perhaps, even dire. You did not hazard the journey to drink weak tea and nibble on stale bread. No. Your purpose must be a *most* strategic one."

How does he know these things? The first speaker thought in utter amazement as the old man let his words hang in the air.

"I wonder what that most strategic purpose might be?" the old man concluded with his chin held high, his steady gaze transfixing them all. Then in one fluid motion he sat before them, cross legged, on the bare floor, and waited.

All in all, Charles judged his entrance and opening monologue a success, one calculated to take command and establish without question the alpha male. Judging from the surprise and general speechlessness of his guests, Charles concluded he had indeed been successful.

Finally, the original speaker found his tongue. "Conjurer, you speak the truth. Our journey has been long and arduous, and our purpose is most serious. We are having difficulties recruiting sufficient true believers to our most righteous cause. They flee their homeland for the allures of the city, where they fall under the *spell* of the western world. If we are to continue our cause, we need your *wisdom* and *assistance* in this matter."

Charles grasped the coded inferences to "spell," "wisdom," and "assistance" in the Afghan's opening statement. That meant these three angled for something that none dared to verbally express, but could only allude to.

"So, it is recruits that you require," the old man concluded pinching his lip theatrically between his thumb and forefinger. "Young men who will do whatever they are told, whenever they are commanded to do so, am I correct? Or, have I misunderstood your *desire*?"

In an almost breathless response, the first speaker answered. "That is our wish, Conjurer. To have obedient and willing recruits for our cause."

"And that cause would be...what?"

"The return of the Caliphate, of course," the first speaker answered.

"Ah, I see. This is both a military matter and one of great mystic prophecy. I now better understand. How might I be of service?" the old man said with a deep bow of his white haired head.

For the first time, the third man spoke. "We require one hundred men within a month's time, as the siege of one of our cities is not going well. Re-enforcements are needed desperately. Otherwise, the many efforts of our brothers in Syria and Iraq will be for naught."

Slowly tapping his front teeth with a boney finger, Charles replied, "One hundred men in one month's time. That, my brothers, is quite a challenge. But this is one I shall embrace...for a price."

"Whatever the price is, we shall pay it!" the second man immediately answered.

Charles looked up and calculated in his head what his fee would be for this "righteous cause."

Then, he coolly said, "I require one hundred kilos of opium, one kilo per man."

Shocked at the sum, only the second man said, "It is agreed. Here is my card. Call me when *it* is done."

*   *   *

Charles did not expect the negotiations to go so smoothly. That told him two things. One, these men were beyond desperate. And two, they dealt in deception, as no respectable mountain Afghani would have so caved during a negotiation, much less in such a shameless manner. So that meant the second man represented the front man, a businessman, the purse strings, perhaps even a banker, of an undermanned operation. His entire demeanor shrieked business school, right down to his flashy business card presented out in this frontier wilderness. The manner in which the third spoke, with clear objectives, marked as the commander desperate for troops. As for the first speaker, he spoke with a respectful tone, hence Charles reasoned, the only true Afghan of the party.

CHAPTER 43
My "Oh Shit!" Moment

THE EIGHTH LESSON

Mortal imagination and their raw emotions of fear and hope fashioned demons and angels. Mortal thought created the energy out of which these constructs came to be. As a consequence, demons and angels are imperfect constructs of mortal mind. They exist solely for a given task, nothing more. They have many forms, many names, and so can be easily conjured into the mortal world by the reckless and foolhardy.

The Knot of Eternity. (trans.) G. L. Love. 2nd. edition with T. Good. (Old Oaks Academy Press, 1960), vol. I.1, 15.

I turned in my thesis outline to Professor Glass several days early. Then, I went back to work on the translation of Tablet C. Again accessing the handy online version of the *Pennsylvania Sumerian Dictionary* by that afternoon I had crafted a pretty good working translation. Not polished, but close. Little did I know.

Lines 1-4

> Mighty Enlil, destroyer, slaughterer, come forth!
>
> Mark this evil one as you would any beast!
>
> Throw this evil one's head from the city wall, open the city-gates and allow all to trample upon it.
>
> Holy Inanna, bless this act.

Lines 4-8

Mighty Enlil, destroyer, slaughterer, come forth!

Cut this evil one as you would sacrifice a willing calf!

Throw this evil one's entrails into the pit and burn them.

Holy Inanna, bless this act.

Lines 8-12

Mighty Enlil, destroyer, slaughterer, come forth!

Name this evil one as it which inhabits the Underworld.

Defile this evil one's name as if it were the name of a traitor.

Remove this evil one's name from all record as if it were befoulment.

Holy Inanna, bless this act.

Lines 13-16

Might Enlil, destroyer, slaughterer, come forth!

Curse the name, MERUSUIK, which inhabits the Underworld.

Defile it as if it were drunk with wine.

Holy Inanna, bless this act.

Lines 17-22

Mighty Enlil, destroyer, slaughterer, come forth!

Banish this evil one back to the Underworld with a draught of spittle, once.

Enlil, the roaring storm that subjugates the entire land, banish this evil one back with a draught of spittle, twice.

Compel this evil one back to the Underworld with a draught of spittle, thrice.

Holy Inanna, bless this act.

In short, the words constructed a powerful conjuring for a minion of the Underworld called MERUSUIK. It called for its marking, cutting, naming, cursing, and banishment. This last accomplished with three "draughts of spittle."

The continuous refrain of "Holy Inanna, bless this act" suggested a connection to the city of Ur, as the guardian deity Inanna resided there. While written in literate Sumerian, the grammar, formation, and vocabulary of the inscription, suggested a later date. Almost as if someone composed today a witch's spell and then wrote it in old English. Regardless, I thought a sound translation of this tablet alone, accompanied by a commentary, would make a fine senior thesis, acceptable for publication.

* * *

"So, Mr. Stone, where should we go for lunch. I'm famished," Professor Makris said first thing.

"Well, ma'am, do you like student dive bars with dynamite hamburgers, or, perhaps something with tables covered in linen?"

"Hmm. Well, since I am on a budget, let's try the

dive bar with burgers."

"Good choice! You won't be disappointed."

As we walked to The Greasy Onion, we talked about a lot of things. She breezily explained that she made a visit to Philly to touch base with Peter, as she had applied for a one year sabbatical at the Met.

Wednesday lunch at The Greasy Onion turned out great. There's nothing like a cheeseburger with all the fixings. While potentially sloppy, when cut in half even a lady like Professor Makris could dig in and come out unscathed.

Our hunger satisfied, the discussion about ancient Near East magic provided me insights that I could not have imagined. After all, only eight complete tablets and three incomplete and unintelligible ones defined my world. Meanwhile, Professor Makris told me about a private compilation of family spells, passed on from generation to generation. I found it all so intriguing, like a family Bible, wherein each generation made their mark.

"So what language is this family book of spells written in?"

"Ancient Egyptian Demotic. But what I am finding is that the later Coptic language borrowed from the Demotic magical vocabulary, and in turn, the Demotic from the pharaonic magical corpus. In essence, secular magic seems to have been very much a hand-me-down industry."

I sat there stunned as I held my head in my hands.

"But enough about me and my research. I heard first-hand your presentation on the soul container in San Francisco. I marveled that your sure delivery and the logic of your conclusions, made such eminent sense.

Are you an adept, Mr. Stone?" Makris angled.

I reacted to that question with beer coming out of my nose. Not exactly good form. As I cleaned myself up, she said, "Can I take that as a 'yes,' Mr. Stone?"

"Professor Makris, I am in no way 'an adept,' and I haven't a clue as to what it takes to become one. So, no, Professor Makris, I am not an adept."

"You know that famous line of Shakespeare that goes, 'The lady doth protest too much, methinks'?"

"I'm sorry, professor, but I know squat about Shakespeare."

"Well, Mr. Stone, what I'm implying is you know far more than you're willing to admit. I believe that your American expression, 'fessing up,' is appropriate here. What I find so intriguing is you're Peter's fair-haired boy and now you're playing coy. Why is that, Mr. Stone?"

I could feel my face redden, as I didn't see me as anybody's "fair-haired boy." Then, I remembered Adam's admonition to stay cool, calm, and collected around the West Coast types.

"I could counter that with one of my own. That's a very personal question. What's your need to know, professor?" I said coolly.

She paused and stared at me. I felt a distinct tingling along my scalp, recognized it, and immediately erected my mental shields to the max. In response, Professor Makris blinked, and blinked again hard.

"Well, Mr. Stone, it seems I have my answer. While you insist you're not an adept, I do believe we have established that you are certainly something. The question now is, what?"

"Why the third degree, professor?"

"Because Mr. Stone, Peter believes you would make a 'fine addition' to our research group on ancient Near Eastern magic. I am trying to find out why."

I looked down at my hands while I considered what would be the best way to approach this delicate subject.

"Professor Makris, I will say this, off-the-record. I have seen and experienced my fair share of special things. From most of those instances, I have learned a lot. But at the same time, I know I have only glimpsed the tip of a vast iceberg. But since your aura is made up of yellow and teal hues, I willing to gamble you're a reasonably safe person to have an extraordinary conversation with."

First, she gulped at my characterization of her aura and what it indicated. And then I let her have it, both barrels, and I told her my entire story. Fifteen minutes later, I finished, and then downed the remainder of my warm beer. Yes, I had become that parched.

"My God," she said. "So that explains your golden aura."

Then she proceeded to tell me her story. In the end I felt relieved. Yes, I had my suspicions about Peter and Running Deer, but they remained foggy notions without clear boundaries. Bottom line: I no longer stood alone in this mysterious paranormal world. While I still didn't know where I was going, it felt comforting that at least one other was in the same boat. Best of all, we parted as friends. Mel is quite a lady.

*　　*　　*

Around five that afternoon, after that heavy lunch with Professor Makris, followed by my German reading class, I staggered back to my office. As I worked on the transliteration of Tablet C, I discovered a beguiling tonal cadence to the conjuring's words. My lips moved unbidden. For some imbecilic reason, perhaps just pure fatigue, I murmured aloud the spell and pronounced the name of the Underworld demon in question.

*　　*　　*

Somewhere within the nourishing embrace of the light realm, Erish started as if struck by a lightning bolt.

Nergal, we must protect J. J.! Erish screamed. *He has done something incredibly unwise!*

*　　*　　*

I first heard it as the strange skittering of chitinous claws crossing the wooden floor of my office. It started by the banquet table beneath Tablet C, which was still nested in its cotton batting. For some reason, I raised my feet above the floor, as the biggest, blackest scorpion I have ever seen passed beneath me.

"Holy shit!" exploded from my lips as I scrambled to the top of my desk, toppling over my chair.

*　　*　　*

Get atop your desk! Nergal commanded.

Then he ordered, *Spit upon it thrice. Quickly, before it begins to grow.*

*　　*　　*

Grow? My brain screamed. *The spell never said anything about that.*

Well, spitting on a scurrying scorpion from the Underworld is not an easy thing to do—much less one you have been told is growing. Fortunately, the demon proved to be dumber than dirt, mindlessly going this way and that, back and forth, across the tiny floor of my office.

Atop my desk on my knees, I waited for it to pass by. I spit, and missed! Then I remembered another important thing. When you're scared shitless, you have no spit, or at least, not a whole bunch. As I hadn't kicked over my water bottle during my daring escape to my desk's top, I took a swig, washed it around, and waited for the demon scorpion to appear.

This time I nailed the sucker as it passed by my overturned chair. The scorpion, now the size of a two pound lobster, squealed in pain and scuttled off again to hit the wall board, bounce, and return again.

The second time I hit it, the demon struck the floor boards several times with its powerful stinger, as it smoldered in agony, clicking and clacking its fore claws in spasmodic desperation. Then, off it ran.

I waited, mouth again full and at the ready. But it too waited under my wooden desk, apparently learning, and didn't want to come out. Okay, so it no longer appeared as dumb as dirt. So I gripped the edge of the desk's top and started jerking the desk to one side in loud jumping, thumps.

The movement startled the demon scorpion into moving. As it emerged from beneath the desk, this denizen from the Underworld had grown to the size of a small dog! Its tail, arched at the ready, struck the desk just below my fingertips. Its impact left behind a gooey, dripping yellowish fluid.

Jesus! I thought as I reflexively jerked my hand back just in time, and spit. Again I nailed that sucker for the third time. Given its larger size, I couldn't miss.

What an odd death. It sort of crumpled in upon itself, shrinking, until nothing remained of it, but an evaporating black haze. Where it had struck the floor with its stinger, the residue of its poison had disappeared as well. Only the impact marks of its stinger on the floor and desk remained.

* * *

Don't do that again! Nergal said in obvious and breathless chastisement.

"No shit," I murmured. Then thought, *Nergal! Where are you?*

Nearby. At least for now, before Erish and I pass on to a new incarnation.

We are tired. This intervention has cost us dearly good friend, J. J., so please remain vigilant.

* * *

I don't remember how long I stayed atop my desk. I had just conjured up an Underworld demon, had Nergal scream into my psychic ear, and then banished the demon scorpion back to wherever. I still knelt there when my office door flew open and Professor Glass appeared.

With a curious look on his face that threatened to split in laughter, me atop my desk, my chair overturned, and with water all over the floor.

He said in his typical accent, "Is everything alright, Mr. Stone? I must say I heard some strange noises."

I got down from my desk, my bones creaking, and my face all lathered in sweat. I wiped it off with my hands, looked at the man, picked up my chair, and offered it to him.

"Sit, sir," I said. "We gotta' talk."

*   *   *

"Professor Glass," I began, gesturing to the tablets arrayed around my office, "these tablets, where did you get them?"

"Where do you think I got them?"

"Well, from the internal evidence from one of them, Ur is a safe bet."

"That is very possible. Now I have a question for you. Why were you kneeling atop your desk?"

"I wasn't praying to Mecca, Professor. I just avoided a demon scorpion I accidentally conjured from the Underworld."

At my direct answer, Glass' face went pale. Then he said in a whisper, "Describe it."

Well, I did, and then placed before him the eight fragments of Tablet C, along with my rough translation of it.

"So, this MERU..."

"Stop right there Professor!" I said with an outstretched palm. "You utter that name and we'll have our hands full again, but this time with the two of us atop my desk."

Now chastened, Glass said, "So the thrice spittle did indeed send this, this thing, back to the Underworld?"

"Professor, that I don't know for sure, but it did shrivel up and disappear, even the poison where it stuck the floor and my desk with its stinger. Here, look for yourself."

We both got down on our hands and knees to inspect the seven sharp, all-too-fresh gouges in my office's wooden floor and desk's side panel.

As Glass felt the marks with the tips of his fingers his face winced as if that alone confirmed my outlandish claim.

Then, getting up and brushing off his slacks he said, "Mr. Stone, I believe every single word you said. And here's why. It's the same story my father told me about a similar tablet."

Then the good professor surprised me, stuck out his hand, and said, "By the way, my name is Peter."

*   *   *

Professor Glass and I met that evening at The Greasy Onion. I felt like I had never left the place since I had been there earlier with Professor Makris. So we grabbed a quiet place in the back—me, who looked like a former dive bar bouncer, and Peter, a young Einstein. It didn't take long before we accumulated a small forest of empty beer bottles.

"For this particular demon," Peter explained, "not only does spittle work, but immersing it in clear water, or drenching it with rain. It seems that these scuttling scorpion demons abound throughout the ancient Near East, a place where the possibility of chance precipitation or immersion remained slight. On the other hand, for a mortal to come into contact with this entity, means demonic possession, and the sending of the mortal's soul, to the Underworld."

"How do you know all of this, Peter?" I asked.

"Well, when you finish reading the rest of the tablets, you will discover clear, fresh running water is a recurring remedy, a powerful force against evil. And that water from the body, spittle, sweat, and especially tears, are even more powerful defensive agents. For those who are possessed, total immersion seems to be the preferred method of casting out the demon and restoring the affected mortal's soul." Peter shifted uncomfortably.

"Remember, J. J., we are speaking of the demons of desert cultures. In the magical world, and that is what we are discussing here, that which is in opposition, is a tool or weapon against evil. This is why early Christian baptisms involved total emersion. A complete purging of anything evil or demonic from the individual. This is one reason why ancient Egyptian priests bathed three times a day. Not only to cleanse themselves, but also to purge themselves from any possibility of possession."

"So how can you tell that someone is possessed? Do they stagger about like zombies?" I asked.

"All the texts I have seen refer to these unfortunates as simple-minded, easily swayed and directed individuals, who often are attracted to acts of extraordinary cruelty, murder, rape, and the like."

"Who else knows about the contents of these tablets?"

"Only the two of us," Peter said. "However, the Nazis acquired them from the Ur and Nippur excavations sometime during the Second World War. Sounds a whole lot like Indiana Jones, doesn't it? Well, presumably, someone read them and perhaps recorded them somewhere. Beyond that, I don't know. But those acquisition numbers on them are not ours. They are those of the *Vorderasiastisches Museum* in Berlin. I have checked out that fact. If you go there today, you will discover a missing run of acquisition numbers in their catalogue that corresponds to the tablets in your office. How they made their way to our university's museum, now that's a story that begs to be told."

"So that explains the German rifle cases the tablets are stored in," I opined.

"Yes, it may indeed. But which Germany? The East or the West? I checked those boxes as well. They are of West German origin. So it seems these tablets somehow, someway, made it from the East to the West. All I can say is that the plot thickens."

I decided to ask a question that had been bugging me ever since lunch. "Peter. Is Professor Makris a witch?"

He chuckled. "Probably, most likely, J. J. I never inquire about those kinds of subjects with my close colleagues. I grant you she certainly has the aura of one, a white witch that is. Why?"

"She grilled me at lunch, that's all."

"Yeah, she can do that. She has a very penetrating mind. But you survived, didn't you?"

"Yes, sir. That I did."

I stopped to take a deep pull from my beer.

"So, Peter. How long have you been able to see auras?"

At first the scholar looked perplexed by the question. Then, as they say, the dawn broke.

"I did say Mel had the aura of a white witch, didn't I." He sheepishly said.

"Well, J. J., I learned how to see them at a young age. My father taught me." He recollected with mist in his eyes. "He told me that being able to do so would help me to tell the difference between friend and foe."

At that, we both drank deeply.

"Now, Peter, for the sixty-four dollar question. What am I to do for a senior thesis?"

"That's a good question, J. J. You could pursue this research or not. If you do choose to continue with the tablets, there is a *way* you can publish them and still be responsible about it. After all, you don't have to include *absolutely* everything. The tablets are broken into fragments. Breakage naturally creates gaps and unclear readings, which do not have to be transcribed and translated. Another way to approach the problem is to exclude from your study any tablet that calls forth a demon. That would leave you with only the publication of the curse tablets.

"Or," Peter sighed, "I can steer you to a safe haven. Something far less lethal. A simple translation project that deals with Biblical historical geography. Ultimately, the choice is up to you."

CHAPTER 44
100 Boys

The so-called Afghanis needed one hundred young men for their latest and greatest cause. So Charles contacted a nearby *madrassa*, or school, that catered to high school-aged males of the middle and upper classes. Given his extensive knowledge of the Koran, the faculty quickly approved a suitable lecture topic. After all, the school rarely had the opportunity to entertain a distinguished scholar, much less one that wished to speak to their student population.

The administration of this high-end institution considered the situation unprecedented, and one which they should try to replicate in the future. Its enthusiastic faculty even suggested they inaugurate an all-encompassing one-day seminar at the end of every school year. The budget could support it. This one a religious philosopher. Why not a scientist next? Or perhaps even an engineer or physician? The possibilities seemed endless.

Eager young faces filled with promise packed the auditorium to the gills the day of the lecture. All dressed in their school's uniform of maroon slacks and jacket, white shirt, and a gold tie, most of them had their iPhones and iPads out and cued to record the special event. No one wanted to miss a thing.

Then, an old, clean-shaven man with long white hair pull back in a long braid entered the hall carrying a cloth bag over one shoulder. Gliding barefoot in his tailored white suit toward the podium, a low buzz broke out among the audience. Many had never before seen such straight, white hair, much less a braid worn by a man. One student, a Christian, thought that he looked like an angel.

Organizing himself, the old man removed two plastic water bottles from his bag, placing them on the shelf beneath the podium for the purpose. Finished, he then placed his hands along the podium's sides, looked up, and waited for everyone's attention. After fifteen seconds, he had them. Not a cough, a drag of a shoe, or the squeak of a chair marred the pure silence.

The old man smiled and began to speak in a language no one could understand. A melodic oration punctuated with odd sounds, pitches, and inflections. As the man spoke, the air in the lecture hall seemed to thicken. Sounds became muffled, even the sound of the old man's strange words became difficult to perceive.

In the very midst of the packed room, something black began skittering about beneath their chairs. With every student's foot it encountered, the scorpion's tail rose and fell like a jackhammer. The many screams, squeals of panic, and calls for help could not be heard beyond the auditorium's walls. Those first afflicted, now held those not, so the ever industrious black scorpion could sting them as well. None escaped the strike of that awful black tail.

In all, by the old man's worn Timex windup wristwatch, the only technological item he allowed on his person, the entire process took a mere three minutes. Meanwhile, a fresh cohort of the damned stood silently by, awaiting their first command.

The vector of this most wicked deed approached the old man as if to claim him too, but the Conjurer had at the ready two open bottles of water, with which he thoroughly doused upon the demonic creature. Slowed and glutted by its vast harvesting of souls, and immersed in clear water, the MERUSUIK drowned, and wilted into nothingness. Only a pool of water remained on the floor to mark its passing.

With all eyes focused upon him, the old man felt like a god, all powerful, all knowing. Then with a smile he said, "Gentlemen, we have a great mission to accomplish. Without delay, exit this auditorium in good order, and get into one of the school buses waiting outside. Then await further instructions from the drivers within." He clapped his hands.

"You are dismissed."

Four associates of the Afghanis drove the four buses. The one hundred Pakistani students, ever-faithful to the old man's single command, mounted the buses in silence. As for the old man, he disappeared. In preparation for this grand spell, he had already removed his entire household to another location across the Afghani frontier. With one hundred kilos of opium, he purchased a new household, a very fine one indeed.

*   *   *

The sudden arrival of one hundred souls caught the Ledger Keeper off guard, but it regrouped, and performed its accounting with impeccable precision.

As for the Devourer of Souls, it rejoiced at the sudden influx into its realm of fresh material. While many of these innocents would not long remain, some would, it calculated, much to its glee and smacking jaws.

The Devourer of Souls also took note of why these souls had appeared. The old man, known to it as the

Conjurer, had performed his most ambitious spell to date. This the Devourer found intriguing, and so chose to communicate. The old man's sensitive psychic ear heard the Devourer's words plainly.

I am most impressed with your innate and well-developed abilities, oh great Conjurer!

To this Charles recognized the devil had again come a-calling. But this time, the adept didn't hang up the line. For a change, he listened to see what might develop.

With proper counseling, oh great Conjurer, your abilities and power could double, triple, reach unheard of levels of influence.

"What must I barter for such 'unheard of' power?"

It is but a trifle.

"And most mysterious one, how do you define 'a trifle'?"

Why your soul, oh great Conjurer.

To all of these things the old man listened, as this was not the first time "the devil had come a-calling."

CHAPTER 45
The Chairman's Oracle

Every CEO on the planet who is worth his or her salt has a go-to advisor to bounce ideas off of. It's just the way it is. Frank feedback from a neutral source is invaluable, especially if that source is itself brilliant, prescient, and gifted with extraordinary paranormal abilities. Giovanni Presto, the Chairman of CMES, had such a secret advisor. But Valeria Costa was so much more.

*   *   *

The pair met as they always did, in the town of Tivoli, for lunch, at a restaurant off the Via Scuole Rurali. Per their unspoken agreement, he paid and listened. She spoke.

"*Signore* Presto," she began with hands folded in her lap, and all business, "an old task, not completed, has come back to roost. As a result, it has grown up to become a considerable force that must be reckoned with. I say 'force,' because he is getting more and more powerful by the day.

"*Signore* Presto, mark my words, this *l'uomo potente*, who you have failed to remove *twice*, has become a dangerous threat both to your family and our Gathering," she said with a widening of her eyes for emphasis.

Merda! In Presto's mind, this luncheon had called him away from a critical F1 race meeting. But now to hear yet again about this elusive *l'uomo potente* from the past...and once again from this shrill *Strega*.

"*Signore* Presto!" Valeria rasped because she had heard Presto's thoughts. "This powerful man is a proven warrior and an *effective* leader." She purposefully emphasized, as a dig.

Breaking his silence, Presto quipped, "And?"

Valeria stopped twirling her fork, which had snared some linguini around it, looked up, and stared at him. "*Signore* Presto. Let there be no mistake. I speak of a man at the very acme of his existence, a powerful man, a man of God," she added with a surprising reverence that unnerved the Roman.

"Is he a priest, perhaps a member of the Vatican?" he quipped with some defensiveness.

"No. But he vexes the Great Dark One below."

Now that raised the hair on the back of Presto's neck.

"How so?" Presto softly asked.

"Because his soul is...old...ancient," she said with a flash of her eyes. "His soul is experienced, wise, and powerful. His soul is the First of Creation. Even the Great Dark One cowers before him."

Whenever Valeria spoke of the Great Dark One Presto shivered, not openly, but in his mind. *How can she remain sane* and *communicate with these powerful things?*

"Quite easily," Valeria smirked across the table, once again discomforting Presto.

His mind is so easy to read.

"But as for this powerful man's soul, must I remind you, yet again, that he must be dealt with?

"*Signore* Presto, do you not remember me telling you about him, what? over thirty years ago when he was but a babe, several times?"

With that, the oracle finished her plate with the swipe of a bread crust, so not to waste any of the oyster sauce. Then she sat back to finish her luscious glass of red wine.

A henpecked Presto thought. *What can I do? This man foiled both Shapiro and the Weasel. I seem to be powerless against such a man. If so, then we are doomed.*

Again Valeria startled the Roman. "Not quite, *Signore* Presto. But if you can break his spirit, somehow induce a deep depression, perhaps he will commit suicide. Then, our problem will be solved."

"Drive him mad?"

"No. Drive him insane with grief. His parents still live..." She suggested with a small, knowing smile.

CHAPTER 46
Cross Roads

My father raised me to face adversity head on and to never run away from anything. That meant I continued on with the restricted tablets, but agreed to publish only the curse texts, and not demon conjuring spells. To this arrangement, Peter assented.

The more I worked with the tablets as a collective, I found myself grouping them into categories, and imagined them as the private collection of an ancient witch or wizard. In the final analysis that seemed to make the most sense, and so I argued for it.

Of the curse tablets, several addressed political topics, the outright cursing of a rival, neighboring city-state, wishing upon them unspeakable bad fortune and disaster. Similar examples exist, like the well-known Old Babylonian text called "The Cursing of Agade." For example, these straightforward texts read: "I curse city-state X. These are the ills that I wish to befall it. X god blesses this invocation."

Others fell under the rubric of personal attack curses, directed at business rivals or against former love interests. Classic set pieces, their motivation and desired result could be found on the headline of any modern tabloid. Any double-crossed Wall Street executive or jilted high school student could have crafted their content. On top of that, these unique texts could be found nowhere else in the extant ancient literature of the Near East. Nowhere else can be found such virulent personal invective.

After four rewrites, Peter signed off on my senior thesis on the document's second sheet. The moment felt like when Professor Gibson had hit the SEND button, transmitting our corrected article off to the editor at *JANES*.

Speaking of that journal, after a bit of reformatting, I sent off my thesis under the title, "Hell Fire from Above. Several Sumerian Curse Tablets." Now I waited to see if it would be accepted for publication.

* * *

Well, I graduated, one semester early, and with honors, *cum laude*. My folks brimmed with pride at the ceremony. Only my grades in mathematics had held me back from anything better.

Before graduation, Peter shared with me his thoughts about the advantages of graduate school that would establish me as a bona fide expert in ancient Near Eastern magic. While I valued his opinion, I decided to leave that door wide open for the moment.

What I needed to do, right now, was to get back into the world. Besides, I knew firsthand all this magical stuff went far, far beyond more than book learning, the translation of cryptic tablets, and the like. It had a practical component to it that required serious attention. So I planned to move to Santa Fe, New Mexico, and study some more under Peter's colleague, John Running Deer.

Why?

Because I wanted to figure out my destiny. I needed to get a firm handle on the answer to the age-old question, "Who am I?"

When I stopped by Peter's office and told him about my plan to study in New Mexico, he got this faraway look on his face. In the military they called it the "Thousand Yard Stare." In the academic world, I suppose, they considered it in more cerebral terms than a sniper ranging his rifle. But when he returned to the here and now, he surprised me by saying, "We have to discuss this plan of yours further. How about this evening at our usual place? Say around five-thirty."

*   *   *

On every Thursday evening, the start of the weekend for the college crowd, The Greasy Onion filled up fast. Experience told me to get there early and grab a table in the back, away from the bar and all the ruckus.

When I got there, I saw that Peter already had found a place in the back with, of all people, Mr. Henry, the university's maintenance man.

At first I didn't recognize him out of his usual whites. Talking in an animated fashion with Peter, the man wore a brown tweed sports jacket and an open-collared dress shirt. Curious, I applied the rules of Marine recon and watched the two of them from a distance. I used the cash register and a redhead for cover. Quickly, that got old, so I sauntered over.

At my arrival, the pair looked up and Mr. Henry said, "It's about time you got your butt over here. We've been waiting for you. By the way, is that redhead as pretty as she smells?"

Come to think of it, she had smelled delicious, and I said so, like strawberries.

How did he know? I asked myself.

"J. J.," Peter began, "Take a chair. Henry and I have been discussing your plans to go to New Mexico. I think you'd be seriously jeopardizing a meaningful career in the academic world, but Henry disagreed. In fact, he supported your plan, all the way down to your choice of Santa Fe."

Here I had just sat down, and already I felt blown out of the water.

"You don't say," I managed.

And since when was Mr. Henry part of my career counseling?

"Starting right now, son," Mr. Henry emphasized with his finger jammed into the table top.

Did Mr. Henry just read my mind?

"It just so happens that Santa Fe is near this long and linear paranormal region–a ley line. In fact, it's so famous among our community that it's called the Silver Nile. That means lots of psychic energy and a great place to train at and test yourself."

This sudden burst of arcane information, coming from a stranger, left me stunned, not to mention the fact that Mr. Henry had just read my mind. Then I noticed their auras. Peter was his usual pale blue of learning and scholarship, but Mr. Henry was this intense deep blue indicating great integrity and inspiration.

"Okay, gentlemen. So why am I here?" I asked.

After a long and awkward pause, Peter and Mr. Henry filled the moment with thoughtful sips from their cold beverages. At this point, Peter broke in.

"J. J., I suppose it's high time for a confession. Henry's an old friend of my father, who died while I was a young man. Henry, however, promised my father he would watch over me until I had reached my...my majority, I suppose you could say, within the spiritual community."

"What was Mr. Henry trying to protect you from?" I asked.

"Mostly myself. From ignorantly stumbling upon something I couldn't handle. Much like that recent incident in your office."

"So, what *is* Mr. Henry?" I probed.

"Henry," Peter said while putting his hand on his shoulder, "technically, is my paranormal guardian. He is rated a Class Four Adept within our spiritual community. The highest rating is a Six. So Henry is well up there."

"So what's this 'spiritual community,' then?" I asked.

Peter said, "J. J., the 'spiritual community' is a hodge-podge of individuals, who for obvious reasons, have gravitated together. Latent and full-blown psychics, telepaths, or those who command telekinetic powers, you name it. For instance, John Running Deer is one of us."

No kidding, I smirked.

"In medieval times we would have been called wizards and witches. Today, we are members of The International Integrated Interface Society, or TIIIS for short. Regardless, all of us have a great desire to see mankind flourish, and not be consumed by the darkness that exists all around us. In short, we are the good guys."

"Is this 'good guy' organization world-wide?"

"Sadly, no," Peter winced. "The society's strongest in the those countries with historical ties to Great Britain. That includes the majority of India and

Indonesia. We meet in the open, under the many umbrellas of national and international paranormal research conferences, like that archaeological meeting in San Francisco where you made your debut." Smiling, he continued, "And I can assure you, J. J., at that conference you made quite an impression."

I felt exposed, like prey caught out in the open, ready to be butchered.

"Now now, son," Mr. Henry picked up, "How could you know that several high white witches sat in that audience? Besides, a powerful youngster like yourself probably got 'em all hot and bothered."

Now wait a minute, did Mr. Henry read my mind again? But before I could ask, Peter continued.

"But to return to TIIIS, the society has been around long before the founding of this country. Many of our founding fathers joined as members-in-good-standing. You have no doubt heard of an organization called the Masons. They are kindred to our spiritual community, a subset of something much larger and more extensive."

"But aren't witches and wizards something more than just gifted?"

"Yes, indeed, they are." Mr. Henry chimed in. "Those sorts have something special going on. It is nothing short of a marvelous merging of the spiritual with the psychic. Belief and ability can be very powerful things, but as with everything, each has its own limits."

"So what about all the pointy hats, sparkly wands, bubbling caldrons, and even cryptic words? Where do they all fit in?"

Mr. Henry smiled. "Marine, they're all camouflage, most are parlor tricks, Hollywood, and myth. But in some cases, those fake and useless trappings do serve a purpose–to help a practitioner to focus."

My face must have given away my confusion as Peter then jumped back into the conversation.

"J. J., when you think of Christmas Eve, what comes to mind?"

"Well, the tree of course, all the decorations, going to church, the lights, the candles, the roaring fire, the music, the presents, dinner, and of course, mom and dad."

"Okay J. J., ask yourself this," Peter continued, "how much of that detail is there to create the mood of the moment? Think for a second. How many of your five senses are being used? From your own description, sight, smell, hearing, and taste. But what is significant is you didn't mention your sense of touch." He held up his hand and continued, "Touch is perhaps the most powerful psychic sense. We feel the room go clammy cold when a ghost passes through. We feel happy or sad in certain situations. We can feel tension in the air, when something is not right."

At this point, Peter paused for a moment to allow his statement to sink in.

"Now imagine training your mind, J. J., as if you had a wand in your hand, to focus your will. It's not that easy. Only the very best of adepts can perform their feats without resorting to some sort of physical focusing device. Mr. Henry is one of them, by the way."

Was I really having this conversion in The Greasy Onion? I asked myself. *Or have I suddenly fallen into the* Twilight Zone?

No doubt reading my mind and seeing the incredulous look on my face, Mr. Henry piped up. "No, Mr. Stone, you not going nuts. It's that the two of us haven't let you in on a few details. But because of recent events that took place in your office, we have since changed our minds."

He leaned forward on his forearms against the table and said with authority, "So with that in mind, Mr. Stone, here are the facts of life.

"Fact. Magic is real, both white and dark varieties, along with two or three shadings in between. I know that sounds strange, but magic is not science, and hence magic, perforce, *is* strange. Magic itself is nothing more than intellect and emotion powered by psychic ability. We are electrochemical beings. Mental effort creates energy, and so any given witch or wizard is limited only by their ability to create this energy, or to harness it from the environment. Ley lines are such conduits of psychic potentiality.

"Fact. Ley lines are real, despite all the crap that is written about them on the Internet. These lines of psychic power crisscross our planet's surface. In some respects, they are like gas stations where physic energy that can be tapped, if of course, you know what you're doing. I know of an instance where a wizard almost fried himself while attempting to tap into a ley line. In another, someone of considerable ignorance, burned off his feet to his ankle bones. The lesson here–under no circumstances screw around with ley lines unless you know what you are doing.

"Fact. Angels and demons exist. They intrude into the mortal world only when summoned by their hidden name. To beckon these creatures, you had better know how to keep them happy, or even better, how to cast them back to wherever they came.

"Fact. God and the Devil exist. They don't intrude into the mortal world, because they have plenty of angels and demons to do their work for them. They also can influence mortals to do their bidding as well."

I nodded. What Mr. Henry said made perfect sense. Then he continued.

"Fact. Telepathy and telekinesis are real. Again, they are a matter of focused ability. Learn to use them, because the bad guys sure as hell will. But be careful, as these can expend your energy. So the key is to learn to manage your energy as efficiently as possible.

"Fact. If you ever find yourself in a tussle with a witch or wizard, be sure to check their feet. As it turns out, some practitioners depend on ley lines when they get into a fight. If they are wearing leather soled shoes, or even better, are barefoot, that means they have little to no endurance for the big magic they conjure, but instead tap into a ley line for the required psychic energy. Lock that one in your memory, my boy, as I guarantee that observation alone will come in handy someday.

"On the other hand, if the witch or wizard you are facing off with is wearing shoes with rubber soles, then you are in for a hell of a fight. Such rubberized foot coverings insulate them from the ley lines, which means that these individuals have great endurance, know how to use their magic in efficient and parsimonious ways, or carry high energies within their very being. Regardless, these individuals are experienced. Avoid them at all costs.

"Fact. Demonic possession is real, as is angelic. Depending on the cultural origin of the demon, its nemesis will be related. For convenience, we refer to this relationship as the Law of Opposites."

I interrupted Mr. Henry by shaping my hands in the T-sign for "time out."

"You said something seminal, Mr. Henry–that demons have a 'cultural origin.' Explain that," I said.

Mr. Henry's eyes took on a misty sort of quality, and then he spoke. "Mr. Stone, the entire discussion about the origin of demons is a very murky one and one fraught with controversy. But perhaps the most neutral answer to your question is this—and Peter please do chime in whenever.

"Let's take your cute little beastie, thousands of years of desert belief created it. Put another way, every culture has its neuroses. Over time, those fears are shaped by their cultural context. The Thunder Bird is a classic example of a sky-dwelling Native American demon, like your scorpion demon for the desert-dwelling Sumerians."

Nodding in understanding, I said, "Mr. Henry, sir, where did you get all of this information from?"

"That is probably best answered by Peter, here."

"J. J.," the academic said while pulling out a thumb drive from his coat pocket, "here, take this. On it you will find a most remarkable book called, *The Knot of Eternity*. Read it. The work is organized into a series of lessons meant to impart wisdom about the Cosmic Order. By all accounts, it seems to have been a sourcebook for those of a priestly status.

"What you now hold in your hand is the best English translation we have of that Sanskrit text, which

369

has been dated to the fifth century BC or earlier. In the translator's notes, you will find all the particulars. The original animal skin scroll that had been found on an East Indian trading ship. Ptolemaic law stipulated that all such works be sent to the Alexandrian Library for its translation into Greek. At that point, an agent of TIIIS came across the text and commissioned a copy. Ever since then, and after God knows how many copies, our society's main library has had a Greek version that dates back to the fourth century of our era."

"You're kidding," I said.

"I am not. In fact, the Roman Church declared the treatise heretical at the Council of Nicaea."

At that we all paused to address our beers. Since Peter and Mr. Henry had shared so much, I decided to do the same on a topic that had been bothering me.

"Gentlemen, given the effect that water has on demons in general, did you know there are holy men in western Asia who haven't bathed for over sixty years. Do you find that a bit odd? Or am I the only one?"

"Mr. Stone," Mr. Henry said, "are you suggesting the current worldwide unrest is not fueled by a radical religious ideology, but rather by something else?"

"Yes, sir. That is what I think, because that conclusion becomes obvious given the auras I have seen on the battlefield.

Ever since I was a kid, Mr. Henry, I could see auras. Early on I learned how to read them–how to access an individual's level of stress, their emotional state, even their health. In sports I had a real advantage. In battle, seeing them became crucial for survival. During my last Iraqi deployment, I ran into a handful of individuals with jet black auras, instead of the usual battle stressed ones. The scary part is that scorpion I conjured possessed a very similar auraic signature."

That statement hung over our table like a funerary pall as the implications sunk in, the brain's tumblers began to turn, and the many connections and possibilities started to accumulate.

"So, Mr. Stone, in your opinion, whose behind all of the worldwide distress?" Mr. Henry asked.

"Well, sir, these individuals with the jet black auras have claimed with their monstrous acts more lives of the Islamic faithful than Christians. Based on that alone, I would say radical Islam is only a convenient front for them. That they are being used as a tool. The real purpose of those carrying the black auras is to foment pure chaos everywhere, regardless of race, religion, or nationality. They delight in anarchy."

"Marine, you seem to have a lot on your mind," Mr. Henry squinted. "But what would you say if I told you there is a name for these anarchistic individuals?"

"What is it?" I asked.

"Have you ever heard of CMES?" Mr. Henry offered.

"Nope. Never. Who are they?"

"The ultimate bad guys, Marine. They have always been the bad guys, since the days of the pyramids, and maybe even before then. They're an international organization of paranormal misfits and monsters. By the way, CMES stands for the *Consilium magorum et sagarum*, The Council of Magicians and Witches."

"You've got to be kidding."

"No, Marine, I'm not. So, Mr. Stone, do you have anything else to get off your chest?" Mr. Henry probed.

"Yes, sir, I do. Peter, Mr. Henry, have either of you ever heard of the Sumerian term *su.mannu.uzuzzu.eli*, 'it which stands apart,' or for that matter, the First Soul of Creation?"

At this the two faces opposite me turned pale.

"Careful, J. J.," Peter said. "Where did you dig up those precious nuggets of information? Surely *not* from among the restricted museum tablets."

"From a conversation I had with a primordial emissary."

"An emissary...?" Mr. Henry whispered in obvious awe.

Then Mr. Henry turned to Peter and said, "My good friend, have you bothered to put two and two together and notice the color of Mr. Stone's aura?"

Then Peter gazed at me with a sort of blank look that transformed. He gasped, "It's the color of ...no! Wait! J. J., you're the *su.mannu.uzuzzu.eli*, 'it which stands apart!' You're carrying the First Soul," the scholar barely breathed.

With an exasperated sigh, Mr. Henry leaned forward and said, "Okay, Mr. Stone. Enough of me telling *you* about the facts of life. It's high time you come clean and fess up."

* * *

Following our discussion at The Greasy Onion, Peter kept his distance. He had become more reserved somehow. As for Mr. Henry, we began having lunch together on a regular basis. By mutual agreement, we agreed on Wednesdays. During those meetings, Mr. Henry shared a ton of information about TIIIS, its many members, their curious forms of etiquette, and how to identify them. I realized Mr. Henry shared all of this with me as prep for admission into their society, complete with its own pecking order.

During my last week on campus prior to graduation, Mr. Henry surprised me at lunch with a business card. When he gave it to me, he did so with both hands, as if a fragile gift. As it turned out, it most definitely was.

"Mr. Stone," he formally stated, "it has been a privilege to have made your acquaintance. This is the first time I have been in the close company of someone with a golden aura. Consequently, on behalf of Peter and myself, we wish to present to you this simple card. We give this to you with our fondest hopes for your future success. Do not be afraid to contact this person, for she has already agreed to meet with you."

I looked down on the plain tan business card. Its thickness as unusual as the scant information printed on it.

Betsy Silver Moon
Santa Fe, New Mexico

"That's all?" I said.

"Mr. Stone. That's all you will ever need. Trust me."

CHAPTER 47
Attack on the Homestead

When Presto ordered the assassination of J. J.'s parents in Denton, Texas, the CMES chairman's assistant in Rome delegated the contract to local talent. From the assistant's point-of-view, that arrangement made far more logistical and operational sense than sending in an Italian CMES team.

The drug dealer assigned the hit to five illegals from Nicaragua, who the dealer felt needed some local seasoning. Their boss, a big, bearded bad-ass who went by Dr. Quick, scheduled the job for that Saturday morning, around ten, perfect for the noontime news.

First they stole a panel van from a small delivery business the night before. They then swapped plates with another vehicle they found on the street.

Their boss' orders said to make a statement. Be messy, destructive, and mutilate the bodies. All five understood, as they had done that kind of work in Nicaragua many times, when messages, for whatever reason, needed to be sent. So the team chose pump shotguns loaded with double-ought buck. With the van gassed up, they only had a forty mile ride up U.S. E 35. What could be easier?

* * *

That Saturday morning, A. R. Stone and his wife of thirty-seven years, Constance, sat at the kitchen table reading the newspaper, drinking coffee. The wall clock said 7:35 a.m.

*   *   *

At 8:30 a.m., Luis started the Chrysler panel van with his four team members seated unseen in the back. As Luis figured it, he'd be at the old folk's address in forty-five minutes, tops. The radio had already declared the day to be a hot one. Best to get this job over with early, then retire to the cool darkness of his boss' favorite bar, get paid, play a little pool, and get wasted.

*   *   *

By 8:38 a.m., Constance had retreated to the coolness of the basement to do some work on a veteran Quilt of Valor she had promised the local VA post. In all, she had twenty-four squares to join on this one, all in various patterns of red, white, and blue. Knowing how hot the day might be, she settled in behind her sewing machine for the long haul.

A. R., on the other hand, a man that Constance often thought more lizard than man, had expressed the desire to work in the garage. On what, his wife didn't know for sure.

He's probably out there futzing with that stubborn old lawn mower of his.

*   *   *

At 9:20 a.m., A. R. sat at his work bench in his open double-door garage. The garage's open screen door allowed a passable breeze. From where he sat at his work bench, A. R. had a clear view of the entire driveway.

As for what he had been doing, A. R. had started in

on his lawn mower and had the darn thing half apart, like he told his wife. But for some reason he couldn't explain, his gut told him to clean his guns–a .45 caliber 1911 automatic and Winchester 1912 pump, a vicious twelve-gauge with a cut-down shorty barrel, all loaded up with six Winchester Super X triple-ought buck shells.

Sometimes an old soldier gets a feeling. Like the smell of rain in the spring, and you just know a storm's coming.

*   *   *

At 9:30 a.m., Luis took the U.S. E 35, 464 exit. Nervous and behind schedule, his colleagues in the back ribbed him unmercifully that he drove like an *anciana*.

*   *   *

At 9:39 a.m., time slowed for A. R. A panel van had overshot the Stone's driveway, stopped, and then backed up into it, deep, right up to its open garage doors, with just enough clearance for the van's rear doors to fully open.

Moments later, the rear doors of the van burst open and four hooded men emerged, all carrying shotguns at the ready. The van's driver stayed put.

At the odd and unexpected sight of the van and its backup lights, A. R.'s adrenalin spiked, he stuck his loaded .45 in his belt, and had his Winchester 1912 pump at the ready. When the van's rear doors opened, and the armed men's hooded heads appeared, A. R. clearly could figure out their intentions.

* * *

"By the look of these five, they're all probably illegals," the Denton police detective commented, after he examined all of their amateurish IDs.

A. R. Stone, sat at his work bench and shook his head in a mixture of shock and disbelief. Why was he a target? He didn't have a clue.

"Mr. Stone, these guys look like a hit squad," the detective continued. "Any reason for that? You have any nasty enemies in your past?"

"None that I know of, sir."

"Well, Mr. Stone, it was a good thing that you were so well prepared. Over the past six weeks we've had several shootings in Dallas that match these guys' style. Hit, hit hard, then run away in a stolen vehicle."

A thoughtful pause.

"Mr. Stone, just so you know, as this is a multiple homicide case, I would normally take you in for questioning, fingerprinting, and such, but today I'm not going to. I've been told that a security organization has vouched for you, and as we speak, has a heavy-duty lawyer in place who is filling out the paperwork. Do you know anything about that, sir?"

"No, detective, I don't. Who are they?

"Some outfit called TIIIS. That's all I know. But they sure as hell have made your life less complicated. However, Mr. Stone, I do have to confiscate your handgun and shotgun as evidence."

"Will I get them back, detective?"

"I wouldn't bet on it."

"That's too bad."

Several minutes later the detective and the

forensics team left, having already removed the yellow crime scene tape, bodies, and towed away the bullet riddled van.

As they disappeared around the corner, A. R. got out the hose and began to wash off his driveway.

*　　*　　*

"*Signore* Presto, I have some rather bad news from the United States," his assistant said with some trepidation.

Now what?

"Speak."

"The Texas operation failed."

"What?"

"Our contacts reported that Stone senior killed the entire hit team of five by himself."

"How is that possible?"

"*Signore* Presto, Stone senior was once a U.S. Marine," his assistant noted.

CHAPTER 48
The Kidnapping

Peter Smithers, president of TIIIS, sat at his office desk in London. The lean and fit ninety-year-old something settled in and gave his attention to his chief of IT and Security, Mr. Ambrose.

"Sir, we have received an urgent message from our contact within the Pakistani Directorate for Inter-Services Intelligence. One hundred school children have been kidnapped from one of their preparatory schools this very morning. On the basis of several phone videos, which the students recorded while the kidnapping took place, it appears that only one elderly male was involved."

"How is that possible, Mr. Ambrose?" replied the TIIIS president. "The sheer numbers alone don't make any sense. And when one adds an elderly male suspect..." the president's voice trailed off as a disturbing thought came to mind.

"Well, sir, based on what I have seen from the videos from ISI, it looks like a scene right out of a cheap horror flick. The suspect turned one hundred students into willing zombies."

"Turned them into zombies?" Smithers' brow furrowed with a mixture of disbelief and then alarm.

It must have been some sort of spell...

"Having reviewed only three videos, and there are others," Ambrose continued, "I would say, yes. And once the elderly male turned them, the students marched right out of the lecture hall and into some school buses. After that, they disappeared off the face of the earth."

"What has our contact within the ISI requested from us?"

"Technical assistance only. But specifically, they have asked us to ID the elderly man. I already have my department scraping off the man's image from the three videos. We'll have a full 3-D composite before noon. Do I have permission to crank up the facial recognition software and perform a full sweep of the usual databases?"

"Make it so, Mr. Ambrose. But just make sure that you're searching for my brother, and not me."

"Understood, Mr. President," his chief of IT and Security grinned.

*   *   *

President Smithers already knew the identity of the perpetrator of this heinous act. The sweep of the EU security databases would only provide him with absolute confirmation. In his mind Smithers knew without question that his twin brother Charles had done this. But Smithers attention remained riveted on the children. Why did he do it and for what purpose? In all of Smithers' tracking of his brother's many illicit escapades, never before had he ever done something of this magnitude. Charles' actions were grossly out of character and that fact troubled his older brother.

*   *   *

As promised, Mr. Ambrose and his technical staff compiled the three videos of the kidnapping from the auditorium. After about thirty-five minutes of cutting and pasting, they had a collage of stills that created a full three-sixty of the suspect's image. This they digitized and submitted for a facial recognition search across a multiplicity of national criminal databases.

After only forty minutes, some promising traffic came in from the BKA, the *Bundeskriminalamt*, or German Federal Criminal Office. They had found several photos of the suspect from the late '60s and early '70s. One from a British passport photo, matched the face with a date, which identified him as none other than Charles Daniel Smithers, date of birth: October 12th, 1948. Several others came from converted documents gleaned from an East German Stasi security archive. These indicated that this individual traveled to East Berlin, and studied an ancient Near Eastern collection for several weeks. His museum *Ausweis*, or ID card, showed up as well, but with the same photo as his British passport. The Stasi had suspected him of smuggling antiquities. Then, a later university ID photo from the Ludwig Maximilian University in Munich popped up. This *Ausweis* indicated his departmental major as *Altorientalistik*, or Ancient Eastern Studies.

Now armed with two photos, a name, DOB, and a British passport number, Ambrose and his team, just to make sure, queried MI-6, hoping to glean more information. Less than an hour later, several more pages of intel appeared about Charles Daniel Smithers, who graduated from Cambridge with a course of study that fit his European M.O.–anthropology and ancient history. Ambrose rang up his boss with all of the good news.

*   *   *

"Mr. President, now consider for a moment," Ambrose began, following a review of all the stabilized videos from the children. "Here is the suspect, your brother, standing and gesturing before these kids with their camera phones. What was he thinking?"

Smithers assessed with deep conviction, "Pure, unadulterated narcissism. That's my take on his behavior. Charles thinks he's invincible."

Then Ambrose asked the question, "So where do you think he is now?"

"Now that is the capital question of the day. Surely not Pakistan. He has burned his bridges there with this stunt. I would wager Afghanistan, most likely somewhere along its southeastern frontier, maybe even near Kabul in one of its suburbs. Mr. Ambrose, you know as well as I that the region is rife with corruption, its political environment chaotic, its tribalism as turbulent as the American Wild West. It would be perfect for him.

"And Mr. Ambrose, consider this as well. He has kidnapped one hundred children. Why? For what purpose? Where do you hide so many children? The fact that no one knows where they are suggests Charles has considerable logistical resources at his disposal. He has moved them somewhere, no doubt for some nefarious purpose."

"Ah, President Smithers, this entire operation must have cost a fortune to pull off. Do you know if your brother has access to those kinds of resources?"

"That too is a capital question. I have no idea as to what Charles' resources are. But to undertake this operation, as you so adroitly put it, suggests to me the involvement of someone else with deep pockets and access to logistical resources."

*   *   *

There existed few secrets within TIIIS. President Smithers had been hunting his wayward twin for decades with no success. On top of that the aging president, who also stood in as his society's enforcer of good against evil, had held that position for more than twenty years. As a consequence, the president considered the following fair question–if he did find his brother, would he be able to best him? Then and there, Smithers decided that he needed an edge, an advantage, and so the search began for an appropriate resource, but he already had an inkling of who that might be.

CHAPTER 49
Return to Santa Fe

Once again I drove cross country in my forever faithful Colorado pickup truck. Along the way, I stopped in Denton to see mom and dad, who for their part remained still busting buttons proud about my college degree. Naturally they inquired about Santa Fe. I have never lied to them and I sure as heck wasn't going to start. So I sat them down, and told them the truth, at least the important parts.

When dad told me about the attempted assassination attempt, I sat in wide-eyed disbelief. When I learned about how an organization named TIIIS had stepped in and taken care of all the legal ramifications, even if they did confiscate dad's guns for evidence, now that got me to thinking.

At the same time, I began wondering how I could ensure their future safety. After all, I remembered from my conversation with the Emissary that family, friends, and loved ones would be prime targets of the unscrupulous. While my parents appreciated having me around, I thanked God that they were just alive.

*　　*　　*

It would not be right to leave Denton without a quick visit to Adam Gibson, the man who started so much of this. I went over to his office, and sure enough, I found him grading three mounds of blue book final exams.

Looking up at my knock on the door, his once sour puss transformed into a big, toothy grin.

"J. J. What a surprise. Come on in boy, and close the damn door while you're at it."

Before I finished doing that, I heard him opening up his hidden treasure chest of frosty beverages and the distinct clink of two bottles being removed.

"Adam, it's only ten-thirty. A little early to start, isn't it?"

"Heck, J. J., if you had to read this stuff, you'd be drunk by now."

Two long necks clinked once, followed by several savory moments, followed by the usual grilling.

"So, how long are you in town?"

"I'm on my way out. Next stop, Santa Fe."

Frown of disappointment.

"Are you going to quiver your chin, too?" I teased.

"Nope. It's unfortunate, that's all. So, tell me all about UPenn, and how's Peter doing?"

"Well, Peter is Peter. One very serious academic. I graduated early."

"I heard."

"I also met Mr. Henry Johnson."

"Heard that too."

"Well then, what don't you know that I'm supposed to be telling you all about?"

A sly smile. Then, "Welcome to TIIIS, my brother."

I think my jaw fell to the floor and shattered.

"You're one of them too?"

"Yep. And as things stand, you'll probably be one of us soon."

"Adam, did you hear about what happened to my folks?"

"Yes, J. J., I did."

"Well, then can you could put in a good word for them? They need either a security detail or to be relocated somewhere safe."

The academic reached over and picked up his phone. "Consider it done."

*　　*　　*

Following my visit with Adam, I said my goodbyes, but only after getting a firm promise about the welfare of my folks.

The rest of the journey to Santa Fe went quickly. My truck seemed to glide on rails. I sat back, drove, listened to some good Texan music, and went over all the stuff for the millionth time that Peter, Mr. Henry, and now Adam had drilled into me.

*　　*　　*

I got a hotel room in preparation for the next day, when my top-to-bottom training with John Running Deer was to kick off. But instead, at eight in the morning, I got a knock on my door. I answered it, and there stood this trim, middle-aged looking Native American woman. All of maybe five foot something.

"Mr. Stone, I presume?" she said.

I had never seen before an aura of bright and shiny metallic silver mixed with aquamarine. The lady glowed. At seeing me, she smiled big and wide.

"Elder Henry Johnson has told me so very much about you, Mr. Stone. I'm Betsy Silver Moon. May I come in?"

*　　*　　*

At first, I didn't know what to make of Ms. Silver Moon's unexpected arrival, but after a few moments, I had settled down. So we went out onto my room's "spacious" balcony to sit in the sun.

"Mr. Stone," Silver Moon began, "Elder Johnson told me that you wish to develop your potential."

"Yes, Ms. Silver Moon, indeed that is my most heartfelt wish. I know I have a purpose. I want a chance to fulfill it. But I thought I had an appointment with John Running Deer today."

As I spoke, Ms. Silver Moon's held her hands together very tightly, to the point her forearm muscles flexed.

"Well, yes, that is true, and John is indeed looking forward to working with you, but, Mr. Stone, I had to meet you. I apologize for my surprise appearance."

While Ms. Silver Moon spoke, she noticed my noticing her hands and so she explained. "Mr. Stone, this might be a strange thing to hear from someone who you have just met, but may I lay my hands on you?"

Surprised by the request, I saw no harm in that. "Sure. Go right ahead."

"As you probably already know, Mr. Stone, touch is a very powerful medium among the members of the spiritual community. Much can be said through touch. The evaluation of an individual's needs can be more swiftly made. Are you ready, Mr. Stone?"

I nodded. Then, Ms. Silver Moon stood up and walked around behind my balcony chair. Ever so gently, like someone testing a hot pot or stove, she placed her fingertips at each of my temples.

I felt a remarkable coolness at her soothing touch. Then, the drowsiness set in, as Ms. Silver Moon held my head up. Then I faded out.

When I woke up, still sitting in the balcony chair, I found myself relaxed beyond belief. The entire experience, Ms. Silver Moon later told me, had only taken a couple of minutes.

Upon my awakening, Ms. Silver Moon appeared exhausted with more than a slight dew on her forehead.

"Mr. Stone. How do you feel?" she asked.

"Very well. Rested. Relaxed. Why?"

"For such a short life, Mr. Stone, yours has been a full one.

"Do you know you have two spiritual guardians?"

"Yes. I do. Nergal and Erish."

"They love you very much. But their guardianship will soon end."

"Yeah, I know, Nergal mentioned that. But are they okay, happy?"

Smiling, "Oh yes, yes, Mr. Stone. It's just it will soon be their time. And once incarnated, they will lose all contact with you. At least, that's how it's supposed to work."

"Wow, that's wonderful news. I've only wanted them to be happy, together."

"Yes, I know, Mr. Stone. You have a remarkably compassionate side for a demon destroyer. Did you know that?"

"No. I did not."

"Your soul, a very old one, wishes to be a warrior in this life. That is why it chose you, Mr. Stone."

"Well," I said as honesty as I could, "I only recently have I been made aware of demons, demon possession, the Underworld, and how the Cosmic Order must function. And now, only last week, a gang of drug thugs tried to kill my folks. There's got to be a connection and I worry about them a lot."

"Yes, I can see that. To put it mildly, Mr. Stone, to date you have been most fortunate. And there is a very simple reason for that. Do you know what that is?"

After a moment of consideration, I said, "Because I carry the First Soul. I enjoy its protection."

"Yes, Mr. Stone. That is correct. But do you know what that means?"

"Yes, I do, but I need guidance as to what I can and cannot do."

"Mr. Stone, what is interesting is you have an inkling of something more, a potential hidden capacity that you wish to know, understand, and tap. Do you know what that 'something' is?"

I shook my head in negation.

"I see. Well, Mr. Stone, I think that we have done enough for today. John Running Deer will be by soon to begin your training. But tomorrow, Mr. Stone, we will begin to discover who you are. I'll pick you up at six in the morning."

* * *

At six I once again heard a knock on my hotel door, and there stood Ms. Silver Moon.

"Okay, I'm ready. Now what?"

"Come with me," Ms. Silver Moon replied over her shoulder. "It's high time you met someone."

"Who?"

"Yourself, Mr. Stone."

After a brief stop for breakfast, we must have

driven in her truck close to an hour, deep into the nearby mountains. We headed northeast into the foothills to a place called Tesuque. Then, we climbed high into the eroded sandstone terrain dominated by mountain scrub, pinyon pine, Douglas fir, and the Oregon pine of the Santa Fe National Forest. She pulled off and bumped along an overgrown rutted track for several minutes until we came to a clearing.

"We're here," she laconically remarked.

Stepping out of the cab, the smell of the heavy pine resin in the high altitude air hit me like an express train. Practically intoxicated, I stood there, eyes closed, and breathing deeply. A profound peace fell upon me.

"Beautiful, isn't it?" the Native American said.

I could only nod and smile as the early morning light spread across the mountain landscape.

"Let's walk."

And we did, for almost a half-hour. At the end of which my flatlander's lungs heaved. Our destination turned out to be two reddish rocky outcrops that stood side-by-side, their low summits maybe thirty feet apart.

"Mr. Stone, climb atop the one on the left. Take a seat and make yourself comfortable."

Mindful not to put my hands or feet in a crevasse or gap, I climbed. Why I stayed so careful, I cannot tell you, except that I sensed something. I went on sheer instinct. I sat down, atop of the world, with a view that reached almost back to Santa Fe. I found myself surrounded by vistas of pine forest, pastel sandstone rock faces, and here and there, flowering explosions in yellow, white, and violet. My head spun. I could not keep from smiling, like a bedazzled little kid on Christmas Eve.

While I enjoyed myself, Ms. Silver Moon scampered like a gazelle to the top of the neighboring outcrop and also plopped herself down.

"I can see you are enjoying yourself, Mr. Stone."

"No kidding! This is great! Does this place have a name?"

"Indeed it does. The name given to it by the local Jicarilla Apache Nation translates something like 'the teaching place of the snakes.'"

"What an odd name."

"No, not really, Mr. Stone. This place is sacred to my people. Here is where young shamans learn the Way. Here they are tested. These tests, in many respects, focus on practical and common sense things, other times cultural rites of passage. But all of them, when taken together, represented a measure, a way to find the strengths and limitations of a candidate." She said as she shifted side to side, adjusting herself into a better position.

"Are you comfortable, Mr. Stone?"

"Yes, I am. And, by the way, my name is J. J. I ask all my friends and family to use it."

"Thank you, Mr. Stone, for that generous invitation. I respect it, but I'm very traditional. To me the knowing of a personal name, Mr. Stone, is an intimate gift. If the wrong individual knew it, their knowledge of it could be dangerous. Do you understand me?"

Thinking a minute, I did see her point. And given my recent experience with a certain Sumerian demonic name, Ms. Silver Moon was right.

"I appreciate what you are saying. Names go far beyond a social use."

That answer earned me a smile of appreciation. And I suspected, I passed some kind of a test, too.

Right again, Mr. Stone. Ms. Silver Moon commented using the wordless tongue.

I blinked at her sudden mental intrusion.

Her too!

For example, she continued, *your immediate appreciation of your surroundings. Think about the first thing you did upon arriving on this sacred ground. You breathed in its wonders. In fact, you almost hyperventilated in the process.*

With your careful ascent of the mound you passed the next test. You instinctively knew not to place your hands or feet into the many inviting hand and foot holds. This bit of field craft and common sense is critical, for beneath where you sit is a vast den of rattlesnakes. And they can get very cranky in the morning's coolness if someone heedlessly intrudes upon their lair.

My God. I thought.

Indeed, Mr. Stone, indeed. Now, Mr. Stone, describe to me, using the wordless tongue, what Iraq smelled like.

An odd question, but one that went to the heart of testing one's senses. So, I shrugged, and started using strings of one word descriptions.

Burning, burning grass, burning wood, trees. Burning houses, plastics. Burning diesel, gasoline clouds. Cordite and black power. Burning flesh. Oh, that god-awful stench. The sometimes sweet, but more often the sharp smell of death. Garbage, human waste. You learned to shut out all the carnage.

My brief description and mental images stunned

Ms. Silver Moon as her face turned white and her breath shortened into quick gasps.

What an impressive display of mental imagery, Mr. Stone. Not only did I see what you had saw, I could smell it as well. But what you probably didn't realize, you also told me of its sounds. The screams, the cries, the pleas for help.

Most remarkable, she whispered in my mind. *I had only gotten a sense of this story yesterday. But the scope of it overwhelms me. Causes me to reconsider my previous beliefs. The Council of Elders must be informed of this.*

Council of Elders? TIIIS has one?

A deep mental sigh. *Of course, Mr. Stone. TIIIS has a governing Council of Elders. How else could we play well together?* And that big smile of hers erupted again. Then she glanced up to locate the sun, which had moved since we had arrived.

Mr. Stone, what do you feel beneath you?

Curious, I closed my eyes. I reached out to sense the den and I found it, big as life, full of life. I could feel their entwined mass. Astonished, I realized almost one third was made up of recent hatchlings. How cool is that?

All of this Ms. Silver Moon listened in on, which prompted her to remark. *Mr. Stone, for a powerful demon slayer, who is responsible for the balance of the Cosmic Order, you certainly have a healthy curiosity and a connection with Nature, even down to rattlesnake hatchlings. Do you find that dichotomy odd?*

I'd never before been asked that. It stumped me. So I sat there thinking about Ms. Silver Moon's question. Then it hit me. I never had been at war with Nature. Far from it. Even as a child I have always been a protective sort. Even when I failed...and then Grace came to mind. She used her body to protect mine. My tears began to flow as they hadn't for quite some time. My Grace, my beautiful Grace.

I do not know how long I sat there with my head down and eyes squeezed tight. But when I had finally come to, I found my body stiff from holding that position for so long. I also felt heavier somehow, like something embraced me, comforted me in my deep sorrow. When I opened my eyes, I discovered basking rattlesnakes covered my entire lap and forearms, and the entire top of my outcrop for that matter.

Knowing to move with glacial speed, I raised my head to see Ms. Silver Moon's smile.

Mr. Stone, I know by now you are stiff and exhausted, but if you move with extreme care, your newly acquired friends will release you from their embrace. And trust me when I say this, this is an embrace that goes far beyond the borrowing of heat from your body. They are protecting you.

Looking at you, Mr. Stone, I am now reminded of a Christian saint, named Daniel, who had lain with wild animals, even lions. So what does that make you?

Silver Moon's statement cause me to pause and think about it. *Demon slayer and friend of Nature. How does that define me?*

While I continued to think about what Ms. Silver Moon had said, I began the slow process of disengaging myself from my predicament. I could lift one reptile off and place it nearby, untroubled at my touch. They all appeared to be dozing, lying about more like bunches of coiled rope than living matter.

*   *   *

By late afternoon I managed to extricate myself from that snake-covered outcrop. While coming down, I remembered thinking that not once did I freak out from the experience. Instead, I felt like I had gotten rid of a powerful head cold. My five senses turned up to the max, and my sixth, felt as sharp as a scalpel.

Once we started back to the truck, all the stiffness and kinks from sitting atop the mound worked themselves out.

We continued on the trail back to the truck without comment, each of us walked deep in our own thoughts, too polite to intrude on the other. As with all things, someone had to break the ice, and Ms. Silver Moon did.

Before she turned the key to fire up the truck, she turned to me and said, "Mr. Stone, you are a very complex man."

*   *   *

Later that evening, Governor Betsy Silver Moon replied to a global e-mail that had originated from TIIIS' London office. Her brief reply said, "Mr. President. I have your man."

CHAPTER 50
Family Feud

"The good Lord works in strange and mysterious ways," my mom always said. In this case, the chirp of my smart phone had caused me to think of that reverent phrase. The e-mail came from none other than P. E. I. Smithers, himself, the President of TIIIS. It read:

Dear Mr. Stone:

I am writing to you as your military background, academic accomplishments, and recent exploits have caused considerable interest within the society.

As you are no doubt very aware, the media have recently reported the kidnapping of one hundred children in Pakistan. While their current whereabouts remains unknown, we have identified and located the man responsible for their abduction. It is hoped that his capture will lead to the rescue of the children.

The individual in question is my twin brother, Charles. He is an extremely dangerous rogue psychic and practitioner of dark magic.

As a consequence, I am flying to Kabul and plan on arriving there within the next twenty-four hours.

If you are so inclined, I would greatly appreciate any support that you can lend me.

Contact Governor Betsy Silver Moon for all of your logistical needs.

Yours sincerely,

P.E.I. Smithers

President
The International Integrated Interface Society

*   *   *

I guess it bears repeating how "the good Lord works," because as soon as I had finished reading President Smithers' e-mail, I received a call from Governor Silver Moon.

"Mr. Stone, have you received an e-mail from President Smithers?"

"Yeah, I just finished reading it. He wants me in Kabul within twenty-four hours. While I'm good with that, how do I pull off that logistical nightmare?"

"Mr. Stone, there's a private jet waiting for you at the Santa Fe airport. Do you have an emergency snatch-and-grab bag?"

"Why...yes, I do."

"Then grab it, and make your way quickly to the private terminal of the airport. Park wherever. I'll take care of your truck. Then, look for me. I'll direct you from there."

*   *   *

Twenty-three minutes later I thought I had dropped into a James Bond movie. True to her word, Governor Silver Moon, all smiles, took my truck keys and squired me through an abbreviated security protocol out onto the tarmac. There sat this drop-dead gorgeous, flat black, private jet that oozed speed. I was impressed.

At its lowered stairs, Governor Silver Moon stopped, looked up into my face, and said, "This is where my hand-holding ends, Mr. Stone. Have a safe journey. Do send my best to President Smithers. And, oh yes, Peter Glass asked me to give you this."

Taking the small DHL package I said, "Governor Silver Moon, could you do me a favor?"

"Certainly, Mr. Stone. What is it?"

"I don't know how to say this, but, could you look in on my folks while I'm away?"

Smiling she answered, "It will be my pleasure, Mr. Stone."

*　　*　　*

Once the plane had taken off I opened the DHL express package. Inside I found a brief note from Mel, wishing me the best of luck and instructions for the object within. She had made me an amulet that looked like a mini-mummy on a leather thong to be worn around the neck.

J. J.–

Inside you will find my mother's very best protection spell. Wear it. You never know!

–The West Coast Witch.

I slipped the leather thong over my head and to my surprise discovered that the mini-mummy amulet nestled into the center crease of my chest.

I have never before slept so well on an aircraft. Perhaps Mel's amulet had something to do with it. Used to the deafening roar and racket of a C-130J Super Hercules transport, here I stretched out on a reclinable leather couch in near silence. I crashed hard, full knowing a battle would find me.

While Running Deer's training of the past weeks had somewhat prepared me for this situation, and Mr. Henry had shared his wisdom with me, I knew this junket would be a stretch, if not a quantum leap.

We flew west from Santa Fe direct into the sun all the way to Honolulu, and from there to Tokyo, Japan. After about sixteen and a half hours that included two refuelings, we flew on from Tokyo to Bangkok, Thailand, and from there to Kabul, another leg of some eleven and half hours. Fortunately, the plane had a full galley and a shower I took full advantage of. The exceptional pilots made it all possible. Along the way, the cabin attendant taught me a god-awful game called cribbage. By the time we touched down in Kabul, I had a serious case of cabin fever.

* * *

The Kabul International Airport has two terminals, one Russian and one modern, complete with Wi-Fi. When we landed, we ignored both and taxied over to the military side of the airport.

There, President Smithers greeted the plane, standing astride the bright yellow taxi marker line, while silhouetted in the fading glare of the setting sun. My pilot knew this game, because our nose wheel followed the taxi line as if playing chicken. As the nose of the plane approached ever nearer, President Smithers didn't move, but the jet did stop with only three feet of clearance.

Mere moments later, the front jet door opened, and its steps descended. At their base stood a lean and fit-looking white haired gentlemen with his hand on the railing. Dressed in an impeccable gray, pin-striped suit, President Smithers had not one crease out of place.

When I placed my hand on the same railing, I received, not an electrical shock, but a strong tingling sensation.

Mr. Stone, I presume. At last we meet. So President Smithers had formally stated in wordless tongue.

Him too!

I bowed my head towards the man, and I don't know why, but I answered, *Sir, you requested my help. I am here.*

Indeed. He remarked while extending his hand. He took mine, and as we both made contact, much was exchanged.

"Mr. Stone, it is a pleasure to meet you. I have heard so very much about you," He said for the benefit of the other men assembled in the hanger's bay.

"No doubt," I wryly responded, which earned me an upraised eyebrow. "Are these your men?"

"No, Mr. Stone, they are on loan from your government to assist us as needed. Mr. Stone, your arrival is well timed. Our encounter with my twin will take place tomorrow, at about 1:00 p.m. local. May I suggest we retire to somewhere less noisy and more comfortable?"

"I'm sorry, sir, but I don't want to leave these men behind." I have never before seen a more rugged and experienced looking bunch. That made them one thing–special ops.

Now with a slight smile and crinkling eyes that could melt ice bergs, President Smithers said, "Oh no, Mr. Stone. You misunderstand me. I meant all of us. You, me, and these soldiers are my guests for dinner, refreshments, and lodging."

Shortly thereafter, a massive air-conditioned tour bus appeared as if out of nowhere. The bus was loaded with all our gear, and we departed for Kabul, a short drive of less than ten miles.

We arrived in style at this huge four-star hotel. The staff wanted to help us with our gear, but we shut them down. Even President Smithers carried his own.

As it turned out, my host had reserved the hotel's entire top floor, a two-story palace, complete with individual bedrooms, with king beds, and private bathrooms with marble and gold fixtures. Talk about swank.

At our arrival, a hot buffet had been set up for grazing. But before I could grab a bite and a beer, President Smithers touched my shoulder, and said, "May I have a moment?"

So I followed him over to a corner arrangement of overstuffed chairs, the kind that you can get lost in and can't get out of.

"Mr. Stone," he began with his long and delicate fingers steepled before him and his gray eyes boring in.

"Tomorrow will be quite a test, for both of us. Part of the issue is the great unknown. I have no idea how developed my brother is. So I am, for the first time in a long time, at a disadvantage."

Throughout this brief verbal interlude, I felt

President Smithers reviewing my thoughts. I found it distracting, and I said so.

Taken aback, the gentleman then apologized, saying, "I am sorry, Mr. Stone. I did not realize your training had progressed so far. I only wished to fill in some blanks."

At that point, my stomach growled loudly. So we broke for some munchies.

*   *   *

Hot food, and lots of it, are a godsend, like manna from heaven. Hot showers are precious commodities. Being squeaky clean sure beats a battlefield communal hose or a box of baby wipes. The sheer luxury of clean sheets cannot be overrated. Despite all the sleep I got on the plane, I slept that evening like a rock and didn't want to wake up.

*   *   *

The next day arrived and President Smithers somehow knew where his twin brother would be. He had elements on the ground casing the location, which turned out to be an orphanage. Apparently, Charles wanted to nab even more kids. President Smithers, in coordination with the orphanage's administration, requested some special arrangements. He even had a Medevac chopper nearby should need be. The man thought of everything.

While the plan had been outlined, its execution would soon become fluid. Enter Commander Frost and his team of ten black ops guys. Their job, as defined, was initially to stay out of sight. If buses arrived, take their drivers out and commandeer them. If the children appeared for transport, mount them up, and deploy to Area A, a local pool reserved and made ready for their arrival. If I or President Smithers did not show up within a half hour at the pool, then Frost and his team would escort the kids into the pool area and order them to jump in, clothes and all—or, throw them in if necessary. I found President Smithers' solution for the children's possession a fine one, as demons and water do not get along. That I knew oh so well. So on the surface, the plan seemed a pretty straightforward special operations gig.

But as for President Smithers and me, our plan remained far sketchier. The target will be escorted with all due respect and courtesies to the auditorium in question. Once there, when the target enters the hall, the school's staff will shutter all the doors behind him. Then we, meaning Peter Smithers and I, will have him, Charles Daniel Smithers, to ourselves, for a family reunion.

I remained confident the orphanage's staff would come through as planned, for I listened in on President Smithers' very careful specific instructions to them. I never thought that someone could be hypnotized over the phone. I guess that there are first times for everything.

As for me, I wore desert AUDs with full body armor, a webbed combat vest with some toys, and a radio with a shoulder mike linked to Commander Frost. While helmetless, and therefore feeling very naked, I armed myself with my trusty 9mm and the bush knife Governor Silver Moon managed to get past airport security.

President Smithers, however, surprised me. He wore a lithe, flat black, one piece leather-looking body suit with padding here and there. One glint from it, however, confirmed its carbon fiber construction. One big zipper ran from his crotch to his chin like a wetsuit. At his waist hung two knives, over his right shoulder hung what looked like a Japanese sword and scabbard. Okay, so he looked like a Ninja, but a very scary-looking Ninja—one who wore the game face of all game faces.

While Commander Frost and his men awaited for the expected arrival of the school buses, President Smithers and I arrived thirty minutes prior to the scheduled event in a common taxi. We entered the facility through its rear service entrance.

Over two hundred moveable lecture desks filled the spacious auditorium. Given its overall size, I felt that two brothers could easily meet here to discuss their differences. So Peter and I took seats in the far back for added surprise value.

It seemed I had just sat down when the doors in the front of the hall opened, allowing in the lone barefoot figure of an old man, with long white hair, and dressed in a white flowing robe. In each hand he carried a plastic bottle of water. With those, he signaled his intent. Also Mr. Henry's admonishment about those traipsing around bare feet rang loudly in my ears.

When the doors closed behind him and their locks engaged by the telekinetic commands of President Smithers, he spun around faster than I thought a human could.

"Hello, Charles," Peter greeted with menace as he stood up, "it has been a long time, my brother." As he drew his sword with a grating hiss. "Such a very long time."

Then it all began. Much of it strained the range of my meagerly tuned senses to follow. Nonetheless, I will try to describe it as best I can.

First off, I had agreed with President Smithers beforehand that I would be the wild card, the supporting distraction to this brotherly street fight. Hence the surprises in my webbing.

As for Charles, he had not come unarmed, or perhaps better said, he came fully armed. As Peter seemed to fly at him like Peter Pan from the back of the lecture hall, Charles raised his arms with a flourish, the open sleeves of his robe fell back, all to reveal magnificent tattoos, inked as full sleeves themselves, of what appeared to be row upon row of some sort of script. They glowed a wicked-looking red.

THEY ENGAGED.

I don't know how better to express it. I beheld twin brothers who, for whatever reason, held considerable animosity, if not outright hatred, for one another. Their falling out seemed to stem from the elder's rank disgust of the younger's excesses and total lack of discipline, while the younger harbored an unbridled jealousy for all things that the elder enjoyed because of his station. Charles, in particular, kept repeating the word "traitor" several times. Peter, in retort, grunted on about his twin's total lack of moral compass.

All of these familial tidbits I picked up during their spirited, grunting conversation.

As for the engagement itself, imagine two individuals attacking one another, showing no let up, offering no quarter whatsoever. The elder wielded a sword that cleaved right through thrown desk chairs with a blue flash. The younger, with arms pumping like jackhammers, threw handfuls of energy, which roiled the air with heat-like convections, that the elder blocked and dodged. There they stood, neither giving in to the other, about eight feet apart, swinging, blocking, thrusting, gesturing, hacking. All in a blur.

All of this occurred during the opening ten seconds of this dysfunctional, family reunion dogfight. Then, I heard Peter Smithers' tense whisper in my mind.

Mr. Stone, now would be a good time.

With my cue to enter into this fraternal free-for-all, for opening giggles I threw a flash bang grenade. That caused a moment's pause in the action as both brothers briefly stopped and looked at me in surprise. Then I began blasting Charles with 147 grain hollow points. Or so I thought, because every one of them ended up in either the floor or the wall around him.

Was I that poor a shot? Nope, and not at this range. Charles had managed, somehow, to deflect them all, while holding his older brother at bay. *Hmm.* That meant I had to up the ante, somehow. So emptying my first clip, I reloaded, and began again. That's when I first began to feel the first impacts, like pillow blows, that attempted to screw up my aim. So I locked my six foot three frame into the floor as rigidly as I could.

I thought about reaching for my third clip when, lo' and behold, I recorded two hits to Charles' center mass. Huge gouts of blood emerged from his back, spraying the blackboard behind him, while two ugly holes decorated the front of his once-pristine white robe. I kept on firing as he continued to stand, how, I didn't have a clue.

Then I remembered Mr. Henry's advice about barefoot encounters with magicians in battle. I figured Charles could not be that strong. That meant he had tapped into some ley line or its tributary for his power. I shifted my targeting accordingly.

I reloaded in record time, resumed firing, and registered Charles' impacts again, several this time with a real sting. Apparently, I had become more than a mere irritant or nuisance. Paying the blows no mind, I continued to blast away, but now moved to my far right along the wall, both to get closer, and to gain a better angle on Charles. This time I shot at his feet. My gun barrel heated up big time, but I kept on firing, relentlessly. I figured I could always replace it. Then, two slugs managed to get through Charles' defenses, that ruined his right foot, unbalancing him.

* * *

Half a world away Melaina sat before a laptop in her departmental office. She too wore an amulet, a twin of the one she had constructed and sent on to J. J. The evening before, Melaina had slept soundly, and had even dreamt about J. J. in vivid and erotic detail.

But right now Melaina gripped her desk for all her worth, because heavy unseen fists pummeled the Alexandrian white witch's torso and arms. The ordeal lasted close to thirty agonizing seconds and ended with a vicious blow to her left, dominant eye.

Panting in quick, short breaths, covered in sweat, and dizzy, Melaina sat in her office chair like a limp wash rag. She had just received the beating of her life. Red marks, the precursors to bruising, appeared on her exposed forearms. The left side of her face felt heavy and bloated. Her vision narrowed as her left eye began to swell. Just breathing hurt her ribs that ached so.

"My God in heaven," she gasped clutching her left side. "J. J. must be taking a terrible beating."

* * *

That unexpected tilt to Charles allowed his older brother to get in with a fierce, swooping blow from his sword. Charles' head lay on the floor, while his body fell and twitched its last.

But even as death commenced to claim him, I saw Charles' lips moving rapidly, and that's when I pulled out my last trick of tricks. I remembered something from biology class, and on pure impulse, I did something barbaric. Using the full weight of my body, I drove the heel of my left boot down, crushing his head utterly. The mess was, well, epic.

How clever, Mr. Stone.

Thank you. I thought. *I think.*

When you crushed in Charles' head, you evacuated all the blood from his brain. When you did that, you broke his death spell.

Surprised at President Smithers' observation, I almost asked about it, when the post-engagement adrenaline rush hit me like a freight train. I staggered to one side in an attempt to stay upright. In the end I lost and slumped against a wall in exhaustion.

The front half of the auditorium looked like a butchery. One body, with two huge slug impacts and a mangled foot, had fallen with its tattooed arms exposed, now just black ink. One head, separated from its torso, lay smashed. Blood and gore splattered across the blackboard and floor. Bullet holes puckered the walls and floor all over the place. Shiny 9mm brass shell casings littered the floor. My left boot looked like pure blood and gore. What a scene–Trenton Tarantino eat your heart out.

President Smithers with sweat cascading down the sides of his face leaned over me. "Mr. Stone, by the look of things, it appears you survived. Congratulations. By the pattern of those bullet holes, might I suggest some time at the firing range." He quirked a smile.

"Yes, sir," I said, although I didn't say what I thought of his recommendation.

Then, Commander Frost, several of his men, and a medic appeared.

President Smithers announced to the room at large.

"Don't anybody touch this man's uncovered arms, much less his tattoos. I suspect they're still active and dangerous. Bag the head and corpse. Then burn them, completely."

No one thought to question those arcane directives so authoritatively stated.

Now looking down at me more clinically, I remember President Smithers saying, "Mr. Stone, I think it is high time I get you out of here before the local constabulary arrives. Can you walk?"

I nodded in the affirmative and levered my sorry ass up off the floor.

"And, Mr. Stone, that's going to be one royally epic black eye."

As President Smithers drove the two of us back to the airfield in a yellow taxi of all things, (where did that come from?), I fought my way out of my battle shock.

"Feeling better, Mr. Stone?"

"Yeah. Just I needed to catch my breath," I lied as I

cradled tender ribs, which shortened my breaths. The vision in my left, dominant eye had narrowed considerably with all the swelling.

"You may not have realized it, Mr. Stone, but you took a bloody beating back there. Charles hit you with everything he had. In comparison, my participation amounted to a mere side show."

Pause.

"Mr. Stone, I could not have taken Charles down without your help. I sincerely thank you."

Then I remembered.

"But President Smithers, how we will find all those kidnapped kids?"

The sweaty and tousled-haired President Smithers looked over at me and for the second time smiled. "Mr. Stone, Governor Silver Moon told me quite a bit about you. Especially, the part about you that is so protective. After your brute force performance today, I would have thought that not possible. It seems you are full of surprises, like that flash bang grenade.

"As for the missing children, before Charles died, he told me, or perhaps better said, I stole that information from his subconscious mind."

* * *

Once at the airport, President Smithers packed me up on the waiting Gulfstream, the very same one that had ferried me to Kabul, heck, what seemed like mere moments ago. Next stop: Santa Fe, New Mexico.

About ten hours en route, the cabin attendant informed me that eighty-four children had been recovered from somewhere in northern Syria. The sixteen missing had died in some horrific confrontation they had participated in.

As for the remaining eighty-four, each had been inoculated with an Africanized honey bee sting that destroyed the demon that possessed them, while restoring their soul. The best part, they're en route back to Pakistan. Their return to their families' just hours away.

Then the attendant shared some good news. He thought Santa Fe would become my permanent home as TIIIS had finished resettling my folks there. New house, new identities, the works. Talk about relief! God bless Governor Silver Moon!

I had plenty of time on the way back to think about the minor part that I played in this much broader drama, which produced such a satisfying result. It felt good. Real good. I was part of a team again.

Two hours later, the attendant again looked in on me, this time with a cellular phone in one hand and a fresh ice bag in the other.

"Mr. Stone, you have a call." He said mysteriously.

"Stone here."

"J. J., are you all right?" A female voice asked that I couldn't place.

"I know you took a beating. Were you wearing my mother's amulet?" She said.

Then the dawn broke.

"Is that you, Mel?"

CHAPTER 51
The Council of Elders

In the olden days, to call together the Council of Elders amounted to a daunting task, one which required considerable courage by the one requesting the meeting. Great distances had to be traveled. Thus, a meeting could not be undertaken at mere whim.

Now things are far speedier and more convenient. With the advent of teleconferencing technologies, secure communications between the many council members became a commonplace.

* * *

Ms. Silver Moon, the Regional Southwest Governor of TIIIS, sat before her computer, while she logged into an encrypted teleconferencing software, which the other members of the council had joined. She took a poll and then began speaking.

"Thank you, council members, for agreeing to meet on such short notice. As you can see by the brief before you, we have been monitoring the individual in question, Jonathan Joseph Stone, since his birth. Mrs. Gloria Hawthorne, a member-in-good-standing, first reported the individual's birth because of his *IPAR* rating of ten. Additionally, the Soul Numeral indicated that the infant carried the First Soul of Creation, which chose to incarnate only one day after its separation."

Governor Silver Moon paused to sip some water and to allow the council members to digest what they just heard.

"Reverend Paul Roberts, deceased, Class Three Level Adept of our society, confirmed Ms. Hawthorne's report and baptized the infant Stone. Thereafter, a member of the Denton, Texas, Fire Department, Mr. Jacob Sapper, deceased, reported the passing of an assassin identified as Irving Shapiro, which coincided with the death of Reverend Roberts. Eighteen years later, another assassin arrived in Denton, Texas. This assassin again targeted Jonathan Joseph Stone, first by an arranged truck crash and second by an aborted sniper attack. The assassin eventually surrendered to the authorities, who released him due to lack of evidence. It is my belief that both assassins were under contract with CMES.

Twelve years later, Professor Adam Gibson, a member-in-good-standing from our Southwestern District, made contact with the candidate and reported his observations. Professor Gibson then encouraged Stone to pursue his university studies at a location in the Northeastern District, under the mentorship of Professor Peter Glass and Class Four Level Adept Henry H. Johnson, both members-in-good-standing. While in the Northeastern District, the individual graduated with honors in his studies. While there, the candidate stupidly conjured an MLSI type, and then managed to return it to its place of origin." Governor Silver Moon paused for another drink of water.

"This heedless conjuring, one which would typically trigger an expulsion from our society, caused John Running Deer, a member-in-good-standing, and myself, to observe the candidate. At that time, we both hesitated to nominate the individual as a candidate for membership in our society."

Pause.

"Upon my second and personal examination of the individual, however, I found that he not only exhibited characteristics that supported the nominations of the members in the Northeastern District, but others as well, including President Smithers. As a consequence, I can now, in good conscience, nominate his candidacy for membership into our society, forthwith, and without any need for a second opinion." The speaker turned another page.

"I further recommend to the council that he be installed at our main headquarters. Then, within an appropriate setting, the council can meet this promising individual. I thank you for your consideration."

All members of the council knew the Regional Southwestern Governor quite well. They took note of her firm tone regarding the candidacy of the individual. Several had never heard Governor Silver Moon advocate so strongly for a candidate's membership. As a result, this piqued their interest even more.

*   *   *

Government bureaucracies plod along like dinosaurs hamstrung by their own regulations. Many times such lassitude prevented them from addressing their avowed purpose. Private bureaucracies, however, especially ones like TIIIS, which embraced technology and paranormal networks, move decisively with near-instantaneous speed come rain or shine. Consequently, the very next day, Mr. Jonathan Joseph Stone received an e-mail invitation.

SUBJECT: Membership Induction to TIIIS

Dear Mr. Jonathan Joseph Stone:

The International Integrated Interface Society (TIIIS) wishes to inform you that Professors Adam Gibson and Peter Glass, Elders Henry Johnson, John Running Deer, and Governor Betsy Silver Moon have nominated you for membership.

You are cordially invited to our new member induction ceremony.

This year the induction ceremony will be held on Saturday, the third of November, from seven p.m. to midnight, at the Smithsonian Castle, 1000 Jefferson Drive, SW, Washington, D.C.

Kindly enter at the Castle's main entrance facing Jefferson Drive, SW.

Black tie and entertainment.

Please RSVP to Geoffrey (212.776.4545) by October 14. He will also provide you with several additional details.

Warmly,

P. E. I. Smithers
President
The International Integrated Interface Society

PEIS/gg

CHAPTER 52
Washington, D.C.

People, who I respected and held dear, had nominated me to become a member of TIIIS, to join with them, to take sides in the struggle between good and evil. I accepted that invitation on trust, without a clue as to what it might mean, because I believed in each one of them. I hoped that some hint or clarification would be forthcoming. I hoped to hear that what they had in mind for me would surface at the induction ceremony.

*　　*　　*

Geoffrey, President Smithers' assistant, provided me with a hotel, limo, and black formal suit. After showing my credentials, my escort led me deep within the multi-towered Smithsonian Castle toward the echoing sounds of a social gathering. We arrived at the Great Hall with its grand columns. Therein someone had arranged chairs, a podium, and a bar. Even though I showed up right on time, I seemed the last one to do so. Perhaps I didn't get the memo.

An amazing menagerie of people packed the Great Hall, all in the formal attire of their native lands. My black formal stood out as rather boring next to some of these colorful peacocks, which prompted me to scan the crowd for their auras. I realized that I stood among the most powerful of individuals. None within this group possessed a hint of a muddied hue, far from it.

A ringing bell, unheard at first, silenced the hall of over one hundred people.

"Good evening, members," President Smithers stated, resplendent in his formal black waistcoat and tails. "Tonight, I am proud to announce an addition to our family. His name is Mr. Jonathan Joseph Stone. This is a name that you should commit to memory. Several championed his membership candidacy, on several occasions, and each time for greater accomplishments, be they of intellectual prowess or unadulterated bravery. So, everyone, please welcome Mr. Stone to our society."

Utter weirdness. I had never before experienced applause directed solely at me. So I did the logical thing. I blushed a bright red and wished that my Grace stood beside me holding my hand. Then President Smithers walked out into the gathered throng, took me by the elbow, and escorted me to the podium.

"Dear Family, as you can see, Mr. Stone's presence can be quite imposing." Mild chuckling broke out with appreciative smiles and appraising looks that cut through me like lasers.

"However, do not let Mr. Stone's physical stature influence your opinion of his intellect. He matriculated from the University of Pennsylvania, *cum laude*, in ancient Near Eastern languages."

Pause.

"His graduation occurred after the publication of his first academic article in a very prestigious journal. That article dealt with the translation of a rare Sumerian magical construct: a soul container. Some of you may have attended his presentation in San Francisco."

Several nodding heads and a low buzz washed throughout the crowd.

"His forthcoming academic article, this one on

417

ancient Sumerian curse texts, I am told by Professor Glass is required reading. So much from one so young.

"You will never find on the Internet the role that Mr. Stone played during a brutal paranormal engagement against a rogue practitioner, much less see in any newspaper. Allow me to be clear. That practitioner was none other than my own twin brother, Charles."

At this news, as one, the intake of breath by the assembled threatened the creation of a vacuum within the spacious hall.

"Dear Family, Mr. Stone provided the difference in that confrontation, for I, as your Lictor of Magic, could not have succeeded alone. Mr. Stone also played his part in the recovery of the kidnapped Pakistani children. That too, you will not find reported anywhere.

"And, consider this–Mr. Stone single-handedly righted the Cosmic Order."

Their reaction could be seen, as some stood more upright, as if at attention. Others wept tears of joy, while the remainder stood with their mouths agape.

"This cosmic imbalance we all have been aware of for most of our lives. Many of us have suffered under its awful psychic overpressure. Many of you have no doubt been relieved by its passing."

Thereafter, the evening blurred. After President Smithers' introduction, a raft of people welcomed me and introduced themselves. A flood of names assaulted me. I tried to remember them all, but failed miserably. One I will never forget, an elderly lady named Gloria Hawthorne. Leaning on a cane, white-haired, and arthritic, Ms. Hawthorne's warm smile radiated like noon-time sunshine.

"Mr. Stone, I am so very honored to finally meet you." She said extending her hand.

As I wrapped my two paws around hers, I felt the gentle tingle of the purest unconditional love, so I asked, "Ma'am, have we ever met before?"

"Oh my yes, Mr. Stone. I discovered you when you first arrived into this world." Then she squeezed my hand continuing. "You see, you're the first time that I ever reported a First Soul incarnation. And now, my life's complete, as I have met its carrier."

She looked up into my face and said, "Your such a handsome young man to carry such a heavy burden. I pray that God may bless you and keep you safe, Mr. Stone."

Then, Ms. Hawthorne turned, disappeared into the crowd, and left me wiping tears from my eyes.

Then Professor Peter Glass appeared out of nowhere, as did Mr. Henry, Governor Betsy Silver Moon, John Running Deer, and Professor Adam Gibson, complete with a beer wrapped in a paper napkin. Just like old home week, I felt that I belonged. Damn, I wish my folks and Grace could have been here.

* * *

All the excitement of the reception had taxed Ms. Hawthorne considerably. When she said that her life had been made complete, she hadn't been kidding. While Ms. Hawthorne dearly loved her mathematics, she also possessed extremely powerful empathic skills. By touching an individual, she could see things that others couldn't. In the case of Mr. Stone, Gloria Hawthorne foresaw when, where, and how he would die. Tears, unbidden, flowed down her cheeks.

"I'm not always right," she whispered. "I do hope so for Mr. Stone. He's such a fine young man."

*   *   *

When President Smithers touched my elbow and asked for a moment, I sensed the coming of closure on several issues. Excusing myself, I followed his lead.

The president of TIIIS led me to a side room, an impressive executive office. Indicating for me to sit, President Smithers rounded the wooden island of a Colonial desk and sat behind it. Folding his hands before him, he began.

"Mr. Stone, I would like to make you a job offer, but first I require answers to some questions."

I nodded for the man to continue.

"I need to know about your moral compass, your emotional maturity, Mr. Stone."

I looked down at my hands and spoke from the heart.

"Mr. President, I was raised a God-fearing Christian. I acknowledge that I have killed many on the battlefield. I assisted in the assassination of your brother. I have protected those who needed protection. I try not to lie, but I know that I do. I do not steal, but I know that I have. Down deep, the guilt of my personal survival eats at me. The loss of my first love and comrades-in-arms consumes me. The constant fear of losing my folks tears at me. But the sheer joy of protecting someone sustains me."

I shook my head and pursed my lips as words, right then, failed me.

"Mr. Stone," the president commanded.

I looked up into the man's hypnotic eyes.

"I am not your priest, so I cannot hand out penance. I do require, however, an adherence to common sense, restraint, justice, and the ability to use lethal force when necessary. Can you do that?"

"Yes, sir."

Pause.

"Second question, Mr. Stone: how trainable are you?"

To this I blinked in surprise. "Very trainable, sir."

Hmph.

"Do you realize, Mr. Stone, that what I have in mind for you will require strenuous, on-going practice, both intellectual and physical?"

"I relish a challenge, sir."

"So you say. For the past twenty years or so, I have been both president of this society and its Lictor of Magic. However, recent events have taken the starch out of me. Further, look at me, twenty years have passed and I'm not as spry as I used to be." He sighed.

"Excuse me, sir, but how old are you?"

"Ninety-seven next month."

My jaw dropped.

"So what I am offering you, Mr. Stone, is to take on the mantel of the Lictor of Magic for the society. You will receive further training and support before you are ever deployed. Do you have any questions?"

"Yes, sir, I do. What do you mean by 'Lictor of Magic'?"

"Mr. Stone, your adventures in central Iraq, at the university, and in Kabul typifies what a lictor does, or perhaps more appropriately, what an enforcer does. Put bluntly, to cast back demons to the underworld or outright destroy them. Or, to remove miscreants...like my wayward brother from this existence.

"But as for the Latin word '*lictor*' itself, it possesses the time-honored connotation of an enforcer of established custom and codified law. Within the Roman government, a *lictor,* an officer of the court, held a station of respect and honor within civilized society.

"Mr. Stone, energy keeps us alive and kicking. If you can learn to harness energy, then one's life extends beyond the norm, your abilities sharpen and aging slows. These things you will learn about during your training. Master your lessons. Their content can mean the difference between life and death. Much like reading an aura to identify friend or foe."

I nodded in acceptance. "I've been told that mine is bright, metallic, and golden."

"Indeed it is, Mr. Stone. Very few have it. But in addition to your aura, you have to ask yourself why you have it. And the answer to that, Mr. Stone, I doubt that you appreciate."

"You mean, sir, that I carry the First Soul?"

"Yes, Mr. Stone, and do you know what that implies?"

"That I ensure balance to the Cosmic Order."

"That is correct, but only in part. During your gestation in the womb, the First Soul decided to join with you. That deliberate choice the First Soul made in order to address needs, the desire to solve problems, and in general, to better the soul.

"Mr. Stone, your soul's foremost purpose, the righting of the cosmic imbalance, you accomplished, for the first time in recorded history. So technically, your soul's purpose has been fulfilled. That said, I suspect Mr. Stone, your destiny lies...elsewhere," he stated.

"So, Mr. Stone, do you realize what you did in Kabul?"

"Not completely, sir."

"Wise answer. Yes, Kabul was a test. But why, Mr. Stone, did you finish off my brother the way you did?"

Pause.

"I acted on impulse, sir. I saw his lips moving and I feared what he might be saying," I replied perhaps a little too hastily.

"'On impulse,' you say. Either, Mr. Stone, you are remarkably intuitive and prescient, or just plain lucky. Regardless, that appropriately barbaric act worked. But my belief is that your soul took direct command of you during that most dangerous moment, which suggests to me that your soul has already encountered such a dire threat.

"But more to the point, when you crushed my brother's head, you stopped Charles' death curse. When you did that you saved me, yourself, and God only knows how many others."

"What do you mean?" I blurted out.

"Death curses, especially those delivered under duress or at the end of one's life, possess exceptional power, Mr. Stone. And given Charles' talent, I would expect a blast radius well beyond fifty feet. Perhaps twice or thrice that range." President Smithers said with his arms extended wide for emphasis.

"A blast radius? With what kind of effects?" My mouth jabbered.

"Mr. Stone, a death curse eradicates all organic life, cancelling it utterly. As its shock wave expands, insects explode, birds plummet from the sky, animals stagger with internal hemorrhaging, and humans die horribly."

"Damnation. But President Smithers, who created such a monstrosity?"

The president of TIIIS paused while he examined his hands as they rested on the delicate wood tooling of the desk top.

"Mr. Stone, sadly, our very own society created it."

"What?"

President Smithers raised his hand to pause any further reaction on my part.

"Allow me to explain, Mr. Stone. During the fourth century of our era, a heretic priest had this dark secret quite literally torn from his being during a Christian examination. This devout unfortunate followed the heretic doctrine of a Christian bishop named Arius. He was the founder of an alternative form of Christianity and the learned minds in Constantinople declared anathema. At the time, only a few of our society knew of the death curse. Think of it like today's nuclear weaponry, dangerous, and therefore available only to a chosen few. Since that fateful Christian examination, however, the curse has become known to far too many."

"Why create such a thing to begin with?" I pleaded.

"Our small society, Mr. Stone, devised the curse with the help of a then sympathetic and impeccable source–the chief high priestess of the Vestal Virgins of Rome. At the time, she foresaw that our society would be a force for good. As for the curse itself, its purpose granted a zealot of our society the ability to devastate, through personal immolation, a large gathering of pagan worshippers, who practiced human sacrifice, and what we now call black magic."

"Just like today's suicide bombers."

"Yes, Mr. Stone. The irony of that observation is not lost on me. As a consequence of the death curse, TIIIS became a credible counter force to CMES. Our opposition's sheer numbers could no longer deter us. A single individual only had to infiltrate their Gathering and snuff it out in an instant. At the First Council of Nicaea in AD 325, Arius had planned to do just that, but his agent's capture prevented him from doing so."

President Smithers, uncomfortable with the unspoken implications of what he had imparted, shifted in his office chair.

"Did that make the heretic bishop Arius a member of TIIIS? Did I get that right?"

"Yes, Mr. Stone, you did. Be aware, however, that the Christianity of the Fourth Century, and present-day Christianity, represent two different institutions. Also remember, at its founding, TIIIS acted as a reactionary pagan organization bent on destroying the practice of human sacrifice and black magic. From the beginning, Early Christianity generated considerable suspicion as to what it stood for. That institutional distrust would only subside during the late second century of our era, when it became clear what the Christian Mass represented a spiritual sacrifice and not a physical one. By that time, however, it was far too late, for Christians did not like us one iota as we represented, and rightly so, another antagonistic pagan institution."

President Smithers then leaned back deep into his chair. Its leather crinkled. Moments passed in silence between us, but I could sense his mounting anxiety. Then, he came to a decision.

"Mr. Stone, if you are ever to understand, much less realize, your true potential, you must turn inward and have a conversation with your soul. You must confront it, find out what it knows and what it wants. I can see no other avenue to ensure your personal development."

"Sir, respectfully, how would you suggest that I go about doing that?"

"Mr. Stone, I have several suggestions, but I can guarantee only one thing–none of them will be very pleasant. As for your guide in these matters, fortunately, you already have met them. Can you guess who?"

I smiled. "Governor Silver Moon and Mr. Henry Johnson."

"Mr. Stone, you do not disappoint." Again sitting back in his chair, he said, "So, Mr. Stone, will you accept my offer, and become our society's next Lictor of Magic?"

"You bet," I said in the blink of an eye.

CHAPTER 53
Bellinzona, Switzerland

The time came. Carla dilated about as far as she could. To her great advantage the maternity hospital employed a sixty degree birthing chair instead of the usual horizontal table with stirrups. Tall, red haired, and athletic, Carla had not only gravity on her side, but the leverage of her runner's limbs. She knew she needed every possible aid, because the ultrasound said she carried twins, a boy and a girl. She had to last out for the both of them.

After considerable effort and strain the first head appeared, then its shoulders, and with a will of its own, the baby girl squirmed free, screaming the entire time, daring the world to ignore her. Then, after about a minute's pause, the second head showed, then a pair of shoulders, and it too fell into the extended hands of the attending physician. After a tense moment, a second cry echoed off the room's tiles, this one of a different timber.

*　　*　　*

Held in their mother's arms, the redheaded pair, washed and swaddled in their pre-warmed blankets, looked at each other for the first time, and smiled toothless, drooling grins.

We made it, Nergal! Erish gushed in complete elation in the wordless tongue.

Indeed we have my love, Nergal blinked. *Now let us enjoy this life together.*

427

*　　*　　*

The Ledger Keeper made note of the passage from the light realm into the mortal of a particularly special pair of twins. If it could have done so, it would have smiled.

ABOUT THE AUTHOR

For W. J. Cherf, this is his first foray into the realm of paranormal adventure literature and urban fantasy. He is best known for his works in "historical science fiction," his award-winning five volume time traveling series, *The Manuscripts of the Richards' Trust*, which take place in ancient Egypt and early medieval France. They are full of adventure, intrigue, and vivid description.

As to why Cherf writes in his retirement years, he says, "I always wanted to write a book without footnotes." This is an oblique reference to his treadmill "publish or perish" days as a professor of ancient history and archaeology.

To find reviews and free chapters to all of his works, not to mention a handy source for the latest breaking news in Egyptology, go to www.wjcherf.com.

ç